MW00966619

A Fine and Private WAR

A NOVEL BY

STUART M. VAN TINE

FORCE BOOKS

A Fine and Private War
by Stuart M. Van Tine

 This is a work of fiction. The characters do not represent real persons, living or dead.

Published by Force Books, Inc. For information, please contact:
Force Books, Inc., P.O. Box 9, Accord, MA 02018-0009
www.forcebooks.com

Cover and Interior Design by Pneuma Books: Complete Publisher's Services. www.pneumadesign.com/books

First Edition First Printing
Printed in the United States of America
Body set in Galliard 11|14.5
09 08 07 06 05 04 03 02 1 2 3 4 5 6 7 8

Publisher's Cataloging-in-Publication
(Provided by Quality Books, Inc.)

Van Tine, Stuart M.
A fine and private war : a novel / by Stuart M. Van Tine.
p. cm.
LCCN 2002091042
ISBN 0-9717394-0-4

1. Terrorism--Fiction. 2. Adventure fiction.
I. Title.

PS3622.A6187F56 2002 813'.6
QBI02-701386

ACKNOWLEDGMENTS

I WISH TO thank Anthony S. Gimbel of Gimbel Music Group, Inc. for granting me permission to quote the line from the song *Watch What Happens* © in Chapter Five.

Special thanks to Pneuma Books for designing and producing this book on the fastest of fast tracks for my publisher.

Professor Bruce Barnett, my college roommate, allowed me to use his name and likeness in a cameo role. Thanks, Moose.

Thanks also to my friends and colleagues, too numerous to name, who took the trouble to read and critique my manuscript in each of its various versions.

My deepest thanks are to my wife, Nancy. Without her help, encouragement, and support, this novel could never have been written.

PREFACE

THIS is a work of fiction. Except for historical figures, all of the characters are imaginary, and are not intended to portray or represent real persons.

Many of the events in this novel actually occurred. For example, the two C-130 Hercules missions described in the Prologue really took place, more or less as I have described them. The pilots of the C-130 missions in the book are not intended to represent the pilots who flew the real missions.

The ships are another matter. They're all real.

THE GRAVE'S A FINE AND PRIVATE PLACE,
BUT NONE, I THINK, DO THERE EMBRACE.

—ANDREW MARVELL—
TO HIS COY MISTRESS,
1650

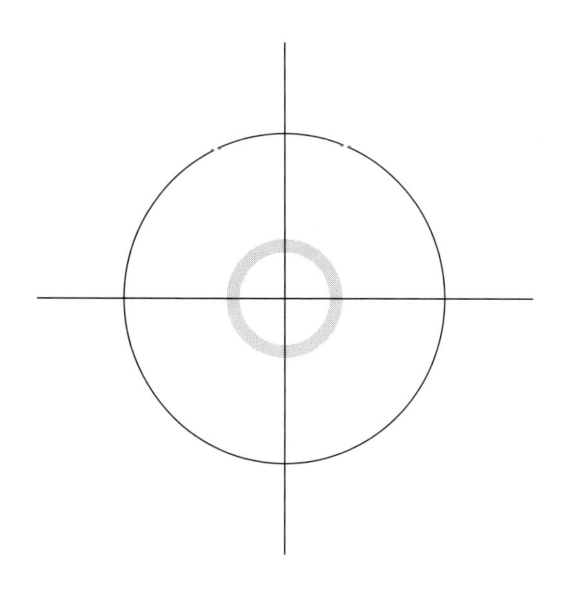

PROLOGUE

GEORGE HOLBROOK advanced the throttle levers, the four Allison T-56 turboprop engines spun up to more than four thousand horsepower each, and the Lockheed C-130 Hercules began to roll. The military transport, nearly a hundred feet long, gathered speed slowly. She was heavy, with twenty tons of iron bars in her cargo bay. The Air Force had modified the plane to land in a very small area. The iron pigs equaled the weight of the men and equipment she would carry on her secret mission.

George had been training in the Herc for three days, requalifying in an aircraft he hadn't flown for years. On those flights, a young first lieutenant had served as copilot. Today, on the modified bird's crucial test flight, Lt. Col. Robert ("Denny") Dennenberg, USAF, was in the copilot's seat, an unusual position for a man in the zone for promotion to bird colonel. Especially since the pilot was a civilian. George was sure that the colonel was pissed off. The thought pleased him.

The Herc reached takeoff velocity. "Rotate," said the colonel.

"Roger," George replied. The big transport continued to roll.

Dennenberg turned to look at Holbrook. He was wearing a brand-new flight suit, with no insignia of any kind. Dennenberg shook his head. Not only is there a civilian driving my bird, he thought, the man thinks he's a hotshot, roaring down the runway when he has speed enough to fly. "One thirty."

"Five more and we're out of here, Colonel," George said. Runway wasn't an issue. The damn thing went on forever.

"One thirty-five."

George hesitated for a second or two longer, then brought the control yoke back smoothly toward his lap. Twenty knots hot for takeoff, the Herc jumped into the sky like a child getting out of school.

Dennenberg sighed. "Don't tell me. Let me guess. You used to be a fighter jock, right?"

George laughed. "Yeah. Long time ago."

Dennenberg looked at Holbrook again. He was smiling, but there had been a hint of bitterness in his answer.

It was a fine day for flying. The sky was clear, but it was still early, so the thermals hadn't built up to make the air lumpy. Holbrook leveled off at one thousand feet and began a gentle turn to the left. He straightened out on a course reciprocal to his takeoff run and trimmed for normal cruise. The Hercules flew arrow straight and rock steady above a patch of American desert called Area 51.

Dennenberg was quiet for a few minutes, as he watched George work. "Looks like you've had some hours in 130s."

"A few."

"'Nam?"

"Yeah."

"Air Force?"

"No. Civilian."

Dennenberg knew what that had to mean: Air America, the bogus airline run by the CIA in Southeast Asia. He decided to leave that topic alone.

"Holbrook, can I ask a question?"

"Why not?"

"Why the hell did they bring you in to fly this mission? This is my bird, damn it. The mission should be mine."

When the boys at the Skunk Works had modified his airplane, Dennenberg had known it was going to be used to rescue the hostages in Tehran. When he'd been told he'd be flying second seat to a ringer, the disappointment had been enormous. He hadn't planned on asking Holbrook why. He hadn't wanted to admit that it mattered to him.

Holbrook took a moment before answering. "'Cause I'm probably the only man alive who can put this thing into the landing zone. I'm certainly the only one crazy enough to try it. And, because the spooks decided a Navy approach was the only way it would work. I'm carrier qualified."

"Carrier qualified! We're not going to land on a ship!"

"Yeah, but the approach is going to be the same. Watch."

As they had been talking, George had flown to a spot several miles downwind of the runway. He turned in a general upwind direction, and meandered about the sky, still at one thousand feet.

"You Air Force guys line up on the runway twelve or thirteen counties out, then glide down a slope two hundred miles long."

Dennenberg grunted. He'd heard this line from Navy fliers before.

"The mission depends on surprise. If somebody sees us coming, and figures out what we're up to, they could kill the hostages before we get there. Have you ever flown a Navy break?"

"No."

"OK, watch how it's done." The Hercules was approaching the end of the runway at an oblique angle. It was still at cruising speed, still at one thousand feet. There was a box painted on the tarmac, about half a mile from the end. It looked impossibly small. The dimensions were the same as the grounds of the United States Embassy in Tehran.

For a moment, it appeared that the C-130 would fly past the end of the runway. At the last moment, Holbrook made a hard starboard turn, and the bird came into line with the strip. The box raced by below. Holbrook shouted, "Break," and his hands flew over the controls. He cut the power to the engines and snapped the bird into a three-gee port turn. With the left wing pointed toward the ground, he held the nose up, keeping the wheeling aircraft at a thousand feet. Dennenberg watched the airspeed indicator as the turn dragged the speed down. George began lowering the flaps, slowing the speed even more.

"One hundred twenty knots," shouted Holbrook. As he said it, he dropped the nose, deployed the flaps all the way, and lowered the wheels.

Dennenberg looked past Holbrook, out the port side window of the cockpit. The Herc was on the downwind leg, parallel to the runway, opposite the box, gliding down through five hundred feet. "Jesus," he said.

"One-eighty, three down and locked," said Holbrook. He sounded happy. The Herc continued to turn.

At fifty feet, the C-130 was over the runway again, a half mile from the box. Holbrook pulled the nose up, flaring the landing, dumping even more airspeed. The stall warning horn sounded a split second before the wheels touched down, just inside the box. Holbrook dropped the nose wheel, powered up the engines and rolled to another takeoff.

Dennenberg was silent until the Herc returned to level cruise at one thousand feet. "Bet you a beer you can't do that again," he said.

Dennenberg lost the bet, and bet again. And again. After an hour of landings, two things had happened. He was convinced that Holbrook was the best pilot he'd ever met, and he owed him a case of beer. Lone Star. Longnecks.

"OK, George," Dennenberg said. "I'm convinced. If anybody can drop this bird into the compound, it's you. Why do you have to be crazy to try it?"

"You know why they installed the rockets?"

"Yeah." The mad scientists at the Skunk Works had installed retrorockets on the Herc. The landing area in the Embassy compound was about a hundred yards long. Not only was the C-130 going to have to land in that small area, it would have to stop before it hit the wall at the far end. The Air Force had installed four rocket engines, stock boosters from antiaircraft missiles, in a ring around the fuselage, in retracting mounts like the headlights on a Corvette. In theory, they would stop the Herc like the wires on an aircraft carrier stop a Tomcat.

"I think the bird will come apart when we fire the rockets. The deceleration will be big, five or six gees, maybe. Carrier jets are built to take that. The builders add extra strength in tailhook versions of any plane. Hercs don't have tailhooks."

"I'm sure the engineers looked at that."

"They say they did," Holbrook replied. "I told them what I thought, and they laughed. But you don't see any of them on board, do you? If you want, I'll drop you off and do the rocket landing alone."

Dennenberg looked at Holbrook for a long moment. "Thanks," he said. "I'll stay for the ride."

While they had been talking, they had been orbiting the runway. People were gathering along both sides of the tarmac, setting up cameras and instrumentation. Fire trucks lined the runway on either side, like an honor guard. It was time. "I hope that's a new poopy suit you're wearing, Denny," Holbrook said. "Fire retardant comes out when you wash 'em."

"Fuck you," replied Dennenberg, and the two men laughed. Dennenberg radioed the troops on the ground to say they were ready.

George flew the break as before, with one difference. At the one-eighty, he deployed the rockets along with the landing gear. Once again, he leveled out at fifty feet half a mile from the box.

"Standby rockets," he said, bringing the nose up.

"Roger." Dennenberg toggled the arming switches. "Rockets armed and ready."

The airspeed dropped and the stall horn sounded. "Fire!" Holbrook shouted, and Dennenberg hit the switch. The retro-rockets fired while the bird was still fifty yards from the box. They took a second or two to develop full thrust. Firing them on touch-down would be too late.

For the rest of his life, George Holbrook would remember the final seconds of the flight in slow motion. The sensation was just like a carrier landing, the bang of touchdown and gut wrenching deceleration, all at once. He held the bird steady on the center-line, watching the painted end zone of the box rushing toward him, but slowing, slowing. They were going to make it! Then the sound of tearing metal as the starboard wing came off at the root.

George fought the controls, only dimly aware that the star-board wing was jack knifing toward the cockpit. He killed the power to the port engines, which were going full astern, to keep them from spinning the Herc like a top. The bird stopped, and the starboard inboard engine, with the prop still turning, slammed into the cockpit, driving aluminum and Plexiglas inward against the side of Denny's helmet.

For an instant, Holbrook was sure he and Dennenberg were going to die. The starboard wing tank had ruptured, and the bird was in a pool of burning JP-5. The firemen couldn't possibly res-cue them. He realized with irony that the damn retrorockets were still firing. "Still firing!" he shouted, wild with hope. He disengaged the brakes, lowered the cargo ramp control handle, and reached for Dennenberg's seat belt.

Years later, men of the Area 51 fire brigade would talk about that day. How they'd known there was no hope of reaching the burning wreck in time to get the pilots out. How they'd watched the huge bird suddenly roll backward, out of the pool of fire, with one wing gone and dead engines on the other. How they'd cheered when the big cargo ramp came down with George Holbrook standing on it, carrying Colonel Dennenberg over his shoulder.

Holbrook promised himself that day he'd never fly another mission for the CIA. He broke the promise, of course. Four months later, he was on the flight deck of another burning C-130, in a patch of Iranian wasteland called Desert One. That time there were no retrorockets, no backing out of the holocaust. That time Holbrook had to leave Dennenberg's dead body in the flames.

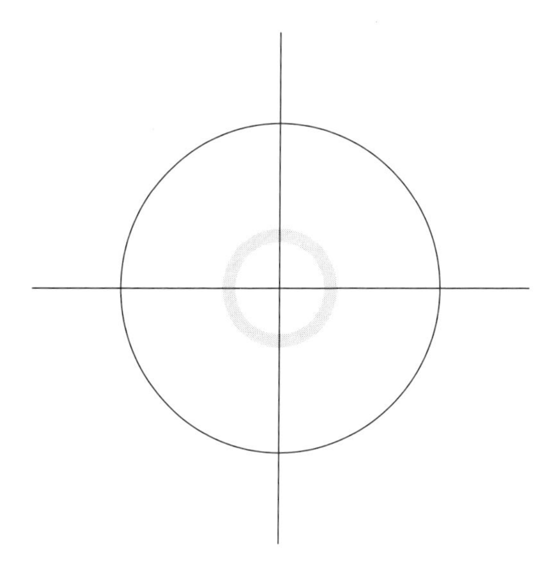

CHAPTER 1

DOLORES BERTOLINI didn't know she was dying. All she knew was fear and pain, and the aching desire to be home. The cracked plaster walls of the room in which she lay, white long ago, were a greasy yellow-brown, the color of cheese left out too long. A single window was covered with paper which kept out the light, but not the cold and damp of the February wind. The only furniture was the old metal bedstead on which the girl was lying, and a filthy bedpan on the floor. She was handcuffed; one metal bracelet encircling her left wrist, the other attached to the cheap brass headboard. Each end of the handcuffs had left its mark, a bright band of polished metal on the headboard, a bloody ring of raw flesh on the wrist. Above the wrist was a crudely bandaged hand, the source of the infection that was killing her. Flies, slow in the cold, commuted lazily between the wrist and the bedpan, but no infection they could transmit could do more harm than the one which already raged in the stumps of her severed fingers. The infection had spread up her arm. Her heart pumped the poison through her veins. Her breaths grew quick and shallow, and in her fevered semi-consciousness her sobs had blended into a ragged harmony with her breathing.

For all but the last few weeks of her thirteen years, Dolores Bertolini had everything she wanted. Her father was immensely rich and he had worshiped the woman who had died giving her birth. Dolores had never asked for anything that had not been given to her. Now all she wanted was her father to come, take her away, and make the pain stop. But he had not come, and as the days passed into weeks, her cries of "Papa!" had grown fainter. In time they, too, had blended into the ragged rhythm of her breathing and her sobs.

The man who called himself Jinnah was in a rage. He had assembled his followers in the stonecutter's showroom. Some of them had been with him since he founded the militant wing of the MLO years ago. They knew he was capable of incredible violence when he was angry. They had come to know and fear him.

Yet none of them had ever seen him in such a rage as he was on this cold Italian afternoon.

For nearly a minute after the men had gathered, Jinnah watched out of the window, with his back to them. Whether he paused to gather control or for theatrical effect, neither he nor they could have said. He often played on the emotions of his followers without consciously meaning to do so. Today's emotional weapon was terror.

Finally, Jinnah turned to face his followers. A handsome man, with strong, sharp features, he was small, even for a Makrani, who tend to be smaller than the Sikhs whom they otherwise resemble. His bright black eyes and snowy white teeth were set against skin the color of oiled teak. His was an expressive face, one that any mime would envy, yet as he faced the group it was unusually impassive.

That frightened them even more.

Jinnah looked over his men fully aware of the effect he was having on them. They weren't a bad looking lot for a small army of liberation. Patriots to some, terrorists to others, such groups are often filled with wild-eyed young firebrands. Not here. The seasoned veterans outnumbered the recruits two to one. Jinnah had worked hard to mold this group of a dozen or so, the elite cadre of his forces, the best he would ever have at his command. The day before he had been intensely proud of them. Today his disappointment was bitter and deep.

"The ransom has been paid," he began. "It is the highest amount ever paid in Italy to ransom a private citizen."

One or two of the newer men began to cheer, but a glare from Jinnah quickly silenced them. "This should be a time for celebration," he continued, "for ours has been a great victory for Makran and our holy *jihad*. Yet our victory has been stolen from us, not by our enemies, but by those of you who chose to disobey me." Jinnah paused again and let his gaze pass slowly over all of the men in the room.

"We live in a world that is not of our making, one that is repugnant to our faith and the teachings of the Prophet. It is an upside-down world, where material things are greatly sought after and the spiritual life is forgotten. Yet, to be effective fighters in it, we must learn to adapt to that world. We cannot challenge the armies of the great powers with scimitars. Our task is not to become martyrs, but to become victors.

"Today, we need two weapons. One is money, capital. The ransom we just earned is not merely a way to buy weapons; that money, used properly, can be a weapon itself. We will use this capital to gain more capital, and then use that capital to gain power. The Vanderbilts and the Rockefellers did it that way, and so shall we."

Jinnah paused again for a moment, doubting that any of these men had any idea of who the Rockefellers had been. Yet, he went on in the same tone, needing to impress them with the solemnity of what was to come.

"The other weapon is world opinion. To succeed, we must make the world aware of us. We must be in the news, we must *be* the news. We must be on television, on the radio, on the Internet, on page one of every newspaper, day after day, night after night. We can shout at governments until we are hoarse. They will ignore us until the masses demand that they pay attention to us. No matter how just our cause, unless the world knows of it and believes it to be just, it will be nothing.

"The average American, or European, has no idea where or what Makran is. Only a few well-educated people know it's an island in the Indian Ocean. And many of them would confuse it with Sri Lanka. If you ask them about the troubles there between Hindus and Muslims, they'll likely reply that Hindus and Muslims are the same thing.

"Today we had a chance to change that. The ransom, the tribute that was paid to us, was a record. The press loves records; no matter what it is, so long as it's the fastest, or the biggest, it's news. When I released the girl, I was going to make a statement to the press. They would have listened, for a change, because of that record ransom. I was going express my deep regret at having to cut the child's fingers off to send to her father as proof that she was my prisoner. I would have said that I hoped that the unfortunate infection in her hand could be cured. If she died, it would be too bad, I would have told them, but it is also too bad that the infant mortality rate for Muslims in Makran is one of the highest in the world, and capitalists like Bertolini are largely to blame. For a while at least, the world would know of our cause. We would be news, a media event. Even after the newsmen forgot us, a few more people in the world would know where Makran is, and that Hindus and Muslims are not the same at all."

Once again, Jinnah paused, and a remarkable thing happened. His face changed, slowly, into a mask of rage. His eyes widened, so that the whites showed all around the pupils, and the muscles in his neck and jaw tightened into taut, knotted ropes. When he spoke again, his voice was an octave lower and there was a tremolo of fury in it. One of his men began to weep uncontrollably.

"That chance is gone. There will be no publicity, no media event. The world must never know that the Makran Liberation Organization had anything to do with the kidnapping of Dolores Bertolini. I thank God that we did not reveal our identity in our ransom demands. For when she was kidnapped, she was a virgin, and she is a virgin no longer.

"Can you imagine how our enemies would use that against us? That we raped a child of thirteen years while she was handcuffed to a bed. That *seven* of us raped her! We, the *Mujahidin*, the holy warriors of God? Can't you hear the Hindu stooges calling us animals and thugs and saying that our *jihad* is but an excuse to rape and plunder? If the men who did this had been Hindu spies, they couldn't have done better. I know each of you who participated in this crime, but one of you bears the gravest guilt: the officer responsible for the girl's safekeeping."

Jinnah turned to look at Mahmoud. He was darker skinned than Jinnah was, but his color was drained now. He was shaking uncontrollably, spittle running down his chin as he tried to speak. He stumbled forward and knelt on the floor at Jinnah's feet.

"Jinnah, please! Forgive me, I didn't know. You had us cut off her fingers, and send them to her father. I thought we just had to keep her alive until the money came, for more fingers, for proof. I didn't think it mattered if we touched her. She is nothing to us, she is not of the faith. I thought she was to die at the end. I didn't disobey you, I never would! I didn't understand. In the name of God, forgive me! I didn't understand."

For a moment the room was silent, except for Mahmoud's spluttering at Jinnah's feet. The other men watched, horrified. Sentence was about to be passed. They knew the terrible meaning of that sentence, why such a brave man as Mahmoud would disgrace himself with fear at its prospect. He was about to lose not only his mortal life, but his immortal one as well. He and the others knew that death in a *jihad* was no death at all. It was a guaranty of eternal life with God. Death as a traitor in the holy war was death for eternity.

Jinnah turned to Syed, another of his officers. "Shoot this traitor. Now."

Syed drew a .45 caliber pistol from the holster on his web belt and pointed it toward Mahmoud.

Mahmoud's last act was to open his mouth, perhaps in disbelief, perhaps to utter one final desperate plea.

Syed shot him through that open mouth. Mahmoud's head virtually exploded with the impact.

Jinnah looked up from his watch, pleased. His order had been carried out in less than five seconds.

As quickly as it arose, Jinnah's rage subsided. The human sacrifice had appeased some demon within him. He dismissed the men and asked Syed to stay with him. The guerrillas left the room quickly, six of them thanking God that there was to be but one execution.

"Syed, I am pleased with you. You show promise. It is too bad that you weren't in charge of keeping the girl. It is well that this was to be our last ordinary kidnapping. The ransom money will be used for a new project. Our targets are people of huge wealth. They will surely provide us with the weapons for final victory."

Jinnah's mood brightened. "It's time to move on. Kill the girl, and dispose of her body so that it will never be found. Mahmoud's as well."

"I suggest that we use the gang saws, the one that the stone cutters used to cut marble into slabs," replied Syed, and Jinnah nodded approval. Syed then asked, "Must the girl be killed immediately? After all, she is attractive, and, as Mahmoud said, she is not of the faith."

Jinnah stared for a moment at Syed, who smiled in return. "If she is to die anyway, why not first let her provide amusement for the men. At least those who didn't touch her before. After all, she really is nothing to us."

For the first time that afternoon, Jinnah, too, allowed himself to smile. "You are a brave man to ask that after what just happened. You show *great* promise."

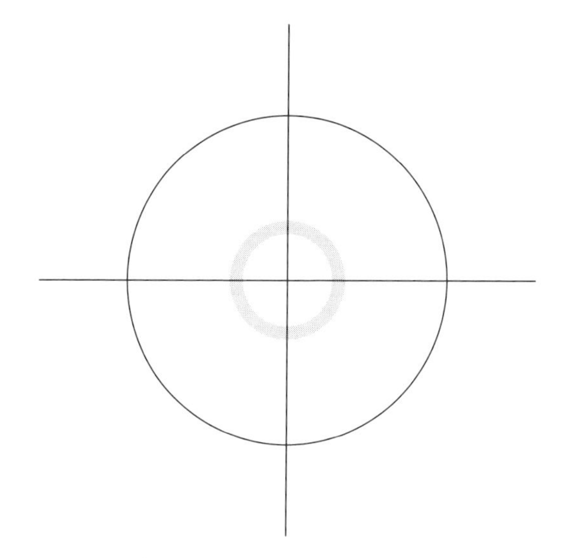

CHAPTER 2

GEORGE HOLBROOK felt the thrill of exhilaration as he brought the Hellcat into line for the final speed run. On each of the three previous passes through the timing gates, the helicopter had exceeded the old rotary wing aircraft speed record by dozens of knots. They were unofficial though, he had wanted it that way. Only the last run was going to be timed. George didn't want just to break the old record. He wanted to smash it to tiny pieces.

The Hellcat thundered across the desert floor. With her tanks nearly empty, she was thousands of pounds lighter than when she'd taken to the turquoise Arizona sky. Less of her awesome power was needed to hold her aloft, more was available to hurl her forward. George felt the adrenaline rush as he dropped altitude to twenty feet and pushed the throttles forward. The airspeed indicator climbed as the low altitude horn sounded. He silenced the horn, dropped a few more feet, and put the throttles past the detents and into the stops.

Three hundred knots and still the machine accelerated. Three fifty. In theory, no helicopter could fly this fast. George smiled. In theory, bumblebees can't fly at all.

The machine began to vibrate. With the airspeed nearing four hundred knots, the tips of the rotor blades were approaching the sound barrier. He adjusted the controls to slow the rotor speed, letting the thrust of the engine exhaust push the aircraft ever faster toward his goal of an even four hundred. The vibration was getting worse, but the gates were only a few seconds away, and George thundered on. The timing crew flashed by beneath the canopy, and he throttled back.

Nothing happened. Then he felt a sudden sensation of horror. The throttles were jammed, and the Hellcat was still accelerating. Four hundred and ten knots. Four fifteen. George fought with the throttle levers. According to the people who had helped him design the Hellcat, she would come apart at four twenty-five.

The Hellcat wasn't just vibrating now. It was shaking, threatening to shake itself apart. Altitude! If I climb, the airspeed will fall off. He pulled back gently on the collective. Too much stick would pull the rotors right out of their hubs. Again, nothing happened, the controls were frozen. The Hellcat was shaking like a wet dog, buffeting him from side to side in his seat …

"Mr. Holbrook, please wake up!"

George opened his eyes. The stewardess had her hand on his shoulder. She'd been shaking him gently. Her face was clouded with concern.

"Are you all right?"

"Yes. Sorry." George could feel his face redden with embarrassment. "I guess I was dreaming. Was I talking in my sleep?"

The stewardess relaxed and smiled. "It wasn't that so much.

You were pulling on the arm of your seat. You nearly tore it off. You were saying something about altitude, and pulling up on the arm."

George looked around. Several of his fellow passengers were looking at him. Their expressions varied from amusement to concern.

"It's an old dream," he said, feeling his flush deepen. "Thanks for waking me before it got to the really bad part." The part about the power lines, George didn't add.

"Are you a pilot?" the stewardess asked.

"Helicopters."

"Oh," she replied, the disappointment clear in her voice.

The noise of the engines changed as the airliner began its descent.

"I don't suppose there's time for one more of those scotch and sodas you've been serving me, is there?"

A tiny frown crossed her face, quickly replaced by the obligatory smile. "Let me see," she said, and disappeared into the galley.

George evaluated his chances of getting the drink. They were good, he was flying first class. In the sardine seating at the rear of the plane, where he usually flew, he wouldn't have had a prayer.

In a moment, the young woman returned with a plastic cup of club soda and a miniature bottle of Johnny Walker Black Label. George rewarded her with a smile.

"Here you are Mr. Holbrook," she said. "We're starting our descent into Gibraltar, so you won't have much time to finish this. I'll have to clear the trays before final approach."

"Don't worry," he said. "I'll finish it."

As the stewardess turned back to the galley, George caught a glimpse of the frown again. She probably thinks I'm a drunk, he said to himself, as he twisted the top off the little bottle. He allowed that she might be right.

The airplane was still heading south, and George watched out his window as the left wing dipped. The secure harbor lay beneath the limestone fortress known as The Rock. From here, Nelson had sailed to victory and death at Trafalgar. From here, the beleaguered British Navy had fought the Axis powers. Now, with the sun setting fast on the British Empire, there were but a few warships in the harbor. They were small ships, frigates and destroyers, mostly, all painted gray. George craned his neck to look at them as the plane swung onto its short final leg.

The stewardess was back. He finished his drink in three big swallows, grinned wickedly at the woman, and handed her the plastic glass. He turned back to the window, pressing his cheek against the plastic pane, peering ahead like a child. "There she is!" he said, half aloud, as he caught a glimpse of the ship he'd been looking for. She was moored among warships, looking at home among them despite her coat of gleaming white paint. George sighed as the aircraft's turn pulled the white ship out of sight. Suddenly, he felt very tired, as the effects of his hurried and unplanned travel caught up with him. Hearing the familiar rumble as the landing carriage was lowered, he raised his seat back to the full upright position, and closed his eyes.

It had been less than fourteen hours since his old friend Ralph Dade had called. George had left in a hurry and had been hurrying ever since. Helicopter to the Houston airport. Houston to Dulles on a Gulfstar owned by the Ferroil Corporation. Dulles to Heathrow on the Concorde. The final leg to Gibraltar on the British Airways 737. The first legs of the trip had been at night, and George had tried in vain to catnap. Now, he was near exhaustion, and jet lag hadn't even begun to take effect. He grunted as the 737 landed hard. Ralph, he said to himself, there damn well better be a good reason to put me through this.

George was traveling light. He had a carry-on case with little wheels, and a garment bag, but no checked baggage. First off the plane, he bypassed the luggage scramble to get through customs and immigration before his fellow travelers could form a line. Ralph Dade was waiting for him as he cleared.

"God, George, you look terrible," Holbrook's old friend said, smiling. Ralph was one of George's few friends. By far the best. They hadn't seen each other for over a year.

"I've got you to thank for it. What the hell is going on?"

"Trouble," Ralph replied, taking George's garment bag and steering him down a corridor. "Major trouble. I can't tell you about it here."

George studied Ralph. He looked terrible himself. He'd gained some weight and lost some hair, but that wasn't it. He appeared haggard, as if he hadn't slept in days. Looks the way I feel, George thought.

Ralph led him through a door marked, "Restricted Access, Authorized Persons Only." It opened outside, onto the apron around the terminal. A serious woman with a uniform, a badge, and a machine pistol blocked their path.

"I'm a pilot," Ralph said to her. "He's my passenger."

The security guard inspected Ralph's line pass as if she were sure it was a forgery. Finally, she grunted something that could have been either, "Have a good day," or, "Get lost and good riddance," and waved them on.

Once they were past the guard, Ralph said, "If you'd rather be the pilot and let me be the passenger, that would be OK. For old times' sake."

"No, thanks," George replied. "I'm not fit to fly. I've come half way round the world and I've drunk enough scotch to put me half way into the bag."

"Suit yourself. Drunk or sober, you're a better pilot than I am."

They turned a corner, and George stopped. There was the ExecuStar. Christ, George thought, this is like a high school reunion. Every time I turn around, there's another old friend. First the ship, then Ralph, now the helicopter.

He joined Ralph as he took his preflight walk around the aircraft. "You've taken good care of her," he said.

"Got to make her last, she's a keeper. Since the company changed hands, the quality's gone down."

George winced, and Ralph regretted his comment. He had meant it as a compliment to the craftsmanship George's father had been famous for. Instead, he obviously had hurt George's feelings. Ralph hastily decided to change the subject.

"How's the aircraft-testing business?"

"Give me a couple of more scotches, and I'll tell you all about it."

"That's twice you've mentioned scotch whiskey in ten minutes. Is this a subtle cry for help? Are you looking for an intervention?"

George couldn't help laughing. "Go to hell, Ralph. If I wanted somebody to tell me to stop drinking, I'd get married. No, I'm not looking for help."

"That's good, 'cause if you were, you've come to the wrong shop."

The flight from the airport to the harbor took barely a minute. George watched in silence as they approached the helo deck on the white ship he'd seen from the air. Long, low, narrow of beam, she was like a stiletto in the water. "God, she's beautiful," he said, remembering the first time he'd seen her, twenty years before at the scrap yard pier. More than half of her diesels were inoperable, and rust was everywhere. But for George, it had been love at first sight. He had proposed to Ralph a total transformation and saved this ship from a scrap yard, and turned her into the gleaming white beauty she was today. Once a fleet destroyer, she was now one of the largest yachts in the world. Her name was *Seafire.*

It took more than a dozen rings of the telephone in the guest cabin to arouse him, and when Holbrook awoke, he was groggy and confused. The clock beside the bunk told him it was just after nine. He spent a moment figuring out where he was, and that it was evening rather than morning. Thanks to a couple of fingers of scotch he'd tossed back before crawling into bed, he'd had three hours of deep and dreamless sleep. It had done little to refresh him, though; he was still feeling the effects of travel. He sat on the edge of his bed. "What?" he shouted into the phone, and instantly regretted it. Loud noises were painful, and his own voice was no exception. He closed his eyes as he listened to Ralph Dade on the other end of the line.

"I'd appreciate it if you could come down to the salon now, George. We're all here and waiting for you. Don't bother getting dressed up, just get decent and come down."

"Damn!" George said. "I was looking forward to showing off my new tux." He hung up before Ralph could reply and dressed quickly in slacks and a sport shirt.

The 'we' Ralph referred to was the syndicate of *Seafire*'s ten owners that Ralph had put together at George's suggestion to pay for the rehab and transformation of the ship. The yacht was set up like a cooperative apartment, with each owner having a private stateroom and jointly owning the rest of it. Ralph liked to call *Seafire* a seagoing condominium.

George wondered what all the secrecy was about. After they had landed aboard *Seafire*, Ralph had stubbornly refused to tell him what the major trouble was all about. Instead, Ralph had urged him to get a couple of hours' sleep until the evening meeting, when he would hear all about it. This secrecy, on top of the huge inconvenience of sudden travel, had infuriated George. Now, still angry, he was curious to learn what had brought him five thousand miles in less than a day. Slipping an old pair of Docksiders onto his feet, George left his stateroom and made his way toward the salon.

Seafire's main salon was forward on the main deck level. It was just aft of the exchange room, the forward most compartment in the superstructure. The salon served as the living room for the ship's owners and their guests. Roughly twenty feet wide by twenty-five feet long, it had been the wardroom when the ship was originally built. George stopped just outside the soundproof door. He hesitated to enter it, knowing the room would be full of people he hardly knew, and cared little about. It was as if he was returning to visit a club he'd dropped out of years ago. He could feel his jaw muscles begin to clench as he opened the door.

When George stepped into the salon, he was amazed at the size of the crowd. His eyes scanned the room, as he silently took attendance. My God, he thought. The gang's all here. Ralph and two or three other people made polite noises of welcome.

"Better fix yourself a drink," Ralph said. "You're going to need it."

George looked at the faces around the room. The men and women had the same haggard look he had noted in Ralph. Deciding that Ralph's suggestion was a good one, he headed for the bar.

"I assume Ralph told you why we're all here," said a familiar voice.

"No, Nick, he didn't," George replied, with his back turned.

"Cut the crap, George. You don't expect us to believe that."

George finished making his drink, and turned to face Nick Argeriardis, one of the world's biggest shipping tycoons. He never had liked the big Greek very much, not even at the beginning. It seemed Nick's manners hadn't improved with age.

"I've been in this room for thirty seconds, and already you're calling me a liar. What's your problem, Nick?"

Nick moved closer to George. The Greek was taller by four inches than George's six feet, and loomed into his personal space. "You flew halfway around the world, and didn't ask why?" His voice was heavy with sarcasm.

George smiled and stood his ground. "I didn't say I didn't ask. I said he didn't tell me."

Argeriardis backed away without reply or apology, and George sat in an overstuffed chair. He took a swallow of his scotch and soda. He was beginning to feel angry again.

"Look, people. I have better things to do than spend my whole day on airplanes. Ralph calls and tells me to get out here, ASAP. Life or death emergency, he says. Can't tell me any more until I get here. Well, I'm here, and somebody damn well better tell me why."

Silence filled the room for five or six seconds as people waited for somebody else to answer.

"Extortion," a woman said, and George turned to face Suvia Ferris. He'd met her before, after her husband's death. Since then, she'd been running Ferroil Industries, the family business. For a decade, Holbrook Helicopters had been a subsidiary of Ferroil, which made Suvia, technically, George's boss. On top of that, she was a beautiful woman. George avoided her as much as possible.

"Who?" George asked, and several people began to speak at once. He raised a hand to silence them, and repeated his question to Suvia.

"All of us," she replied. "We had a visit from Jinnah. The terrorist. He wants a billion dollars."

George was stunned. Jinnah! Of all the terrorists in the world, Jinnah was best known for ruthless, senseless slaughter. He was generally believed to be crazier, in terms of pure blood lust, than the leaders of the IRA and the PLO combined.

George was about to ask another question when Alex Wilson interrupted.

"Hold on, Suvia. Let's not get ahead of ourselves. We agreed not to tell George the whole story before we got into deliberations."

George regarded Wilson sourly. The Englishman had a long face and straight nose, the mark of British aristocracy and the horses they ride. The newest of *Seafire*'s owners, he'd bought his share three or four years earlier. George didn't know him well, but well enough to think he was an arrogant jerk.

"Was it your idea to drag me out here without telling me why?" George asked.

"Yes." There was neither defensiveness nor apology in the answer.

"Why?"

"We have to decide what to do. Some of us think we need your advice. For the record, I don't. In any case, we didn't want you to start off with any preconceived notions."

"Are you sure it really was Jinnah? There aren't any known photographs of him, as I recall."

It was Peter Carson who replied. He had aged well since George had last seen him. He was handsome and firmly dedicated to looking distinguished at all times. The steel gray hair helped a lot. "That's right, George," he said. "I called one of my papers and had the file pulled on the guy. There aren't any pictures, but the man who was here last night matches what's known about him."

"What did he look like?"

"Small," Carson said. "Middle age. Forty, maybe. Dark skin, black hair. Looked like an Indian or a Pakistani."

"He was good looking, like Omar Sharif, when he was young," said Jacqueline Girard.

"Jacqueline!" said her financier husband, Henri, in a tone of outrage. He pronounced the name the French way, Zhock-a-leen.

"It's true, *mon cher*," she replied. "I didn't say he was a nice man. Just good looking."

Emily Carson whispered into her husband's ear, "They all look good to Jacqueline." He ignored the remark.

"I think English is a second language, although he spoke it very well," Carson continued. "He had a British accent, as if he went to school there. Very BBC, very upper class."

"Talked like he had a broomstick up his ass," said Ralph Dade. "Like Alex, only worse."

Wilson glared at Dade, but didn't say anything.

George rubbed his temples and took another swallow of his drink. "How did he get aboard? How did he get back off? Was he alone? Jesus Christ, where was security?"

Nick Argeriardis answered George's first question with a growl. "Harold and Patty Phelps brought him aboard," he said, glaring at them. "Like he was a fucking honored guest."

Patricia Phelps was another person that George didn't care for, much. She had a thin, shrewish face and an even thinner, nasal voice. When she replied, she was in full whine.

"That's not fair, Nick! You know we had no choice. Jinnah could have used you and Frances as easily as us to get aboard. You wouldn't have been able to stop him."

Nick snorted in derision.

"When was this?" George asked Patty.

"Last night. Close to midnight."

Ralph spoke up again. "Helen and I were playing bridge with Suvia and Joe Langone. Jinnah came in with the Phelpses. He had me call the other owners and told us to assemble in the exchange room ."

"Did he call it by that name?" George asked.

"Yes. Pretty good intelligence, right?"

"Right."

"It gets worse. There are the folders ..."

"Bloody hell!" shouted Alex Wilson. "This is all wrong. We agreed on the agenda. We'll tell George the facts as they happened and talk about implications afterward."

"Stuff your agenda, Alex," said George. "I'll ask any question I damn well want." He turned back to Ralph. "How come nobody pushed a panic button?" There were three hidden buttons in the salon. If somebody had pushed one, silent alarms would have summoned the ship's security force. George had planned for dealing with intruders when he drew the first designs for *Seafire's* conversion. The panic alarms were just one of the countermeasures he had put in place.

"Funny you should mention that," Ralph replied, looking at Patty. "I tried to. Patty told Jinnah what I was doing and he pulled a gun."

George turned and gazed at Patty Phelps. She got out of her chair and started pacing about in agitation.

"I had to tell him," she said, whining again. "Jinnah only came to talk to us. He told Harold and me before we came aboard that if we interfered with him, if anybody decided to be a hero and grabbed him, or shot him, or had him arrested, we'd regret it for the rest of our lives."

Patty sat, shaking, at one of the tables and buried her face in her hands. Harold stepped over and placed a comforting hand on his wife's shoulder. She clasped her hand over his and began to sob quietly. George wondered if it was an act.

"We should stop talking about Patty as if she were a traitor," said Peter Carson. "Jinnah made his demands and left. Nobody got hurt. God knows what would have happened if Ralph had pushed the button. Think about the folders."

George had to swivel around to face Peter. "What folders?"

"Why don't we move this meeting into the exchange room?" Suvia Ferris asked. "We can all sit around the big table. This room isn't set up for a conference." There were several murmurs of agreement, and the group headed for the exchange room door.

Seafire's exchange room was a good deal larger than her salon, running the full width of the superstructure, which the salon did not. Situated at the forward end of the deckhouse, its corners were slightly rounded at the end of the room nearest the bow. Otherwise, it was roughly twenty-five feet square. There were several small desks around the perimeter of the room. Each one had a telephone and a computer terminal mounted securely on it, and two small combination safes built into the single pedestal. Mounted against the aft bulkhead was a large rack full of radios, satellite telephones, fax and telex machines, and other communications equipment. Most of this gear was designed to provide continuous stock, bond and commodity trading information. If it had been earlier in New York, NYSE, NASDAQ and AMEX stock tickers would have been crawling across electronic display boards. At the moment, the displays were dark.

A long conference table stood in the middle of the room. It looked massive and solid, built of rich, dark wood and beautifully polished. Nineteen people sat around it in varied dress, ranging from Alex Wilson in a jogging suit to Peter Carson in a blue blazer, white shirt, and a club tie.

"Jinnah claimed that his troops were holding several of our children hostage," Ralph said, once everyone was seated. "He wouldn't say who or how many. He was here only to make initial contact and basic demands. After that, he said he'd leave, to give us time to decide whether or not to meet the demands."

"Excuse me," said Bob Knight. "There's an easier way to do this. I could play the videotape."

"What?" said Ralph, in a chorus with three or four others. There were security cameras all over the ship. In the exchange room, however, privacy concerns had outweighed the desire for security. No cameras were installed there, or so everyone had thought.

Bob looked uneasy. He was small and boyish, with fair skin and thick glasses. He looked like a computer nerd, which was exactly what he was. "I put a camera in here a couple of days ago. It's a new project Steve and I are working on." He glanced at Steve Roth.

"What the hell were you two doing," Nick Argeriardis growled, "spying on us?"

"No," Bob replied, defensively. "It was never turned on unless I was in here alone. It's voice controlled. I needed a big room to test the control system. When Jinnah had us come in here last night, I switched it on. It seemed like a good idea. Later, I wondered if maybe it wasn't. I've been trying to decide whether to tell you about it, or just erase the tape."

"This is terrible," said Harold Phelps. "If Jinnah finds out we have him on tape, he'll go nuts."

"We could use the tape as a threat," Nick Argeriardis replied. "Tell him to fuck off or we give the tape to Interpol. If there aren't any pictures of him, the tape could nail his ass."

"No, we can't!" Harold shouted. "We have to destroy it."

"Let's be quiet and watch it," George said in exasperation. "We can decide what to do with it later."

Bob Knight picked up a hand-held remote, and the TV came on. It had a huge flat screen, flush mounted on the forward bulkhead. It showed the familiar pattern of electronic snow as Bob put a tape into the VCR.

"How did you turn on the camera without anybody knowing?" George asked.

"The microphone is always on. It's hooked to a computer that recognizes my voice. When I say a code word, the computer turns on the camera and rolls tape."

"What's the code word?"

"It can be anything I program in. Last night, it was, 'candid,' like in Candid Camera." Knight grinned at his own humor. "I said something about 'candid discussions' to Steve as we were filing in, and the machine turned itself on."

Suddenly, the snow disappeared, and the screen filled with a view of the exchange room. The camera position was forward, pointing aft toward the door to the salon. A dark-haired man was leaning nonchalantly against the communications rack, watching as *Seafire*'s co-owners took seats around the table. George watched the image, aware of an eerie feeling of deja vu. The TV screen was like a mirror, showing the room in which he sat, and the people with whom he was sitting. The only difference was that the stranger was there, and George wasn't.

The intruder waited until everyone was seated. "Mr. Dade," he said, "please call the quarterdeck. Tell the watch that there is an important meeting of the steering committee in progress and it is not to be disturbed." When Ralph made no move to comply, he added, "If some stupid security guard blunders in here, I shall shoot him first and your wife second. After that, I shall improvise. Now, Mr. Dade, are you going to make the call, or are you willing to risk a bloodbath?"

"I'll call," Suvia Ferris said, and started to get up from her chair.

"No!" the man shouted with such vehemence that Suvia sat down hard. "Not you! Him!" The gun was out again.

The TV was silent for a minute as it showed Ralph walking to a desk, speaking inaudibly into a telephone, and returning to his seat at the table. George glanced at the faces around him. No wonder they look haggard, he thought, and returned his attention to the TV.

As Ralph sat, the visitor opened the briefcase he had been carrying. He pulled out a stack of blue folders and placed them on the table.

"Please pass these to the proper persons," he directed, "but don't open them until I tell you so. Husbands and wives will have to share; there are only ten dossiers." The people around the table shuffled the folders for a moment, until each was in its place.

The man continued. "I know a great deal about each of you, as I will soon demonstrate. You don't know me. I shall not tell you my real name, very few people know it. The name by which I have come to be known lately is Jinnah."

The tape recording was excellent. George could see the shock register in the faces around the table. It was the same feeling of shock he had felt when Suvia had spoken Jinnah's name a few minutes ago. He noticed something else, too.

"Hold it, Bob. Can you back the tape up ten seconds or so?"

"Sure."

The screen flickered briefly, and once again Jinnah was speaking. "Here good enough?" Bob asked, and George nodded.

"...Very few people know it. The name by which I have come to be known lately is Jinnah." Once again, the faces registered shock, but George was not watching those faces. He watched Jinnah's face, watched his expression of satisfaction, of almost sexual pleasure. You are one son of a bitch, George thought. Scaring people turns you on.

Jinnah continued. "I see by your expressions that you know of me. Excellent! However, your knowledge of me does not obviate the necessity of my demonstrating my knowledge of you."

George had been puzzling over the man's use of English. Ralph had been right about the broomstick. Did he really talk like that all the time, or was it part of the production?

"Nicholas and Frances Argeriardis," Jinnah said, nodding slightly in their direction. "Nicholas' fleet of ships is nearly as large as that of the late Mr. Onassis. Additional holdings include docking and warehousing facilities in several major ports, and interests in surface transportation industries. He also holds a minority interest in an airline.

"Sealed in an envelope at the end of your folder, Mr. Argeriardis, there is an approximate accounting of your assets and liabilities. It is for your information only. You may show it to your friends, or not, that is up to you. It is included to prove that I am fully aware of your financial circumstances. A similar accounting of the net worth of the other owners is included in their respective folders."

There was a murmur in the room. Nick picked up his folder and began to open it.

"Mr. Argeriardis, please! Do not open the folder until I tell you to."

"What happens if I do?"

"You might make me angry. Your family would regret that."

Nick's jaw clenched as he put the folder down on the table.

Jinnah turned. "Mr. and Mrs. Peter Carson. The Carson chain of newspapers is not the largest in the United States, but it is one of the most profitable. It owns or controls a number of television and radio stations. Additional ventures include two book-publishing houses and a TV production company.

"Ralph C. Dade, and his wife, Helen. Mr. Dade is a developer of real estate. Currently, most of Mr. Dade's holdings are in the Miami area, in a part of Florida known as Dade County. The similarity of names is not a coincidence. Since so much of Mr. Dade's property is in the form of undeveloped land, and is therefore somewhat illiquid, estimates of his net worth tend to be inaccurate. The figure in the Dade dossier will suffice for our purposes, however."

"Hold it," George said, and Jinnah's image froze again on the screen. "He's going through everybody in alphabetical order. Do I need to watch this?"

"Probably not," Ralph said. "Let's fast forward to where Joe punches Jinnah on the nose."

"Great," George said, looking curiously at Joe Langone. "I certainly want to see that."

Once again the screen flickered, then the images came to rest. "Each of you profits from your association with the others," Jinnah was saying. "Ms. Ferris' petroleum is shipped in Argeriardis hulls. Argeriardis ships and aircraft run on Ferroil fuels. Langone Construction builds Mr. Dade's condominiums. Mr. Phelps and Mr. Wilson handle the trading in your personal accounts and in various trust accounts as well. You share investment opportunities and pool your resources to exert leverage. Acting together, you have helped each other to amass more capital than you could have if you had acted alone. Together, also, you shall part with a portion of that wealth.

"Earlier this evening I told you that my associates had young hostages in their custody. Technically, that is untrue. I have taken no one prisoner, nor will I. Yet, I hold as hostages *all* of your children, *all* of your grandchildren. The fate of your heirs is in my hands. The proof of this is in the several folders before you. In each, you will find a number of photographs. You have my personal assurance that there has been no retouching or other tampering with the images. The cross hairs are quite genuine, the photographs were indeed taken through telescopic rifle sights."

"Here it comes, George," Ralph said. "Watch Joe."

Joe had opened his folder, but Jinnah hadn't noticed. Joe was looking at a photograph in it, and his face was turning red. George and the others watched the screen in fascination.

Joe closed the folder, making strangling noises deep in his throat. "You little piece of shit, you get out of here! I swear to God I'll kill you with my own fucking hands. I'll take that toy gun away from you and ram it right up your scrawny ass. Get out of here!" As suddenly as he had begun, Joe was finished. Incredibly, he was still seated. The knuckles on his clenched fists were white, the tendons stood out on his neck like the roots of a cypress tree, but he had managed to stay in his seat. For Joe Langone, a man with a bad temper, it had been an amazing display of self-control.

For a good three seconds, the room was totally silent. Jinnah took two steps around the end of the table, and stood beside Langone's chair. "Shut your filthy mouth, old man." He slapped Joe across the mouth with the back of his hand.

The sixty-year-old flowed up and out of his chair, catching Jinnah completely by surprise. He threw only one punch, a left. It was a roundhouse left that started somewhere in the deep pile of the carpet, and ended about three feet behind where Jinnah's head had been. The terrorist went down in a heap.

Jinnah was slow in regaining his feet, giving Nick and Alex time to restrain Joe. Wiping blood from his mouth and nose, Jinnah spoke again.

"If it were not for my duty to my people, I would leave you now, and let each of you die over the years, childless and alone, of old age."

Still mopping at the blood, he looked at his wristwatch. "Time is short. The ransom is one billion U.S. dollars plus this ship and some other minor contributions in kind. A week from now, the ship will be in Palma de Mallorca. Further details will be delivered to you at that time. Two weeks from tonight, the ship will be in Malta, where you are planning to host a dinner dance. I will come aboard then, after midnight. If you have decided to meet my demands, I will tell you the final details. If you refuse, my associates will begin to shoot bullets instead of film.

"One final item. If you agree to comply, you will have with you in Malta the equivalent, in gold coin or bullion, of one million American dollars. This will serve as a down payment, a token of your good faith."

Gesturing to Harold Phelps to accompany him, Jinnah left the room. "That's it," Bob Knight said, and the TV went dark.

"Christ, Joe," George said, "What brought that on? You came out of your chair like lava out of a volcano."

Joe didn't answer. Instead he went to one of the desks, opened a safe, pulled out a blue folder, and handed it to George.

George looked at the folder, a binder such as salesman use to present brochures and proposals. Joe Langone's name was embossed in gold letters at the lower right corner. George opened it.

The folder was thin. It held only three or four typed sheets and a single photograph, an eight by ten color glossy. It was a full-length shot of Chrissy Langone, Joe's only grandchild and the light of his life, on roller skates. Pretty and smiling, she was gliding almost directly toward the camera, wearing shorts and a halter, dark hair flying, skin deeply tanned. A beautiful picture of a child poised on the brink of womanhood. With the cross hairs of a gun sight intersecting at her left breast.

As George looked at the picture, he could feel his eyes fill with tears of rage. "Are all the folders like this?"

"Yes," Ralph replied.

George looked at the typed pages. He realized with embarrassment that he was looking at a statement of Joe Langone's net worth. "Sorry," he said to Joe, and closed the folder.

"No, please, look at it," Joe said. "Look at the last part." His voice was low and gravelly.

George scanned the figures, and came to the last sentence. "Mr. Joseph R. Langone's contribution to the cause of justice in Makran shall be fifty million United States dollars."

Neither George nor anyone else said anything, and Ralph handed him another folder. It had Ralph and Helen's names embossed on it. He opened it and scanned the financials to the end.

Ralph's ransom was to be sixty-five million. Then he looked at the Dade family photographs. Ralph's sons, the twins, Ralph Jr. and George. The "boys," young men now, each with an identical touch of early gray at the temples. Their wives, and their young children, all of them, in the pictures. All taken through gun sights. George felt the rage return. For several moments, he said nothing. Then he stood up and began to pace around the table.

"Well, it looks like you people have a decision to make. As I see it, you have two choices. You can give the man what he wants, or kill the son of a bitch."

"That's crazy, George," Patty Phelps wailed. "If anything happens to Jinnah, his men will kill our children!"

"I was coming to that point, Patty. If you kill him, you'll have to kill his men, too."

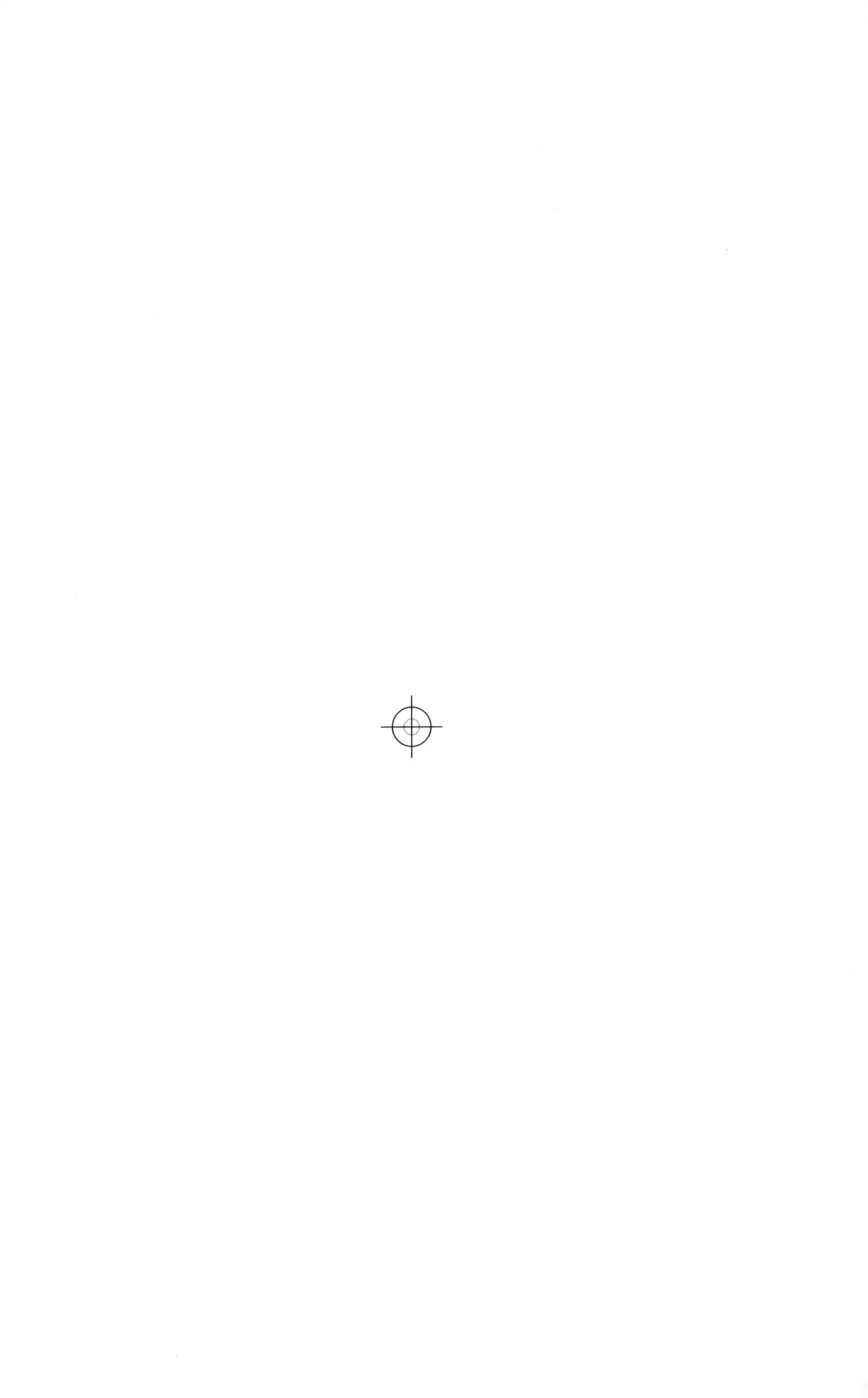

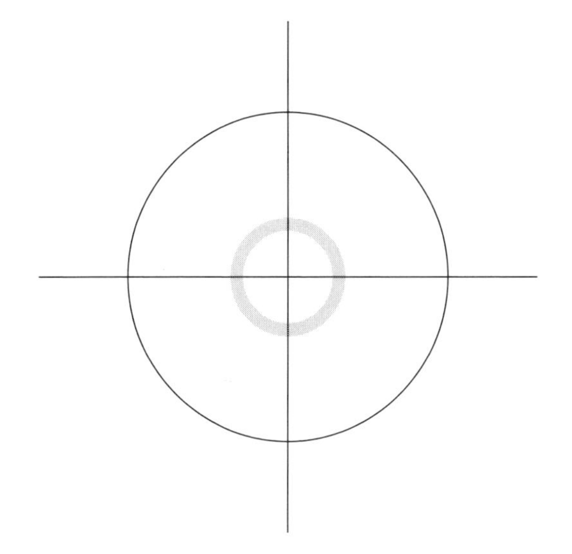

CHAPTER 3

FOR NEARLY a minute, nobody spoke. George Holbrook stopped pacing and got back into his chair.

Alex Wilson broke the silence. "I'd say the so-called terrorism expert missed an obvious third choice."

"What's that?" George asked.

"Go to the authorities, of course. Maybe they could catch Jinnah in Malta. At least, we should let them know what he's up to."

"Well, Alex," George replied, "if you're thinking about doing that, then there's a fourth choice, too."

"What's that?"

"Buy a gun and shoot your kids yourself."

Alex's face turned red with anger. "What do you mean by that?"

"Calling the authorities would be stupid. It would surely get some of your kids killed. Maybe all of them."

"I've had enough of this," Alex said, looking around the room. "I'll not be insulted by Suvia Ferris' bloody paid flyboy. The last thing we need is advice from the likes of him!"

George got out of his chair, and headed for the door. "Alex is right," he said, with his hand on the doorknob. "I don't have a dog in this fight. I don't have any money and I don't have any family. Nothing at risk. Nothing to lose. Whatever you decide to do can't possibly affect me. I don't understand why you dragged me out here to tell me this." He opened the door.

"George," Suvia Ferris said. "I watched your face when you were looking at Ralph and Helen's folder. The twins are your godsons, aren't they? Do you care if they're killed or not? If it came to it, would you fight to save them? Would you?"

George looked at Suvia. Her gaze was level and steady, her expression calmly questioning. He sensed, vaguely, that she was probing for more than an answer to her simple question.

"I would, if I thought it was the right thing to do."

Suvia nodded slowly, and George turned back to Ralph.

"I still don't see why I had to fly here. You could have faxed me the folder and asked for advice over the phone."

"We don't know what to do," Helen Dade said. "Ralph says you've had experience with terrorists and guerillas. We thought you could help us better to decide if we talked face to face."

"Just what we don't need," said Alex Wilson.

"Alex, stop being rude," said Polly Harrington. The elderly widow was another newcomer to *Seafire*, having bought her share after her husband's death. George was fond of her. "Please sit down, George," she said, "and tell us why you think going to the authorities is such a bad idea."

George sat. "OK, Polly. What do we know about Jinnah? Peter, correct me if I'm wrong on any of this.

"He's a Muslim terrorist. Specializes in bombs. Big ones. He's got a name in Arabic that translates as The Technician or The Engineer, or some such. As a bomb designer, he's not half bad.

"His first big bomb, people think, was the one that took down the Marine Corps barracks in Beirut. Very sophisticated blast enhancement technique. If I remember right, the flatbed of the suicide truck was lined with marble slabs, to focus the blast upward. Very effective. Jinnah's generally given credit for that design.

"Terrorism cops think the Khobar Towers was his work, too. Story is that Jinnah had planned that as a suicide mission like Beirut. Run the truck right in under the building and bring it down like a house of cards. The local fanatics couldn't find a suicide bomber, though, so they parked the truck as close as they could and ran off. Blew the front off the building, but left it standing.

"His latest exploit supposedly was the synchronized bombing of the U.S. embassies in East Africa. Acted as a consultant to Osama bin Laden, gratis. Normally, he gets paid for his work. He did this one for free, as his contribution to the *jihad*."

George hesitated, and turned to Peter Carson. "How am I doing?"

"Absolutely right, so far."

"OK. Now to answer Polly's question. This guy's been designing bombs for years. His devices have killed over three hundred Americans. Yet, the CIA and the FBI and Interpol and the whole lot haven't caught him. Don't even know what he looks like. Are you with me so far?"

George's question was directed at Alex. He didn't respond.

"So, you go to the authorities and say, 'Oh my! Jinnah is threatening us.' What's going to happen? They're already trying to find him. Do you think they'll try harder just because a bunch of rich people want him caught?

"What *will* happen is that Jinnah will learn you ratted him out and carry out his threats."

"Your opinion," said Alex Wilson.

"Yeah, Alex," George replied, "My opinion. That's all it is."

"Alex, you're being rude again," said Polly.

"I'm not offended," George said. "Alex is right. I'm not an expert on terrorists. Rumors of my skills in counterinsurgency are greatly exaggerated."

"I thought you worked for the CIA," Alex said.

"I should sue you for slander," George said, with a bitter laugh. "As far as I'm concerned, CIA stands for criminally incompetent assassins. No, I don't work for the CIA."

"Jesus, George," Nick Argeriardis said. "If you don't have any experience with terrorists, what do we need you for?"

George waved his hand in a gesture of impatience. "Have you gone deaf in your old age, Nick? Haven't I been asking you people that?"

"George, we owe you an apology," Alex said. "It was a mistake bringing you out here. Certainly not your fault. Why don't you leave us to talk, get a good night's sleep, and fly back to the States tomorrow?"

Suvia Ferris said, "Be quiet Alex." He looked at her in surprise. "Tell them about Peru, George," she said, and it was his turn to look surprised.

"I don't want to talk about that, Mrs. Ferris." Her eyes widened briefly at his icy tone and formal address.

"I'm sorry, George. There are lives at stake here. People we love could die if we make bad decisions. Everybody here needs to know about Peru. If you don't tell them, I will."

George stared coolly at Suvia and said nothing. She stared back. After a moment, he got up and left the room.

"Damn," Suvia said.

"He works for you, Suvia," said Steve Roth. "I'll go after him if you want. Tell him you want his ass back in here. I'll even drag him in." Roth, a big, bear-like man, with broad shoulders and jet-black hair, looked as if he might enjoy doing it.

"I don't think that would be a good idea," said Ralph Dade.

"Tell us about Peru," said Joe Langone. "Maybe that will help us decide whether to ask him back or let him go."

"After Dick died," Suvia began, "and I took over running Ferroil Industries, I decided to steer clear of George Holbrook. I thought it would be awkward to deal with him. Here he was an engineer and test pilot in the Holbrook Helicopters Division. An employee in the company his father had founded. He did good work, so I just left him alone.

"There was another reason. There were rumors about him. If he had no projects to work on, he'd disappear. Weeks at a time. Nobody knew where he went. Very mysterious."

"You can imagine the rumors. He was a mercenary, an assassin, a spy. He smuggled guns, drugs, illegal immigrants, all of the above. No one knew what he did, but everyone was sure he was a rogue.

"Six months after Dick died, the Shining Path guerillas kidnapped a bunch of my people. They'd been negotiating for drilling rights in Peru. If the kidnappers had wanted money, I would have paid. They didn't want money, they wanted the Peruvian government to let their comrades out of prison. The government wouldn't do that, and negotiations for release of the hostages were going nowhere.

"One day George showed up in my office. I'd never met him, but I knew his reputation. He said he could get the hostages out, so long as I didn't care or want to know how he did it. I was shocked. I got all outraged and huffy and sent him away. Three days later I got a video from the guerillas. One of my people, a woman, was being gang raped and tortured. The day after that, George was on his way to Peru.

"I still don't know what he did there. There were protests lodged with the State Department. Vague threats of prosecution. That's died down. The former hostages won't talk about what he did. They're all very grateful to George for rescuing them, but they've seen him in action and don't want him for a friend. Ally, yes. Friend, no. When his name is mentioned, they shudder and change the subject."

The room was quiet for several moments. "I think we need him to help us," Polly Harrington said. Several people made vague noises of agreement. "How do we get him to do it?"

"Offer to pay him, of course," Peter Carson said. "A couple of million bucks should do. I'm sure that's what he's angling for, walking out in a phony huff. He wants us to open the bidding."

"If you want him to walk out in a real huff and never come back, all you have to do is insult him by offering him money," said Ralph.

"Is he crazy?" asked Steve Roth.

"Of course he's crazy. Weren't you listening to Suvia's story? That's what makes him so good at what he does."

Ralph found George in the salon, just outside the exchange room. He'd mixed himself a scotch and soda — a tall, dark one, the color of iced tea. He hadn't drunk any of it yet. He sat looking at it, as if challenging it to a duel.

"Hello, Ralph," he said. "Come to twist my arm?"

"Actually, I've come to beg."

"Ralph, if it were just you and Helen, you wouldn't have to beg. Hell, you wouldn't even have to ask. I'd be here, telling you what to do, whether you wanted me to or not. But this crowd, how can I work with them? They're all assholes! Most of 'em, anyway. Nick's a bully. Alex is a spoiled brat, born with athletic ability and a lot of money, who thinks he's God's gift to mankind. Carson's a stuffed shirt. None of those people are going to listen to me. They'll second-guess me a hundred times a day.

"Bob Knight's brilliant. At least it said so in *Time* when he was Man of the Year. But he looks like a pencil-necked wimp to me. If we have to fight, take risks, will he be with me? I doubt it. The rest of them, who knows?

"I'm sorry, Ralph. It won't work. Find somebody else."

"You're probably right, but I want you to try, anyway. The twins are your godsons, George. If Helen and I die, you're supposed to look out for their souls. Helen takes that religious stuff seriously, she put a lot of trust in you when she asked you to do that. *I'm* asking you, as an old friend, to look out for their lives.

"You saved my life once. Try to save theirs. Even if it's not easy. Even if you have to save a bunch of assholes' kids along with them. Please."

George looked at his old friend and saw tears in his eyes. He'd never seen Ralph cry. The sight made him feel awkward and embarrassed. And ashamed.

"Tell you what I'm gonna do," George said, pretending not to notice Ralph's tears. "I take the job, consultant or whatever, on an interim basis. A couple of weeks. Until they can find somebody better qualified."

"Or until you can't stand working with assholes any more."

"Or until then. Would that be OK?"

"That would be great, George." Ralph's huge relief was obvious. For a horrible moment, George was afraid Ralph would give him a hug.

"Pretty good job of arm twisting, Ralph. I'm surprised they didn't send you in here to offer me money. My father would have. People like that usually assume everybody's for sale."

"A couple of people suggested that. I talked them out of it."

George entered the exchange room and looked around. The people at the table watched him with a curiosity that he found annoying and amusing all at once. "All right," he said, sitting down.

"I've agreed to serve as chairman of the what-do-we-do-about-Jinnah committee."

"Thank you," said Suvia. Most of the others voiced agreement. Alex Wilson grunted in disgust.

"I'll do it for a week or two at most. By then, you'll have decided the direction you're going to take. After then, somebody else has to take over. I'll stay on as a consultant, if you want, but I'm not going to be in charge."

George looked around, making eye contact with the people, one by one, gauging their reactions. Mostly, he decided, it was relief.

"OK, let's get started," he said. "First, we have to assume there's a spy among us. Some of the stuff Jinnah knew probably came from somebody in this room. Before anything of substance gets decided, or even discussed, we have to find the spy or be damn sure there isn't one."

Muffled gasps and groans filled the room.

"Think about it," George continued. "Ninety-nine percent of what Jinnah knows about you is in *Who's Who* or *Forbes.* Most of the rest could have come from someone in the crew, or even guesswork. The alarm systems, for example. Anyone who thought about it would assume we had them; we'd be crazy not to. But some of his info sounds like it came from one of the people sitting here."

"Give us an example," Suvia said.

"The steering committee's one. He used that term. Actually, there's no such committee. Every so often, people who care enough to bother get together to plan the ship's itinerary. Years ago, Ralph called one of these sessions a meeting of the steering committee, since we were deciding where to steer the ship. It was a pun. Very funny."

"I'd never heard the term until Jinnah used it last night," said Bob Knight.

"Neither did I," said Alex Wilson.

"You newcomers haven't been around long enough," George

replied. "I doubt that anybody in the crew has, either. The joke got old after a while, and people stopped using it. It tells me one thing, though. It tells me neither of you is the spy."

George looked around the table. "We're not going to figure out tonight if there's a spy or not, let alone who it is. I don't think we should discuss the main issue before we do."

"What do you mean?" asked Henri Girard.

"What are you going to do about Jinnah? Pay him? Call the cops? Threaten to release the videotape as Nick suggested? That's the main issue. Everything else is secondary.

"So long as there might be an informer here, it's dangerous for any of you to discuss those options. Suppose Jinnah's spy tells him Nick wants to use the videotape to blackmail him. Whose kids does Jinnah go after first to teach us not to mess with him?"

"Jesus Christ!" Nick shouted.

"OK. Let's talk about generalities for a while. Peter, what can you tell us about Jinnah?"

"He's a terrorist. His group is called the Makrani Liberation Organization — the MLO. Its goal is independence for Makran, an island that belongs to India. Muslims make up a majority of the population of the island, but the Hindu minority controls it. That's because Hindus are the majority in India as a whole. Once free, the island would become an Islamic state."

"Does he have the manpower to carry out the threats he made tonight?" asked George.

"Hard to say. I doubt it. There are ten shares in *Seafire*, ten family units. Maintaining a constant tailing watch on that many families is a big undertaking. At a minimum, for watch rotation and all that, you'd need four people per unit, I'd think. That's forty, at least.

"I can't see the bastard fielding that many people on a sustained basis. He's a hit and run operator, the classic guerilla. I would guess that his threat is part truth and part bluff. Mostly bluff. He may have two or three teams lurking about, waiting for orders to assassinate somebody. Does he have a constant tail on all our children and grandchildren? No way."

"Thanks, Peter," George said. "I'm no shrink, but did anybody other than me think that our boy Jinnah was more than a little bit nuts?"

"Jesus, George," replied Bob Knight, "terrorists are all crazy. They blow people up for the glory of God. If they can't find innocent people to kill, they kill themselves to become martyrs. They're all nuts. It's in the job description."

"Agreed, agreed," said George. "I'm looking for specific hang-ups, though. Control seems to be an issue, for example. He likes ordering people around. Pulled his damn pistol out when Suvia was going to do something he'd told Ralph to do."

"Why do we care about his hang-ups?" asked Ralph.

"I have an idea that if we can get a handle on them, we can avoid making any disastrous mistakes like Joe did."

"What do you mean?" Joe asked.

"You insulted him. Called him a piece of shit. A 'little' piece of shit. It drove him wild. Maybe he's sensitive about his size. I'd like to know what else sets him off, so we won't do it unless we have reason to." George looked at his watch. It was after three in the morning, and he suddenly felt terribly tired.

"There are one or two things," he said, "that we have to decide before we go to bed.

"First, did you warn your families to take cover?"

"No," Ralph replied, "Not yet anyway. We were afraid it might provoke Jinnah. We put off making a final decision about that."

"I think we should warn them," said Peter Carson. "Tell them to adopt strict security measures. No point in letting them be easier targets than they have to be." Bob Knight and Nick Argeriardis nodded vigorous agreement.

Steve Roth shook his head. "I still say we shouldn't. It's useless. Those folders have over a hundred pictures in them. We can't keep everybody safe forever. Jinnah can sit and wait until one of the kids gets careless and then ..."

Suvia Ferris broke in. "Steve's right. We can't lock them up indefinitely. What about the ones in college? Do they abandon their education and come home? Hide in their bedrooms? If they take precautions, Jinnah's agents will notice. He'll regard it as a challenge and pick off a couple of stragglers just to prove he's invincible."

"Good point, Suvia," George said. "I think for now you shouldn't tell your families about the threat. Do we all agree?" George looked around. "Good. It's unanimous. However, I think Joe Langone should be an exception."

"Why?" asked Ralph.

"Joe gave Jinnah a bloody nose. He might take personal revenge on Joe's family, regardless of its effect on the extortion plan. I think Joe should warn his son to take cover for a while." Again, everyone nodded agreement.

"We shouldn't try to decide anything more tonight. Why don't we adjourn and talk some more tomorrow?"

George remained seated as people left the room. "Ralph," he said. "I'd appreciate it if you and Helen would stay for a minute. I need to talk to you about a problem."

Ralph and Helen Dade returned to their seats. Suvia Ferris was last in line to leave the room. George asked her to close the door.

"Shall I close it behind me, or would you like me to stay?" she asked.

George hesitated for several seconds. "Stay if you like. You need to hear this as much as anyone." Suvia nodded, closed the door, and sat down.

"I have a suggestion. Think about it before we talk more. I wish I could say this to everybody, but I can't risk Jinnah hearing about it. Whatever you decide to do, try to maximize your options. Never commit to a single course of action.

"This down payment in two weeks, for example. Pay it. That's a tactic blackmailers have used for years. When they make the first demand, they make it small.

"A million dollars is more than I'll ever see. Even for you it isn't chump change, but if you divide it up among all of you, it isn't a king's ransom, either. Do you see what he's doing? He wants to make it easy for you to pay the first installment. Once you've gotten over that initial psychological barrier, once you've agreed to submit to extortion, the rest is just a matter of degree.

"I suggest you decide soon, tomorrow or the next day, to pay the million bucks as the purchase price for two weeks' time. Two weeks to learn everything you can about Jinnah and his damn guerrillas. Two weeks to plan. Does that make sense?"

"OK," said George, when nobody replied. "I'll suggest that to some of the others. The ones I'm sure can't be the spy."

"Assuming there's only one," said Suvia.

"If there's more than one, we're finished, and it doesn't matter what Jinnah finds out. We have to assume there's only one."

Suvia nodded. George couldn't tell if it meant she agreed with his logic, or merely understood it.

Suvia and the Dades left the exchange room, with George behind them. Passing through the salon, he passed Alex Wilson, who was pouring himself a very large brandy. Alex offered to pour George one as well. George knew that it was a gesture of reconciliation, but for an instant he felt an awful craving for alcohol, and the power of it frightened him. He knew he had been drinking a lot lately, but the physical longing for booze was something new, or at least something he hadn't allowed himself to notice until now. No, he told himself, now of all times I need as clear a head as I can muster. He turned down the invitation, as politely as he could, and returned to his stateroom. For the first time in several weeks he went to bed without placing a drink on his bedside table. And, for the first time since he'd first set foot aboard *Seafire*, he locked his stateroom door.

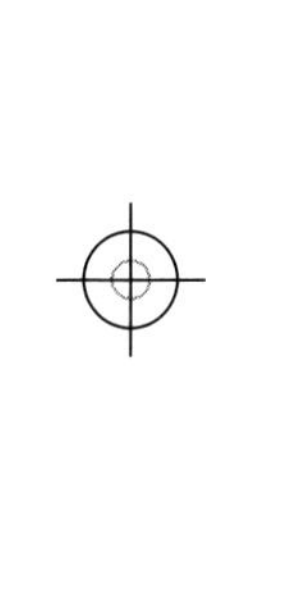

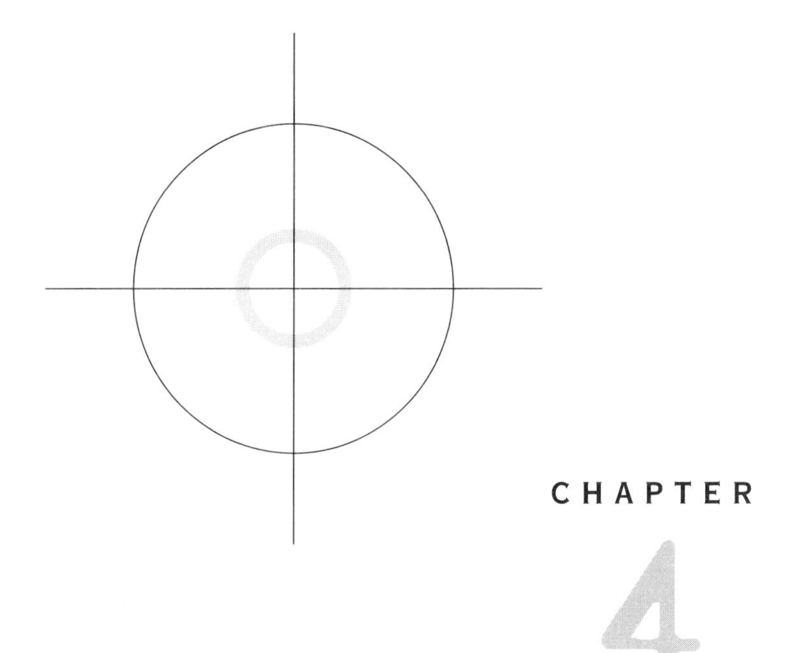

CHAPTER 4

CHRISTINE LANGONE hurried to the car so she could open her own door. She hated it when Billy opened doors for her. She knew he was only being polite, but he worked for her father, and it made her feel creepy. Like she was a countess, or something, and Billy was her footman. Since the men had tried to kidnap her two years ago, there had been a lot of changes in her life. She blamed herself for all of them, and hated most. The one exception was Billy Borowski. She loved Billy Borowski.

She truly detested the car. It was a Cadillac Fleetwood, big and black, over ten years old. Daddy had bought it because the new ones were lighter, and heavier was better. Chrissy had cried when she saw it. It looked like a funeral car. Even after two years, when it arrived at Rosarian Academy, some of the girls would hum the theme from *The Godfather*. It was mortifying.

"Sometimes, kidnappers force cars off the road," Daddy had said. "Good luck to them if they try it with the Fleetwood."

The biggest change, and the one Chrissy regretted most, was the move. She had loved the old house in West Palm Beach. It was right on the Intracoastal Waterway, with broad lawns running down to the water, and big, old oak trees she could climb and sit in all day. She could look across at the mansions in Palm Beach, where Ringo Starr and the really rich people lived. After the men had tried to abduct her, her family had moved to Singer Island, to live in the Village of Hidden Tree.

Christine Langone hated Hidden Tree. The place reminded her of a prison. It had fences around it fifteen feet high, and guardhouses at the entrances. There was hardly anyone her age around, and everybody was filthy rich. She knew that Daddy was rich too, and so was Grandpa Joe, but they didn't show their money like these people did. She even hated the house. The old house in West Palm was a Mizner house, with Spanish architecture and a red tile roof. It was incredibly romantic. The new house was big and comfortable, and about as romantic as a Burger King. It was all her fault. If only she had stayed away from the men in that car.

The man who saved her was an off duty policeman. He brought her home and made some phone calls. A doctor came and determined in two minutes that Chrissy was fine. He spent over an hour tending to Mommy. Daddy and a police detective named Borowski talked in the library, and Chrissy listened outside the door. He gave Daddy advice, and Chrissy cried as she heard it. The Mizner house was indefensible, Borowski said. It went on the market the next day.

On Borowski's recommendation, Daddy hired Billy, the detective's younger brother, as a driver and bodyguard. They bought the Fleetwood, and sent Billy to a special school to learn evasive driving. For four months, he was her constant companion, and she developed a huge crush on him. Then, once they were settled in Hidden Tree, Mommy started driving the Fleetwood and Billy's assignment was over.

When the call came from Grandpa Joe, Daddy called to see if Billy was available as a driver. He was pleased to get the call. He needed work, and he looked forward to seeing Chrissy Langone again. She was a neat kid. It made him regret never having had a little sister. And, she'd had that huge crush on him, which he found amusing and endearing. Yes, it would be fun to work for the Langones again.

Billy knew he had to vary his route as much as possible when driving Chrissy around. On the mainland, that was easy; there were dozens of possible routes to Chrissy's school. Getting to the mainland was the problem. There are only two ways to get off of Singer Island by car — the bridges either end. Billy flipped a coin. On this morning, the route would be south, over the Blue Heron bridge.

The Fleetwood was warmed up and waiting when Christine came out of the house. He was ready to roll. One of their favorite tapes was playing, the first Who? album. Chrissy got into the front seat, as usual. She would never ride in the back like a rich old lady with big diamonds and blue hair.

⁍ ⁍ ⁍ ⁍ ⁍

The man with the telescope was two miles away. On the balcony of a condominium, fourteen floors above the flat Florida landscape, he watched the huge black car turn south onto A1A. He spoke briefly into a small radio, using a code name, Jake. Then he swung the telescope toward the undeveloped part of the island, and focused on a white van. It was a windowless Chevrolet C-10 with an enormous plastic termite on the roof and the name of an exterminating company on the doors. It was the perfect anonymous vehicle, so outrageously conspicuous as to look friendly and harmless. Of course, it was neither. It flashed its headlights in response to the radio call, and the man who called himself Jake began to pack his gear.

• • • • •

The traffic on A1A was light. Billy drove carefully as he approached the wildlife refuge in the narrow part of the island. The ocean dunes to the east were covered with pines and palmetto. Mangroves lined the shallow water to the west. As Billy passed the white termite truck, it pulled onto the road behind the Fleetwood, but he paid it little attention. He didn't notice the motorcycle which had been alongside the truck, as it pulled onto the roadway. The truck accelerated quickly, and within seconds, it was close behind the car, with the motorcycle, invisible to Billy and Christine, just behind.

Near the end of the wildlife refuge, Billy slowed for some S-curves. The motorcyclist pulled out from behind the truck and quickly passed both vehicles. "Jesus," Billy said, startled. "That guy must be nuts, passing on curves like that!"

As Billy spoke, the motorcycle began to fishtail. In a second, it was sideways and then down, bike and rider sliding along the blacktop, and coming to rest on the sandy shoulder of the road. Billy's reaction was immediate, instinctive, and terribly wrong. He stopped just behind the motionless rider, shielding him from traffic with the heavy car. Then he got out to help, closing the car's door behind him. The white van also pulled over, stopping with its bumper nearly touching that of the Cadillac.

Billy was nearly to the prone cyclist when he began to realize, too late, that something was wrong. The man was wearing a helmet and full leathers, and he hadn't hit his head. How come he wasn't moving? With a sudden, awful certainty, Billy realized that it was a trap, and turned back toward the car. He almost made it there, almost had his gun out, when the cyclist rose and shot him in the back.

Inside the car Christine watched with horror as Billy pitched forward, supporting himself on the hood of the car for a moment before slumping out of sight in front of it. She screamed, "BILLY!" so loud that her throat hurt. Then, she watched as two men got out of the van, and with the cyclist, walked toward the car. Forcing herself not to scream again, forcing herself to think, she slid behind the wheel of the car. She pushed the button for the automatic door locks, and felt a small comfort when they engaged with a solid thunk. She pushed the horn button, held it down, and with the horn blaring, used her other hand to call the police on the car phone. It would take the men a minute or two to get into the car, she thought.

The cyclist saw the girl trying to use the car phone. "Fuck that," he said, and ripped the cellular antenna from the car's roof. He waved the antenna at Chrissy in triumph.

The car's engine was running, and Chrissy put it in gear, still blaring the horn. Ahead lay freedom, escape from the men who terrified her. Yet ahead also lay Billy, possibly alive. (Please, God, still alive, she thought.) She could not, would not drive over his body to escape. She put the car into reverse, trying to push the van backward. The Fleetwood's tires spun on the loose Florida sand while the man in leather smashed through the window of the car. The cyclist reached in and turned off the ignition. Chrissy put her face in her hands and wept.

Seafire was at anchor in the harbor at Palma de Mallorca when word of Chrissy Langone's kidnapping arrived. The news hit her people like a torpedo amidships.

Morale was bad enough before the news came. The possibility that Jinnah had a spy aboard made communication difficult.

George knew that a quick consensus was needed, but group discussion was impossible. For three days, George had been meeting with the owners, singly or in pairs, to sound them out. The process had been unproductive. Everyone's mood had been somber, and the sense of camaraderie had vanished. In its place were uneasiness and distrust. Few wanted to make a decision, nobody wanted to leave decision making to others. Most, George realized, were simply in denial.

Nick Argeriardis had been an exception. He'd been decisive, and his mood had been pure rage.

"Fuck the little bastard," Nick said, while his wife winced at his fury. "I say we go to war with the son of a bitch."

"What do you mean?"

"Christ, George, beat him at his own game. If we've got a billion dollars, why not use it against him? Makran's a poor country. Life's cheap there. Tell him we'll hire mercenaries to kill Makrani Muslims by the thousands if he fucks with us. Touch one of our kids and we'll blow up the biggest mosque in his rat hole of a country!"

George was appalled, not so much by the tirade but by the fact that he, George, had been thinking along similar lines. George saw something in Nick he hadn't wanted to see — a reflection of part of himself.

"Nick," George said, "I agree with you. If we decide to fight Jinnah, we'll fight as hard and as dirty as we can. I don't know about bombing mosques, though."

"Then maybe we need another chairman," Nick had replied, crowding into George's face. "Alex Wilson, maybe. He won a gold medal in the biathlon. Somebody like that wouldn't be afraid to fight an all out war."

George knew that Alex was lobbying people to take over as chairman. Obviously, Nick had been one of them.

"Maybe so," George said, pushing his own face forward so his nose was nearly touching Nick's. "Maybe, like you, he's stupid enough to blow up a mosque, create a bunch of martyrs, and have every Muslim on the planet after your kids." Nick had stormed out, with Frances trailing behind him in tears.

Between meetings with the ship's owners, George was gathering information on Jinnah and his followers. Peter Carson had received a thick report, brought to the ship by courier shortly after she had dropped anchor in Palma. Peter gave it to George, two nights before Chrissy Langone's kidnapping, as the two men sat together in Seafire's library.

"If you want to understand a man," Peter said, "find out who his heroes are. Jinnah has only one — Muhammad Ali Jinnah, the man whose name he adopted."

"Who was that? I don't think I've heard of him." George replied.

"Ever hear of Mahatma Gandhi?"

"Sure. He practically invented nonviolent political action. Won India's freedom from Great Britain. He's India's George Washington."

"Muhammad Ali Jinnah was Pakistan's George Washington. It's all in here," Peter said, brandishing the folder.

"The British had ruled India as a single colony," Peter explained, "despite the fact that many religious and ethnic groups populated it. They didn't mix and they treated each other with suspicion and animosity, with religious differences generating the deepest hatred. Throughout British rule part of the 'white man's burden' was keeping Muslims and Hindus from slaughtering each other.

"In 1947, Britain granted India independence. To prevent bloodshed, the British partitioned India into two nations before they left. Hindus in one country, Muslims in the other.

"Gandhi, a Hindu, opposed partition. He believed Hindus and Muslims could live together in peace. Jinnah, Gandhi's Muslim counterpart, favored partition. Freedom from Great Britain would mean nothing if Muslims had to live in a Hindu state. He led the All-Indian Muslim League, whose goal was to carve an Islamic nation out of India. It was to be called Pakistan, meaning land of the pure. The Muslim League told the British, 'divide India now, or we'll divide it later.'

"They were the two most powerful men in India, one a man of peace, the other a man of confrontation. Gandhi said, 'You shall have to divide my body before you divide India.' Jinnah said, 'We shall have India divided, or we shall have India destroyed.' Gandhi used nonviolent methods of persuasion. He went on pilgrimages, he fasted, and he spoke of brotherhood. Jinnah's followers responded with riots. In one day, in the city of Calcutta alone, mob violence between Hindus and Muslims claimed six thousand lives. In the end, Jinnah won, and Pakistan was created.

"I'm amazed that I've never heard about this Jinnah character," George said.

"Not many westerners have. It pisses Muslims off. We all know about Gandhi, the Hindu, and what a great man he was. Jinnah, the Muslim? Never heard of him."

To divide India into Hindustan and Pakistan, Peter explained, the British drew boundary lines. There were areas which were almost entirely Hindu, others predominantly Muslim. Those parts were easy, but there also were vast areas of evenly mixed population. When the final map was drawn, Hindus and Muslims were equally outraged. At midnight, on August 14, 1947, two new nations were born, and the period that followed was one of the most violent in the history of mankind. The bloodshed was inevitable, and not due to any fault in the method of division.

Later, people realized that there had been two blunders in the partition. They were like time bombs. The first was the creation of East Pakistan, what is now Bangladesh. After the partition, Pakistan was one nation with two parts, East and West, separated by the full width of India. East Pakistan, the eastern part of the old Province of Bengal, was much smaller than West Pakistan. The Eastern Bengalis, though Muslims, were a world apart ethnically and economically from the people in the west, who they regarded as oppressors. The revolution that created Bangladesh was inevitable. India, delighted to see her archenemy tear itself apart, secretly aided the rebels and happily watched them create an impoverished fragment state.

Meanwhile, Makran, the second time bomb, was ticking on the eastern rim of the Bay of Bengal. The partition left millions of Muslims stranded in Hindustan, but nowhere as concentrated as on Makran. More than sixty percent of the island's population was Muslim, the rest were mostly Hindu, plus a few Buddhists. From the first day after independence, the Muslims on Makran were a majority population with minority status.

"If the Brits were so careful about drawing the lines," George asked at that point, "why did they include Makran on the Hindu side?"

"Money," said Peter. "Makran is rich in natural resources. The Hindus, with the political power, control those resources. The British thought they could to do business with Hindus more easily than with Muslims. They made sure Makran was under Hindu control even though Muslims are in the majority."

"I don't understand," said George. "If the Muslims were a majority population with minority status from the beginning, how come it took them forty years to get a revolution going?"

Peter frowned, "Indecision as to where to go. Some wanted independence, some wanted to join Pakistan. Then came the Bangladesh troubles. Nobody in Makran wanted to be a part of Bangladesh. All those people had to offer was poverty and cyclones. When Bangladesh split off, what was left of Pakistan was too remote. Many Makranis thought their island was too small to survive as an independent nation, and had to join with somebody. Plenty of people hated the status quo, but there was no agreement on an alternative."

The Makran Liberation Organization was formed even before the partition, Peter explained. Today, it's a lot like the PLO or the IRA. It wasn't always that way. In the beginning, its methods were more like Gandhi's than Jinnah's. The Muslims had the majority. They thought they could achieve independence through the political process. There were the usual calls for a holy war from the hotheads, but they were largely ignored until recently.

It was money that transformed the MLO into a terrorist organization. After the Bangladesh war, oil and gas were discovered under the seabed near Makran, in what oilmen call the Andaman Basin. Makran is now the world's third largest exporter of liquefied natural gas. If the island became independent, the Andaman and Nicobar islands would go with it, along with control of the Basin. That changed everything. Indian resistance to demands for Makrani independence intensified, she wanted to keep the oil and gas revenue. The poor Muslims of Makran, dreaming of becoming rich like the Saudis, became more determined to be free. The squabbling among Muslims ended. Nobody wanted to join Pakistan, or Bangladesh, or anywhere else and share the wealth. Third parties got involved. Libya and Iran became interested — creation of a new, wealthy, Islamic state would suit their purposes nicely. They, and possibly others, covertly funded the radical factions of the MLO. During the struggle for its control, each faction had its own backers. Ultimately, the group headed by Jinnah came to control the organization and mold it into the terrorist organization it has become.

"The fact that he chose Jinnah as his pseudonym tells us what he wants and how he intends to get it," Peter concluded.

Peter was quiet for a moment, as the two men considered what he had said. "It looks like there's more to the report," George said. "What's in the rest of it?"

"Background information about Jinnah. Known associates, methods of operation, things like that. Scary stuff."

After Peter left, George read the report. Then he read it again, hoping to find a key to some weakness in Jinnah or his organization, a way to fight him. He didn't.

George sat alone in the library, waiting for news of Chrissy Langone and wondering what the group would decide to do about Jinnah. The Phelpses and a couple of others wanted to give in to Jinnah's demands, to pay the money and hope for the best. Paying a billion dollars would cost each of the ship's owners about a third of their fortunes. A financial blow, but not a disaster. It wouldn't change their lives, let alone ruin them. So, why not just give in? George knew the answer. We can't give him the money until we know what he's going to do with it.

"Hello, George," said Suvia as she entered the library. "I thought I'd find you here."

"Hi, Suvia," he replied. "Any news of Chrissy Langone?"

"They found the truck that the kidnappers used. Or had you heard that?"

George had heard. The exterminator's truck had been found in the parking garage of a condo complex less than a mile from the site of the kidnapping. The kidnappers obviously had switched vehicles to get off of Singer Island. That it took the police thirty-six hours to locate a truck with a huge plastic termite on the roof had angered and baffled George. The discovery had killed any hope that Chrissy would be found quickly, and word of it had added to the mood of depression aboard *Seafire*. Especially since it had come less than a day after Chrissy's bodyguard had died.

"I came to talk about your job as chairman of the Jinnah committee. The week is almost up. Will you stay on?"

George hadn't been expecting the question and hesitated before answering. "I've decided to let somebody else take over. Alex, maybe, he seems to want the job pretty badly. I shouldn't be in charge of dealing with Jinnah. I think you should fight him, but how can I say that without being a hypocrite? Whose kid will he grab to retaliate? Not mine, that's for sure! I don't have any. You need a new leader. One with something at stake."

"George," Suvia replied, "you're wrong. I don't have any children, either. I don't think that disqualifies me from making rational decisions about Jinnah and his threats."

"I thought you had two sons."

"Stepsons. Richard's by his first wife. They were teenagers when she died, and they weren't pleased when he married me. I'm fond of them, but I don't imagine they're more important to me than Ralph and Helen's boys are to you.

"Your not having any children is an advantage. If you resign as chairman, somebody has to replace you. His family automatically goes to the top of Jinnah's hit list. You can run things with the best interests of everybody in mind, and not worry about that. Please don't give up, George. We need you."

Not in years had anyone said to George, please help us, we need you. The effect was compelling, yet he realized she was right. Of all the people aboard, he was least likely to be subverted by Jinnah, as someone probably had been already. He was vulnerable through the Dade family, of course, but only indirectly.

George became aware that Suvia was watching him. Her gaze was direct, her expression one of polite curiosity. He'd seen that expression before, on the night he'd arrived in Gibraltar. She was waiting for him to respond and was giving him all the time he needed.

"I hadn't thought of it that way. Maybe I was just looking for a way to drop out and let somebody else deal with the problem."

"Then, you'll keep the job?"

"Yes. For the time being, at least. Until Alex Wilson stages a coup."

Suvia laughed. "Good," she said. "George, your judgment had been perfect so far. You were right about Jinnah going after Joe Langone's family. You just looked at the tape and knew he was going to do it."

"That was easy. Jinnah's a control freak. I spotted it right away. Hitting him was the worst thing Joe could have done. Calling him a little piece of shit wasn't too swift, either."

"How do you know he's a control freak?"

"Lifelong experience. My father was the grand champion of control freaks."

"Ouch, George. Speak no ill of the dead."

"It's OK, Suvia. He's been dead ten years. I'm through mourning him."

Suvia got out of her chair. "I trust your judgment, George. I'm glad you'll stay in charge. Thank you."

George watched her go. She was an attractive woman. He wondered why he had just lied to her.

George was back in the library several hours later, waiting for Ralph Dade to bring a message from Jinnah. He knew he should have felt curiosity and excitement about it, instead, he just felt tired.

He hadn't been sleeping well. The Hellcat dream had been recurring, several times every night. Each time it was the same, the feelings of fear and helplessness as the helicopter hurtled, controls frozen, toward the power lines. Each time George had awoken, heart pounding, bathed in sweat, just before the inevitable crash.

He was considering the meaning of the nightmares when Ralph arrived with a sealed envelope marked confidential. He handed it to George and waited as he opened it. Inside were the instructions Jinnah had promised. George read them aloud.

"There's no salutation," George said. "It gets right to the point. 'These are the major details of the transactions that are to occur. They are provided at this time to permit your full agreement in Malta in one week. At that time, minor matters will be addressed. Among these will be specific dates and locations, banking details, etc.

"'During the next six months you will pay the sum of one billion U.S. dollars into my account at a Swiss bank. In order to generate that amount of liquid cash without arousing government suspicion and interference, you may use the entire six-month period. Periodic deposits into the designated account shall be not less than $150 million per month.

"'In addition, during the six months, you will have the ship *Seafire* converted into, and fully outfitted as, an oceanographic research vessel. On the last day of this year, you will donate the ship to a nonprofit foundation to be designated later, at a location to be specified when we meet in Malta.

"'The gold is to be provided in coin and/or bars of not more than ten troy ounces each. Based on a recent price of three hundred U.S. dollars per ounce, it will consist of 3,333 troy ounces, or 103 kilograms. It will be divided into four equal portions, each to be placed in an attaché case.

"'It has come to my attention that a videotape was made during my visit in Gibraltar. You will give me the original tape in Malta. If there are copies, they are to be destroyed. You will not tape my associates or me ever again. If any of these directives are disobeyed, your children will die.

"'I look forward to our next meeting, at which all of the owners of the ship *Seafire* are to be present. Upon delivery of the gold and your agreement to all of my terms, and after my departure without interference, Christine Langone will be released to her parents.'"

"That's it?" asked Ralph.

"That's it. No signature. No final threats. Nothing."

"There's really not much new here, is there? Giving us time to come up with the cash is a nice touch, but not surprising. He seemed to know as much about our liquidity as he did about our net worth."

"You can thank your spy for that," said George.

"You're sure there is one?"

"Yes. Jinnah didn't know about the camera in the exchange room when he was here. He avoids being photographed. If he'd known about it, he'd have made somebody turn it off. It's obvious that he learned about it after he left."

"It has to be one of the owners," Ralph said.

"Or me."

"Nah, George, couldn't be you."

"Why not, my unimpeachable character?"

"Nope. Jinnah knew our itinerary. You couldn't have given him that. I doubt that you know our net worth, either. Or care.

"Anyway," continued Ralph, "the only other new demand is the research vessel business. I wonder what that's all about."

"Cover," replied George. "Very clever cover."

"I don't understand."

"Jinnah's wanted by police all over the world. Even in Makran. Hell, especially in Makran. He takes a risk every time he enters a country, every time he gets on an airplane. Disguises, phony passports, whatever he uses, there's always a chance something will go wrong and he'll be arrested. With *Seafire*, he'd have his own navy. He can set up some phony research foundation, dedicated to world peace and saving the whales or whatever, and travel anywhere. He wouldn't have to be captain or anything. On the contrary. He'd be an engine room snipe whenever the ship cleared customs. Nobody ever looks closely at crew."

"Sure, it would work," said Ralph. "And with a billion dollars, he could buy a lot of fuel."

"With a cover like that the United Nations would probably buy his fuel for him! He could sneak bombs, terrorists, guns, whatever into any country in the world that isn't landlocked. No, it's not hard to figure out why he wants *Seafire*." George paused for a moment. "We need to tell the others about this. Would you get them together? Exchange room in half an hour?"

"Sure."

"Thanks."

Ralph turned to leave the library, then hesitated at the door to the passageway. "I think you're right about Jinnah's plans for *Seafire*. What do you think he's going to do with the billion dollars?"

"I keep asking myself that," George replied. "I don't know yet. Whatever it is, I'm sure it's nasty."

CHAPTER 5

USS *Watson*, DD 482, a Fletcher class destroyer, motored southwestward across the blue Mediterranean Sea, riding easily through the gentle morning swells. Like all the Fletcher class 'cans,' she was three hundred seventy-six feet, six inches in length, and less than forty feet of beam. Her powerful engines could drive her long, narrow hull at nearly forty knots. Such speeds were required by the destroyer tactics of her day. The slim ships had virtually no armor, relying on speed and agility to protect them from enemy gunfire. To many with an eye for the beauty of warships, the Fletchers were loveliest of all American destroyers. Unlike other ships of the same vintage, the line of their main deck was unbroken, sweeping from the low and slightly raked stem to the even lower stern. Whoever first used the term 'greyhound of the sea' must have had one of the Fletchers in mind.

Watson was the black sheep of the Fletcher family. Now over fifty years old, she had never seen battle, never fired a shot in anger. In fact, she had never fired a shot at all. She was an experimental warship. Her keel was laid along with those of her sisters who would be launched to find death and glory in the Second World War. She had been building when Pearl Harbor was bombed. She had been building still when Hiroshima and Nagasaki were bombed. All around her, at the Federal Shipbuilding and Dry-dock Company in Kearney, New Jersey, her sister ships were begun, completed, and launched. Yet, as the war raged and the years passed, *Watson* limped toward her completion. It was never to come.

When *Watson* was designed, all United States Navy destroyers had steam engines. Steam power had disadvantages. The boilers take a long time to be brought on line in an emergency. The Navy learned that too well at Pearl Harbor. Safety was another factor. Relatively minor battle damage in a boiler room could release high-pressure steam and scald dozens of men to death. For years, the German Navy had been experimenting with huge diesels in some of their large combatants, including the pocket battleships. The United States Navy, long on tradition and short on innovation as usual, belatedly decided to give diesels a chance. *Watson* was to be built with diesel electric drive.

The engines chosen for DD 482 were General Electric locomotive diesels, stock units already in production. Each engine had thirty-two cylinders, delivered 2,500 horsepower, and drove its own electric generator. *Watson*'s twin propellers would be driven by electric motors. The power plant was like that of a submarine, but without the batteries a submarine needs for underwater operation. The plan was hardly radical. During the war, Federal Shipbuilding and other yards built and delivered dozens of destroyer escort types that used the diesel electric drive system.

The problem with *Watson*, however, was that she was not a destroyer escort. Slow and small, those ships made do with five or six thousand horsepower. A fleet destroyer required ten times as much. *Watson* was going to need a lot of those railroad engines to make her go, and a lot of fancy switching gear to handle the electricity. The engineering problems were enormous, requiring endless recalculations and reworking of the plans. Before the project was completed, the war had ended, and the experiment was scrapped.

On January 7, 1946, USS *Watson* slid gently down the ways at the Federal Shipyard, into the cold, brackish waters of the Passaic River. It was an ignominious event. She was nearly completed, yet she carried no armament of any kind. No flags flew, no bands played, and nobody broke a champagne bottle on her bow. She wasn't even named *Watson*. Not officially. Never christened, never commissioned, she was a nameless hulk from the instant her keel first tasted salt water. In fact, she'd already been sold as scrap. The launching had been the most practical way to get her out of the yard. At the foot of the ways, tugs were waiting to tow her to Hoboken.

Consolidated Edison, the electric utility company, had bought *Watson*. A bright young executive had realized that her diesel engines could be a source of enormous backup generating capacity. She could, after all, produce forty megawatts of power on extremely short notice. Yet, not even in this was she to succeed. She arrived at her berth on the Hudson amid a storm of union trouble over who would man her, and how. For three years she sat alongside her pier, never tied into the power grid, never manned except by a caretaker crew, with her engines idle and her generators cold. All the while labor and management squabbled over manning levels, work rules, and whether the maritime or shore side trades would get the work. In 1949, the company gave up. The bright young executive was fired, and *Watson* was sold again.

Bubba Caulfield was a native-born Texan who worked hard

living like one. He enjoyed playing the red-necked blowhard that many people expected Texans to be, even to calling himself Bubba despite being an only child. He drove an enormous Cadillac convertible with steer horns on the hood, wore a ridiculously large hat, and generally played the part as best he could. When he first heard about the ship those Yankees up in New Jersey had for sale, he had his people look into it. It was big and cheap and might be useful in his offshore oil drilling operations. Once he saw the specifications, however, he saw its real potential. Bubba Caulfield was going to own the biggest, fastest private yacht in the world. A real Texas yacht. He would name her *Yellow Rose.*

William Jackson, captain of the yacht *Seafire*, ex-*Watson*, ex-*Yellow Rose*, was at his accustomed place on the bridge. Over the years, successive owners and successive conversions had altered much of the old destroyer, yet her pilothouse and bridge wings were largely unchanged. Jackson liked it that way. Here he felt at home, in a small world filled with familiar and comforting objects from the past, like the Bendix engine room telegraph. From here, he could watch the sea and sky, an occupation of which he never tired. As captain, he was not assigned a rotation on the watch roster. Instead, he was on constant call and usually quite busy. Yet, whenever the ship was underway, he spent as much time as possible on the bridge. Like *Watson*, Jackson was ex-Navy, an ex-destroyerman, and a seagoing relic of what might have been. Where *Watson*'s career had been stillborn, Jackson's had died an early death. Discharged in disgrace only three years after being commissioned, Bill Jackson had found a home aboard *Seafire*, the yacht that might have been a destroyer.

Using the pylorus on the port bridge wing, Jackson checked the ship's heading. It was 219 degrees true; she was on course. The ship's autopilot was accurate to less than half a degree, yet

Jackson still checked the heading himself, from time to time, to make sure. Moving at her normal cruising speed of twelve knots, *Seafire* would be at the entrance to Grand Harbor, Valletta, well before her nine o'clock rendezvous with the tug that would lead her in. During the early morning, she had crossed the Malta Channel, having rounded the southern tip of Sicily at midnight.

On the wing of the bridge, Bill Jackson was enjoying himself. The sky was clear, the gentle southwest breeze was warm, and it was promising to be a fine day. Two hours earlier, the sun had risen off of Seafire's port quarter, and the island of Malta gleamed bright ahead in the golden morning light. For a moment, Jackson was disturbed by the arrival of George Holbrook and Suvia Ferris. Jackson secretly resented any intrusion by the owners or their guests onto "his" bridge, although he usually managed not to show it. After all, it was their ship, and they could go anywhere aboard her that they pleased. Still, he was relieved to see Suvia and George climb to the flying bridge above the pilothouse, leaving Jackson alone once again.

If George had been alone, Jackson would have felt differently. Holbrook had hired him years before, quietly accepting his word that the old court martial charges were false. Jackson's gratitude for the job was still enormous, but his gratitude for the belief in his innocence was even greater. Holbrook was ex-Navy and knew how to keep out of the way on the bridge of a ship underway. Jackson liked and admired George and would have shared the bridge with him happily. One owner and one guest, though, would be too much.

The flying bridge was originally designed as a secondary steering station. It still fulfilled that function, occasionally during docking maneuvers, but was primarily a lounging area for members of the owners' party. Occasionally used for sunbathing when the ship was in port, its most frequent use was as a sightseeing platform when she was underway. Unlike the bridge immediately below, this area of the ship which had undergone radical alteration during her conversion to a yacht. The turret-like gunfire control director, common to all destroyers, was missing. Like the gun mounts, it had never been installed, although its circular base was in place. All around were tables and comfortable chairs in friendly groupings, and aft there was a wet bar and a dumb-waiter. The latter allowed meals to be sent up from the galley, four decks below.

George had invited Suvia to join him on the flying bridge, to watch the entry into Grand Harbor. They chose two of several chairs that were located on the raised platform where the fire control director would have been. From these, they could see over the spray deflector and bulwarks. They looked at the fortress island ten miles ahead. The light brown sandstone was golden in the morning sunlight, and the island, which was normally so bleak and barren in appearance, showed a surprising amount of early summer green.

"It's beautiful," said Suvia after a few minutes. "I've never seen Malta before. Thank you for asking me to come and see it."

"Wait until we're closer, and we can see the fortifications around Valletta," George replied. "They're incredible. I think they're more spectacular than the pyramids." George was silent for a moment. "I asked you to come up here partly because I wanted to talk. I've been working on our problem for days now, and I have the outlines of a plan."

"Shouldn't you call a meeting and go over it with everybody?"

"No. I want to discuss it with you, only."

"OK. I'm listening."

"The gold's aboard. I flew to Rome yesterday and picked it up. While I was there, I got another report on Jinnah. I can't tell you how. I still have a couple of contacts in the spy trade that you don't want to know about.

"I've been trying to find out why, all of a sudden, Jinnah needs a billion dollars. He's been operating for years, quietly funded by Iran and Libya and who knows whom else, and supplementing his income extorting the odd million here and there. Why a billion? Why now?"

"Maybe he's just greedy," Suvia said. "Maybe this is the first chance he's gotten to blackmail a boat load of millionaires at once."

"Maybe. I had my friends try to find out."

"Did they?"

"No, they're still working on it. In the meantime, though, they gave me some interesting news. Do you remember hearing about the Bertolini kidnapping?"

"Vaguely."

"The victim was the daughter of a wealthy Italian. She was held for several weeks. The kidnappers sent her father two of her fingers to prove she was still alive. About six weeks ago, he paid a huge ransom, but the girl wasn't released. No word from the kidnappers. Nothing. Total silence.

"About a week ago, the police in Naples were investigating the disappearance of a marble dealer and his family. They found fragments of human bone in the stone cutting equipment at his factory. They had DNA testing done. The pieces of bone had come from four related individuals. The family, probably. But there also were fragments from a two other people that were unrelated to the other four or to each other. On a chance, they checked the fifth and sixth samples against one of the Bertolini girl's fingers. One was a match."

"God, how gruesome! But what does this mean to us? Do you think Jinnah was the kidnapper?"

"The police say he's high on their list of suspects. I think it's a near certainty. The tactics used in the Bertolini kidnapping were nearly identical to those used to grab Chrissy Langone. Even down to the fake motorcycle crash."

George paused. "You have to fight Jinnah. He can't be trusted to keep his word. If you pay, he may still attack you. Paying him may only provide him with the money to hire the attackers."

"That makes sense, George. But I think we should keep our options open, as you suggested."

"Of course. As I said, I've been working on the outlines of a plan. Keeping options open is the main goal. Redundancy is a close second. I want two, three, or four lines of defense. If any one holds, we win, even if the others fail. I don't want to let success or failure rest on only one tactic.

"Whatever we do, we'll chop it up into separate phases. We'll put one or two people in charge of each phase. For security, only the people involved in a phase would know its details. Only I would know the complete plan, and how the phases would mesh with each other."

"You've been reading too much LeCarre, George," said Suvia. "Isolated cells, no less. Do I get a cyanide capsule?"

"Very funny. We know we have a spy. Even if we figure out who it is, it could happen again."

"OK. Sorry. This all seems so... well, grim. Why are you telling me all of this?"

"I need your help. There should be a vice-chairman. I'd like it to be you."

For several seconds, Suvia said nothing. "Why?"

"Why do I need a vice chairman, or why do I need Suvia Ferris?"

"Both."

"There has to be more than one person who knows the whole plan. In case something happens to me. Mostly, I'll need a second opinion about a lot of things. Did I forget something? Is phase three going to screw up phase five?"

"That makes sense. But why me? Why not Ralph? You've been friends forever. You and I hardly know each other."

"First, you're single. No spouse as a potential security leak. But that's not the main reason. I know how you got control of Ferroil, how you handled the trustees of Richard's estate and the company executives who wanted to take over. They thought Suvia Ferris was a poor widow-woman without a lick of sense. You cleaned their clocks before they realized they had any real opposition. I'm going to fight dirty, Suvia. I need someone like you on my team."

"I suppose I should take that as a compliment. Would you really ask for advice from a woman?" Suvia asked, only partly in jest.

"Why wouldn't I?"

"I don't know. Something I heard about you, I guess. You're over fifty, never married..." She trailed off. "Sorry. It's none of my business." Her cheeks reddened.

"You're blushing," George said, amused.

"No, I'm not," she said, her whole face turning crimson.

"Seriously, Suvia, I need your help. Twice since Jinnah showed up, you've caught points that I've missed. When I wanted to resign as chairman, you told me not to chicken out. I really do need you to help me."

"OK," Suvia said, after a moment's reflection, "you have a vice-chairman. Tell me about this plan of yours."

Before George could answer, Peter and Emily Carson arrived on the flying bridge, followed immediately by Alex Wilson and the Dades. They had come up to watch the approach to Malta.

"Suvia's never been to Malta before," George said. "I've been pointing out the sights.

"The city on top of the rock is Valletta," George continued. Suvia responded with a small smile. "Named after Grand Master la Valette, of the Knights of St. John. He led the defense against a Muslim siege in 1565. The island was a bastion of Christianity that stood in the way of Sultan Suleiman and the Ottoman Empire. If Malta had fallen, all of Europe might have been overrun by the Turks and their allies."

Suvia was amazed at the extent of the fortifications in and around the city. Stone walls, sheer manmade cliffs, rose from the water's edge to the city itself, a hundred or more feet above. Everywhere were bastions and battlements, the angled walls of interlocking fortifications. The massive scale of it all was breathtaking. Here, four hundred years ago, people had built this fortress to protect themselves from Muslim attackers. What sort of stronghold will we build against Jinnah? She would wait to hear George's plan.

In the three days since *Seafire* had moored at Valletta, Suvia had seen a lot of George Holbrook. He'd been busy with his planning and scheming. He'd spent hours in secret meetings with one or another of the ship's owners, sending and receiving scrambled faxes all over the world. Still, much of George's time had been spent with Suvia. Tentatively, he had explained to her the basic framework of his plan. They had discussed it as they explored the cities of Valletta and Floriana, and the Three Cities across Grand Harbor. They'd walked about, with guidebooks in hand, pretending to be tourists, as they talked about it.

"The most important feature of the plan is flexibility, like the option play in football, where the quarterback can run with the ball, pass it, or pitch it back to another runner. Even as the play begins, the quarterback doesn't know which of the three options he will choose. Only at the last moment will he commit to one of them, after he's had a chance to analyze the defense." Suvia nodded in understanding as George explained.

George finished dividing the plan into phases. The earlier ones consisted of planning and preparation. Later would come the action phases. These would be the options available to George in his role as quarterback. Suvia was impressed with George's reasoning and agreed with him on all but one point — the last phase.

In the earlier phases, *Seafire*'s owners would agree to Jinnah's demands and convince him that they were complying with them. At all times, actual compliance would be an available option. At no time was Jinnah to know that they were considering anything else. The first action phase would be a tactical assault on Jinnah himself. Neither George nor Suvia yet had any clear idea how they would do it, but using mercenaries seemed most likely. The next phase would be defensive. The teams of terrorists following the owner's families would be identified and followed. When the attack on Jinnah was launched, they would be killed, again by mercenaries. Following that was the strategic weapons phase. Again, George wasn't sure what final form it would take, but it would be some sort of counter threat against Jinnah's followers. Perhaps it might be a threat against Makran itself. Finally, there was the final, all-out warfare phase. Suvia was dead set against it, while George insisted it had to be available as a last resort. The threat of strategic action, in whatever form, would be carried out. Once more, there was no specific plan, but the concept was of a massive explosion, causing huge loss of life in Makran. It would be done in such a way that Jinnah would be blamed for it. He would be discredited, perhaps even assassinated by his own followers. In any case no one would be following his orders after such an outrage, and *Seafire*'s people would be safe.

Of all the aspects of the plan, this one caused the only disagreement between George and Suvia. Their last discussion of it was over dinner, Friday night, in the Hotel Phoenicia. "God, George," she said, "we can't do that. Kill innocent people just to make Jinnah look bad? We can't!" Suvia became angry, and George tried to calm her down.

"I don't like the idea, either. It's just an option I've been considering as a last resort. The whole plan is flexible, anyway. We'll probably come up with something better long before we implement any of it. Let's forget it for a while and enjoy our dinner."

Suvia tried, but was only partly successful. In the two days they had spent together, Suvia had learned a lot about the island and its history from George, and in the process she had learned much about him as well. Just over six feet tall, he was trim and fit, looking younger than his age. His dark hair was graying to a salt and pepper mix, but it had neither thinned nor receded. His skin was tanned enough to earn him a stern reproach from a good dermatologist, and it made his light blue eyes even more startling by contrast. She liked the way he treated her, as a friend and confidante, without a hint of condescension. Yet, as she sat across from him at dinner, she was deeply troubled by his last phase. It hinted at a dark side of him that frightened her. She thought back to the incident in Peru.

- - - - -

Suvia Ferris looked at herself in the full-length mirror in her stateroom and was satisfied with what she saw. Her hair and jewelry were just right, and her dress was perfect. It was Saturday night, and she was going to a party. Another time, she would have been looking forward to it. After midnight, she and her friends would have to face Jinnah again. She could think of little else and certainly wasn't in a party mood. But the event had been scheduled for months, and George had insisted that things aboard *Seafire* appear as normal as possible.

Suvia could hear the music from the party. She could feel the strong bass beat through the metal deck. She decided it was time to join in. With a last glance in the mirror, she turned off the lights, locked her door behind her, and headed aft to the helicopter deck determined to look like she was having a good time. There had been good luck in the weather. The air was warm, with a gentle southwesterly breeze blowing across the sea from Tunisia. It was going to be a lovely night.

Seafire was moored in Grand Harbor, and, like Suvia, she was dressed up. She was wearing her Med lights, a string of bright white bulbs running from her stem up to the top of her mast, then down to her stern. The helicopter had been flown ashore, and the hangar had been decorated for the party. The effect, as always, was reminiscent of a high school gym decked out for the prom. The landing deck, covered by a white awning, was the dance floor. The lifelines had been raised to keep errant dancers from falling into the harbor, and these, too, were strung with white lights. The ship shimmered in the harbor, white above her own reflection, beckoning to her guests as they assembled on the quay.

The annual spring party aboard *Seafire* had become one of the premier social events of the Mediterranean cruising season. Invitations were coveted and regrets were few. Each year, the party was held in a different harbor and this was the first time it had been in Malta. Several guests had come to the island on their own yachts, which were moored or berthed in Marsamxett Harbor, just to the north of Valletta. They arrived on their own launches, coming around the corner past Fort St. Elmo. Others had flown in and were staying ashore. For them, fifty rooms had been booked at the Hotel Phoenicia. They now waited on the quay, while *Seafire*'s launches, *Seamist* and *Seasmoke*, ferried them out to the ship.

It was still early, not yet nine o'clock, and while dozens of guests were already aboard, there would soon be hundreds. Some were dancing, others were serving themselves at one of several buffet tables. Suvia stood at the edge of the dance floor for a moment and listened to the music, realizing how long it had been since she had gone dancing. The musicians were good and the music danceable. The band, flown in from Brazil, played songs with the rich beat of the samba and the old bossa nova. She stood awkwardly for a minute or two. She was out of practice at this, she realized.

Just as she started toward a likely looking group of guests, George appeared. "Suvia, you look great," he said.

"Thank you, George," she replied. A waiter offered them champagne. George declined, and Suvia noted this with interest. At dinner the night before, he'd had wine with dinner, but no cocktail before nor brandy afterward. Tonight, apparently, he was drinking nothing. Keeping himself in shape for Jinnah, she thought. Good for you, George. The waiter was hovering by her with the champagne, and she waved him away. "No thanks," she said, "I'm wearing heels tonight."

George laughed. "Great line, Suvia. Too bad I can't use it." Then, he took her by the arm and turned her toward the dance floor. "Let's pretend to dance."

"Pretend to dance?"

"I need to talk to you. I'm afraid Jinnah may have spies in the crowd."

Suvia looked around. There were dozens of strangers, but party crashers had always been a problem and invitations were carefully checked. She didn't argue, though, and they began to dance. "George, you amaze me," she said. "You're a very good dancer. I thought you weren't supposed to be a ladies' man."

George smiled at the gentle teasing. "This is just a holdover from my Don Juan days. You're lucky you missed them. I hate to think what a fool I made of myself back then. I guess dancing is something you don't forget how to do. Like riding a bicycle."

They continued to dance, neither saying anything, each simply enjoying the night and the music. When the song ended and another began, George remembered why he'd asked Suvia to dance in the first place.

"I think I'm going to have a problem later tonight," he said. It was a slow dance; he held her close and spoke softly, so no one could hear. "I think you'll be able to help.

"Jinnah wants the billion in installments. I don't want to give anything but the million in gold before the end of the year."

"Why?"

"If we fight, we can use the money to fight him. If we've given him millions of dollars, he can use the money to fight us."

"He'll never go for it."

"I think there's a way to sell it to him."

George explained what he had in mind. When he was finished, Suvia looked into his eyes.

"You're a cynical man, George Holbrook."

"Too true. Will you do it?"

"Of course."

"Thanks. See, picking a woman as my vice chairman wasn't so dumb after all, was it?"

"Pig," said Suvia. With her head resting on his shoulder she felt, rather than heard, his chuckle in response.

The band was beginning another tune. This time it was "Watch What Happens," a song familiar to both George and Suvia, and they danced to it with mock abandon. "After this dance, I should leave," said George.

"Why?'

"I still have things to work out."

"George, relax. At midnight, Jinnah is going to come aboard, and our coach will turn into a pumpkin. He'll give us a bunch of boring details and, hopefully, make arrangements to release Chrissy Langone. We'll offer him our compromise on the money and he'll take it or leave it. What more can you do to prepare for that?"

"I don't know. You're right, of course. I just need to be doing something, I suppose."

"What you need to do is relax. Let your mind rest. Stay at the party. Be my date. We can have some supper, and if you need to talk about Jinnah, we can talk. When the time comes, we'll go in there together and ram the compromise down his damned throat. What do you say?"

"Suvia, that's the best idea I've heard in weeks. I'd love to be your date."

The music played on, and they continued to dance. The singer, an exotic looking creature, had lovely green eyes. George noticed that they were the same color as Suvia's. She had a silky, sexy voice with an intriguing accent, and George and Suvia listened to the words as they danced. Suddenly, Suvia stopped dancing, and stood still. George, who had been stepping forward at that instant, caromed into her. He had to catch her to keep her from falling down. She stared at him for a moment, as if seeing him for the first time.

"Are you all right?"

"Yes. Sorry," Suvia replied, embarrassed. They had nearly knocked over another couple, and had gotten several curious looks from nearby dancers. "Something just struck me. It wasn't important."

As they began to dance again, Suvia knew that she had lied. What had struck her had been important. Listening to the music, she had suddenly found the answer to a question she hadn't known she'd been asking. She smiled, listening to the familiar refrain, as the singer returned to the words that had stopped her in her tracks.

"Cold, no I won't believe your heart is cold. Maybe just afraid to be broken again."

Jinnah arrived almost precisely at midnight, pulling alongside in a black hulled motor launch. George, who had been waiting for him at the top of the accommodation ladder, wondered if Jinnah had chosen the boat for its sinister look. He probably had, George decided, for effect or, more likely, because it would suit his self-image. With Jinnah were Syed and two other men. Syed carried a large briefcase; the others were empty-handed. Without introducing himself, George led all four forward to the main salon. Aft, on the fantail and helicopter deck, the party was still in full swing. It would continue nearly until dawn.

The owners were assembled once again in the salon. As Jinnah entered the room, he glanced quickly around, mentally taking attendance. George sat down next to Suvia, but Jinnah and his three companions remained standing.

"Why are you here, Mr. Holbrook? You are not needed here."

"Mrs. Ferris and the others have asked me to act as their spokesman."

"A helicopter pilot!?"

"Yes. Would you like to hear the story of my life, or do you want to talk business?"

George had used the sarcasm deliberately, and he saw anger flash in Jinnah's eyes.

"Have you produced the gold?"

"Yes, we have," replied George. He rose from his chair and stepped to an intercom handset. After speaking briefly, he returned to his chair. In less than a minute, two of *Seafire*'s uniformed crewmen brought four heavy attaché cases into the salon, set them down in a row on the floor, and left.

"Three thousand three hundred thirty-three troy ounces of gold," George said. "One million dollars, at three hundred dollars per ounce. Do you want to count it?"

"No. I do not think you would be foolish enough to cheat me." Jinnah gestured to his men. Two of them picked up two cases each and wordlessly left the salon, leaving Jinnah and Syed behind.

George motioned to the bar. There was a VCR cassette on it. "There's the videotape of your last visit," he said. "Nobody but the people in this room has seen it. That's the original, and there are no copies."

Jinnah nodded toward Syed, who picked up the tape and put it into a pocket.

"I take it you have agreed to my demands," Jinnah said, smiling with the white teeth.

"In principle, we have," George replied. "We haven't heard all the details yet. Unless there's something in those that can't be done, then yes, we agree to pay the ransom. But we have some demands of our own."

"You will demand nothing of me!" The smile was gone in an instant.

"Conditions, then," said George. He was still seated, speaking in a firm, even tone.

"And these are ...," said Jinnah.

"First, Christine Langone must be released unharmed, immediately. Second, there must be assurances that you will never make further demands upon our families or us. We will pay a ransom once, and once only. Finally, we will turn over the ship and the one billion dollars at the end of this year, at one time. We will not pay you in installments."

Jinnah looked into George's eyes as if to find a clue as to what lay behind them. All he found was a level, passionless gaze. "As for the girl," he said, looking at his watch, "she will be released in precisely thirteen minutes, regardless of the outcome of this meeting. As a gesture of my good faith. And as a lesson. As to further demands, there will be none. I thought I had made that clear. You will pay the ransom and you will never hear from my people or me again. I am a man of honor, Mr. Holbrook. You have my word that I will never seek anything more.

"While I am not a capitalist, I understand liquidity problems — liquidating a large stock holding can depress the price of the remaining shares. I agreed to allow you to raise the billion dollars over time. In the meantime, however, I want the funds that you liquidate. So, while I can agree to the first two of your conditions, I will not agree to the third. The requirement that payment begin at once is not negotiable."

"I'm sorry," said George, "but our position is likewise nonnegotiable. We will pay you one billion U.S. dollars on December 31st. Other than the gold we just gave you, we will give you nothing until then."

Jinnah's complexion darkened. "You will not dictate terms to me," he shouted. "You will do precisely as I say, or you will regret it!"

George finally rose to his feet, color in his face as well. "Listen to me, Jinnah. You call yourself a man of honor. I don't believe you. I don't trust you any farther than I could throw this ship. The decision to pay the ransom was a very close one. Many of us believe that you'll attack us even if we pay you. We know that your men kidnapped the Bertolini girl. Her father paid a huge ransom, but you killed her anyway. Some man of honor!"

George took a breath to calm himself. "We're not going to pay you piecemeal and have you use our own money to hire assassins against us. We'll pay you once, in December. At that time we'll obtain sufficient guarantees of your so-called good faith. And that, my friend, is not a demand. It's a fact. You get your money in December, or never."

"Your information is erroneous. We had nothing to do with the Bertolini kidnapping. These are lies!"

"No, Jinnah. We know it's you who's the liar. You were sloppy. You left traces of evidence. You ground the girl into dog food in your hideout in Naples. We know you did it."

As George said this, he quickly glanced at Syed. A look of horror and surprise flashed across his face. It was as good as a confession. Jinnah saw it too.

"We will pay the ransom our way, or not at all." George said.

"There will be no negotiation," Jinnah shouted. "My terms will be obeyed, or the children will die."

By this time, George was shaking with rage, fighting to control himself. He'd deliberately set out to display anger. Now, the genuine article was threatening to destroy his composure. "Then fuck you, asshole!" he shouted. "We go to Plan B. We'll spend half the billion dollars on security and the rest on mercenaries. Hindu criminals, freelance Sikhs, a regular Death Squad. Pay them big bucks for every Muslim they kill on Makran. Double for women of childbearing age. Triple for mullahs. I'm sure we can afford it. The life of a Muslim isn't worth much on Makran, is it? And we'll be sure to let the mullahs know that all this is happening because Jinnah's terrorism is coming home to roost. I bet you run out of followers before we run out of money. If you want a war, you fucking little piece of pig shit, you've got it! A war of attrition!"

Jinnah was shocked into momentary speechlessness by George's vehemence and obscenity, as was everyone else in the room. Other than during Nick Argeriardis' brief argument with George, Plan B had never been discussed. George's friends were appalled by the concept. The irony of a terrorist being threatened by counter terrorism hadn't struck Jinnah. His immediate reaction was to try to gauge whether George was bluffing. He concluded that he wasn't. The description of Plan B had a terrible ring of truth to it. That was what he had seen in Holbrook, Jinnah realized, that vaguely dangerous attitude. It was Holbrook's knowledge that he had the means to fight back. A dangerous commodity in an intended victim of extortion, Jinnah realized. He has his Plan B worked out, thought Jinnah, and he looks damn eager to try it.

Now, it was Jinnah's turn to fight for control as he responded to Holbrook's outburst. Carefully, and as calmly as possible he said, "Your threats are nothing to me. You are correct, the life of a Muslim on Makran is quite worthless. To be born a Muslim there is to be born a slave, without hope, without a future. It is a living death. If my brethren cannot be free of the Hindu oppression, then they are better dead. Then they will live forever in freedom and happiness with God. If you wish to join the Hindus in their genocide, then do so. But I will not wait until December to commence *my* war of attrition, as you so aptly call it, against you. I will not let you liquidate your billion dollars and then tell me six months hence that you have opted for Plan B after all. I trust you no more than you trust me."

Turning away from George, he shouted, "So, you fools, do you want to follow this helicopter pilot into war with me? It is a war you will surely lose. Despite your precautions, my men took Christine Langone as easily as a cat takes a baby bird. So it shall be with the rest. You insult me, you call me names, and you threaten my people. You will regret this night for the rest of your lives."

For a moment, there was silence in the room as the two men faced one another, as if challenging each other to combat at dawn. Then, Suvia Ferris stood up and shouted, "For God's sake, stop it! Both of you!"

Jinnah and George turned toward her, startled by the outburst, each having been so intensely focused on the other that they'd forgotten anyone else was present. Suvia's eyes flashed genuine anger of her own. "Two minutes ago we handed over a million dollars in gold and agreed to pay a billion dollar ransom. Now you two are hung up on details and are screaming threats at each other. 'I can kill your people faster than you can kill mine,' you're saying. You're crazy, both of you. Crazy with hate. Nobody needs to be killed, don't you understand that? If you start this damned war of attrition the only thing I know for sure is that both sides will be killing a bunch of innocent people. Is that what you really want? There has to be a way to work this out, even if you don't trust each other."

Jinnah and Holbrook stared at Suvia as she continued. "Put the money into Jinnah's account, George. A hundred and fifty million, or whatever, a month. But make him put a hold on the account until December, so he can't get any money out until we close the deal. No withdrawals, no loans against the account, nothing. We'll know he's not using the money against us. He'll know we're not holding out."

The room was silent for several seconds. George and Jinnah remained standing. Suvia sat down and said, "Well?"

At this, George, too, sat down, with an audible sigh. "That would be acceptable to me," he said, rather stiffly.

"To me also," Jinnah said, looking at George Holbrook. For a brief instant, Jinnah felt a small feeling of kinship with George. He handed George a slip of paper with the name of a Zurich bank and an account number on it. "The funds are to be deposited into this account. I had not planned to make any periodic withdrawals. Monsieur Girard is a banker. I am sure he can arrange a hold on the account. It will not inconvenience me.

"Now, this ship. It will be delivered to me also on the thirty-first day of December. On December 25, it will anchor in Eclipse Bay on the island of Diego Garcia. I will board there to assume command. I expect that some of the owners will be aboard at that time, but it is not necessary for all of you to be there. For a week, your crew will train mine to operate the ship as it proceeds to the delivery point. Then you and your crew will be transported to an island with an airport, and we shall never meet again.

"Between now and December, the ship is to be overhauled completely. It must be ready for extended cruising at sea. Fuel tankage, water making and provision storage capacity are to be increased. Finally, the ship is to be outfitted with the latest equipment for oceanographic research. I shall provide details of these requirements within a few weeks. Are there any questions?"

"No," George replied. "It will be done. Is that all?"

"Not quite," Jinnah said, looking at his watch again. He turned toward Joe Langone who, like nearly everyone else in the room, had remained silent throughout the discussion. "Your grandchild, Christine, has just been released. When I have left, I am sure you will want to verify that fact. She was taken as a lesson that opposition to me was useless and would not be tolerated. As I said earlier, I was pleased that she had been in the company of a bodyguard. The fact that I was able to capture her despite such precautions only served to demonstrate to you the folly of trying to hide behind guards and fences. Now that the lesson has been taught, the girl will be released, more or less intact." Jinnah paused for a moment, for effect.

"More or less," he continued. "So that this lesson will not be quickly forgotten, I have brought a reminder, this small package. Please do not open it until I have left. And, no, it is not a bomb. If I had wished to kill you I could have done so long ago."

With a small mock bow, Jinnah handed the parcel to Joe Langone, who accepted it with a horrible premonition of what it might contain. Jinnah motioned to George to remain, turned, and left the room with Syed behind him. George called the quarterdeck, and alerted the watch that two of the guests would be departing. Then he, along with the others watched Joe open the package and begin to weep tears of rage. In it was the frozen, severed hand of a child. The left hand. Joe looked at his own left hand, the one he had used to knock Jinnah down.

As soon as he had seen the contents of Joe's package, George Holbrook bolted from the salon. Racing aft to the quarterdeck, he saw Jinnah's sinister black launch pulling away, with Jinnah and his three men aboard. *Seasmoke* was just coming alongside, and several guests were waiting for her to take them ashore. "Sorry," said George, "I need this boat for a minute. I'll be right back." He jumped into the launch, even before it was alongside the accommodation ladder, and told the crewman to get out. In seconds, he was away, alone in the boat, in pursuit of Jinnah.

Syed, who had dedicated his life to being Jinnah's personal bodyguard, was the first to notice the pursuing boat. During the confrontation between Jinnah and George Holbrook, Syed had kept his hand on his weapon. Now, seeing the white bow wave of the boat behind them, Syed took the gun out. He whispered to the man at the helm, and Jinnah's launch accelerated, heading out of Grand Harbor toward the breakwater and the open Mediterranean beyond.

George watched as the black boat ahead climbed onto a plane, and smiled as he thrust *Seasmoke*'s throttles forward. The supercharged engines drove the big Magnum up and out of the water with the ease and grace of a leaping dolphin, and in seconds she was skipping over the wave tops at well over sixty knots. Jinnah's boat, laboring at no more than forty, was alongside in less than a minute.

Jinnah and his men watched as George maneuvered his boat to within six feet of theirs. Syed still had his pistol at the ready, but Jinnah, seeing that Holbrook was alone and showing no weapon, motioned for him to put it away. Then he told his helmsman to heave to. The boats slowed, then stopped, side by side on the black water of Grand Harbor, and for a minute they were rocked violently by the passing of their own wakes. When the motion had eased, George brought *Seasmoke* right alongside Jinnah's black boat, then tied the two boats together with a mooring line.

"Please come aboard for a minute," said George. "I have one more thing to tell you."

"I don't believe there is anything more to say," Jinnah replied.

"It's important. Please."

Jinnah glanced at Syed, as if to say, "Cover me," and climbed over the gunwales into George's boat. For a moment the two men stood facing each other, while Syed and his two men watched apprehensively.

"You didn't have to do that," George said.

"It was necessary." He hesitated. "Have you come to lecture me, or demand an apology?"

"No. Only to give you a warning."

"More threats?"

"No. I've had enough of those for this evening. I came to tell you there's no Plan B. There never was. We considered something like it early on. We rejected the idea at once."

George looked around him. The moon was high in the sky, and the fortifications surrounding Grand Harbor were bathed in bluish light. He asked Jinnah, "Do you know the history of the Great Siege of 1565?"

"Of course. Had Malta fallen, the Ottoman Empire would have conquered all of Europe."

"That's Fort St. Elmo," George said, gesturing to the fortress at the tip of the peninsula beneath Valletta. "During the Great Siege, it held out for a month. It should have fallen in three days. By resisting for so long, inflicting huge losses on the attackers, it turned the tide against the Turkish Army.

"When St. Elmo fell, the Turks tortured and killed its survivors. Grand Master La Valette was in Fort St. Angelo across the harbor, right up there." George pointed. "He'd known that St. Elmo was going to be overrun. He had hundreds of Turkish prisoners in his dungeons. He was waiting to exchange them for the survivors of Fort St. Elmo.

"La Valette wasn't a butcher. The Knights of St. John weren't warriors like the Knights Templar. They were hospital builders, men of peace and compassion. Yet when La Valette saw the brave men of St. Elmo butchered, he responded in kind. He had all of the Turkish prisoners beheaded. He had their heads loaded into his cannons, and fired into the Turkish lines. It was a plain statement. Today we'd say, 'If you want to play hardball, so will I.'

"I'm not the Grand Master aboard *Seafire.* The owners decide things, not me. As I said, there's no Plan B. But your needless mutilation of that child makes me wonder whether there should be. I'm sure Joe Langone thinks there should. Others may be thinking that way, too.

"That's why I followed you, to give some advice. Don't teach us any more lessons, Jinnah. Don't hurt any more children. If you do, you might piss us off. When people get pissed off enough, they can do nasty things. Things they wouldn't do otherwise, things against their nature, their religion, and their conscience. Like La Valette."

"It's an interesting story, Mr. Holbrook," Jinnah said, "but it still sounds like a threat."

"Take it as you will. It was meant as a warning."

Neither man had anything further to say. Jinnah climbed over the gunwales into his boat, and George untied the mooring line. He motored slowly toward *Seafire.* She was ablaze with lights, surrounded by the fortifications La Valette had built to withstand a second siege, which had never come. He remembered that the launch was needed to ferry guests ashore and sped up once again.

When George returned to the salon, only Suvia Ferris and Joe Langone remained. The others had left to rejoin the party for the sake of appearance, or to go to bed. As George entered, Joe got out of his chair to leave, taking his pitiful package with him. George started to offer condolences, but Joe brushed them aside with a wave of his hand.

"No words, George, no sympathy" he said. "Make plans. The call came while you were gone. My Chrissy is alive! Safe! This," he said, brandishing the package, "this is a sad thing, a terrible thing, but it is nothing compared to her being safe. I was afraid they would kill her. The doctors can give her a new hand, one that will be almost as good." Joe paused, fighting tears, his voice choking with emotion.

"He didn't have to do this, George. He could have taken her and then just let her go." Joe stopped speaking, unable to continue, and sobbed openly. Both George and Suvia started to get up, but Joe waved them back into their seats with an angry gesture.

"No words! Plans! Make good plans, George. But in the end, you must plan one thing. You must let me be the one to kill him." Joe abruptly left the room, taking the package with him.

"Shouldn't that thing go into the freezer?" said George. "Maybe it could be shipped back to the States and reattached."

"No," replied Suvia. "We asked that when Joe got the call from Florida. Chrissy was in the hospital when the call came in, and Joe asked the doctors about that. It's been too long. We have to keep it, though. Chrissy wants it saved so when she dies it can be buried along with the rest of her."

"God," George said, "what a shame. What a night!"

"What did you do when you went tearing out of here?"

"I caught up with Jinnah and we had a little talk. I told him that if anything like Chrissy Langone happened we might retaliate."

"What did he say?"

"Not much. He took it well enough." George lapsed into silence, then visibly brightened. "The meeting went well. We got the concessions we needed, even though I nearly lost it."

"Nearly?"

"OK, I guess I did get carried away for a minute or so. But it worked out in the end. You were great! You should have gone into acting. You really sounded furious with me when you broke in. For a minute, it actually sounded like you were taking Jinnah's side."

"I really was angry, George. Maybe your own act was too good. You had me convinced, and I think you convinced yourself a bit too much, too, with that Plan B nonsense. You sounded so damned bloodthirsty that for a minute or two I couldn't tell who was worse, you or Jinnah. And do you want to know something really awful? After seeing Chrissy's hand, wrapped and frozen like a leg of lamb, Plan B doesn't sound so bad."

Suvia was silent for a moment, considering the implications of what she had just said. "Enough of that. Why don't you explain to me just what we accomplished tonight. Why the hell did we have to go through all of this grief to put a hold on Jinnah's bank account? I've been thinking about what you said about keeping our options open. I still don't understand how this accomplishes that."

"As I said, if we decide to fight, he'll be a lot more dangerous opponent with all of that money at his disposal."

"But sooner or later the hold will come off the account, and he can fight us then."

"Not if we've cleaned out the account."

"So you're retaining the option to double-cross him?"

"That's right."

"But how?"

"I'm meeting with Henri Girard in the library in ten minutes to work that out," George said. "It will probably involve breaking several Swiss banking laws. It's all part of phase two of the plan."

"Phase two!" Suvia said. "What's phase one?"

"Tonight was phase one."

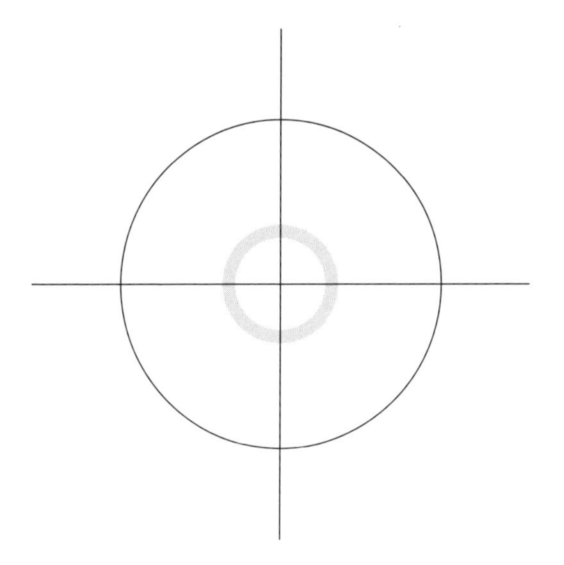

CHAPTER 6

THE EXECUSTAR was cruising at an altitude of five thousand feet. Ralph Dade was in the pilot's seat, and George sat to his right. Joe Langone, Nick Argeriardis, and Dick Phelps were in passenger seats behind them. It was a fine afternoon for a sightseeing trip. A tanker had gone aground off the coast of Algeria. Nick had asked Ralph to fly him over to have a look. They'd invited the other men along for the ride.

George looked around. They were out of sight of *Seafire*, and Africa was a vague mass of land miles away. As good a place as any, he decided, and unbuckled his seat belt.

"Have fun," Ralph said, as George moved aft.

George settled into a seat next to Dick. "Flight to the wreck's over an hour," he said. "Might as well talk on the way. Why don't you tell us how long you've been spying for Jinnah?"

For a moment, Dick said nothing, not believing he'd heard right. "What?" he said.

"You heard me."

"I don't know what you're talking about." Dick's tone was defiant.

George got up and stood in front of Phelps. "Liar," he said, and slapped him in the face with his open right hand. The blow landed with a loud smack, hard enough to shock, not hard enough to injure. Dick opened his mouth to protest, and George said, "Traitor," and slapped him again with a left. Dick looked at Joe and Nick. They were watching impassively.

Dick's face was beet red, from outrage as well as the blows. He started to speak, then winced in anticipation of another slap. None came. "What did you do that for?"

"To prove a point. I just committed assault and battery. Back home, you could sue me or have me arrested. Up here, there's jack shit you can do about it. I hit you so you'd understand that. Now, answer my question."

"You're crazy, Holbrook. I'm not a spy for Jinnah. If you think you can get away with assault, you're completely nuts. The minute we get back to the ship, I'm going to call the police!"

"No you're not," George said, and hit him again, as hard as he could, but still with an open hand.

"Slow down, Ralph," George said. After a moment, George slid the door open. Wash from the rotors swirled in the cabin.

"When I was in 'Nam, some of our people didn't always follow the Geneva Convention when they interrogated Viet Cong prisoners. You know what I mean? Sometimes they took Charlie up in a Huey. Say about five thousand feet, like we are now. They'd ask him some questions. What's your battalion strength? How do you get supplies? Stuff like that. If he didn't answer, they'd throw his ass out of the Huey. They had a name for it: flying lessons. Big joke. See if he learns to fly before he hits the ground."

George had been speaking in a conversational tone, as if he were telling war stories to some buddies in a bar. Suddenly, he wheeled on Phelps, slapped him again, and grabbed him by the front of his shirt.

"Now, you worthless sack of shit, tell us just what you've told Jinnah, or by Christ I'm gonna teach you how to fly."

Phelps was terrified. "Nick, Joe, get this madman off of me!" he wailed.

"The arrogant son of a bitch isn't going to talk, George," Nick said. "Thinks he can bullshit us. Let's quit wasting time and throw him out." Nick grabbed Dick's arms from behind his chair. Joe unlatched his seat belt. The two men hauled Dick to his feet and to the door.

"This is murder!" he screamed. "You can't get away with this."

"Sure we can," George said. He picked up Dick's camera bag and opened it. "Tragic accident. You opened the door to take pictures. You got disoriented looking through the viewfinder. Pitched right out the door." George took a camera out of the bag. "Oops," he said, and tossed it out. Nick and Joe held Dick so he could watch it fall. It shrank to a tiny dot, then disappeared. The sea was a mile below. Too far to see a splash.

"I swear ..."

"OK, let's do it," George said. He opened a duffel bag, and pulled out a black cloth hood. He put it over Dick's head, and tied it securely under his chin.

"No! No!" Dick shouted. The hood muffled his voice. George took a roll of duct tape out of the bag and used it to bind Dick's wrists together in front of him. Then, he secured a heavy belt around Dick's waist.

"What's that?" Dick asked as he felt the belt tighten. Panic was clear in his voice.

"Diver's weights," George said. "Make sure you sink and stay sunk."

"Please!" he screamed. "No!"

"My granddaughter probably pleaded not to have her hand cut off," Joe Langone said. His voice was pure venom. "Just like you're pleading now. You helped make it happen."

Hatred rang in Joe's voice, and Dick believed at last that he really was about to die. His legs turned to rubber, his knees began to buckle. "No," he said. It was a whimper.

"Goodbye, Dick," said George. He nodded. Nick and Joe threw Phelps out the door. They could hear him screaming all the way down to the water.

The whole twelve feet.

He was still screaming when they pulled in the line attached to the web belt, and hauled him back into the helicopter.

Seafire motored west, making good speed toward the silver-gold Mediterranean sun as she approached the Straits of Gibraltar. The Rock loomed above her starboard bow, the sheer eastern face dark against the late afternoon sky. Insurance salesmen around the world would have wept at the beauty of it. From above, *Seafire* looked as if she were cutting through a sea of diamonds, as the tops of the short, choppy swells threw off shards of sparkling light.

The conditions were nearly ideal for an underway landing, but George Holbrook wasn't satisfied; nearly ideal conditions were unacceptable if they could be improved upon. He called the ship on the radio and Bill Jackson, on the bridge as usual, replied. George asked him to alter course to starboard about thirty degrees. As *Seafire* turned, the relative wind shifted and the flight deck was no longer in the turbulent wind shadow of the superstructure and stacks. Once the ship was steady on her new heading, George brought the helicopter aboard with smooth precision. As the ship resumed her former course, and the deck crew prepared to wheel the aircraft into the hangar, George got out and went below.

He made his way quickly forward to the salon and asked the duty steward to invite all the owners to join him there in an hour. "Also, please ask Mrs. Ferris to meet me in the ship's library immediately." Then he climbed the ladder to the library on the 01 level.

Of all the living areas aboard *Seafire*, the library was George's favorite. It was a blend of quiet elegance and seagoing efficiency. The bookcases were burnished aluminum, and each shelf had a discreet retainer bar to keep books from spilling out when the ship rolled. Since the library was above the main deck, excess weight would diminish the ship's stability. The decor was Art Deco, with aluminum being the dominant material rather than mahogany or oak. The walls were a vibrant aquamarine, and the room was accented in the rich pastels of the classic Miami Beach style. The effect was bright and pleasantly serene.

The reading alcove was small, with two comfortable chairs bolted to the deck. George sank into one of them and sighed. He was tired. It had been three days since Dick Phelps' tearful confession to treason. For the past two, he had been ashore, flying the ExecuStar from city to city, calling in old favors and piecing together information. He knew now why Jinnah needed a billion dollars. It was just what he had suspected.

And infinitely worse.

Suvia Ferris came in and sat next to him in the alcove. She studied him for a moment. "You look tired," she said. "Are you all right?"

"I'm fine," he replied. "I haven't been sleeping well lately. I lay awake scheming, and when I do get to sleep, I have stupid nightmares. They should take me out and shoot me." George forced a lame laugh.

"What did you find out about Jinnah?"

"About six months ago, some ordnance was stolen from a U.S.

Army armory in Europe. The Army thinks some former Baader-Meinhopf people did it, maybe with inside help. The motive was profit rather than politics. The thieves are offering the entire package to the highest bidder. All the terrorist groups are interested. Well they might be! Part of the loot was a dozen or so Mini-Stingers, small infrared anti-aircraft missiles. Just enough range to take out an airliner on final approach. Imagine what a terrorist would give for those babies.

"The missiles aren't the best part, though. The thieves also took three low-yield tactical nuclear devices. They're called atomic satchel charges. Every terrorist in the world wants them. One of 'em can tear the heart out of a small city. Level buildings for blocks. Kill tens, maybe hundreds of thousands of people. Jinnah has the inside track on the purchase. His bid is supposedly a billion U.S. dollars."

"Oh, God," said Suvia.

"Jinnah apparently plans to use *Seafire* as his headquarters for terrorism. I'd suspected as much. He's been trying to set himself up as leader of a worldwide council of terrorists. If we give him the ship, he'll have a mobile base of operations. If we give him the billion dollars, he'll be a nuclear power."

"No wonder you looked so glum when I came in. We can't pay the man, George, and you know it. I think you've known it, or suspected it, all along. We can't give Jinnah the ability to blow up three cities. We have to fight."

"Of course. I've thought so all along. And I know that you've thought, on one or two occasions, that I was a typical bloodthirsty male, looking for a fight."

"That's not fair, George! I never said that!"

"OK, maybe not. Tell me, would you have given him the money if it were only going to buy the anti-aircraft missiles? If there were no nukes in the deal?"

"I don't know. Probably not. George, why are you asking me this? Are you mad at me, or something?"

"How about just one missile? Or a car bomb? Or a one-shot, sawed off shotgun? Would you have bought one of those for him? I know I would."

"What's your damn point, George?"

"All along I've been sure that if we gave Jinnah a billion dollars, he'd do something terrible with it. I just didn't know what. He's a terrorist, for Christ's sake! What's he going to do with the money, find a cure for cancer? Hell no, he's going to use it to hurt people. A lot of people. I knew that.

"What's bothering me is that for three weeks now, since you first told me about Jinnah, I've been keeping open the option to pay him. Not just for show, for Jinnah's sake, but open as a viable option in my mind. Even though I knew that if we did pay him, he'd use the money to hurt lots of people we'd never know.

"When I found out what he was going to buy with the money, I was relieved. I knew there would be no debate, no second thoughts. None of us would allow such a thing to happen. Then, I started wondering what kind of weapons we would have bought for him. How much suffering would we have pushed off onto strangers to save ourselves?"

"George Holbrook, you should stay out of this library," Suvia said. "Every time I come in here to talk to you, you've worked yourself into a depression. What would we have done if Jinnah were just going to buy one or two missiles? Would we have done the right thing? Who knows? Who cares? If you start hating yourself for things you might have done and didn't, you're finished. I agree that three atom bombs is too much to give a terrorist. It's convenient that some lesser weapon isn't at issue. We don't have tough choices to make. So, I'm a moral coward. So, what?"

George laughed. "Damn, you have a way of cutting through bullshit. You're right. We have enough decisions to make without regretting choices that we never made. I just keep questioning what I'm doing. I know it's not productive, but I do it all the same."

"What's this about nightmares?" Suvia asked.

George's first reaction was not to tell her. After a moment, he changed his mind. He told her all of it — the Hellcat, the frozen controls, crashing into the power lines, burning alive.

"Poor George. That's gruesome," she said. "It can't have been too bad, though. You survived, and you don't have any scars from the fire."

"I thought you knew, Suvia. I wasn't flying the Hellcat when it crashed. That's the crazy part. I've been in flaming wrecks of my own, but the one I dream about is the one that killed my father."

They were both silent for a moment. "I wish you weren't leaving in the morning," George said. "I'll miss you."

"I have to go, George. I've already overstayed my vacation by two weeks. How long will it take to cross to Boston? Ten days? I can't be gone that long. I've got a company to run."

"It's not as if you'd be on the moons of Jupiter," said George. "There's the satellite telephones, and a secure fax. You could keep in touch."

"I just spent two years fighting tooth and nail to establish control of Ferroil. There are people who would stab me in the back in a nanosecond to take my place. Who knows what palace coups they're plotting. I need to be there, and not just by satellite link!"

"OK, Suvia, you know better than I what you need to do."

"If you ask me," Suvia said, "I think your crossing the Atlantic with the ship is a waste of time. Why do you need to be aboard, anyway? Couldn't you plot and scheme just as well in the States?"

"I really do need to be aboard, Suvia. This ship has to be modified in a shipyard, relaunched, and taken half way around the world, all in less than six months. There's planning that has to be done before the work even begins."

"What kind of work, George? Turning *Seafire* into a phony research vessel? Hell, that should be easy enough."

George grinned. "You're right," he said. "That will be easy. The hard part will be turning her into a Trojan horse."

The owners gathered in the salon as George had asked. The meeting with them took little over an hour. As he expected, the decision to fight Jinnah was unanimous. No one was willing to pay him, and the abduction of Christine Langone had removed going to the authorities from the list of options. Once that had been decided, George delivered his ultimatum.

"Throughout my life I've done a number of things that others had told me to do, even when I thought it was a bad idea. Among other calamities, there have been three aircraft crashes. In each case, I'd known in advance that disaster was likely, but had deferred to the judgment of others. The last time, when my father was killed on a flight I should have made, I vowed never to let such a thing happen again.

"I have a plan to fight Jinnah," George said. "If you want me to, I'll stay aboard and carry it out to the end. On one condition. Today you must give me complete autonomy and control of the operation. I can't fight this war if I'm a private and you're a committee of generals. I'm going to be in charge, or you're going to have to fight this war without me."

Alex Wilson was the first to protest. "I'm certainly not going to delegate authority to George," he said. Before he could," continue, George interrupted him. "I don't need to hear this, he said. "I'll wait outside the door for fifteen minutes. You'll be able to speak freely. If it takes you longer than that to decide, then I don't want the job in any case."

George stood in the passageway outside *Seafire*'s salon. He looked at his watch. The fifteen minutes was almost up. He was about to leave for his stateroom and start packing when Polly Harrington came out, and closed the door behind her.

"Oh, good, George! You're still here. I was afraid you'd leave as soon as the time was up."

"I was about to."

"George, you're like your father. So proud, so stubborn. Give us a few more minutes. It's a big decision."

"It's not pride, Polly. To do this right, I need the group's support. If it takes forever to decide, it means the support really isn't there."

"You are so like Jim," she said, fondly. "So full of logic, so quick to deny the existence of any emotion."

"I didn't realize you knew him well,"

"Far better than you think," Polly's blue eyes sparkled, and George could see, for an instant, the beautiful woman she once had been.

"This was after your mother died, of course," she lowered her eyes in mock modesty, but her smile grew wider.

"You have my full support, George. And that of most of the others. Alex is being a prig, as usual. He has an ally or two. It should only take another minute or two for Suvia and me to whip them into line."

"Thanks, Polly." She turned toward the door.

"Polly?" George said, tentatively. "Were you, uh, friendly with Dad when he crashed the Hellcat?"

"Yes." The smile faded and the blue eyes turned steely.

"Do you believe it really was an accident?"

"Of course not. Do you?"

The helicopter flight to Lisbon had been a pleasant one for George. Now, alone on the return flight, loneliness made him wish he'd let the ship's paid helicopter pilot do the flying. He'd taken off from *Seafire* in the early afternoon, shortly after she had rounded Cape San Vincent. The Carsons, the Argeriardises, Alex Wilson, Joe Langone, and Henri Girard rode in back. Suvia was up front with George, in the co-pilot's seat. To the mild concern of the other passengers, George had spent most of the trip teaching her to fly the aircraft. He'd noted with approval that she had a light and firm touch on the controls, rather than the usual white knuckled grip of a novice. She would make a good pilot, he had thought and he'd told her so. She'd laughed, kissed him lightly on the cheek, and made him promise to teach her how to fly. Peter Carson had told him, partly in jest, to keep his eyes on the road. Emily Carson had giggled.

There hadn't been much discussion of Jinnah on the flight. The owners had given George a free hand and an open checkbook to wage war against him. They seemed content, even relieved, that he had assumed the task.

George landed the ExecuStar on the flight deck, and stayed with it as it was stowed. He watched the crew roll it into place in the hangar, and personally supervised as it was secured to the tie-downs on the hangar deck. Even in summer, storms are common in the North Atlantic, and destroyer hulls can roll through a ninety-degree arc in a crossing sea. Satisfied that the helicopter would stay put in a blow, George went forward to the library, to talk with his old friend, Ralph Dade. George smiled to himself as he thought of Suvia's comment, and resolved not to work himself into a depression.

George found Ralph in *Seafire*'s library, slouched in a leather wing chair, legs dangling over the arm, and a book resting on his chest. Ralph was in the same contortion when they first met in Pensacola during flight training. He called it his serious study position and fell into it whenever he needed a nap. Ralph Dade could hardly be charged with having a military mind, but George wanted to discuss strategy, and Ralph would have to do. Old habits die hard, George thought as he leaned over to wake up his long time friend.

"Suppose," George said, settling into one of the chairs in the reading alcove, "that we decide to fight Jinnah at the last minute, when we're delivering the ship. Jump him, bag his whole entourage. How would you propose to bring that off?"

"Are we preparing to do that?"

"Maybe. I want to consider it as an option. How would we do it?"

"Christ, George, it depends on how many men he has with him where we meet up with them."

"Well," George said, "some of that we know and some we can figure out. Intelligence reports say there are no more than twenty or thirty men in his group. If we eliminate all of them, we don't need to worry about anyone wanting to avenge Jinnah. No one will know we had anything to do with his death.

"As for the place, it's got to be within six day's range of Diego Garcia. There's a big U.S. Navy presence, it would be too risky for him to bring his entire organization there. He'll probably come aboard, maybe with two or three guys, and lead us to a rendezvous. That's where he'll meet up with the main group of his supporters. They'll probably be on a ship or a remote island. He'd want to stay away from civilization to avoid being captured."

"OK," Ralph said, "that makes sense. What we need is an amphibious assault team. Mercenary commandos. Rent 'em out of the ads in *Soldier of Fortune*. Hell, we could use *Seafire* as the assault ship. Her hangar will hold two helicopters. We could drop a couple of squads of troops on Jinnah's base or ship or whatever in a matter of seconds. Wipe out the entire Makran Liberation Organization in two minutes flat!"

"Anything else?"

"It would be great if we could put a couple of heavy weapons aboard the ship. Too bad she doesn't still have her five-inch battery, eh? We could stand off and sink Jinnah's ship or pound his island into dust and not even have to mess with commandos."

"Not messing with commandos would be good," George said. "What I'm thinking about is illegal. Wherever Jinnah's base is, it's bound to be in somebody's jurisdiction. We're talking about going in like vigilantes and killing the bad guys. We can call it neutralizing or eliminating or whatever we want, but it amounts to murder. Who are we going to hire to do this that we can trust not to blackmail us with it later?"

"Jeez, George, I dunno," said Ralph, grinning. "Those guys in *Soldier of Fortune* are supposed to be pretty discreet."

"Sure," George replied, chuckling.

"I sure as hell hope you're not planning a do-it-yourself operation, George," Ralph said, seriously. "I'm too old for that kind of shit."

"So am I, Ralph. Here's the problem. Our options are limited. Suppose we train our crew to fight. I doubt they'll be very good. Even our own security people have police backgrounds, not military. We'll be asking them to risk their lives doing something they're poorly trained to do. If the worst happens, they'll be killed. Or, maybe, that's not the worst. Maybe they'll get captured and executed as terrorists. Can we ask them to risk that?"

"I don't like where this is going," said Ralph.

"I don't like the idea of mercenaries, either. I don't think they're trustworthy."

"Which leaves..."

"Which leaves us."

"I think you're crazy. We could hire the best private army in the world. You want to put on an old set of cammies and fight the bad guys yourself? You're certifiably nuts!"

"Remember, this is just a contingency plan. The more we can handle ourselves and the less we have to farm out to strangers, the less chance there will be that Jinnah will find out that we even have a contingency plan."

"Jesus, George. We're talking about twenty or thirty young guerrillas, full of religious zeal, well trained and well armed. Who do we have in the opposite corner? A dozen geriatric Geronimos who don't know which end of a piece the bullets come out of? Give me a break!"

"If you've noted a certain glumness in my mood recently, now you know why. Everything you say is true. You and I had some basic weapons training a long time ago. What little you remember is out of date and nobody else on our side even learned what we did. How on God's green Earth are we going to take on a trained paramilitary operation? But, the more I thought about it, the more I realized that mercenaries aren't the answer.

"People who take up arms for money do it for just that — the money. If we bring a bunch of them aboard, what's to prevent a mutiny? They could take over the ship and hold *us* hostage. Rob us blind. We couldn't even call for help without getting arrested ourselves. Even if our plan succeeds, they could blackmail us later.

"If we go to the mat with Jinnah, I can see us getting some hired talent in the States to protect our families. Maybe, even, to take out some of Jinnah's hit teams if we identify them. The people we hire for that wouldn't need to know whom they're working for. But the battle group, if there's a battle, has to be us."

"George, you're having delusions of adequacy again."

"Right. Keep thinking about heavy weapons. We're going to need an equalizer if we have to go up against Jinnah's troops. No, not just an equalizer. An edge."

Most often, when *Seafire* had crossed the Atlantic Ocean, she had done it without any of her owners aboard. The crossing is long, boring, and frequently uncomfortable. On this trip, the Dades were aboard, as were the Roths, and the Knights, Mrs. Harrington, and a guest, Mr. Holbrook. It was all that the crew could talk about.

Aboard any yacht, large or small, life begins for the crew when the owners depart. Work has to be done, of course, and the ship's captain sees to that. Still, the overall atmosphere is far more relaxed when the people who pay the bills aren't around to pick and poke, to bitch and moan, and wonder if they're getting their money's worth. When the crew learned that *Seafire* was bound for Boston, there had been a feeling of pleasant anticipation for the trip — ten relaxed days crossing an empty ocean with little to do but routine maintenance. The news that there would be a small crowd in the owners' party had swept through the ship like a whirlwind. Disappointment and dismay reigned, and rumors flew about the meaning of this unprecedented trip.

On the fifth night out, more or less in the middle of the North Atlantic, George put a tape into the VCR. The movie was the re-released version of *Star Wars*. As they had watched the spaceships exchange laser fire, George had asked Bob Knight whether the real world was catching up to these movies. Had the Star Wars program been just a Ronnie Reagan bluff, or were there real weapons like that?

"Steve Roth could tell you better than I," Bob said. "His company did a lot of work on the lasers. Some on contract to the Air Force, some spec work on his own. I worked with him, some. On the computers."

"Computers?"

"Yeah. We were working on a really powerful laser. Steve called it Big Dumb Laser. He got the name from the Big Dumb Booster concept that some people in the space program thought would be better than the shuttle. He figured that if we could build a huge laser, we could shoot down incoming warheads from the ground. We wouldn't have to worry about building space stations or any of that complicated bullshit. Just put a really big laser on the Mall in D.C. and shoot down anything the bad guys throw at us."

"Engagingly simple," George said. "I'm sure the military types made short work of that."

"Actually, they listened politely for a lot longer than I thought. Bob actually built the laser. Two of them, in fact. Two different prototypes. A big ruby crystal unit and a blue-green argon monster that you wouldn't believe! The problem was in aiming the suckers. That was my job, and I blew it."

"What do you mean?"

"Here's the problem. You're shooting at a target that's moving at several thousand miles an hour. It's a hundred miles away, and it's only five or six feet long. The energy beam is only inches across. Unless you score a direct hit, you've missed. A millionth of a degree in deflection of the beam is all it takes to miss. No matter how hard we tried, we couldn't design a computer and a program fast enough to aim the laser and hit the target. The gun had the range. The sights just weren't good enough."

"Why didn't you put the laser in space? Get closer to the targets?"

"Power, mostly. These lasers were monsters. They deliver huge amounts of energy, so they need huge amounts of electricity to run them. We'd have to put a power plant in space along with the lasers."

"How much power would they need?" George asked.

"Tremendous amounts. Megawatts. Many megawatts."

"Would forty megawatts do the trick?"

"Oh, yes," Knight replied, "but where are you going to get forty megawatts of power?"

The bridge was wrapped in the warm sort of quiet that comes in the midwatch on a ship underway. The autopilot was steering, and the pilothouse was darkened to preserve night vision. Bill Jackson stared out over the bow, into the night, talking quietly to himself. His lips moved only slightly and no words could be made out, but emotions were clear on his face and in his eyes — anger, determination, pleasure, sadness.

George Holbrook entered the pilothouse, but Jackson was unaware of his arrival for a moment or two. For another moment, both men were embarrassed, Jackson for his emotions and George for intruding. George apologized, a lame effort even for him, explaining that he had come onto the bridge to recheck his navigational computations. He was about to leave, but Jackson asked him to wait.

"Mr. Holbrook, I want to know what's going on. You built this yacht and you've supervised her overhauls for over fifteen years. You never took any interest in running the ship. Not until a month ago. Now, you're up here every night. You fiddle with the autopilot, you plot positions, and you read charts. You're even studying celestial navigation, for Christ's sake. We've got Loran Charlie, SatNav, GPS, the works. The computers on this thing can tell you where we are within fifty feet, anywhere on the planet, and you're out there dawn and dusk with a sextant stuck in your eye like the Ancient Mariner.

"And it's not just you. Mr. Roth is running around with a clipboard measuring and mumbling and he spends more time in the engine room than he does on deck. He's got some scheme, Finnerty says, to control the entire engineering plant from up here on the bridge. Mr. Dade has been asking more questions about supplies and fuel than a team of auditors. He's like an ensign fresh out of supply officers school.

"We want to know what's going on, Mr. Holbrook. Finnerty and I both do. You owe us that, at least. Finnerty has run the engine room since Bubba Caulfield bought this thing, over forty years. I've been the captain for over ten. We know that we're going to Boston for a refit. When the ship comes out of dry-dock, Finnerty and I are going to be left behind on the beach, aren't we?"

For a moment, George didn't reply. He looked toward Jackson, and then away, unable to look him in the eye.

"*Seafire* is finished, Bill. This is her last cruise as a private yacht. The owners are going to turn her into an oceanographic research ship and donate her to a foundation. Get a big tax write-off. The foundation will staff her with its own people. Part of the refit will be remote control and automation, so the research organization won't have to hire sailors, just scientists. A couple of us will take her out of Boston to the delivery point. That's why I'm learning to run her."

Jackson said nothing in reply, and George turned to leave. He could see, even in the dim light, that Jackson was again staring out over the bow.

"The ghosts you're watching," asked George, "are they friendlies?"

Without turning, Jackson said, "I suppose you might say that."

"War stories? Sea stories? I'd like to hear them, sometime, if you wouldn't mind telling me."

"I'd rather not," replied Jackson, "they're sort of private, you know?"

"Oh, yes, I know. I've got a couple of my own that I keep pretty much to myself.

"Don't worry about getting a job, Bill. Ralph Dade is going to be getting a yacht of his own. A big Bennetti or something. If you want the job of captain, it's yours. Finnerty can run the engines. I'm sure that a couple of the others will offer you the same deal. They'll probably end up fighting among themselves over who gets to hire you."

Jackson didn't reply. Once again George started to leave, and once again he hesitated. After a moment, he sighed, and sat on the edge of the chart table.

"Ralph and I were in the Navy together. I guess you knew that. We were on our first real mission, flying jets. Basic fighters, nothing like the flying computers the Navy has now. We'd been in Pensacola together, and we'd just joined the squadron. Neither of us was particularly good as a pilot. Ralph's gunnery was so bad that after a few weeks they gave up and put him in photo recon. One day they sent us on a mission that was supposed to be a milk run, Ralph in an unarmed camera ship and me flying shotgun. We weren't supposed to be there. Officially, we never were. If they had thought there would be a MIG within five hundred miles of us they'd have sent people who knew what they were doing.

"We were in the middle of nowhere when the MIGs showed up. Four of them, diving on us. I tried to warn Ralph, but his radio wasn't working. I figured he'd get the message when the bullets started going by, anyway.

"As bad as Ralph's gunnery was, his combat maneuvers were worse. He was hopeless! Whenever somebody jumped him he'd instinctively go through the exact same maneuver. A little climbing turn to the right and then a full-power diving turn to the left. Not a bad maneuver, really, but when somebody's done it eight times in a row, the enemy sort of catches on, you know? That's where he got the name Old Predictable Ralph."

"So here we were with four MIGs on us, and only one of us with guns, and we can't talk to each other. At that instant something happened to me that I still can't explain. For the first time in my life, I was flying, not pushing on the controls to make the airplane fly. It was me that was flying, and the airplane was an extension of my body. Fear, adrenaline, who knows what it was, but somehow, suddenly, I could feel the control surfaces as if they were a part of me.

"I was like a halfback running for a hole in the line that wasn't open yet, but would be when I got there. I knew what Ralph was going to do, where he would end up, and how I was going to get to that point in the sky. I was already starting to climb when the MIGs fired and Ralph started into his old shuffle."

Without realizing it, George was gesturing with his hands, rolling and twisting his flattened palms to mimic the maneuvers of the airplanes. "I was a quarter of the way into a loop, going straight up, and I rolled 180 degrees and then continued the loop.

I Immelmaned out level at the top for two or three seconds, and then I split-essed over onto my back and into the loop again. Two of the MIGs were trying to follow me through all this but they got lost for a couple of seconds. When Ralph finished his turns, the other two MIGs were behind him, and I was right on top of them. I blew them both to pieces before either of them knew I was there.

"My two MIG drivers took one look at this and took off for home. I chased them. Now how's that for a dumb move, when I'm supposed to be escorting Ralph? But the adrenaline was pumping and I didn't want to let them get away. Crazy!

"So, I caught them and shot them both down. They never had a chance. I flew that day like I've never flown, before or since. On the way back home, I kept waiting for the feeling to go away, for the airplane to start feeling like a machine again. It never happened.

"Most good pilots come to a point when they stop thinking about flying and suddenly they know how to fly, like a bird knows. I still fly that way. I can still feel the airplane around me, as if it were a part of me, no matter if it's a helicopter or a glider or what. But, it's never been as exciting as it was that first time. And, I've never been as good a pilot as I was that afternoon.

"Four MIGs in one day. All confirmed kills. I never saw another MIG, so I didn't get to be an ace. I got a commendation for the first two kills and a general discharge for the others. And I got about ten minutes of memories that I've been living off of for the rest of my life.

"It's a hell of a note, isn't it? I'm a test pilot, and the only real pleasure I seem to get in life is reliving ten minutes that happened years ago. The same damn ten minutes every time. If it's not too private, I think I'd like to hear another story, even if it's out of somebody else's life. Tell me about your ghosts, Bill. Please."

Jackson still hadn't looked at George. He began to speak; at first in a sort of monotone, but as he spoke, the emotion returned.

"I was an ensign, six weeks out of the Academy, on my first ship. A destroyer out of Newport. I was junior officer of the deck on the midwatch. We were steaming south off the coast of New Jersey, heading for Annapolis to pick up a bunch of midshipmen for their summer cruise.

"The officer of the deck was a lieutenant named Sykes. He was the weapons officer, my department head. He was the senior watch standing officer, too, so he made up the watch bills. I don't think I've ever hated a man as much as I hated Ron Sykes.

"It wasn't just me, either, everyone aboard hated him. He was an asshole, there's no other way to describe him. But on top of that, he was morally convinced that there was no room in the Navy for black officers. He never came right out and said anything, of course, but he made sure I knew how he felt.

"This was nothing new to me, I'd run across prejudice before. The Academy had its share of bigots when I was there. I'd learned to put up with them, mostly by staying out of their way. But since Sykes was my boss, I couldn't put any distance between us. I can hear his voice to this day. 'MISter Jackson, this. MISter Jackson, that. He's the only man I know who could call you mister and have it come out sounding like boy.

"He made sure I got more than my share of night watches. Whenever he stood the midwatch, he had me with him. It gave him four uninterrupted hours to give me a full ration of shit.

"So there we were, on the bridge, just like this one. He was quizzing me on stuff I had no way of knowing so I'd look like an idiot in front of the enlisted men. Then one of the lookouts reported that he thought he saw a light.

"Sykes and I spotted it. It was blinking on and off. Faint, irregular, you know? We were a good fifteen miles off Atlantic City and it was seaward of us. I thought it looked like a boat in trouble. Sykes didn't agree. He thought it was somebody fishing with a light, and the blinking was because the boat was bobbing up and down on the swells. I watched for a while, and the longer I looked, the surer I was it was a distress signal. It looked to me like ragged groups of three. Three long, three short, three long, three short. Sykes, of course, thought I was out of my mind. I tried to convince him that we ought to check it out, but he wasn't about to listen.

"Then I did the unforgivable thing. I told Sykes he should wake up the captain. Sykes went ape. He told me that he'd been standing watches for five years and no punk like me was going to tell him how to run his bridge. The captain had trouble getting back to sleep if you woke him up. Then he'd come out on the bridge and lurk around for hours. No way did Sykes want the old man looking over his shoulder the whole watch.

"Then I told Sykes that he was violating the captain's night orders, Navy regs, CRU DES LANT op-orders, and the unwritten rule of the sea. I can't remember exactly what all I said but I suppose it was quite a speech.

"Sykes changed then. He quit ranting and raving and he got very angry and very calm all at the same time. He took me aside, out on the wing of the bridge, where the enlisted types couldn't hear. He was so furious I could hear his heart pounding in his chest. It made little toc-toc-toc sounds when he opened his mouth. He reminded me that he wrote my fitness reports and assigned me my duties. He promised that if I said another word for the duration of the watch he'd personally see to it that I'd never make my first promotion.

"I don't know how I got there, but suddenly I was back on the open bridge. There was a phone set there to the captain's sea cabin, and a button to push to ring a buzzer next to his bunk. Sykes was still talking to me, but I wasn't hearing what he was saying. I put my thumb on the button and I pushed it. I mashed that button so hard my thumb hurt, and I held it down, as if I was trying to squash a beetle — as if by pushing harder I'd get the buzzer to ring louder.

"I picked up the phone set and held it out to Sykes. I was still holding the button down and you could hear the buzzer all the way out on the bridge. I asked Sykes if he wanted to talk to the captain or should I?

"Then the captain stepped out of the shadows and said, 'If either of you gentlemen have anything to say to me, why don't you just come right out and say it?' God knows how long he'd been there, and I don't know who was more startled, Sykes or me. Then the captain told me that since he was already up, I should quit buzzing his buzzer. I still had my thumb on the button and didn't realize it. Sykes started to say something but the captain shut him up and told him to go below.

"And then the captain said to the bridge watch, 'This is the captain, I have the deck; Mister Jackson has the conn...'"

Jackson's eyes were glistening, and he hesitated before repeating, "'...Mister Jackson has the conn...'"

He took a breath, and continued, "So I put on left standard rudder and we went over there to see what was what. It was a boat all right, with four people aboard. An old guy who'd had a stroke or something, his wife and daughter and a boy about ten years old. The guy was barely conscious, the two women were so seasick they couldn't move, and the engine and radio were dead. There was just this kid who knew that Morse 'S' and 'O' were three long and three short, but he didn't know which was which, so he was sending O-S-O-S-O-S and hoping somebody would catch on. A brave kid. He said later that he never cried once until he saw our running lights change and he knew we were turning toward him.

"The Coast Guard came out with a helo and flew the old guy to a hospital, and he ultimately made it OK. We put the other three ashore at Annapolis. It turned out to be a lucky night. The old guy's brother was a Senator with a lot of pull in armed services appropriations. Sykes was transferred three days later, the captain got his fourth stripe a hell of a lot sooner than he ever expected, and I got a good fitness report.

"But that's not what I instant replay up here at night, Mr. Holbrook. It's three things that happened after we'd taken the people aboard. First the captain took me aside and said that my performance gave him renewed faith in the quality of officers the Academy was turning out. Those are the words he used, renewed faith. Then he took me down to the mess decks where the kid was, and introduced me as the one who was responsible for picking him up, and the kid said, 'Thanks, Mister'."

Jackson hesitated again, fighting to control his emotions. "And the third thing was the best of all. If I have to think of the proudest moment in my life, this was it. As I was heading for officers' country, I ran into one of the men who had been on the bridge. A Seaman Deuce who probably was no farther out of boot camp than I was out of the Academy. Messenger of the watch. A southern redhead about eighteen years old. He looked me right in the eye and said, 'Nice goin,' Mister J.' It was the finest compliment I've ever had, and that mister didn't sound one bit like boy."

Jackson was silent for a moment, then turned and looked again out over the bow. Without saying a word, George left the bridge.

GEORGE HOLBROOK stood on the wing of *Seafire*'s bridge and watched the land rise above the western horizon. It was a beautiful morning, the sun high and bright, the sky a brilliant blue. The wind and seas were light, and the ship glided effortlessly at twelve knots. Off the port bow, George could see an orange and white buoy. As it got closer he used his binoculars to identify it. It was marked BE — Boston Entrance.

George stepped into the pilothouse and looked at the chart table. The NOAA chart for Massachusetts Bay was taped down. He fingered the edge of the chart, the top one in a stack of three. He knew what the other two were without looking. The chart for Boston Harbor would be the second in the stack, with the Boston

Inner Harbor chart on the bottom. George smiled. Jackson was incredible, always prepared, always attentive to the details. He'd taped down the charts in sequence, each squared with the parallel motion protractor, while the ship was miles at sea. There would be no wasted time setting up the new charts while the ship was navigating in restricted waters. Peel off the top one, and the next is ready. Charts set up the Navy way by a man out of the Navy for decades, George thought. Soon to be out of a job. His smile disappeared.

George busied himself with checking the ship's position. Taking a reading from the GPS unit, he plotted a fix, which fell almost exactly on the course which Jackson had laid out on the chart. Sure enough, buoy BE was right where it was supposed to be. The ship was in the inbound traffic lane to Boston Harbor, about twenty-five miles to the northwest. At twelve knots, that would take about two hours. *Seafire* had an eleven o'clock rendezvous with the harbor pilot and tugs that would guide her to the shipyard for her overhaul. She was precisely on schedule.

Jackson stepped into the pilothouse and interrupted George's thoughts. "There may be a delay. *Rene Descartes* is due to enter harbor the same time as we are. We're probably going to have to wait for her to clear."

"Can't we just go around her?"

Jackson looked at his watch. "Listen for yourself, Mr. Holbrook. They've been broadcasting this message every ten minutes for the last half-hour. It's about time for the next one."

Jackson switched one of the pilothouse radios to VHF Channel 9. For a moment they listened to the usual idle chatter on the channel. Then a female voice came on. "*Securite, Securite, Securite.* This is United States Coast Guard Group Boston. The LNG ship *Rene Descartes* will transit Boston Harbor between eleven hundred and twelve hundred hours eastern daylight time, enroute the Distrigas terminal in Everett. Group Boston has declared a moving security zone ahead and astern of this ship as follows: Two miles ahead, one mile astern, and one mile on either beam. No moving traffic is to enter the security zone without express permission of Coast Guard Group Boston. All traffic is directed to monitor this channel for updated information on the progress of the LNG ship in order to comply with this directive. Group Boston, out."

"LNG, that means liquid natural gas, right?" George asked.

"Liquefied, actually."

"And the Coast Guard doesn't want anybody near it because a collision would cause an explosion?"

"Not exactly," said Jackson. "The gas can't explode. There's no oxygen source. If the tanks ruptured, the liquid gas would flow out over the water. It's lighter than water, so it would float. It's cold, near absolute zero. The water, which is warm by comparison, would heat up the liquid gas and turn it into vapor. Then it would mix with the oxygen in the air. If a spark or something ignited it, a column of flame would build up. The flame would radiate energy, which would heat up the floating liquid gas even faster. Then the flame would get bigger, the gas would boil even faster, and pretty soon, you've got a firestorm."

"Jesus."

"The government did a computer analysis. A lot depends on whether the water freezes where it meets the gas. The scientists can't agree on that. If the water freezes, that slows down the boiling of the gas. The best guess is that the water wouldn't freeze solid, just get slushy, and the gas would boil pretty fast."

"How the hell do you know all this?" asked George.

"It came up in a naval architecture course at the Academy. I got interested and read up on it."

"Tell me about the firestorm."

"Well, there are a lot of variables, like wind and how much gas gets spilled. As I recall, if a ship the size of the *Descartes* were to go up completely, you'd get a column of fire about a mile high and a quarter of a mile wide. Anything two or three miles away would burst into flame just from the radiant energy. Houses, cars, people, anything. The reports I read had lots of graphs and charts. 'A lightly clothed person x miles away will be fatally burned in y seconds,' and so forth."

"Jesus!" George said again. "It sounds like a nuclear bomb."

"It would be like the air burst at Hiroshima," replied Jackson. "The nuke releases a flash of heat and light in billionths of a second, and it's incredibly intense. The firestorm energy would be far less intense, but it would go on much longer, probably four or five minutes. So the cumulative effect, as far as flash burns go, would be just as severe. There are only two differences. One is that with an LNG fire there's no radioactivity. The other is that your average LNG ship packs about five times the energy of the Hiroshima bomb."

George was silent for a moment, then stepped back out onto the wing of the bridge.

"Well," said George Holbrook to himself. "Well, well, well." He made a mental list of things to do. First, he would talk with Nick Argeriardis. There was a worldwide surplus of shipping, dozens of ships were idle for want of cargoes. George wondered if there were any LNG carriers on the market. He guessed that there were. "By God," he said, "I think we've found our strategic weapon."

George climbed the ladder to the flying bridge. Off the starboard quarter, a helicopter was making its approach to the flight deck. He recognized it at once. It was a Holbrook ExecuStar, painted in the colors of the Ferroil Corporation. George watched as it landed. A single passenger got out and scurried forward and out of sight behind the hangar. The helicopter immediately lifted off. The entire operation had taken less than a minute.

Suvia Ferris climbed the ladder to the flying bridge several minutes later. George's "Hello!" to her was so bright and cheery that she replied, "God, George, you're in high spirits! You look like a man whose just gotten good news."

"A good idea. At least I think it is. I'll tell you about it in a couple of days when I've checked out the details, if they can be worked out. I've had a couple of ideas during the crossing, in fact. I'm glad you're back, Suvia. I missed you."

"Thank you," she said. "I missed you too. I remembered being up here with you when we were approaching Malta. I thought it would be nice to be here when we came into Boston."

George was pleased that Suvia had come. Arranging for the Ferroil helicopter to meet her at Logan Airport must have involved a significant effort on her part.

On the horizon was a dark hulled ship with LNG painted in large white letters on her side. George studied her through his binoculars.

The summer in Boston was a beautiful one, unless you were a farmer. Weeks went by without rain, yet there wasn't a hint of a heat wave. Day after sunny day passed by, perfect vacation weather, and throughout the city, Bostonians reveled in it. For George Holbrook, however, it passed in a blur. Planning, scheming, supervising repairs and renovations to the ship, George hardly noticed the lovely weather. On the rare occasions that he did, he was with Suvia Ferris.

Suvia's flying lessons were going well. As George had suspected, she had natural ability. Helicopters are the most awkward and demanding of flying machines, and the usual tendency is to fight them. From the beginning, Suvia controlled the aircraft with a smooth and gentle touch and economical use of the controls. In mid-July, he asked her to go soaring. With Suvia at the controls, they took Ralph Dade's helicopter to Plymouth Airport, thirty miles to the southeast of Boston. There, George showed Suvia the Caproni.

George Holbrook had always thought that, when it came to

machines that moved, the Italians built the most elegant ones in the world. Donzi and Baglietto boats, Ferrari and Lamborghini cars, and the Caproni airplane. It was, to George's eye, quite simply the most beautiful aircraft ever built. A contradiction in terms, the Caproni was a jet powered glider.

"I bought her as part of phase five," George said, then he laughed. "Actually, you did. It's a poor man's U-2. Once we find out where Jinnah's base is, I can overfly it in the Caproni, and take pictures. Then we'll be able to refine our assault plan."

"George," Suvia said, "it's a beautiful day and that's a beautiful airplane. Why don't we forget Jinnah for an afternoon and just go flying?"

George smiled and relaxed. He helped her into the cockpit, and got in beside her. Starting the tiny turbojet engine, he taxied the airplane to the duty runway, and took off. They climbed to five thousand feet in a series of lazy circles. Then, George shut off the engine. The quiet was glorious, as George retracted the turbojet into the bay behind the cockpit. Now, the Caproni was a sailplane, gliding silently through the sky.

As she had been with the helicopter, Suvia was a quick study in the glider. She maintained the steady fifty-knot airspeed with precision, and her turns were smooth and coordinated from the start. She seemed to have an instinctive ability to find green air, the rising currents that kept the vertical airspeed indicator in the green climb sector. Through the afternoon they flew, searching for thermals over the dunes of Cape Cod, looking for soaring birds to give the thermals away. The southwest wind was blowing up Buzzards Bay, and they played for an hour in a ridge of green air over the bluffs at Falmouth. Finally, they headed back toward Plymouth. When they got there, they were still at five thousand feet.

"OK," George said, "are you up for a loop?"

"Yes! Can we do one?"

"Sure. You have the aircraft."

Suvia waggled the controls in acknowledgment, as George had taught her. "Shouldn't you do one first, to show me how?"

"Nope. More fun when you do it yourself the first time. Are you game?"

"Of course."

"OK. Throughout the loop, the wings have to be parallel to the deck. They have to be level at the top, and you can't come out going west if you were going north when you started."

"Right."

"You need a frame of reference on the ground. That's easier in Texas, where everything is laid out on a grid. Around here, the ground doesn't have many straight lines on it. Let's use Route 3. Ease over and fly above it."

"OK," Suvia said, turning the plane in a smooth bank.

"Once we're lined up, you're going to put her into a shallow dive. When we hit a hundred and twenty knots, you'll pull back hard on the stick. Your two reference points are the G-meter and the horizon. You're going to hold three Gs. No more, no less. As the nose comes up, the airspeed is going to drop. It's a tradeoff, pure physics, airspeed for altitude. As the airspeed drops, you're going to have to pull back more on the stick to hold the three Gs."

"Got it."

"As we come up, keep the wings level to the horizon, and the plane lined up with the road. As you reach the top, you won't be able to see the horizon any more. Throw your head back, and you'll be able to see the opposite horizon coming up the other way. Keep the wings level, keep the G's up, and everything will be fine."

"What happens if I do it wrong?"

"The worst thing is not to pull enough Gs. The plane runs out of airspeed upside down at the top of the loop and stalls. You end up in an inverted spin. Some aircraft can't recover from an inverted spin. I don't know if this one can or not."

"Very funny, George!"

"I'm not kidding. But I'll be watching the G-meter and the airspeed indicator. You'll do fine."

They had reached Route 3, and were flying above the asphalt ribbon a mile below them. George said, "Whenever you're ready," and Suvia pushed the stick forward. The wind noise increased as the aircraft gained speed, and the altimeter spun down through four thousand feet. "One twenty," said Suvia, as the airspeed indicator passed that mark. "Go for it!" said George, and Suvia pulled the stick back.

The nose came up, and Suvia felt the G-force pushing her into her seat. "More stick," said George, and she pulled back a bit more, concentrating on keeping the wings aligned with the horizon. Suddenly, it was gone, and she looked back and up, seeing the earth coming up behind her, the ribbon of the highway running toward the Cape. Now, she was headed straight down, the airspeed increasing again.

"Now, ease off the stick," George said. "As the airspeed comes back up you have to ease off or you'll pull too many Gs."

"Got it." Suvia eased the aircraft back to level flight. Once again they were flying above Route 3, heading north, in much the same position as they had been before the loop. The entire maneuver had cost them two hundred feet of altitude.

"Not bad for a first loop," George said. "A little sloppy on the top, but overall not bad."

"What happens if we pull too many Gs coming down?"

"The wings come off."

"Oh, great! Too few Gs going up and we're in an inverted spin. Too many coming down and the wings are off!"

George laughed. "You've got the idea. Would you like to try again?"

Suvia laughed, too. "You bet." She flew ten more loops, each more precise than the one before.

George could have wished that all his efforts had gone as well as Suvia's flying lessons. Some things had gone well enough, others less so. Nick Argeriardis was negotiating, through a dummy company, to buy an LNG tanker. It was one of the Zodiac class that had been built by General Dynamics at Quincy, Massachusetts. Each of them had been named for a sign of the zodiac, and *Aries* and *Virgo* were both for sale. Nick was confident that he'd have one of them in plenty of time for its intended use. That wasn't the problem. Suvia was the problem.

When George told Suvia, "You'll love this idea," he couldn't have been more wrong. She hated it. She'd been against the idea of a strategic weapon from the beginning. Now that she knew the particulars of the LNG option, she was even more firmly against it. She was dismayed by the idea, dismayed even more that George would even consider it, much less put it into operation. The more George tried to convince her of its necessity, the more adamant she was in her opposition.

"George, I don't care what Jinnah is or what he might do," she said. "We can't drive a ship full of liquid gas into the harbor at Makranpur, and blow it up! We'd kill tens of thousands of innocent people. How could you even consider doing it?"

"Innocent people? Ho Chi Minh said that a guerilla is like a fish. He swims in a sea of popular support. If the sea of support dries up, he dies. Without the support of the Muslims in Makran, Jinnah would not exist. He's a creature of their anger and hatred. They approve of his acts of terrorism, he's their hero."

"But why? Are you going to say, 'Leave us alone or we'll blow Makran up'?"

"No, of course not. Phase six is a last resort, Suvia. One I hope and believe we'll never have to use. I don't plan to threaten Jinnah with it. He won't even know it exists as a possibility. If all else fails, we'll use it. Even then, only if the majority of us decides it has to happen. We'll blow up the ship, and make everyone think Jinnah did it. He will be a pariah in the Muslim world, and everywhere else. His followers will desert him, and our families will be safe."

"At a cost of how many lives?"

"At the cost of the lives of a lot of people who support a terrorist. If you want my opinion, the more the better!" George instantly regretted his last remark, but it was too late. Suvia's response had been simply to leave the room.

Phase two was moving along well, after a rocky start. Henri Girard had finagled a way to have dummy deposits made to the Swiss bank. Jinnah was getting reports of deposits being made, but which really weren't. It was a massive fraud.

Girard's initial attempts to arrange this had been met with icy resistance by the officials at the bank. Even though the only victim of the fraud would be a terrorist and his associates, fraud was fraud. It was as if Henri had asked them to commit an unnatural act. The more he attempted to reason, the haughtier they became. So, Henri did the only thing he could. He put together a small consortium of his friends and his wife's relatives, formed a closed corporation, and quietly bought the bank. Shortly thereafter the bank officers had begun to see his point of view.

The ship was awash with cables. Hardware engineers and software engineers were bustling about from dawn to dusk, muttering in a language that George found incomprehensible. Their goal was the installation of a single computer that could control the entire ship. It would navigate and steer, start and secure the engines as needed, and control the flow of electric power to the motors that drove the screws. More important, it would control the lasers. In bits and pieces, truckload by truckload, Bob Knight had brought aboard the computer he had built for the Star Wars program. It might not be able hit an incoming nuclear warhead, but Bob was sure he could hit a ship with it.

Steve Roth's lasers had come aboard, too. The ruby laser,

mounted in a housing about the size of a commercial freezer, had been installed on the flying bridge, where the USS *Watson* would have carried her fire control director. The argon laser, a huge unit, was mounted on the main deck, forward of the superstructure. For structural reasons, it was located where the forward five-inch gun would have been. It too, had a custom built housing, a gumdrop-shaped affair ten feet high and eight feet in diameter. Each of the laser housings was festooned with antennas and TV cameras. More of these had been installed on the mast. Day by day, *Seafire* was looking more like a research vessel, although Suvia remarked it looked more suited for the search for extraterrestrial intelligence.

Ralph Dade had enjoyed great success in his negotiations with a number of arms merchants in the Miami area. His shopping list included several M-60 machine guns, as well as a pair of 50-caliber weapons. These, together with a large quantity of ammunition, had been brought aboard quietly and stored in hidden compartments below decks. Ralph was especially proud of one shipment of laser aimed automatic rifles. These were of the type used by the Miami riot police. The laser sight projects a dime-sized circle of light precisely where the bullets are going to go. A prison guard, who'd helped put down a riot, had told Ralph that even the most hardened convict turns into a model prisoner when he sees the dot of red light on his chest.

By late September, *Seafire* had been floated out of the drydock, where her hull had been stripped and repainted, and her underwater machinery serviced, and a sonar array installed. Now, she was moored alongside a pier, while the work on her superstructure went on. While the work was in progress, many of the owners had continued to live aboard. The crew, all having been given their notice, had mostly dispersed. A few remained, however, to tend to the housekeeping needs of the owners. They were living ashore, in apartments rented for the purpose, since the crew's quarters were being rebuilt. Aside from the owners, only

Jackson, the captain, and Finnerty, the chief engineer, continued to live aboard *Seafire*.

One afternoon, Bill Jackson took George aside on *Seafire*'s main deck, out of earshot of the yard workers. "Mr. Holbrook," he began. "I'd like to talk to you if I could. It's about these lasers."

"What about them?"

"They're supposed to be 'Doppler lasers for high accuracy cartography.' That's what I've been told, anyway."

"That's right. Third World countries need accurate charts of their waters."

"Mr. Holbrook, I'm a graduate of the Naval Academy. You know, at Annapolis. In Maryland."

"I knew that," said George, smiling at the sarcasm.

"They teach science at the Academy. Physics and stuff. I've seen the power cables for those lasers. Copper wire as thick as my wrist. Those lasers aren't for making maps. They're weapons. Heavy weapons. Judging by the power supply, you could carve your initials on the moon with those babies."

George started to speak, but Jackson continued before he could. "I've seen the secret armory down by after steering, too. The one with the concealed door, where Mr. Dade has been stashing all those machine-guns. I suppose they're for research, too?

"Look, Mr. Holbrook, I've served for years on *Seafire* while she was a floating motel. You guys are turning her back into a warship. Whatever you're up to, wherever *Seafire's* going, there's no way she's leaving without me. I don't care who she's going to fight. I want to be there when it happens."

George was quiet for a moment. Having Jackson aboard would be invaluable. Yet, how could he ask him to take such risks? "You don't know what we're going to do, Jackson. We don't even know, for sure. It may be illegal, and it will probably be dangerous. All of us have a stake in it that makes the risks acceptable. There's nothing in it for you but the potential for disaster. It wouldn't be fair of us to ask you to come."

"You gave me a job after I got thrown out of the Navy, Mr. Holbrook. For all these years, you've trusted me despite what it says on my discharge papers. I've been a part of this ship, and it's been a part of me. It's been my life and my home. Wherever you're going, please let me go with you. It wouldn't be fair to ask me to come, you say? It wouldn't be fair to leave me behind!"

George thought for a minute or two before responding. "You're making a big mistake. Don't you remember what they said in the Navy about volunteering?"

"I don't think I'm making a mistake. Whatever happens, at least I'll be there."

"It's not my decision, alone. The owners have a say in everything we do. I'll recommend bringing you along, but I can't guarantee they'll agree."

"I understand. When you talk to them, say a word for Finnerty, too."

"Finnerty!"

"He's been aboard this ship for over forty years. He was with the crew that brought her to Texas when Mr. Caulfield first bought her. He's seen the wiring and the computers that are supposed to run his engines without him. He wants to come, too. Says the minute you're out of the sight of land, you're going to wish he was aboard to fix something. He's probably right. Even if he's not, he should come. This ship has been his whole life longer than it's been mine. He deserves to be around when things finally get interesting."

"Does he know he could end up dead, or rotting in a Third World prison for the rest of his life?"

"I don't suppose he cares, Mr. Holbrook. I know I don't."

The conversation with Jackson had left George with mixed feelings. He was pleased that Jackson and Finnerty wanted to join

Seafire's mission. Both men would be invaluable and their willingness to assume unknown risks was touching. He was disturbed, however, that the two men had figured out that the ship was arming for combat. He was glad that the rest of the crew had dispersed before any of them could have caught on.

There had been numerous press releases concerning the promised donation of the ship to the research foundation. The organization had been set up and was already soliciting donations for funds to operate the ship once she was completed. The foundation was called Hands Across the Oceans, and it was getting a fair amount of publicity.

U.S. Customs had taken an interest in the project. Customs agents had requested a list of all of the technology which was being incorporated into the research vessel, to make sure that nothing on the restricted list was leaving the country. It wasn't until September, however, that anyone from customs actually came to look around. By coincidence, he arrived two days after Holbrook's conversation with Jackson. George was feeling somewhat insecure about the ship's cover at the time and wasn't particularly happy to have customs aboard.

The man introduced himself as Bill Christmann. Jackson had recognized him instantly as a threat and had arranged for Holbrook to meet with him, rather than letting him poke around on his own. George was giving Christmann the full dog-and-pony show, talking a lot to avoid answering questions. The strategy was meeting with limited success.

"These are the mapping computers," said George, showing Christmann around a space in the superstructure above the salon. "They process all the information from the radar, sonar, lasers, and GPS. The data will be stored on ROM, and the computers can actually produce charts when sufficient data has been collected."

"Why all this to make charts? Most of the world is charted."

"Lack of accurate charts is a big problem in emerging nations. Lots of places have virtually no chart coverage. Others are based on old British Admiralty surveys a hundred years old. The British Navy's cartographers were good, but they had no electronic equipment, of course, and there are huge gaps that were never filled in. Bad charts can have a huge economic impact. Uncharted rocks cause shipwrecks and oil spills. Poorly charted harbors can't attract international trade. As you would expect, the poorest nations have the poorest charts and can least afford the cost of oceanographic surveys.

"It's not just the poor countries that have problems with charts. A couple of years ago the *Queen Elizabeth II* hit an uncharted rock in Buzzards Bay, less than fifty miles from here. Did millions of dollars in damage. The water was seven feet shallower than that shown on the chart. The last survey of that area had been done more than fifty years ago. We're talking about coastal waters of the United States in a high traffic area. You can imagine what the charts of the coast of Bangladesh must be like."

"Why all the fancy gear, though?" Christmann asked. "Why not just use the GPS satellites? Why the lasers?"

"GPS is great for telling you where you are. Once we know that, we have our position on the chart we're making. Then, we can aim the lasers at the shoreline, and measure the distance from the ship to every inch of the shore. The computer can then draw the shape of the shoreline. In ten minutes we can produce a shore profile that would take a surveying party a week to duplicate.

"The problem is that GPS reads out latitude and longitude on its own theoretical world grid. In a lot of places, you can be anchored in the harbor, and the GPS will tell you that you're up in the foothills outside town. The trouble is that the local charts have a grid reference difference. They think they're closer to the Prime Meridian than GPS thinks they are. Or farther away from the Equator. Or both. Until GPS came along, nobody knew those grid differences existed. Now, they're becoming a problem as more and more people are using GPS to navigate. Hell, there are huge crude carriers running around with the GPS controlling the autopilot. The latitude and longitude of a reef on a chart might differ from its coordinates on the GPS grid. Big problem! The lasers can be used to measure those differences. If one laser tells you you're a certain distance from one fixed point, a lighthouse, say, and the other laser says you're another distance from another fixed point, then there's only one place you can be."

"Two," Christmann said.

"What?" George asked.

"Two points. If two circles intersect, they must intersect at two points. Unless they're tangent of course, but that only happens on a line connecting the two centers."

Alarm bells were going off in George's mind. Christmann had been absorbing the technical information awfully smoothly, he thought. If customs were looking for high-tech gear that shouldn't be exported, they'd probably send somebody with a technical background to look for it. Still, this guy seemed too smart to be what he claimed to be.

As they left the computer room, a group of men was wrestling a large console into the space across the passageway. It had a large TV screen and was marked *Donkey Kong*. "What's that?" Christmann asked, with a tone of amused surprise.

"Video games," George replied. "This used to be the ship's library. We tore it out to make it into a game room. The crew of this ship is going to spend months, perhaps years at sea. There will be books aboard, too, of course, and a physical fitness room, but this is going to be their penny arcade."

Once the men had gotten the "Donkey Kong" unit through the doorway, Holbrook and Christmann went inside. There were rows of video games lined up, and workmen were busy bolting them to the deck. Most of them were the classics, like "Pac Man," "Ms. Pac Man," and "Frogger." There was "Star Castle," an old black-and-white cursor scan unit, and war games like "Armor Battle" and "Submarine Attack!" Mixed in were a few of the more modern machines, such as "Mortal Kombat," but the majority were a decade or more old.

"Steve Roth collects these things," Holbrook explained. "He thought it would be good for the crew to be able to relax with them and donated a few machines out of his collection. If we were on land, we'd have pinball machines in here, too. Pinball machines on a ship are not a good idea. Every time the ship rolls, the ball goes over to one side and stays there. Very frustrating."

Christmann laughed. "Not to mention the TILT alarm going off all the time."

"Right," George agreed, as they headed toward the door to leave the game room. "Billiards are out, too, of course."

Just then they passed the "Ms. Pac Man" unit. Its front panel was off, and a workman was rummaging about inside. Christmann noticed the dozens of circuit boards arrayed in racks below the control panel. "I had no idea that the circuits in these games were so complex."

"Neither did I," said George. "This game is pretty old, though. Memory chips had a lot less capacity then. Probably took a bunch of boards to store a program that would fit on one chip, today."

"I'd like to look at the lasers," said Christmann.

"Certainly," George replied, as offhandedly as he could. He led Christmann up to the flying bridge, to show him the ruby laser, the smaller of the two lasers aboard *Seafire*. Neither man said anything as Christmann followed Holbrook up the ladders and out into the September sunlight.

The laser unit was encased in a weatherproof housing, and not much could be seen of it. All the optics, including the laser itself, were behind remotely operated ports, all of which were closed. George professed ignorance of how to open any of them, and suggested that opening any of the inspection doors might cause a problem. This didn't seem to bother Christmann, who appeared to be content just to walk around the housing and look at it.

"Pretty big," said Christmann. The housing was eight feet

high, and topped with three small radar dishes. Mounted where the fire control director would have stood aboard *Watson*, it sat on its own training ring. Christmann studied this, and grunted. "Must be pretty powerful."

"Has to be. You can tell I'm excited about this project, I keep talking as if I were going on it. The foundation is going to convert local maps and charts to a single world grid. To do that, you start with a known point on the accepted grid. Then you actually measure along the earth until you get to the questioned grid. They'll put a reflector on a known point on a mountaintop. They'll put another reflector on a mountaintop a hundred miles away. With both lasers going at once, they can measure the distance between those two points to within an inch. Simple triangulation will enable the ship to map any place in the world on a single, GPS-compatible grid."

Christmann seemed to be losing interest in George's explanations, a fact that George noted with approval. He recalled the old joke: if you can't dazzle 'em with brilliance, baffle 'em with bullshit.

Christmann had stopped looking at the ruby laser housing and was now gazing down at the larger laser on the foredeck. Without turning to George, he said, "What the fuck is this thing, Holbrook? Another *Glomar Explorer*?"

George was so startled by the question that he nearly gasped aloud. His response was lame. "*Glomar Explorer*? What's that?"

"She was another phony research ship. Supposed to be looking for manganese nodules or some such nonsense. Her real mission was to salvage a Soviet nuclear sub that had sunk in water about five miles deep. You must have heard about it."

George had, of course. "Right. I'd forgotten the name. What do you mean another phony research ship? That was a CIA project. I can assure you we're not working for the CIA!"

"We know that," Christmann said, then hesitated for a fraction of a second. George noted the hesitation. Just how, George wondered, does a Customs agent know who is or isn't working for the CIA? He smiled at Christmann. It was a large and toothy smile.

George Holbrook was alone in the salon several weeks later, when Bill Christmann came in. He'd been back aboard one or two times since his initial tour of the ship, but hadn't spoken to Holbrook, or anyone else, so far as George knew.

"Mind if I come in for a minute?"

"Come ahead," replied George.

Christmann strolled about the room for a minute, and George sensed he was trying to decide whether or not to say something. Finally, he turned abruptly and looked directly at George, picking up the glass from which George had been drinking. He sniffed the glass.

"There's no alcohol in this."

"That's right."

"By this time in the afternoon you're supposed to be half crocked."

George sighed with resignation. The spook has decided to make trouble, he thought. "The ignorance of the CIA is legendary. For example: your ignorance of geography. The CIA is supposed to operate only outside the United States. Boston is part of Massachusetts, one of those United States. So what are you here for, Christmann?"

"People say your friends have big pull in D.C. They're right on that one, for sure."

Christmann turned to face George, barely controlled anger in his voice. "Something stinks on this boat, Holbrook. I've just been told by headquarters to let you guys alone. I talked to a couple of friends of mine in the FBI and they say that you're off limits to them, too.

"Some guys down in Miami think there's going to be a new

improved Bay of Pigs some day. Despite the fact that Florida's also a part of the United States, we agency types talk to a couple of those guys once in a while. Word is that your boy Ralph Dade has been buying machine guns. Fancy jobs with lasers on them for aiming. I know that rich guys like you are fond of big game hunting, but machine guns aren't the kind of weapon a real sportsman uses, are they? Smells like gun-running to me, and you've asked somebody, or bought somebody to pull off the heat."

George replied, "You'd better see a shrink, Christmann, you're getting paranoid. You're right about one thing, though; you've been called off. Not as the result of any sinister plot. You're out of your jurisdiction, and I've filed a formal complaint, as a citizen. You should be off giving Fidel Castro an exploding cigar or something rather than harassing citizens in the continental U. S. Or, maybe you should be redesigning the famous remote control, exploding cat with the antenna in its tail. Don't talk to me about the Bay of Pigs. CIA? Certifiably Insane Assassins. You make me puke!"

Christmann turned to leave, jaws so tightly clenched that George could see white spots in the hollow of his cheeks. With a hand on the doorknob, he said to George, "I don't care who you own, in the agency or out of it. Neither you nor anybody else is going to shake me off your tail."

George replied, "Then you'll do it as a private citizen, Christmann. Such a waste. You have such a fine career going for you. Tehran, Beirut, Baghdad — all brilliant work. Now you're about to throw it all away because you can't tell the good guys from the bad guys. Such a stupid waste."

Christmann froze, standing motionless for ten or more seconds in bewildered amazement. "Where did you get that information? There aren't twenty people in the world that know that I was in any of those places, let alone all three. Those missions are still classified top secret."

George said nothing, and Christmann continued, having

stepped away from the door and back to face Holbrook. "You have a lot of information for a guy who seems to hate the agency so much. What's your beef with the CIA, anyway?"

George laughed. "You really don't know? I took the trouble to look you up Christmann, and you didn't bother to do the same with me. Incompetence, Agent Christmann, that's my beef with the CIA."

The personal insult angered Christmann, and he tried to hide it. "So you're one of the good guys, huh? How do you explain the fact that your Captain Jackson was kicked out of the Navy for dealing in drugs?"

"I was waiting for you to drag that up," replied George. "He was framed. He was in Vietnam, and he discovered one of the Khaki Mafia smuggling operations. They were shipping heroin and God knows what else back into the States in body bags. They had a whole graves registration team in on the scam. Jackson figured out what was going on, and went to his CO with the evidence. Unfortunately, the CO was in on it, too. So, they framed Jackson on this phony drug charge to keep him quiet."

"You must be kidding me, Holbrook. Those guys didn't frame people to shut them up. They killed them."

"Jackson wasn't totally naive. He'd sent off a few 'to be opened in the event of my death' letters. There was a deal with the prosecutor and Jackson got a dishonorable discharge but no brig time. And the letters didn't go out."

"So you believed in his innocence and gave him a job, I suppose, to help make up for the terrible wrong." Sarcasm was heavy in Christmann's voice.

"Something like that."

"Sorry, Holbrook. I don't buy your good guy image. Your sources of information are impressive, but I guess money can buy anything these days. The fairy tale about Jackson is laughable. I still haven't heard anything which changes my mind."

George hesitated for a moment. It was time to make a decision. He sighed and gestured for Christmann to sit down. The agent shook his head and remained standing.

"About a year ago some interesting items turned up missing in an armory in Germany. You hear about that?"

"Yes," said Christmann. Suddenly, George had his complete attention, and he sat down.

"What were they?" asked George.

"You tell me."

"Well, let's see. There were some hand-held infrared anti-aircraft missiles. Mini-Stingers, I think they're called. Simpler and smaller than the full size Stinger, but with a lot less range. Some rifles, ammo, a few cases of grenades, stuff like that. But those weren't the most interesting things, were they?"

"No."

"No, you bet your ass they weren't. There were three nuclear devices taken too. Not the real biggies, but big enough to tear the guts right out of a city. Nuclear satchel charges. Tactical jobs one guy can plant and set to go off later. I'll bet you CIA types would really like to get them back, wouldn't you?"

"We and every other intelligence service on the planet."

"I'm going to offer you a deal, Christmann. A while ago you asked if this ship was another *Glomar Explorer*. Well, I hate to admit it, but you were pretty damn close. My friends and I are going to go out and collect those missing special items. All three of them. I'm not going to tell you how, and I'll let you try to figure out why, but that's what we're going to do. I won't give you any proof or any details. You're going to have to decide whether or not I'm telling you another fairy tale. There are one or two things that I'd like you and your colleagues to do for me. If you do, the CIA in general and you in particular get the credit for recovering the missing nukes. It would do wonders for your career. Put you on the fast track for director. Otherwise you can fight us and two days later you're unemployed. Think it over and let me know."

For fifteen or twenty seconds, Christmann stared at George. It fit, of course. Christmann saw that in an instant. The modifications to the ship, the machine guns, all of it. "Christ, Holbrook," he said, "you have to tell me more than that! You can't just say trust me."

"Wrong, Christmann. I just did."

"If you know who has those devices, or where they are...if you have any information at all you have a duty..."

"Forget it, Christmann," interrupted George, "I've said all I'm going to say. Probably too much."

"You can't do this on your own! Work with us. We have trained agents. We could operate together."

"Not a chance," Holbrook said, the anger returning to his voice. "This is one operation the CIA is *not* going to fuck up!"

"OK, we'll let that pass for a minute. What is it that you want us to do?"

"I thought you'd never ask."

GEORGE HOLBROOK brought the ExecuStar smoothly down into one of the circles painted on the tarmac. The private game preserve's airport, suitable for helicopters and small jets, was an impressive facility. Given the kind of clientele the preserve attracted, George guessed, the airport was probably its main entrance.

The ExecuStar's twin rotors were still turning when three vehicles pulled up next to it. George stifled a laugh. They were identical Land Rovers, all done up in camouflage paint, and the drivers were wearing khaki bush jackets. The people who come here must be real jerks, George decided. Fat cats that pay big bucks to shoot semi-domestic deer while the help calls them bwana. Fortunately, he wouldn't have to meet any of them. He'd rented the entire facility, on a strictly exclusive basis, for a week.

The Land Rover drivers helped George's passengers disembark, loaded their luggage onto the roof racks, and two of the vehicles took them off toward the lodge. The third driver waited patiently while George secured the aircraft.

"Mr. Holbrook?" the man asked when George was finished.

"Yes."

"There's a lady waiting for you in the bar. She asked me to bring you there. Said it was very important."

George looked down the flight line at a parked Holbrook Sparrow. The two-seat helicopter, another Ferroil corporate aircraft, was the one Suvia had been flying since she'd gotten her license. He smiled, she was learning fast. He turned to the man in the safari outfit.

"Let me guess the name of this bar," George said, still smiling. "It's the Oasis, right?"

The driver frowned, sensing George's sarcasm. "No," he said, "it's the Watering Hole."

"Silly me," George said, getting into the Land Rover. The driver slammed the door behind him, and George's smile became a grin.

The Watering Hole was everything George expected it to be. It had dark, rough-hewn wood walls and taxidermists had done most of the decorating. The bar was small, and almost empty. The only patrons were two women seated in a corner. George was pleased to see one of them. The other was Patricia Phelps.

Suvia beckoned George to the table, and he could feel his jaws beginning to clench even before he sat down. A waitress drifted by, and George ordered an Amstel Light beer. Patty asked for another scotch and soda, while Suvia shook her head. She was drinking white wine and had barely touched it.

"Hello, Suvia," George said, pleasantly. "It's good to see you." He turned to Patty. Equally pleasantly, he said, "What the fuck are you doing here?"

"George!" Suvia squawked. He ignored her. So did Patty.

"I'm moving aboard the ship, George. I'm staying until this Jinnah business is played out."

George stifled the angry response that quickly came to mind. "That's not possible," he said.

"It's not only possible, it's happening. If necessary, my attorneys will get a court order. I'm a part owner of that ship, and you have no right to keep me off."

The threat pushed George's anger level up several notches. "While they're at it, they'd better update your will. First night at sea, you're fish food!"

The waitress arrived with the drinks before anyone could reply to George's outburst, and no one spoke until she had left.

"George, you're a fraud," Patty said after she'd taken a big swallow of her new drink. "You try to sound so dangerous, so ruthless. You couldn't even kill my ex-husband. Hauled him into your helicopter like a tuna. I would have let him drown. I'm not afraid of you, George."

"Ex-husband?" said Suvia.

"The divorce was final last week. I should have done it years ago." Patty turned to George. "It would have saved me a bundle if you had drowned the spineless son of a bitch. Even with the antenup, it cost a lot to get rid of him."

Suvia was clearly bewildered. "The money was all mine," Patty explained. "I guess I knew all along that was why Dick married me, but I loved him and pretended he loved me, too..."

Patty was silent for several seconds. She took another swallow of her drink. It was half full, but she beckoned to the waitress anyway. "He'd been unfaithful, a couple of times that I knew about. I suspected there were more. It's funny, but no matter how much it hurt, I made myself live with it. I was tough enough to take it.

"Betraying our friends, though, that was too much. The brokerage house had been my father's, and his father's before. Dick gave Jinnah information that our friends had provided, *to the firm*, in confidence. Thank God Father's not alive to see his name disgraced."

Patty finished her drink at a gulp and looked around for the waitress. "I should have married somebody like you, George. You never gave a rat's ass about money. Sure as hell wouldn't marry for it. And, unlike Dick, you seem to be a man. Maybe not as ruthless as you'd like to be, but nobody's perfect."

Patty paused while her fresh drink arrived. She sipped it with obvious relief. "I know you don't trust me. If Dick Phelps was Jinnah's spy, Patty must be, too. That's what you're thinking, right?"

"Something like that."

"Well, I trust you, George. Maybe that will help you trust me. Here." Patty opened her purse, and pulled out a laminated card. "It's a Swiss bank account," she said, passing him the card. "It's in your name. You can do what you want with it. Use it to pay Jinnah, use it to fight him. Whatever you're planning to do. One nice thing about getting divorced is you can move a lot of money around, and nobody thinks it's unusual."

"When we asked you and Dick to leave," Suvia said, "we agreed to divide the ransom up between the rest of us. We didn't expect you to contribute."

"I know. That was very generous. Also, humiliating. And you didn't ask us to leave. You kicked us out. But, I'm back in now, like it or not, and George has my contribution. All seventy million dollars of it."

The predawn air was cold in northern New York state, even though fall was only three weeks old. George felt invigorated. He inspected his troops. They just looked cold. The sun wouldn't rise for another half-hour.

"OK , people. Listen up!" He said in his best drill sergeant's voice. "Today we learn to shoot."

George got the reaction he expected, groans and snorts of derision. He'd told then, singly or in small groups, the real purpose of their retreat. Several had thought the idea was crazy, but most of them had come anyway. Bob Knight had shown up without Linda, and hadn't volunteered an explanation, so George hadn't asked why. Polly Harrington had brought a grandson along. Her explanation had been simple and honest. He was a professional student who'd run out of courses to take and had nothing better to do. As with Patty Phelps, George let him stay because he didn't have the authority to make him leave.

George studied the group for a moment, taking note of who was standing with whom. Joe Langone was off to one side with Alex Wilson. Probably plotting a mutiny, George guessed. Suvia Ferris, the Dades, Polly Harrington and her grandson were in another distinct group. The Roths and Bob Knight were together. Patty Phelps was standing next to Bob saying something to him that he found amusing. The Carsons stood far to one side, keeping to themselves. They looked like models from the Eddie Bauer catalog. They also looked bored.

"All right," George said, raising an assault rifle high so everyone could see it. "This is an AR-15. By the end of the week, you'll all be as good a shot with it as Alex."

This brought more derision. George smiled, it was just the reaction he'd been hoping for. He gestured toward two targets, shaped as human silhouettes, about fifty yards away. "Alex, did you bring your target rifle?"

"Yes."

"Great. Load it, and tell me when you're ready."

"What's this all about, George?"

"A demonstration. Bear with me, OK?"

"All right," Alex said, and began loading rounds into the magazine of his Mannlicher target rifle. George slapped a twenty round clip into the AR-15 and cycled the operating lever to chamber a round. He made a small show of waiting for Alex to finish loading.

"What happens when the FBI shows up thinking we're some right-wing militia group?" Polly Harrington asked. "With a bunch of illegal assault rifles."

George laughed. "This one is legal. Semiautomatic only. Don't worry, Polly. We're no more heavily armed than the usual customers in this place."

"Now Alex," George continued, "we're going to pretend that we've been surprised by hostile forces. We'll hold our rifles at the ready, safeties on, until Suvia says go. When she does, we'll take out our targets as quickly as we can. You take the guy on the left. First one to put three rounds in the kill zone wins."

"What's the kill zone?" Alex asked.

"Center torso, neck to navel," George said, silently thanking Alex for making his point. Alex was one of the finest marksmen in the world, but to him, rifles were sporting goods, not weapons.

"I'm ready," Alex said. He planted his feet shoulder width apart and held the rifle at a loose port arms position.

"Any time, Suvia," George said, and after two or three seconds, she said, "Go!"

Alex was just beginning to bring his scope onto the target when George started firing. It startled Alex, and George had fired four or five rounds before Alex got his first shot off. George kept squeezing off the rounds as fast as he could. After five seconds, George had emptied his twenty round magazine. Alex had fired twice.

"OK, stop," George said. "In a real firefight, if you haven't killed the opposition by this time, they've killed you. Let's look at the targets."

George and Alex trudged the fifty yards to the targets, with the rest of the group trailing behind them. George looked first at the one on the left. There was one hole in it, high on the right shoulder. "Not bad, Alex," George said. "Not a killing shot, but enough to put him out of action for a while. Pretty good shooting in this crummy light."

Alex said nothing, and George sensed that he was seething with anger and embarrassment. George shrugged. He hadn't meant to be condescending, but if Alex wanted to take it that way, tough. He walked over to the other target. It looked like a Swiss cheese. There were fourteen bullet holes in it. Eleven were in the kill zone.

"How did you do that?" Alex said. Even in the dim light, George could see his face reddening.

"I cheated," George said. He raised his rifle and pointed it at Alex's target. A dime size circle of ruby colored light appeared in the middle of the kill zone. "Laser sight," George said. "The light beam is parallel to the rifle bore. When the red dot is on the target, you pull the trigger. Simple. It let me start shooting while you were still getting your eyeball into the sight."

"Not very sporting," Alex said in a vaguely petulant tone.

"Absolutely not. That's how I like it. If we go up against Jinnah's troops, the last thing we want is to be fair and honorable. We just want to kill the sons of bitches any way we can."

Bob Knight took a tentative half step forward. It was the most assertive thing George had ever seen him do. "Are we planning on going up against Jinnah's troops?" he asked. He didn't sound as if he was looking forward to it.

"It's not part of the plan, but it might happen. I want us to be as ready as possible if it does."

"Are we going to spend the whole damn week doing target practice?" Joe Langone asked. "It's not even six o'clock yet. What is this, boot camp?"

George laughed. "No, it's not boot camp. We're too old for that. I came out here before dawn so I could show you the laser sight. They don't work too well in broad daylight. By the time the week's over, you'll be able to handle small arms, and you'll have a little tactical training. Nothing fancy."

"Just what is the plan?" Steve Roth asked. The bear-like man moved up next to Bob Knight. "Isn't it time you told us?"

"I can't, Steve. A leak could croak us."

"Speaking of leaks," Joe Langone said, "what the hell is Patty Phelps doing here?"

"Harold was talking to Jinnah. Patty wasn't. At least, that's what she says. I have no reason to disbelieve her. She's helping to pay for this operation. She has a right to be here."

"She may be telling the truth," Langone conceded. "Who knows? The less she knows, though, the happier I'll be."

Suvia Ferris spoke up. "Here we are, out in the woods, before sunup, playing with laser-aimed rifles. If Patty's spying for Jinnah, all she has to do is tell him that much, and the game is over."

George said nothing. He hadn't asked Patty who'd invited her to the retreat. He suspected that she'd come with Suvia, but he hadn't asked her, either.

"Suvia's right, George," Steve Roth said. Grace was standing next to him, and he put his arm around her. "We have a lot at stake, here. Our lives, our children's lives. We want to know how you plan to handle Jinnah."

George looked at the sky. It was brightening quickly, dawn was only a couple of minutes away. They were right, he realized. Perhaps a part of his secrecy had been reluctance to submit his schemes to scrutiny and debate. As the sun rose over the hills of upstate New York, George Holbrook told his friends how he intended to defeat Jinnah. When he was finished, it was daylight, and nobody said a thing. The only sound was Suvia Ferris' sobbing.

George Holbrook scanned the clearing through his binoculars. The night was dark, with heavy clouds covering the moon. The night glasses intensified the feeble light thirty thousand times, and George saw the world as in a greenish, glowing dream. The shadowy figure of a woman appeared at the clearing's edge. In the fuzzy glow, George made her out to be Suvia Ferris. She hesitated, and George watched as she raised an identical set of night goggles to her eyes.

"Here they come," he said.

Two more figures joined the first.

"What do you think?" George said, and handed the night glasses to Patty Phelps.

Patty studied the three people at the edge of the clearing for over a minute. "Looks pretty good. They're staying low, and taking their time going into the clearing."

"What are they doing wrong?"

"Nothing, that I can see. Are they?"

"Yes. They're too close together. One burst from an automatic weapon could take out all of them. Also, all three of them are looking around, but nobody has a weapon ready to shoot. There should be one looker and two shooters."

"Jesus, George, you do this for a living, don't you?" Patty handed the Night Mariner glasses back to him. In Desert Storm, such glasses had been highly classified. George had bought them through a civilian marine supply catalog. Top secret to dirt cheap in a decade.

"I take the Fifth," George replied as he watched the group enter the clearing at last.

"Do you still think I'm a spy for Jinnah?"

"I don't know. I have to admit that the money was a hell of a gesture of good faith."

"You've verified that it's really there, I suppose."

"Oh, yes. I've already spent some of it."

"Good. Can you tell me how?"

"Nope. You might be a spy for Jinnah."

Patty laughed. "You probably bought yourself a villa in the south of France."

"The thought did cross my mind."

George watched the group of three near the center of the clearing. He was pleased. They were moving carefully and keeping low. They were making mistakes, of course, lots of them, like heading for the middle of the clearing rather than keeping to the edges. For civilians with less than a week of training, though, they were doing surprisingly well.

It was hard to tell who was who in the blurry green light of the Night Mariners, but George was pretty sure that the two people moving through the clearing with Suvia were Helen Dade and the Harrington kid. There were two more members in Suvia's aggressor unit, but they were nowhere to be seen. George wondered what Suvia was up to.

As on the previous three nights, George had set up the skirmish assignments in secret. The leaders were Suvia and Alex Wilson, but neither knew who the other leader was or how many people were in the opposing force. To confuse them, George took a random number of people out of the action, using them as observers. This was the last skirmish of the last night, the grand finale. George had set it up as a fair fight, with equal numbers on each side, but only he and his observers knew that.

George saw movement at the edge of the clearing, as Alex sprang his ambush on Suvia's group. She reacted quickly, hitting the dirt at the first sight of the laser beams. The brush in the clearing was knee high, and as Suvia and her two companions lay prone, Alex's troops were unable to focus the beams on them. Firing deliberately, they advanced into the clearing. Suvia and her two companions stayed down. George Holbrook began to laugh a deep, rumbling chuckle. "I think I'm in love," he said.

Patty turned toward him. "What?"

George was still laughing. "Watch."

Alex's group of five was thirty yards into the clearing when two more laser beams lit up, and two more rifles began firing from cover at opposite edges of the clearing. Alex's group was precisely between them, caught in a perfect crossfire. George watched as the two new gunners fired, trying to gauge whether the laser beams were on target as the blank rounds were fired.

He guessed that at least two of Alex's group would be down if the rounds were real — all of them if the rifles had been fully automatic.

"Jesus," said Patty Phelps, as she watched Alex's group turn and run for the tree line. It was the worst thing they could have done. They were running at right angles to the hidden gunners, presenting crossing targets, which was good. But, they were running directly away from Suvia, which was very bad. She and her two companions rose and fired at five easy targets, blazing away as the laser beams flickered on the backs of their enemy.

"Game, set, match," George said. He stood up and blew a whistle.

The conference room was decorated like the rest of the buildings in the preserve — Paul Bunyan chic. Everything was rustic, dark, and heavy. It made George's group, still dressed in tiger stripe cammies, look like something out of Terry and the Pirates. Bob Knight cruised the room with a piece of electronic gear in his hands, pointing it here and there like a dowser in search of water. Finally he gave George a nod of his carrot-topped head. The room was free of bugging devices.

George took a closer look at Knight. The little engineer looked happy. He was relaxed, he was smiling, and there was bounce in his footsteps. Proud of himself, George realized. Well he might be. He'd been one of the two gunners who had caught Alex's troops in the crossfire. Getting into position undetected had been a real physical and mental accomplishment, and Knight knew it. George was pleased.

George studied the people in the room for a few moments. He noted with satisfaction that the distinct groups of the first cold morning were gone. The groupings were fluid with everyone wanting to say something to everyone else. The most obvious change was in the Carsons. Peter was full of animation, dragging Emily around the room so he could brag about her exploits. She'd been Suvia's other point gunner, Bob Knight's twin in the crossfire. Peter had been a observer, and had watched her move into position like a ninja. He was as proud of her as if she'd just won a Pulitzer Prize. Emily's face was flushed with pleasure and embarrassment.

George shifted his attention to Alex Wilson, who was wearing a sour expression. The Brit's in a snit, George said to himself, and this pleased him, too.

"What are you smirking at, Holbrook?" Wilson asked.

"I wasn't. Tonight's exercise went well. I was going to say so, and I was smiling. You're just not used to seeing me smile." George smiled as hard as he could at Alex, an enormous grin that made his jaw muscles ache. George knew he was pissing Alex off. He loved it.

"Bloody nonsense. The exercise was a farce. You set it up so my team would lose."

"Why would I do that?"

"You tell me. My guess is that you wanted to toady up to your boss, Suvia, by making her look good. Maybe you wanted to get into her knickers. Maybe you already are."

George felt a red hot flash of anger, and his jaw muscles got another workout, but Bob Knight spoke before he could.

"God, you're an insufferable bastard," Knight said, standing up and facing Wilson. "We beat you fair and square, and now you're whining about it. You may be an Olympic champion, but you're no sportsman. Probably got your medal by cheating."

Wilson took two steps toward Knight and threw a punch at his head. The little engineer ducked under the punch, and moved right in under the far larger man. Bracing his feet in a tee stance, he grabbed Wilson and threw him on the floor. The throw was amateurish, and Wilson landed more on his head than his back. He took a few seconds to orient himself, then tried to get up.

Knight pivoted and delivered a karate kick to his head. Wilson went back down and stayed down.

George hurried over to put himself between the two men before there could be any further violence. "Jesus" he said, looking at Wilson. "I think you broke his nose."

"I was trying to break his neck."

Wilson struggled to his knees, then to his feet. "You'll regret this," he said, and left the room. George couldn't tell whom the threat had been directed at, and didn't much care. He turned to Knight, and saw him smiling.

"I didn't know you knew karate."

"I didn't until this week. During the free time, Patty was teaching me some of the basic stuff."

"Patty?" George asked, glancing in her direction.

"Yeah. She's pretty good at it. Does it to keep herself in shape. She says aerobic dancing is boring."

"Really?" George was starting to smile again.

"It works, too, don't you think? Keeping her in shape, I mean." Knight paused, realized what he'd said, and blushed as only a redhead can blush. George's smile gave his jaw muscles their third workout of the evening.

The Wednesday after Columbus Day was a glorious day, sunny, clear and mild. After lunch, Suvia Ferris asked Helen Dade and Polly Harrington to come with her on a boat ride. Later in the week, *Seafire*'s launches were going to be hauled aboard and secured on deck, ready for sea. Suvia was taking *Seasmoke* up to Marblehead to pick up a package at Ted Hood's sail loft. Polly and Helen allowed that it was as good an excuse as any to be on the water on an Indian Summer afternoon, and off they went.

Suvia had been living aboard *Seafire* off and on throughout the summer. Keeping Ferroil running and coup-free was a full-time job, and she'd been in Houston far more than in Boston. Still, the shipyard was less than a mile from Logan Airport, and the Ferroil Gulfstream could fly from Houston to Boston in less than three hours. She'd managed to spend one or two days a week aboard *Seafire*. Besides learning to fly, she'd spent a lot of time messing around in boats. The big Magnum was her favorite, and this might be her last chance to play with it.

Seasmoke was moored alongside a floating dock near *Seafire*'s berth. The three women climbed down the gangway from the pier to the dock and got aboard. Most of *Seafire*'s crew had been laid off; only a skeleton housekeeping staff remained. The deck crewmen, whose tasks included driving the launches, were long gone. Since July, when the owners wanted to ride in *Seafire*'s small boats, they'd had to drive them themselves. Relearning old skills, they'd become adept at it. Polly and Helen took in and stowed the dock lines as Suvia expertly piloted the big Magnum away from the floating dock, and out into Boston Harbor.

Suvia obeyed the speed limit in the Inner Harbor, keeping the twin engines at little more than idle speed. Once they were in the Outer Harbor, she told Helen and Polly to hang on and opened the throttles. The Magnum surged forward, screaming across the anchorage area, past the enormous egg-shaped tanks at Deer Island, and out Presidents' Roads. *Seasmoke* charged down the North Channel at sixty-five knots, leaping from wave top to wave top into the easterly breeze, as the two passengers held on for dear life and Suvia yelled, "Yee Hah!" in sheer exhilaration. They were halfway to Marblehead when Helen shouted over the engine noise, "I know you didn't ask us along on this ride just to destroy our kidneys. What do you want to talk about?"

Suvia throttled back to a more sedate speed, and the Magnum dropped into a semi-displacement mode, shouldering through the swells rather than leaping across them. "George Holbrook. What else?" she replied.

Helen regarded Suvia dubiously. "I've known George for a

long time, Suvia. I won't betray any of his confidences. What do you want to know?"

"Are you asking if my intentions are honorable?" Suvia asked, with a grin. Helen grinned back, and Suvia went on. "I want to know why people say he's a woman-hater. He gets along fine with me. He never says anything chauvinistic, except on purpose when he's trying to be funny. He trusts my judgment, he respects my ideas, yet all his friends tell me he's a woman-hater. How come?"

Helen thought for a moment before she replied. "George was never a woman-hater. He actually used to be something of a romantic. He was engaged once. The girl assumed that George had money, or was going to inherit it. When she discovered that he wasn't, she took a hike. It happened to him again a few years later. Not exactly the same way but, you know, same song, different verse.

"No, Suvia, George doesn't hate women. He's just decided not to let himself get hurt by one again. Until a few years ago he had a Blonde-of-the-Month Club going. Each girl was two years younger and two shades blonder than the one before. So long as it was strictly physical, it was OK with George. When he thought he might be falling in love with one of them, it was, 'Goodbye, Blondie.' He finally got tired of this, or maybe too old. He's been out of circulation since then. I think he's a virgin, in a way. He's been in the sack often enough, but never with anyone he's been in love with."

Helen paused for a moment, and Polly Harrington spoke up. "I think there's more to it than that. I knew George's father, Jim. I loved him, but he was a stubborn man. So was George. They fought a lot, mostly about the helicopter business. Jim had worked for Howard Hughes and was determined to become as rich as Hughes had been. George could see the obsession for what it was, but he kept quiet and let his father run the business. Then the obsession killed Jim and ruined the company. George is still blaming himself for not stopping it."

"What does that have to do with women?" Suvia asked.

"Nothing, directly. It just makes him that much more reluctant to commit to any relationship — love, friendship, anything."

"How do you know so much about George?"

"If Jim hadn't crashed the Hellcat, I'd be George's stepmother."

"And when Jim died, the company was worth nothing at all?" Suvia's tone said she found it hard to believe.

"No, not nothing," Polly replied. "The key man insurance on Jim's life carried the company for a few months. I've always suspected that Jim crashed on purpose, to save the company from bankruptcy. I think George has the same suspicion."

Polly was silent for a moment, remembering. "George got the stock. He could have sold it to Hughes or Bell for a few million. All they wanted was the designs and the patents, though. They would have closed the plant and fired the people in a week. Instead, he sold to your late husband Richard for one dollar. Richard gave him a handshake promise to keep the plant open."

"He walked away from millions to keep the plant open?" Suvia was amazed.

"He was a test pilot. He worked with the people in the plant every day. He bet his life on their work every time he flew. They were the closest thing to family he had. Certainly closer than his father. I'm not surprised at what he did. Didn't you know?"

"No. It was before I married Richard. I knew he bought the company for short money, but..." her voice trailed off.

Suvia and Polly were quiet for a moment. "Are you going to try to melt George's heart of stone, my dear?" Helen asked.

Suvia was annoyed by the tone. "Of course not," she snapped. "It's just that I've never known a man who liked me and could see that I liked him, who just sat there without making a move or two. I was just wondering why, that's all. Now I know. Thanks."

Suvia said nothing more, but Helen wouldn't let the matter drop. "So why don't you make a move or two of your own, Suvia? You're younger than George is. Blonde too. You're definitely his type. You could get one of those nighties that doesn't reveal too much, just sort of gives a hint here and there..."

Helen hesitated. Polly was snickering and Suvia was glaring at her. "Oh," Helen said, "I see. You know about such nighties."

"I'm just an old fashioned girl from the South, I guess. Women don't do the chasing where I come from."

"Bullshit," said Helen. "You're in love with George. It's been obvious for months." Helen turned to Polly. Polly nodded. "Even Ralph noticed, for God's sake!" Helen continued. "You love George because he's one of the few men who's as smart as you are, and because he admires you for being as smart as he is. You love talking with him and being with him and flying with him. You'd really like to have your wicked way with him but you're afraid you'll scare him off if you try. Right?"

"I don't think I want to talk about this any more," replied Suvia. She pushed the throttles ahead, and *Seasmoke* accelerated again, leaping from wave top to wave top at a bone-jarring sixty-five knots. Helen Dade managed to keep herself from falling backward by grabbing a handhold at the last moment. She and Polly laughed all the way to Marblehead.

▬ ▬ ▬ ▬ ▬

When Suvia returned from her errand in Marblehead, her anger had passed. "Got time for a short sightseeing tour?" she asked.

Polly and Helen eyed her warily.

"Won't take more than thirty extra minutes," Suvia said, punching numbers into the GPS unit as she piloted the Magnum out of Marblehead Harbor. Once *Seasmoke* was clear of the harbor entrance, Suvia advanced the throttles again, and the Magnum roared off to the south. Fifteen minutes later, Suvia brought the boat to a stop, next to a lighthouse. "Here we are," she said.

"Where is here?" Helen asked.

"Minot's Ledge," replied Suvia, and the three women were

quiet for a moment as they looked at the lighthouse, a gray granite tower, seeming to rise directly out of the sea. Looking more closely, Polly and Helen could see that it was built on a massive submerged ledge. Helen glanced nervously at the fathometer, and was amazed that *Seasmoke* was sitting in over fifty feet of water. The ledge, barely awash, seemed terribly close.

"That's Minot's Light," Suvia said. Some people call it the Lovers' Light. When the light is on, it flashes one-four-three, like the letters in I love you. When I was a little girl, my mother told me a story about it. There was another lighthouse on this same ledge that was knocked down in a storm. When the lighthouse keeper knew it was about to go over, he banged one, four, three on the bell to say goodbye to his lover ashore. When they built the new lighthouse, they gave the light the same code. It still makes me tear up to think about it."

"Two hundred years ago, there was a terrible shipwreck and the only survivor was a little girl who washed ashore in a lifeboat not far from Minot's. She was barely old enough to talk, and when they asked her name, she said 'Suvia'. That was probably baby talk for Sylvia, but Suvia became her name. My mother's name was Suvia, so was her mother's. For generations in my family, mothers have passed the name down to their daughters.

The women gazed across the water at the lighthouse, clutching their arms around their shoulders as the boat bobbed up and down.

"I dreamed of having a little girl of my own someday, and naming her Suvia, and telling her the story about the lighthouse. But Richard and I had no time, and little Suvia had to wait. Then Richard died and it was too late."

"I know you don't have to be married to have a baby, but that wouldn't work for me. I'm a southern girl with roots in stodgy old New England. No husband, no baby.

"Stupid of me, isn't it, to be so concerned about not carrying on the family name? Women have had the right idea all along, not passing on names. Leave that guilt trip to the men. This Suvia business was a fluke, anyway. It's probably better that it will die with me."

Neither Helen nor Polly could think of anything to say, and Suvia headed the Magnum back toward Boston.

* * * * *

When Suvia got to her stateroom later in the day, there was a small package propped against the door. A note attached to it said, "Suvia, sorry I was bitchy today. Hope you'll put this to good use. Helen."

Suvia took the package into her stateroom and unwrapped it. The box was from an expensive Boston shop. The silk nightgown inside was the color and texture of heavy cream. Suvia laughed until she cried.

* * * * *

In a secure room in Langley, Virginia, Agent William Christmann of the Central Intelligence Agency closed a moderately thick file folder. He was smiling, amazed and amused at what he'd read. So, George Holbrook, he thought, I know who you are. You're the guy who told Jimmy Carter, beforehand, that the Iran hostage rescue mission was a recipe for disaster. The company has never forgiven you for being right.

GEORGE & SUVIA were in the exchange room when the alarm on the secure fax machine rang. She'd been in Houston most of the past two weeks, and he was briefing her on preparations that had been completed while she'd been gone. She was expecting a report from one of her loyal executives at Ferroil, and took the paper as it came out of the machine. "It's for you, George," she said, handing him the single page. George looked at her apprehensively. There had been a quaver in her voice and her hand was shaking.

"Urgent and confidential to George Holbrook," it began. "Boarding and search are imminent. Warrants have been issued, ATF and FBI agents are en route. All your telephone lines are tapped and constantly monitored. Any calls indicating awareness of boarding will advance the action sked."

"Boarding now sked for 1630 hours EST. Search and seizure warrants are legitimate. Recommend emergency sortie."

George stared at the unsigned fax. *Seafire* was loaded to the gunwales with machine guns and other illegal weapons. There was a fully armed Holbrook SparrowHawk helicopter, the small anti-tank model, stowed in *Seafire*'s hangar. Suvia's helicopter company was licensed to export SparrowHawks, but having one fully armed with rockets and machine guns aboard her yacht in Boston Harbor would be tough to explain. The boys from ATF were going to have a field day.

"There's only one person who could have sent this," he said to Suvia, "Christmann." George had told Suvia about the CIA agent when he had first appeared.

"How could he send us a scrambled fax? How would he get our code?"

I don't know. Maybe the CIA can do something right, after all." George was quiet for a moment. "Amazing."

"What?"

"If the telephone lines are tapped, then the fax lines must be, too. The FBI probably recorded the scrambled transmission. They should be able to decode it and print it out in a few hours, a day at the most. Once that's done, Christmann could be traced as the sender. He must know the risk he's taking by sending this."

"By God," Suvia said, "he's signed on!"

Feeling a little better, George assessed the situation. "There's no question about getting underway by four-thirty," he said. "We're going to leave at all costs. The question is, who and what will get left behind?

"The fuel tanks are full," he continued. "So are the water tanks. Ditto the freezers. Odd things are going to be missing. We'll have strawberries but no shortcake, but what we have will last for weeks. Especially since we won't have a crew to feed."

"We can't take this ship to sea without a crew, can we?" Suvia asked in disbelief.

"We've got no choice," George replied. He looked at his watch. "In less than three hours, we're going to be fleeing felons. We can't ask the crew to be our partners in crime. Either we do this ourselves, or not at all. I hope there are enough of us. I don't know who's aboard and who's ashore. Damn! Christmann didn't say what the warrants were for. Are they just plain search warrants, or are there arrest warrants, too?"

George used the intercom to call the security guard at the quarterdeck. "This is Holbrook," he told the guard. "Something's come up. Please stop any of the owners if they're planning to go ashore, and ask them to come to the salon. It will only take a minute or two." Then he called Bill Jackson, while Suvia went off to find out who was aboard and who wasn't.

Ten minutes later George and Jackson were discussing the situation as the owners straggled in. "Look, Bill," said George, "if the Feds are going to be here at four-thirty we damn well can't be alongside the pier singling up our lines and pulling in the brow. We've got to be gone before then, four at the latest. Sooner than that if we can manage."

"Too much sooner won't do us much good," replied Jackson. "If they've got our phones tapped, they're probably watching us, too. As soon as we show signs of getting underway, they'll scramble to get aboard. They won't wait until four-thirty."

"Right," said George. "The ship has to look like nothing is happening one minute and be underway the next. We'll cut the mooring lines, fire up the engines and go like hell, all at once. Let the brow fall into the water, snap the telephone lines, and just go. By the time they figure out what's going on, we'll be halfway out of President Roads. What time is sunset tonight?"

"Four forty-two," said Jackson.

George looked at his watch. "That explains why they're coming at four-thirty. Still daylight, but there won't be any shipyard workers aboard. The Feds would want to keep as many civilians out of the picture as possible. I still think we should use 1600 as a target. If 1630 is party time, they'll be moving their agents into place before then. The closer they are when we make our move, the better their chances of stopping us."

Suvia had just returned. "Steve and Grace Roth are aboard. They'll be here in a minute or two. So will Bob Knight. Linda's at home in Cambridge and Bob says she's not coming." George and Suvia exchanged a glance. "Joe Langone and Alex Wilson both are aboard. So are Peter and Emily Carson." They walked in just as she was saying their names. She paused and looked around the room. Polly Harrington, her grandson, and Patty Phelps were already there.

"Nick and Frances Argeriardis are out of the country," Suvia continued. "So is Henri Girard. Jacqueline is ashore but she'll be back in a few minutes. That leaves Ralph and Helen Dade. They're ashore and not expected back until dinner time."

"That's a problem," said George. "We need Ralph badly. He's had Navy experience, which we need if we're going to run this ship by ourselves. My plan to bag Jinnah requires two helicopter pilots. Ralph and me. I don't want to leave him behind to get arrested by a bunch of pissed off ATF agents who have just missed their primary target. The people who are out of the country can lay low for a while, but Ralph and Helen would be sitting ducks."

"I agree that we shouldn't leave Ralph behind to be arrested," Suvia said. "But why do we need two helicopter pilots? We only have one helo aboard."

"That's another problem," George replied. "Not having the ExecuStar is a big setback. The Caproni sailplane is in Plymouth, being crated. That's going to hurt us, but not as much as losing the ExecuStar."

"Leaving the Caproni behind is no loss at all," Suvia said. "Your plan to launch it at sea was suicidal."

"You may be right. I'll worry about the ExecuStar later. Right now I have to risk calling Ralph and Helen."

George was reaching for the phone when the door to the salon opened with a bang and a red-faced Alex Wilson strode in. "What in bloody hell is going on, Holbrook?" he shouted.

George said nothing as he handed Wilson a copy of Christmann's fax. Wilson read it in a rush, then balled it up and threw it on the deck.

"Well, this tears it, doesn't it?" Wilson said. "So much for your brilliant plans. What do you propose to do now?"

Normally, George would have reacted with anger to Wilson's shouting. This time, he didn't. Instead, he felt calm, almost serene. For a second or two, he wondered why. "What I propose to do," he said, "is run away. Emergency sortie, as they call it in the Navy. You can come along for the ride if you like."

"You must be quite mad, Holbrook. This ship can't possibly leave port without being stopped."

"You may be right. What do you suggest as an alternative?"

"I don't know. You've made a right bloody mess of things."

"Well, until you have a suggestion, please shut up. For weeks now, you've been telling everybody but me that my plan sucks. You know what? You're right. It does suck." George bent down and picked up the balled up copy of the fax. He waved it at Wilson. "I thought of a hundred things that could go wrong, including something like this. I'm sure there's a thousand I haven't thought of.

"The trouble is, Alex, that even if my plan sucks, it's the only one I've got. If you have a better one, great. If you can improve on mine, tell me how, for God's sake. If you can't, keep quiet. Going around behind my back and telling people we're doomed is counter productive. Bad for morale."

Wilson said nothing for several seconds. He looked around the room, as the people in it watched him. There was disapproval in their expressions. A spot of red appeared on each of his cheekbones. "Are the others going?"

George realized that he hadn't asked them. He, too, looked around the room. "Of course," said Patty Phelps and Suvia Ferris almost simultaneously. The rest nodded.

The color in Alex's cheeks deepened. "If I'm so bad for morale, why do you want me along?"

"You're a sneaky, mean-spirited son of a bitch, Wilson. Sort of like me. You're also the best rifleman I've ever met. You could be a great sniper. We might need one of those, some day."

"You might, at that," Wilson said, gruffly, and moved away from the door. George picked up the telephone.

Ted Miller, the FBI agent monitoring the live telephone tap, turned to his superior. "Outgoing call, Mr. Norton. It's Holbrook, calling Dade on his car phone. Holbrook wants him to return to the ship right away."

Norton's eyes narrowed. "Did he give a reason for wanting Dade back?"

"Something about heavy activity on the commodity exchange and that Dade should get there before the close of trading. Could be bullshit, could be legitimate. If I had to pick, I'd go with the bullshit."

"You may be right. When does the commodity exchange close?"

"I don't know. It's in Chicago, right?"

"Did Dade say when he'd get there?" Norton asked.

"Four-thirty, he thinks."

Norton stretched and yawned, and flashed Miller a wicked smile. "Well, then, so much the better. We have a warrant for the arrest of our Mr. Dade and I can't think of anything more convenient than having him drive right onto that pier just as we board his ship. Beats having to track him to hell and gone. So it really doesn't matter, does it?"

* * * * *

"Ralph's alone in his car," George said. "He's going to try to get back here by four, but he thinks four-thirty is more likely. Helen's out shopping with Jacqueline Girard. They should be back soon. That leaves Ralph as the only straggler. I think I can deal with that, and another problem at the same time, but that can wait. Who's aboard that needs to go ashore?"

Again it was Suvia who answered. George realized that she was operating like an XO, and a good one, at that. "There's the crew. We can send them ashore in one's and two's and not have it look unusual. There are only a dozen or so aboard, and people are coming and going all the time."

George nodded. The crew had moved ashore when the crew's quarters were being rebuilt. They hadn't moved back yet. The only crewmembers actually living aboard are Jackson, Finnerty, and Finnerty's grandson, Kevin. There were kitchen and housekeeping staff physically aboard, but none of their personal belongings were on the ship.

"Several of Steve Roth's technicians are still aboard," Suvia continued. "They're supposedly checking over his computers, but they seem to spend more time in the old library playing with those silly video games than doing anything else. They normally leave at four, but sending them ashore five minutes early wouldn't arouse much suspicion, either. The shipyard workers have been gone since last week. That leaves Jackson, Finnerty, and young Kevin Finnerty to get ashore."

"I'm staying aboard for the ride," said Jackson. "Mr. Holbrook and I discussed that several weeks ago. Emergency sortie out of Boston Harbor? I wouldn't miss that to save my life!"

"Welcome aboard, Bill," George said. "I hope it doesn't come to that. I suppose the same still goes for Finnerty as well?"

"Doubly. If you tried to put him ashore he'd hide in the engine room and you'd never find him."

"Well, he won't have to do that. We need both of you badly, and we deeply appreciate your volunteering." There was a murmur of assent from the other owners. "Kevin's another matter. He goes ashore. Tell Finnerty to send him home. I'll cut him a check for travel and severance while he's packing."

"That will be a problem, Mr. Holbrook," Jackson said. "He doesn't have a home. He has to stay with his grandfather."

"We'll give him enough money to rent an apartment for a year, for Christ's sake," George said. "What do you mean, he has to stay with his grandfather?"

"It's a condition of his probation."

Suddenly, for the first time since the alarm had rung on the fax machine, George Holbrook found himself laughing. Suvia and several others were laughing as well. "Get Finnerty up here," he said. "I've got things to discuss with him."

Finnerty arrived about ten minutes later. It was nearly three o'clock. Most of the owners had left the exchange room to carry out last minute tasks. "We're leaving harbor at four," said George. "We can't take your grandson with us. I'm sorry."

"If I go, he goes," Finnerty said. "I'm all the family he's got."

"Then you both have to go ashore," George replied. "We need you and we'd like to have you along. We appreciate your willingness to take all kinds of risks with us. But, one hour from now, we're going to commit a crime. It's called 'flight to avoid arrest' and it's a felony. If Kevin is aboard, he'll be aiding and abetting. That'll violate his parole and he'll go to prison for the parole violation, just for openers. Anything he gets for the 'aiding flight' charge will be added on top. We can't ask him to do that!"

"I appreciate your concern, Mr. Holbrook. You're an honorable man. The trouble is, I can't seem to find Kevin."

"Is he ashore?"

"No. He's just off somewhere listening to his Walkman, probably."

"We'll page him on the loudspeaker."

"That won't do much good. There are a lot of places in the engine rooms where you can't hear the loudspeakers; and with those earphones on, well..."

"How old is Kevin?" George asked.

"Nineteen."

"Does he know the risks; that he could get himself killed, or go to prison?"

"He knows. I tried to talk him out of coming, but he's even more stubborn than I am."

"If you see him before four, tell him to get his ass off this ship. In the meantime, we need you to do about fifty things in the space of an hour. First, do we have a chain saw?"

Jackson and Holbrook stood on *Seafire*'s quarterdeck, fighting the temptation to peer about in search of hidden watchers. They had just come down from the flying bridge where, as discreetly as possible, they had used binoculars to study the Coast Guard Piers across the Inner Harbor from *Seafire*'s stern. There, a scant six hundred yards away, had been the Coast Guard cutters, *Escanaba*, *Seneca*, and *Spencer*. To Holbrook and Jackson, they represented a triple threat.

As Jackson and Holbrook played 'What if...?' with each other, they kept coming back to the Coast Guard. What if we really do get underway before the FBI gets here? What if we're backing out of our berth, and one of those cutters starts backing out at the same time. "We could get hip checked by the white hull navy," said Jackson, "and, Tilt! the game is over."

In the locker where the books had been stowed after the library's demise, Jackson had found a two-year-old edition of *Jane's Fighting Ships* with data on the Coast Guard near the end. It provided both good and bad news. The bad news was that any of the three cutters could blow *Seafire* out of the water, if it got close enough. The good news was that *Seafire*, given enough of a head start to stay out of gun range, could do a horizon job on the whole pack of cutters with half her engines in mothballs.

Holbrook had looked through the ships' specifications. The three cutters were all of the Medium Endurance type, about a hundred feet shorter than *Seafire*, with a maximum speed of twenty knots. George had been pleased that none of the High Endurance *Hamilton* class of cutters had been in town. They were a foot and a half longer than *Seafire*, destroyer size. They could push thirty knots, destroyer speed. Worst of all, they carried Harpoon anti-ship missiles. Thankfully, according to *Jane's*, they were all in the Pacific. Just about far enough away, George thought.

For what seemed like the hundredth time, Holbrook looked at his watch. It was three forty-two. The last hour had been full of frantic activity, all of it carefully concealed. Finnerty had quietly lit off two of the ship's generators, and *Seafire* was now free of shore power. The power lines, though disconnected, were still in place, bridging the gap between the ship and the pier. Each one had been checked carefully for a fair lead, so that it would slide overboard without binding when the ship began to move. The telephone lines were still in place. Their connectors had been loosened in their sockets, but they hadn't been disconnected since that would alert the Feds listening to the wiretap. Hopefully, the phone lines would pull out cleanly when the ship got underway. Even if they didn't, the damage would be slight, since the wires weren't particularly strong.

Finnerty had primed and cold-cranked four of the main propulsion motor-generators. He would have liked to have started them and run them for a while, so they would be warm. That had been vetoed since the exhaust might arouse suspicion.

Finnerty was sure that they would start right away. If they didn't start, there would still be plenty more power to draw upon. One benefit of *Seafire*'s peculiar power plant was that you never had to worry about getting several engines started.

They had done one thing that carried a high risk of arousing suspicion — a risk that Jackson insisted had to be taken. At three-thirty, a five-man working party, consisting of Wilson, Holbrook, Langone, Roth and Knight had crossed the brow onto the pier. Then, looking as nonchalant as possible, they had singled up mooring line number two. Two of them had uncleated the line on *Seafire*'s foredeck, and for a time, it had been completely undone. The eye was passed back, through the chock, and over the shipboard bitt. The bitter end, now ashore, was cleated to the dock with the extra line coiled beside it. It was perfectly backward from they way the line should have been placed, and any seaman would have recognized that fact in an instant. The sight of a helicopter pilot and four very wealthy men humping a two-inch nylon hawser around might have aroused some interest as well. Still, Jackson had insisted it was necessary, and it had been done.

Three forty-five, said George's watch, as he looked at it again. The minutes had flown by as *Seafire*'s impromptu crew had raced to get her ready for sea. Now that there was nothing more to do, the seconds were creeping along. The bridge was manned and would be ready as soon as Jackson got up there. Knight and Roth had the new computers up and running. *Seafire* was as ready to depart as she was going to be. To everyone's immense relief, Helen Dade and Jacqueline Girard had returned to the ship a few minutes after three, leaving Ralph Dade as the only one still ashore. And to Jackson's dismay, George Holbrook was preparing to leave the ship.

"Look, Bill," said George, "we've been through all of this. We only have the small helicopter aboard, and we need the big one, too. I've got to go over to Logan and get it. You get the ship underway at 1600, and I'll fly aboard while you're passing Winthrop."

Jackson was upset. "Suppose they've impounded the helicopter? Suppose they arrest you before you get it off the ground? We need you. You're the guy with the plan, remember? We can't afford to leave you, of all people, on the beach when we go. You're not expendable."

"Suvia knows the plan as well as I do. What she doesn't know, she can figure out. You can do without me a whole lot easier than you can do without that aircraft." Once again, George looked at his watch. Then he turned and crossed the brow to the pier.

"There goes Holbrook," said Norton, more to himself than to Miller. From the balcony of the waterfront condominium in Charlestown, Norton had a commanding view of the piers and of *Seafire* across the narrow inner harbor. "I hope to hell he doesn't get away."

"Don't worry, Mr. Norton, the guys at the shipyard should be able to follow him."

"You don't know those ATF stiffs on the shipyard detail. They couldn't track a bitch in heat even if they had Rin Tin Tin with them. If Holbrook gets into that rush-hour traffic, he's gone."

Norton raised the powerful binoculars to his eyes once again. Something about the ship had caught his attention. Focusing on the forward stack, he could see smoke coming out of it. A lot of smoke. "Now what the fuck is going on?'" he said.

"What's happening?" Miller asked.

"I think they're starting their engines!"

"What time is it?"

"Five minutes to four," Norton replied, agitated. The last time he'd been on a joint operation with the ATF troops, it had been in Waco, Texas. If this operation turned into a disaster like that one, he didn't want to be sharing any blame for it.

"Christ," said Miller, "that thing's an old World War Two destroyer. You can't just turn the key on one of those babies and drive off like it was a Chevy or something. They have to get up steam, and that takes hours! Relax. Even if they are trying to get away, they'll still be there at four thirty. You can bet your career on it."

Norton had a sick feeling that he might be doing just that. He looked more closely at the ship. One more weird thing happens over there, he said to himself, and I'm going to call for the raid to go down right away.

As he drove out of the shipyard, George Holbrook forced himself to give the appearance of calm. The distance from the shipyard to Logan Airport was a little over a mile. Hardly enough distance to lose a tail if there is one, George thought. There was no alternative to going as if he weren't being followed, so on he went. Just drive like you're going to the store for a loaf of bread. You won't be a fleeing felon until five minutes from now. Then you can drive like a fleeing felon.

Jeff Stern, the senior ATF agent at the shipyard, was also a veteran of the Great Siege at Waco, Texas. He knew that being involved in another high-profile disaster would put his career into the burn bag. When the FBI agent had called on the radio to say that Holbrook was leaving, Stern was about to have him followed. Then, Holbrook had turned right onto Maverick Street, heading for the airport. It was six minutes to four, over half an hour away from the assault time. What if they followed Holbrook to a dead end? He had a phone in his car. If they moved in to arrest him, he might be able to warn the others, and give them time to destroy evidence. Surprise was essential, Stern thought. Look what had happened in Waco when those fruitcake Branch Davidians got advance word of the raid! Going after Holbrook could spook the others on the ship. Better to risk losing Holbrook than to risk blowing the main operation, Stern decided. Convinced of the soundness of his logic, he watched through binoculars as George drove serenely toward Logan Airport, not followed and unopposed.

Norton was becoming agitated. The smoke from the stack was no longer black. It was a faint gray, nearly clear. The ship's engines were still running, only more smoothly and efficiently than before. It could be a test of the engines, he supposed. Somebody could be tuning them up. He looked at his watch. Precisely four o'clock. Who tunes up ships' engines at four o'clock? The shipyard shift gets off at four o'clock, and every one of those union stiffs has his card through the time clock by four-oh-one. Something definitely was going on.

Suddenly and explosively, Norton exclaimed, "Holy shit!," dropped his binoculars, and grabbed the radio. He had momentarily shifted his gaze from the smokestack to the ship's main deck. There, Roth, Langone and another man whom Norton didn't recognize were undoing the mooring lines from *Seafire*'s bitts and simply dropping them into the water. Of the six lines, three were undone and the men were working on the fourth.

"All agents, all agents!" he screamed into the radio. "Move in now! They're untying the fucking boat!"

On *Seafire*'s bridge, Bill Jackson paced about in agitation as he planned the departure. They had been lucky in the ship's placement, starboard side to and bow in at the outer end of the pier. They had only to kick the stern slightly to the left, and then back out into the fairway. The biggest problem was the lack of dockhands. Dropping the lines overboard was the obvious solution, but that carried the risk of wrapping a line around one or both props. Jackson's plan had been simple and elegant. With the stern out, only lines four and six could possibly foul the props. These had to be cast off and cleared, and that would be first. Peter Carson and Paul Harrington had raced over the brow, and frantically pulled four and six up onto the pier as Steve Roth and Kevin Finnerty had cast them off. Then, Carson and Harrington had run back aboard, cutting the lashings on the ship end of the brow, but leaving the other end of it tied down on the pier. Then the three men had undone lines five, three and one, in that order, while Kevin Finnerty fired up his chain saw. The redheaded youngster saluted the bridge with the saw to signal that they were ready.

Bill Jackson took a deep breath. Through the soles of his feet, he could feel the gentle vibration of the idling engines. He had taken *Seafire* to sea a hundred or more times before, yet never had he felt so wonderfully alive as he had done it. In the wheelhouse, Bob Knight was at the control station, while others of the owners' party waited to carry out their assigned tasks. At the entrance to the shipyard, Jackson could see a commotion: speeding cars and flashing lights. The Feds were on the way. Jackson smiled. Too little too late, fellahs. "Right standard rudder," he said to Knight. "Port engine ahead one third." With mooring lines in the water on the starboard side, he wasn't going to use the starboard prop until he got clear of the mess alongside the pier.

Brown water, the color of a coffee milk shake, frothed under the stern, and the ship began to move. Number two mooring line, cleated to the ship near the bow, took the strain, groaning as it stretched and chafed in the chock, while the stern moved away from the pier. "Port engine stop," Jackson said. Police cars appeared at the head of the pier. "Port engine back standard. Rudder amidships," said Jackson. He looked at the pier and verified that the ship had slight sternway, then picked up the loudspeaker system microphone. "Cast off line number two," he said. With a flourish, Kevin Finnerty cut the hawser with his chain saw. Like a huge rubber band, the stretched nylon line snapped back onto the pier, the brow fell into the water, and *Seafire* was free. "Underway," said Jackson on the loudspeaker. "Shift colors!"

On Seafire's fantail, Paul Harrington took down the ensign, quickly folded it, and took it inside the ship, all as Jackson had asked him to do. On the bow, young Finnerty did the same with the jack. At the same time, on the signal bridge, Emily Carson hauled a new ensign up to the masthead. Jackson, still in the wheelhouse, pushed a button that activated the ship's siren. Since she wasn't a steamship, she had no steam whistle. Instead, she had a huge siren, a monstrous electric klaxon that Bubba Caulfield had installed forty years before. High on the mast, just beneath the weathered steer horns, it screamed one long blast, then three short ones. *Seafire* was underway. Jackson smiled to himself. Perhaps it had been silly to shift colors with Navy precision. He'd done it because he knew that a lot of people were watching. Some of them might know how such things ought to be done. In any case, it had been sharp and crisp, and he was glad he'd done it.

Jackson turned his attention to the Feds on the pier, who were boiling out of their cars like scalded ants. He could see at once that they weren't going to get close. Already, *Seafire*'s stern had cleared the end of the pier, and at the nearest point there was fifteen feet of open water between it and the foredeck. The ship was gaining sternway rapidly, and the gap was widening fast. There was no way anyone could jump aboard, but Jackson was concerned that the cops might fire a few parting shots. He ordered everyone to stay well within the protection of the pilothouse, which still carried the original inch and a half of armor. He watched as the bow cleared the end of the pier. "Left standard rudder," he said.

Jackson turned and looked astern. The Inner Harbor was narrow, and the ship was backing toward the Coast Guard piers in Boston's North End. The nearest ship was the cutter *Escanaba*.

There were a number of whitehats aboard her, two dozen or so, watching *Seafire*'s departure. Several of them were waving their hats and capering about, obviously amused by the show. Jackson gave them a salute, and the Coasties waved and cheered in response. "Stop engines," Jackson said. He waited as the ship's momentum carried her into the channel, the bow swinging toward the open sea. "All engines ahead standard. Turns for fifteen knots. Steer course one eight zero."

Once again, Jackson pushed the klaxon button, held it down long and hard, and *Seafire*'s strident voice wailed across Boston Harbor. It was an ear-splitting, tooth-grating, triumphant sound. Jackson looked back at the Feds lined up on the end of the pier, staring impotently at *Seafire*'s stern and looking forlorn. "You just saw a warship being born, you turkeys!" he shouted to them. "You just heard her cry."

So much for the FBI and the ATF, Jackson thought. Now all we have to do is outrun the Coast Guard, the Navy, and the Air Force.

CHAPTER 10

THE BOSTON TRAFFIC was more horrendous than usual. At ten after four on the last Tuesday in October, it was the worst Ralph Dade had seen in months. The Central Artery was clogged in both directions, and the Mystic River Bridge and Callahan Tunnel were both hopeless.

Ralph, waiting in line to enter the Callahan Tunnel to East Boston, was beside himself with frustration. The leased Jaguar he was driving, with its V-12 engine, could attain speeds in excess of one hundred and fifty miles per hour. But Ralph was going absolutely nowhere. At the center of the steering wheel, encased in Lucite, was the Jaguar symbol, a bronze disk in the shape of a snarling cat's head. Ralph hated cats, and this one seemed to be sneering at him. He pounded at it with his fist in frustration, and the horn squawked. The driver of the car ahead of him turned around, glared, and gave Ralph the finger. "Christ," Ralph said to the cat, "if I keep this up I'll have a stroke."

Ralph didn't notice the blue and white Boston Police cruiser four cars behind his Jag. Fortunately for Ralph, the officers in it didn't notice him either, probably because the Jaguar was so low to the ground. Five minutes before, an alert had been radioed to the entire Boston Police force, as well as to several other jurisdictions, concerning one Ralph Dade, urgently sought as a material witness by the Federal Bureau of Investigation and the Bureau of Alcohol, Tobacco, and Firearms. Believed to be driving a Jaguar XJS coupe, color black. All over the greater Boston area, V-12 Jags were being pulled over for something other than excessive speed for a change.

Ralph sourly considered the situation. George's message about the commodity market had been so transparent that it had bordered on the asinine. Radio waves travel faster than cars, even XJS Jaguars. If the deal of a lifetime really was out there, George could have told Ralph about it on the phone, and Ralph then could have called his broker on the car phone, right there on I-95.

Ralph was worried. Obviously, something was wrong and he was needed back at the pier in East Boston ASAP. The buzzer sounded on the console, and Ralph picked up the cellular telephone.

It was George. "Where are you?"

Lt.(j.g.) Giulia Monaco, USCG, had been having a fine day. She had just qualified as a command duty officer aboard the United States Coast Guard Cutter *Escanaba*, and this was to be her first night of duty as such. It was a milestone in her career, evidence of confidence placed in her by the ship's captain and senior officers. Until about six minutes after four, she had been savoring it.

As command duty officer, Lieutenant (j.g.) Monaco was the senior officer of the duty section which would stay aboard the ship until the formal changing of the watch, at eight the following morning. Being a CDO meant that in the opinion of the captain, she was capable of taking the ship to sea in an emergency, with just the duty watch as a crew, and carrying out any missions she might be called upon to perform. It meant that, in the eyes of her superiors, she was qualified to command a ship at sea. Giulia Monaco had been born and raised in the North End not a quarter of a mile from the pier to which *Escanaba* was moored. All her life she'd dreamed of a career in the Coast Guard. Now, one more part of that dream was coming true.

By quiet tradition aboard *Escanaba*, the captain, XO, and other senior officers had found excuses to go home early, to leave the new CDO some time to appreciate her new responsibility. One by one they had left the ship, congratulating Monaco, and remembering the times in their own careers when this milestone had been passed. By four o'clock, Lieutenant Monaco was the senior officer aboard. She'd been standing on the port wing of the bridge, thinking about the day when she would take a ship like this to sea under her own command. The air was mild and clear, with the sun low in the west. Over the port quarter, the East Boston waterfront was bathed in the golden afternoon sun. Monaco was appreciating the view when the duty quartermaster, having just congratulated her on her new status in the watch bill, said, "Hey, Lieutenant Monaco! Check this out. They're doing something funny on that big yacht!"

Lieutenant Monaco and the quartermaster watched the sideshow across the Inner Harbor with amazement. He leaned over the wing of the bridge and called out to several of his shipmates on deck. The word quickly passed, and soon dozens of men were lining the rail. "Knock off ship's work" had just been passed, and several of the men had been skylarking in the late afternoon sun. They watched with professional interest and sheer disbelief as

Seafire got underway. The bo'suns mates shouted derision as the yacht's lines were loosened on her bitts and thrown overboard; yet they could appreciate the smart way the old destroyer's stern kicked out from the pier as she drove ahead against her spring. "Christ, they forgot the fuckin' brow!" one deck hand exclaimed and watched in awe as it dropped into the harbor, with one end still tied to the pier. The climax of the display, which the deck hands enjoyed especially, had been the use of a chain saw to cast off the spring line. This, followed by the parade-ground perfect shifting of colors, brought such mirth to *Escanaba*'s crew that several of them were unable to remain standing, and the cutter's deck erupted in a mock cheer.

On the bridge, Lieutenant Monaco was more than interested in the evolution, she was stupefied. She had noticed the big yacht, off and on, over the summer. When it had first pulled into the East Boston shipyard in May, she had mistaken it for a Coast Guard cutter, with its military lines and its brilliant white paint. Professional interest had piqued her curiosity, and she had noted the progress of the refit as the months had passed. The hasty and frenzied departure from the dock had her totally baffled. Then, she saw the flashing blue lights on the pier, and she began to understand. At six minutes after four, when she got the orders from District Headquarters, they didn't come as a complete surprise. Her first decision in a position of command was a brilliant one. She called the bo'suns mate of the watch and said, "Chief, get us out of here!" Then she called the duty snipe in main control and said more or less the same thing.

▬ ▬ ▬ ▬ ▬

The two vehicular tunnels between Boston to East Boston run side by side. The Sumner Tunnel carries traffic into the city while its twin, the Callahan Tunnel, carries the outbound flow. From the helicopter above the Boston end of the tunnels, George Holbrook quickly picked out the Jaguar, about a hundred yards from the entrance to the Callahan.

George had been lucky for a change. He had exited the shipyard six minutes before four o'clock, without apparent pursuit. He'd driven out to Maverick Street, then turned right toward the airport. The trip had taken eight minutes; he had been at the helicopter pad at two minutes after four. His fears about impoundment of the aircraft had been groundless. The ExecuStar had been in its normal position, fueled and ready to fly, with no law enforcement types anywhere in sight. By four ten he was airborne and had swung out over the Inner Harbor to watch *Seafire* accelerating toward the open sea. So far, there was no sign of any pursuit. He had then flown over to the Coast Guard Base in the North End, a scant half-mile from the pier that *Seafire* had just vacated, to take a look at the cutters. There was frantic activity aboard *Escanaba*, with groups of white hats milling about on deck. It was apparent that she was making hasty preparations to put to sea. George calculated that it would be a good twenty minutes before she could clear the pier. Like *Seafire*, she had diesel engines, so getting steam up wasn't an issue. Getting organized would be. Judging by the number of people running fore and aft on her main deck, it might be close to an hour before she got her act together, George thought.

From his vantage point over the harbor, George could see both ends of the tunnels. Ralph was going to be stuck for a long while. Traffic was coming out at the East Boston end of the Callahan at a trickle. There had to be an accident or a breakdown inside. George looked around, and noticed the Quincy Market parking garage, only five hundred yards from where Ralph was sitting. If Ralph could just get to the roof of that garage.

"OK Ralph, you've got to reverse your field and head back into the city," George shouted into his microphone. "Get to the left and do a U-turn into the inbound flow coming out of the other tunnel."

"Jesus, George, how the hell can I do that? I haven't moved five feet in the last ten minutes."

"Play bumper cars, for God's sake. Just get the hell out of there. You've got to get someplace where I can pick you up in the next ten minutes."

Ralph looked around. To his left was an opening nearly as wide as the Jaguar. He proceeded to widen it.

The driver of the police cruiser couldn't believe what he was seeing. A black sports car had sprung out of the line of traffic. It had cut violently to the left, between two cars, simultaneously hitting one on the front bumper and the other in the rear, accelerating as it went. Horns blared, brakes squealed, but the black car moved on. Then, doing God knows what damage to its low-slung undercarriage, it jumped the median, knocked down two or three traffic pylons, and completed a U-turn into the inbound lanes coming out of the Sumner Tunnel.

Ralph had switched the car phone to the speaker mode, so he could listen to George while using both hands to drive. He knew that he had done at least five thousand in damage to the coachwork back there. His ears told him that the mufflers were gone, and he had serious doubts about the oil pan. The car was still moving, though. So far, so good.

"Get right, get right!" George shouted. "Go under the expressway, as if you were going to go up onto it southbound!"

Now, Ralph had to cross two lanes of traffic. The drivers just spent half an hour in a smoky tunnel and were not about to allow anyone to cut in. Ralph picked his target carefully. Hitting the Buick slightly abaft the left front wheel, he backed, then swung forward and around the car, which had stopped in reaction to the impact. The next lane was easier. The driver of a Chevy compact had seen the Buick episode and decided to be chivalrous.

"Don't look now, Ralph, but the gendarmes are in pursuit. Bear left under the expressway, then straight and slightly right. Whatever you do, don't go up the ramp."

Those few yards, a short block and a half along the surface artery, were the longest Ralph Dade would ever drive in his life. Trying to cross lanes against a flow of Boston drivers eager to get home after a day's work. No salmon swimming upstream to spawn ever had to work harder. The Jaguar was low slung and small in appearance, yet it outweighed the full-sized Oldsmobiles and Chevrolets it came upon, and, so, after three more collisions, it turned right onto Clinton Street, fifty feet from the entrance to the parking garage.

The police cruiser had made a valiant effort to follow the Jag, but it required larger openings in traffic and they just weren't there. Its driver had managed to make the U-turn into the inbound traffic and had noted the right turn under the artery. A radio call had alerted Precinct One headquarters, about three blocks away, and more units were called. As Ralph pulled into the entrance and stopped at the ticket gate, no fewer than four police cruisers were on his tail. The gate was automatic, with a time clock that dispensed tickets when you pushed a button. Ralph, hearing sirens behind him, was tempted to ram through the gate, but the Jag was so low-slung that the gate was just at windshield height. Ralph decided against it.

Stopping alongside the ticket dispenser, Ralph tried to lower the window. He pushed the button, but the electric mechanism wasn't working. The door was jammed as well, only opening a few inches, and he wasted precious seconds awkwardly groping for the ticket. The sirens were louder, and in his rear view mirror, he could see flashing blue lights reflected in the Quincy Market shop windows across the street. Finally the gate lifted with painful slowness and Ralph accelerated onto level one. As he raced down the long aisle he saw the first police car reach the entrance. It hit the gate without even slowing down, taking the wooden board square on the grille and smashing it into splinters. Ralph swung left to head up to level two, with the police no more than ten seconds behind him. Not enough time. There were five levels between Ralph and the roof, and each level represented the opportunity for him to add precious seconds to his slim lead over the police. There were pedestrians in the aisles, people walking to their cars, but the unmuffled roar of the Jaguar kept them back and out of the way. Ralph hoped that no one would back out of a parking place at the wrong moment. Forcing himself to ignore that possibility, he drove on.

The police cars were no match for the Jaguar. They were superior in gate smashing, but outclassed in all other respects. Ralph was about to make the turn onto level five as the lead cruiser was half way along the straightaway on three. Ralph was on the roof before the police reached level four.

The Jag swung through the turn off of the last sloping ramp and screeched to a stop alongside the helicopter. Ralph scrambled and half-rolled out of the passenger door, landing in a heap. "Move it!" George shouted, as he saw the first of the police cruisers appear at the top of the ramp.

The passenger door of the ExecuStar was open, and Ralph dove in headfirst. George hauled back on the collective and was airborne before Ralph was settled in his seat, and long before the helicopter door was closed. Ah, well, he thought, another safety violation. Doubtless, there will be more.

As the helicopter gained altitude, one of the policemen drew his service revolver and aimed it at the aircraft. His sergeant grabbed his arm before he could shoot. "Are you fuckin' nuts? Shoot down a helicopter in the middle of downtown at fuckin' rush hour? Kill a million fuckin' civilians?"

■ ■ ■ ■ ■

As George swung the ExecuStar over the North End toward the harbor, his elation faded. He'd underestimated the seamanship of the Coast Guardsmen. *Escanaba* was just getting underway, beginning to back into the Inner Harbor. George looked at his watch. Four twenty, ten minutes before the time the warrants were supposed to have been served. *Seafire* had a twenty-minute head start on *Escanaba*. It was going to be an interesting evening.

George watched *Escanaba* back clear of her pier. She would have to complete backing, turn, stop, and then gather headway. This would take four or five minutes. *Seafire* was passing the Castle Island container ship facility, three miles ahead of *Escanaba*, and she had good way on, twelve knots or more. By the time *Escanaba* got moving, *Seafire*'s lead would be at least four miles. The Coast Guard would never catch up with her.

But, George knew, *Escanaba* didn't have to catch up with *Seafire* to cause trouble. *Escanaba* carried a three-inch, rapid-fire gun mount on her foredeck, with an effective range of approximately four miles. Where it really mattered, Seafire's head start amounted to nothing, the two ships were in a dead heat. The Coasties weren't going to blaze away with their primary battery right in the middle of Boston Harbor, of course. Especially with a bunch of civilian airliners flying around. Once both ships were out past the harbor approaches, though, if *Seafire* wasn't out of range of Escanaba's three-inch gun, *Seafire* was going to be in a bad way.

Escanaba wasn't the only problem. George could see two fast moving boats coming up from the south. He guessed that they were Coast Guard forty-one-footers and they appeared to be on a course to intercept *Seafire*. It looked to George as if they would catch the yacht just off of the Graves. Finally, there were now two helicopters flying on either beam of *Seafire*, and these worried

George a great deal until he recognized them as TV news camera ships. It wasn't even four-thirty yet, so these guys would have their videotape ready for the six o'clock news, George thought.

Of all the threats, George regarded *Escanaba* as the most serious. The forty-one-footers probably came from the Allerton Station in Hull. One or two more of them were probably being dispatched from Scituate, farther to the southeast. Even if they could catch up with *Seafire*, there was little they could do to stop her. Their mission was to catch boaters with inadequate safety equipment or illegal marine toilets, to bag the occasional lobster poacher, and to intercept drug runners. Their heaviest weapon was probably the Thompson forty-five caliber sub-machine gun, effective against small boats but not against a fleet destroyer. Destroyers don't carry much armor, but *Seafire* still had every ounce she'd been born with. The shell of her pilothouse was almost two inches thick, and soft lead slugs would never pierce it. *Escanaba*'s three-inch gun would be another matter.

George decided to do a reconnaissance run on the cutter. Swinging wide to port over the outer anchorage area, he turned back toward the city. With the wind out of the northeast, Runways Four Left and Four Right were active at Logan, and George was about to fly through the landing approach lanes to both of them. Switching back to the Logan approach control frequency, he called the tower. "Logan Approach, this is Holbrook Two Three Delta, over."

"Holbrook Two Three Delta, this is the senior controller. Your flight clearance is canceled. You are ordered and directed to return to Logan immediately. Indicate your intention to comply and await instructions, over."

"Well," George said to Ralph, "we tried." Then, on the radio, "Logan Tower, this is Holbrook Two Three Delta, I am reading you strong but broken, am unable to copy, over. I will stay low to avoid danger to other aircraft. Out." He then dropped altitude and crossed the approach lane with the skids less than three feet above the water. The radio squawked in outrage. George stabbed at a button, and it went silent. Down on the deck, George was well under the approach slope of any incoming airliners.

George eased off on the airspeed as he came upon the Coast Guard cutter, which had aligned herself toward the outer harbor and was just beginning to accelerate. He transitioned into a stationary hover off her port bow, and it was the ship that passed the helicopter rather than vice versa. As she slid past, George could see that preparations for flight ops were underway. *Escanaba*'s helicopter was being rolled out in preparation for launch. If they got her airborne with the same efficiency that they had gotten the ship away from the pier, she'd be in the air in ten minutes.

More ominous than the action on the flight deck, however, was what was happening on the fo'c'sle. The three-inch gun was depressed, its barrel lowered and close to the deck. Two men were attending the muzzle, and there was only one thing that they could be doing: removing the brass tompion. *Escanaba* was getting ready to shoot.

George had seen enough. He swung the helicopter wide around the cutter's stern, still staying low to avoid intruding into active airspace around Logan. He watched the white ship gain speed for a few more moments, then punched in a prearranged frequency into the radio. "Bill, this is George, over," he said.

"Go ahead, George," came the reply. Holbrook recognized Jackson's voice. By agreement, they were using first names, in case the frequency was monitored. Failure to identify themselves on the radio was yet another violation of law, but by now, George had lost count.

"I have our wayward friend aboard, and we're coming home. We'll be there in two minutes. Meanwhile, shake a leg. The six foot tall sailors are going to sea." The reference was to an old Navy joke. You have to be tall to join the Coast Guard, so you can wade ashore if your ship sinks. George was sure Jackson would understand, but most people wouldn't.

Approaching *Seafire*, George could see that she'd increased speed. He'd never seen her move so fast. The forty-one footers from Hull were closer, but it was clear that by the time they got to the end of the Narrows, *Seafire* would be well beyond that point. Obviously, they weren't going to intercept. Whether or not *Seafire* was matching *Escanaba*'s speed was questionable, it was close either way. The big yacht had just executed a gentle left turn, and was approaching Deer Island Light, heading outbound from President Roads. George guessed that it would be fifteen or twenty minutes before the cutter would have a clear shot at her.

George thought about staying airborne for a while so he and Ralph could act as observers. He decided to go aboard. "We're unarmed, so we can't act as defenders," he explained to Ralph. "We already know they're after us, so we're not needed for early warning. *Seafire*'s still in flat water in the lee of Winthrop, but with the northeast wind, it's going to get lumpy as soon as she clears Deer Island. We might not be able to land later without making her slow down. On top of that, *Escanaba* is about to get her helicopter up, and with an empty helo platform on *Seafire*, they might be tempted to land a boarding party. With this bird sitting on the deck, they can hover around all they want, but they won't be able to land."

"They could lower men on the cable hoist," Ralph said.

"Not likely. If they had a squad of Rangers or Seals aboard, they might try it. I doubt that the average Coastie is trained for commando stuff. By the time they could get ready, it'll be dark. *Seafire* will be out into the open ocean, making twenty knots or more. She'll be bouncing around like a newlywed on a waterbed. Lowering a man on a rope could kill the guy or wreck the helicopter, most likely both. I think keeping our flight deck foul is all we need, at least until dawn tomorrow."

As he spoke, George was lining up his approach to *Seafire*'s helicopter platform. Steve Roth and young Finnerty were waiting with the tethers. The landing was uneventful, and the four men quickly tied the ExecuStar down.

Bill Jackson was waiting when George and Ralph got to the bridge. "We've been listening on the radio to the reports of your exploits."

George ignored the comment. "*Escanaba*'s about four miles astern of us and she's packing on the knots. She's getting ready to launch her helo and her three-inch gun is cleared for action. Once we get clear of the harbor, I think she's going to start throwing shells at us. That's just for openers; God knows what they're strapping onto that helicopter. We'd better put on all the speed we can muster."

Steve Roth said, "Our weapons systems are on line, George. They haven't been tested, of course, but I'm sure they're operational. I doubt that we can sink the *Escanaba*, but we can make short work of any helicopter."

"Christ, Steve, we can't do that," said George. "They're the good guys. If we can't outrun them, the whole deal is off.

"If the Air Force flies by with a couple of their Tomcats or whatever, that's another story. Shoot up one of those babies and the pilot pushes a button and out he pops. His chute opens, his life raft inflates, and his emergency bottle of champagne is automatically chilled to the proper temperature just as he hits the water. Nobody gets hurt. But if you shoot down a helicopter, people get killed every time."

"Speak of the Devil," Ralph Dade said, gesturing out the port bridge door. *Escanaba's* helicopter was coming up astern. It circled *Seafire* twice, then took station on her starboard beam.

"Great," George said. "They're probably waiting for instructions."

Bill Jackson had been studying the chart. "There's a shortcut out of here, if you don't mind a narrow channel with a lot of rocks on the sides of it. We could pick up a mile on the cutter if we took it. Maybe two."

George stepped over to the chart table. "Show me," he said.

"The main ship channel runs northeast, actually a little north of northeast, for over two miles. You can't turn southeast, which is where we want to go, until you're here," he said, pointing at a buoy symbol on the chart. "Then you can begin to turn southward, and go north of the Graves." Pointing again, he said, "We're here. If we turn southeast now, we can go south of Aldrich Ledge, and out through Hypocrite Channel. We'd save two miles of running at right angles to our final course. If we do it, it's got to be now."

"Do it," George said.

"Steer zero-eight-five," Jackson said to Bob Knight, who was still at the controls, and *Seafire* swung into a smooth right turn.

Once the ship was on her new heading, George asked Jackson, "Won't *Escanaba* follow us? They don't draw any more water than we do."

"The sun set two minutes ago. There will be enough light for us to go through there, but just barely. *Escanaba* is a good twenty minutes behind us. It'll be dark by the time she gets to this point, and the buoys aren't lighted. It's nearly low tide. There's no way the Coast Guard will go through this water at eighteen knots in the dark."

Suvia Ferris had been on the bridge since George had arrived. "What happened to your friends in Washington, George, the ones who were supposed to keep the heat off? Even if we outrun the Coast Guard, there's still the Navy and the Air Force. What went wrong?"

"I don't know, Suvia. Maybe it was the guns that Ralph bought in Miami. Someone probably thinks we're arms merchants. My friends in Washington are politicians. They'll put in a good word for you, especially if you're a regular campaign contributor. But if there's the slightest chance you'll cause them embarrassment or bad publicity, suddenly they've never heard of you."

"Well, Mr. Holbrook," said Jackson, "I'd like to make a suggestion. I'm the paid captain here, and when it comes to running away, I can do that without your help. I bet you could do a lot more good than you're doing up here, if you were down on the telephone telling your senator friends that it ain't so."

"If they'll take my calls," said George.

"If they'll take your calls," said Jackson.

As George turned to leave the bridge, Steve Roth said, "It will be completely dark in a half hour or so, George. Don't worry, we'll lose them. Unless, of course, you object to my messing about with the good guys' radar."

"Christ, you didn't put Satan's Cloak on board, did you? That thing is cosmic top secret. Even taking it out of the United States could set us up for espionage charges!" George had given Roth free rein to install any electronic gear he thought they might need. George had kept up with the progress on the lasers, but he had no idea of what else was on board. He decided that he had better learn fast.

"Yeah, I know," Roth was saying. "I invented it. I built it, but the government was too cheap to buy it. Instead, they classified it top secret so I couldn't sell it to anybody else and said that if I tried to, they'd arrest me as a spy. Well, hell, I'm no spy. I'm just an aggressive salesman. I'm about to give the United States government a practical demonstration of my product's usefulness. Hopefully this will induce them to reconsider their decision not to purchase it. What could be more innocent? I'm acting in the true American tradition of capitalism and free enterprise."

"Cut the crap, Steve. Does it work?"

"You bet your ass, George."

"I think I have."

George Holbrook tried to keep the exasperation out of his voice. "Look, Hal, you know who I work for. You know how much money they have. Suvia Ferris earns two million dollars a month on her investments alone. Do you really think she'd waste her time and risk her freedom to smuggle three crates of machine guns to some generalissimo with a small army and a big hat? If she'd gone loony, she'd sell the plans for the Scimitar attack helicopter to the Red Chinese or somebody and make some real bucks. The guns we're supposed to be smuggling are available on the black market all over the world, and the maximum gross profit before shipping expense is less than a hundred grand. How the hell far do you think we have to go in *Seafire* before the whole hundred thou is eaten up in gas money and the profit is zip? Come on, Hal. I'm not asking you to accept on faith that I'm an honest man. I just want you to believe that if I ever turn into a crook, I'll be an efficient one."

George listened to the words, empty politician's words, which came in reply. Hal Granger had been listening, but he hadn't been hearing what George had said. Or, maybe he just didn't care. Perhaps George's innocence or guilt weren't important to Senator Granger. Currently, George and his friends on *Seafire* were a political liability, a potential embarrassment to be avoided regardless of guilt or innocence. At least, George reflected, Granger had accepted the call. That was more than several of his colleagues had done.

Granger droned on, and George looked around at the equipment in the exchange room, Telex and fax machines, and satellite communications gear with secure voice and data links. Machines for communicating with people, all totally useless if no one wants to communicate with you. Twenty-four hours ago, most politicians would have been delighted to take a call from any one of the people who owned *Seafire*, or somebody who worked for them. Not now. Now, the only people willing to talk to George were those who didn't know what was going on.

Senator Granger was winding down his "Sorry-but-I-can't-help-you" speech, and George decided to make one final, shameless appeal. "Hal," he said, interrupting, "Do you remember my father's funeral?"

"Of course." The senator's tone was wary.

"You told me, afterward, that he was your first major supporter. Without his help at the beginning, you said, you wouldn't have gotten your start in politics."

"That's true."

"You told me that if I ever needed a favor, just call. I never took you up on that, Hal. Not until now. This is important. I need that favor. Please."

There was a second or two of silence on the line. "I wish I could help, George, but ..."

George didn't let him finish. "Hal, I'm sorry to have embarrassed you this way. Let's pretend I never called. I should have known better. Say hello to Carol and the kids for me." Before Granger could reply, George hung up.

Suvia Ferris was the first to see George when he returned to the bridge. She read disappointment in the way he carried himself. "You look a little down. Your friends not taking your calls?"

"Friendship is like love," he said. "It should be avoided at all costs." He tried to grin, to make a joke of his bitterness. It didn't work, the grin was more of a grimace. "That way, you won't get hurt when people let you down."

"You did what!?!"

Malloy's question was clearly rhetorical, so Christmann didn't reply. He'd heard Malloy sound a lot angrier. What was ominous, though, was that shortly after Christmann had begun his report, Malloy had told him to stop and had called another agent into the room. A witness. That had never happened before. Malloy clearly believed that indictments were possible.

"Let me get this straight," Malloy continued. "You discovered that the Federal Bureau of Investigation and the Bureau of Alcohol, Tobacco and Firearms were about to raid a ship. They were investigating possible illegal arms shipments, and they had valid search and arrest warrants. You took it upon yourself to warn the operators of this ship in time for them to sail and thus avoid arrest. Is that a fair summary of what you told me?"

"Yes, sir," Christmann replied. Malloy waited for Christmann to say more. Christmann disappointed him, and said nothing. Malloy looked at Tolman, the young agent he'd called in to cover his ass. For a second or two Malloy regretted doing that. Perhaps he'd been too quick to make that play, perhaps he was getting overly defensive in his old age. No, he concluded, he had done the right thing. The climate in Washington vis-a-vis the Central Intelligence Agency had changed, and not for the better. No longer was there an alumnus of the shop sitting in the Oval Office. The current president was anti-war, anti-military, and certainly anti-spy. Being down on the CIA was politically correct these days. Covering your ass was definitely the wisest program, if you happened to work in a certain large building in Langley, VA. Malloy sighed, sat down, and looked at Christmann, one of the best men in the agency.

"OK, Bill, you win. I'll come right out and ask. Why did you do it?"

"It was a judgment call, Jim. Bizarre as it seems, I think it was the right one. I know it was a risky move, for the agency and myself. That's why I did it unilaterally. I didn't tell you or anyone else in advance. Any blame will be mine alone."

"I don't know if I should appreciate the cover, Bill. You're still under my supervision, and your screwups are going to blow up in my face, whether I give prior approval or not. And, you still haven't told me why you did it."

"Do you know who George Holbrook is?" Christmann asked.

"Sure. Test pilot. His father was a defense contractor, died in a helicopter crash. Some conglomerate bought out the company and he still works for them. They make mean little attack helicopters for the Army and the Navy. He was one of the guys the FBI wanted to talk to, right?"

"Right. What else do you know about him?"

"Not much, why?"

"Did you know we had a dossier on him going back for years?"

"No. You pulled the file on this guy? What authority did you have to do that? Jesus! This gets worse and worse."

"I'm surprised you haven't heard of him. He's one of the biggest CIA-bashers around. He never says CIA. He always calls us something like 'Certifiably Insane Assassins' or 'Cretins, Imbeciles, and Assholes'. He has a million of 'em."

"Well, that explains it," said Malloy, rolling his eyes at Tolman. "Good friend of the agency like that, of course we'd warn him if his ass is about to be tossed in jail. What did we do to make him so angry at us?"

"We screwed up the hostage rescue in Tehran."

"Why should he be so agitated about that?"

"We tried to blame him for it."

• • • • •

"Where the hell are we?" George Holbrook directed the question to no one in particular, but it was Bill Jackson who replied.

"We're in the shipping channel, outbound lane. We'll be passing the tip of Cape Cod in about a half-hour. Another half-hour beyond that, and we're in international waters. *Escanaba's* still calling us on the VHF radio, by the way, telling us to heave to. You think they'd get tired of that."

"What's our speed?"

"Twenty-four knots. Maybe a half knot more."

"Tell Finnerty he's a genius," replied George, as he looked around the bridge for the first time.

Suvia Ferris had left. George had the odd feeling that something he had said had offended her, but he had no idea of what it might have been. Ralph was there, as well as Jackson, Steve Roth, and both of the Carsons. The rest of the crowd which had been there earlier had dispersed.

George said, "Excuse me for a moment," and stepped out onto the port wing of the bridge. He was grateful that no one followed him, he needed a few moments to himself.

For a minute or two, George simply enjoyed the view, not thinking, planning, or scheming, just letting himself absorb the beauty of his surroundings. The ship's motion was gentle for the speed she was making. The water slid by with an audible hiss as *Seafire* drove forward at nearly half a mile a minute. Off the port quarter, the North Shore was drawing away, Salem and Gloucester and the wealthy suburbs between were hunkering down on the horizon. Off the starboard quarter was the South Shore, its low hills silhouetted against the dying red glow of the sunset. The beauty of the late autumn evening calmed and soothed George, and made him nostalgic all at once. Nothing in the world is as exciting as an evening sortie. The land and the light fade away into the wake. The night and the open sea lie ahead, with dark promises of adventure.

What adventure is in store for us, George wondered. What future for my friends and me? Nineteen warm bodies on a ship built for a complement of three hundred. Four guys who spent a couple of years in the Navy long ago, a bunch of rich people, and one juvenile delinquent. Capture and arrest in a few hours at most, probably. Almost certainly. The Coast Guard helicopter was still keeping station on the beam. Sooner or later somebody was going to get up the nerve to authorize her crew to start shooting. It was amazing that it hadn't happened already. Jesus Christ, thought George, what have I gotten us into?

For an instant, George waited for an answer to his own question, without realizing that he was doing so. The answer came to him from the sea itself. The hiss of the passing wake was loud and insistent, the bow wave foamed white and proud in a narrow vee, narrower than he'd ever seen it. "Damn," said George, "we must be doing something right. We're going like a bat out of hell, faster than we ever did with a boat load of hired hands." He looked astern. The Coast Guard cutter was still there, but she was falling back. George stuck his head into the pilothouse. "We still doing twenty-four knots?"

"Closer to twenty-five," replied Jackson.

"What's *Escanaba* doing?"

"Eighteen or nineteen at most."

"Difference between the professionals and the amateurs," said George, stepping inside and smiling broadly as he closed the door behind him. He looked at his watch. It was nearly six o'clock. It would be completely dark by the time they would reach international waters, if they got that far.

"What the hell is the story on the Coast Guard?" asked George. "They should be doing better than this."

"According to *Jane's*, *Escanaba*'s top speed is twenty knots. Unless her bottom's been scraped recently, eighteen and a half, nineteen is about all she can be expected to produce," Jackson replied. "Mr. Roth intercepted a message from her a few minutes ago. Her captain believes he can maintain contact with us and ultimately intercept us. He doubts that we can maintain our present speed, and he's, quote, confident, unquote, that his ship, which is far newer, can outlast us in the stretch."

George felt a surge of hope. "How would you translate that, Bill, you being an ex-Navy man?"

"This is my baby and I can handle it by myself."

"Right," said Holbrook. "Which explains why the Massachusetts Air National Guard isn't dropping napalm on our foredeck. The black shoe Coast Guard still thinks they can bag us all by themselves; so they aren't about to call in the Navy or the Air Force or even their own Airedales to share the glory with them. We never needed a friendly senator to keep the Tomcats off of our backs, we just needed a little inter-service rivalry in the right place at the right time."

George looked at the radar repeater. The hook of Cape Cod was clearly visible to the south, Cape Ann to the north. He asked Jackson, "Where's *Escanaba*?" Jackson pointed out the blip, and George checked it with the range cursor. Seven miles.

"Lets slow a bit, Bill. We don't want to leave him in the dust. The longer he thinks that he can catch us, the longer he's going to hold off calling in the cavalry."

George looked at the chart, which was taped down on the navigation table near the port bridge wing door. The ship's course and track were neatly pencilled in, with good, solid radar fixes marked every five minutes. With all the electronic navigation equipment aboard, the pencil plot was an anachronism. Yet it comforted George to see it, to know it was there as a backup if the nav computers went down. It somehow reinforced George's belief that they actually might succeed.

"I'm going to operate on the assumption that we'll get out of here somehow," George said. "That means we need a watch bill. I had one worked out in rough, anyway, and we were lucky that not too many of us were left on the beach. I knew that Henri Girard and the Argeriardises weren't going to be aboard. Nick's working on a special project and Henri is still in Geneva keeping us liquid. That leaves nineteen here — fourteen owners, me, Polly's grandson Paul, plus Jackson, Finnerty, and his grandson Kevin.

"I look at sixteen watch standers, the fourteen owners, me, and the Harrington kid. The three professionals won't stand watch. As the captain, Bill, you have to be on call twenty-four hours a day. You can't afford to tire yourself out standing watches. The snipes, Finnerty and Kevin, we'll leave to themselves. All the engine controls and alarms are duplicated on the bridge. We don't need them hanging around in main control. So long as the machines keep running, Finnerty can decide where he and his grandson need to be.

"Ralph and I both did time in the Navy. Alex Wilson has been around the world on two Whitbread races; he knows more about navigation and seamanship than anyone else here, except for you, Bill. The three of us will rotate as officer of the deck. I'd like to have Suvia as my JOOD, so we can use the time to talk over our plans. You figure out the rest of the assignments, OK?"

"Sure," Jackson replied.

"Next, assignments for general quarters. Ralph and I here on the bridge along with you. Suvia, Polly, and Helen here, or in the exchange room, as needed. The Roths, Bob, Patty, Jacqueline, and the Carsons all in Combat. Alex, Paul Harrington, and Joe Langone will be down in main control as a damage control party with the Finnertys. Agreed?"

George looked around him and saw the agreement that he had hoped for. He took a moment to look at the radar repeater. *Escanaba* had gained about a quarter of a mile in the past ten minutes. Good, he thought, that'll give them a little encouragement. *Seafire*'s speed was down to sixteen knots. Again, George checked the chart just as Jackson was plotting a new GPS fix. Using a pair of dividers, George measured the distance to the imaginary line that marked the twelve-mile limit, the boundary of international waters. Even outside that boundary, the Coast Guard had authority to stop and seize suspicious vessels, especially those that, like *Seafire*, flew the flag of the United States. Yet, George also knew, stopping a vessel on the high seas was a significant event. In territorial waters the Coast Guard could and would stop anyone at random to check if they had sufficient life jackets on board. To order a three hundred and seventy-foot yacht to heave to in the open ocean required a damn good reason.

George's plan, if it could be called that, was to do a lame bird routine until they got close to the boundary line, than go like hell for it. Once into international waters, he'd call on the radio full of outrage and ask *Escanaba*'s skipper for his name, rank and serial number. Threaten to sue. Bluff. If that didn't work, Roth would use Satan's Cloak.

George explained his plan to the people on the bridge and withstood far less derision than he'd expected. He picked up the handset to call Roth.

"Steve, I think I finally have a need to know. Just what the hell is this Satan's Cloak? I know it's a radar-jamming device, but they've been around for forty years. What's so special about this one?"

"The power, George. It's got a tunable magnetron with immense power, something we just developed. It's a maser, like a laser except it shoots microwaves instead of light. Lasers 'lase' at a fixed frequency. Ruby lasers produce red light, argon lasers are blue-green, and so on. It's the same with masers and particle beam weapons. They shoot waves on the frequency that they're designed to shoot at.

"Satan's Cloak is different. It transmits radar energy in a laser-like beam at a wide range of frequencies. It has a diagnostic receiver that locks onto an enemy radar. Any kind of radar, air search, fire control, you name it. Then it tunes the magnetron to the same frequency as the other guy's radar, and zap!"

"What do you mean, zap?"

"Shit, George, you know how radar works. You blast out a bunch of microwaves with your transmitter. Then the transmitter shuts down, and the receiver comes on. This all takes a couple of millionths of a second, you understand. Then a little tiny bit of the energy you transmitted bounces back off of the target and your receiver picks it up. *Voila*, you see the echo as a blip on your scope. The receiver's a delicate machine, it has to pick up extremely small amounts of energy. It's all tuned up to grab every microwatt of signal that comes in on the right frequency and amplify the bejaysus out of it. You with me so far?"

"Steve, I'm a pilot, for God's sake," replied George. "I know how radar works. Spare me the basic theory and tell me what the damn Cloak does."

"So the radar transmitter is off and the receiver is listening for an echo, and along comes a signal that is absolutely dead-nuts on frequency. Only it's about a hundred billion times more powerful than this poor machine was designed to receive. So what do you think happens?"

"I give up," said George.

"It melts the son-of-a-bitch."

"Swell." George hung up.

Bill Jackson had been fiddling with the radar repeater on the bridge, marking on the face of the scope with a grease pencil. George asked him what was happening.

"It's going to be close, Mr. Holbrook. They're six miles astern of us now. I calculate their speed to be close to twenty knots. We're doing eighteen. It's a little over ten miles to the boundary of international waters, so it'll take us over half an hour to get there. In that half-hour they'll pick up another mile on us. We'd be in range for a lucky shot. They've almost got a chance now."

"What does Finnerty say we can do if we have to?"

"He says we can outrun them. Whatever they do, we can match it and more. We're still a destroyer hull, and that cutter is a glorified DE."

"He forgets that this destroyer hull is fifty years old and the glorified DE is brand new."

"He says what he says. I'm just a deck officer. I don't know nuthin' 'bout no engines."

George Holbrook looked up from the chart, and for an instant his gaze met Jackson's. There was a spark in Jackson's eye, a twinkle that George had never seen before. What was it, excitement, amusement? Both, George thought, and more. And, it was infectious. George felt his jaw muscles relax; he hadn't realized before that he had been clenching them. Mischief! That was the feeling. The delight he'd felt as a kid, running like mad from the guy whose car he'd just pounded with snowballs. That was the damn twinkle in Jackson's eye. He was enjoying the chase.

And so, George Holbrook thought, am I.

"Let's increase to turns for twenty knots, Mr. Jackson. I think six miles is as close as we want to get to that three-inch gun."

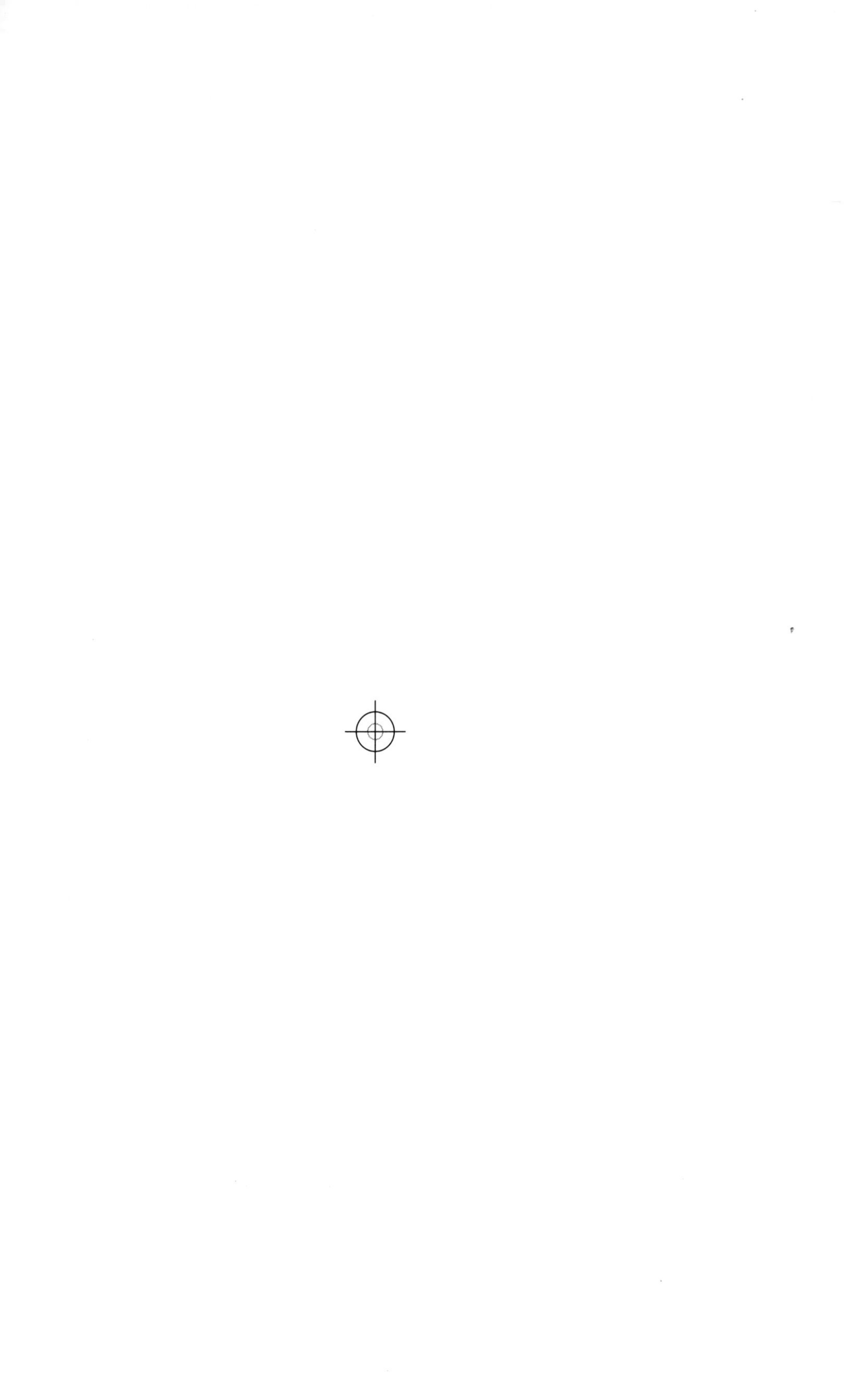

CHAPTER 11

"THE IRAN HOSTAGE RESCUE!" said Tolman, unable to remain quiet any longer. "How could he have messed that up? Wasn't there a sandstorm, or something, that screwed up the airplanes?"

Malloy had sent for Holbrook's dossier, and at that moment a file clerk brought it into the room. Malloy signed the receipt, and waited for the clerk to leave before replying. "Tolman's right Bill. That's how I remember it, and I was here when it happened. The whole fiasco was blamed on lack of adequate contingency planning. Which, of course, was blamed on the CIA. Christ, what a horror show."

"Read the file, Jim. Holbrook was there. Not officially, of course, but he was there."

Malloy regarded the file sourly, then put it aside. "Why don't you just tell us about it."

"Sure. As you recall, the American Embassy got taken over by Iranian Revolutionary Guards in 1979. Everybody there was taken hostage. By early '80, the situation was becoming a major political liability for Jimmy Carter. Every night there were TV reports with names like 'America Held Hostage.' It was an election year, and Carter's advisors were telling him his chances for reelection would be zip unless he resolved the situation.

"The CIA and the joint chiefs came up with a rescue plan. Airborne assault on the embassy, catch the guards asleep, kill 'em before they can kill the hostages, take our people out by helo.

"Enter George Holbrook, pilot extraordinaire. He'd been a Navy fighter jock. Got a general discharge from the Navy for chasing some MIGs into Laos or Cambodia or someplace and violating their sacred neutrality."

"The scoundrel," said Malloy.

"Yeah, shocking, isn't it? Anyway, we picked him up as contract labor. Flew black missions, Air America, you know the story."

"I do indeed. I imagine he violated some neutrality for us, too."

"I'm afraid so," Christmann said. "He was a good pilot. One of our best — maybe *the* best. Especially in a C-130 Hercules. In pitch darkness, people said, he could land a Herc on a handball court. Called him Batman. If a mission was really dicey, and insertion and extraction was going to be really tough, our people would say, 'Batman flies it or I don't go.'

"When we realized we needed a really good Herc pilot for the hostage rescue, we tracked down Holbrook. He was working for his father, but the two of them never got along, so he took a sabbatical. He hated the plan from the beginning. Thought it more likely that we'd get the hostages killed than get them out. Said that to everybody who'd listen. A regular Cassandra. He crashed and burned twice on this mission, once during the planning stage and once in the desert in Iran. So, when the mission came apart, who better to blame than Holbrook?"

"Standard agency procedure," Malloy said, directing his sarcasm to Tolman. "Silence your critics and give yourself a scapegoat, all at once." Malloy turned back to Christmann. "Did it stick?"

"No. Tolman was right. The problem was sandstorms. There were eight big Navy helicopters flying across the desert. They couldn't fly high enough to get over the sandstorms, and they sucked a ton of grit into their turbines. One crashed. Two others had to turn back. Then Holbrook had his C-130 parked on a makeshift runway, and somebody drove a helicopter right into it. Both birds burned and a lot of people with them. The mission was stripped of reserves for contingencies, and Carter aborted it."

"So, none of this was Holbrook's fault," Tolman said.

"Of course not. That didn't stop us from trying to blame it on him, of course," Christmann replied. "What really made people mad was that the raid failed almost exactly as Holbrook had been warning people it would. He'd made them look bad, so they had to make him look bad. Problem was, enough people survived the desert crash to tell the congressional committees that Holbrook wasn't the one to blame. His big black Herc was parked where it belonged. Some other guy blundered into it in the dark."

"Does this have any bearing on why you warned him that the fibbies were about to pounce?" Malloy asked.

"Indirectly, yes. I'd been looking at him for several weeks. There was something funny going on. The people he works for on that yacht were moving a lot of money around. Really huge amounts, hundreds of millions of dollars, in and out of Swiss accounts. Then they sent out a press release about how they were converting their yacht into an oceanographic research ship. All of this had started happening shortly after the granddaughter of one of the other owners got kidnapped, held for a week, and then returned minus a hand.

"I suspected that they were the target of some extortion plot, and were going along rather than calling in the law. I know that our mission doesn't include foiling extortion plots, but a couple of these guys are big defense contractors. In their case, there's potential for security leaks. Anyway, I began to snoop around a little, then my fearless leader, James Malloy, tells me to lay off."

"Word came down from upstairs," said Malloy. "'These are good people. Leave them alone.' I passed it along."

"Right. That pissed me off, so I went and really leaned on Holbrook. Made him tell me what's going on."

"Note how well this agent follows orders," Malloy said to Tolman. "If you want a good career in the company, you should emulate him."

Christman laughed. "He wouldn't tell me everything. He still doesn't trust the agency. Few do. He did tell me that he has a plan to retrieve three nukes that were stolen in Germany last year. Asked us politely to leave him alone to do it. Refused all offers of help. And said that if I did him one small favor, he'd give all the credit for retrieving the boom-booms to the good old CIA."

"And you believed him?" Malloy asked, in a tone of awe and disbelief.

"I did, partly because of the favor he asked, and partly because of what's in his dossier. If you want my opinion, the guy's a fucking Boy Scout. I'm certain that he really is going after those nukes. Strangely enough, I think he actually might have a chance to succeed. So when the fibbies were about to screw things up, I warned him."

The HH-65 Dolphin helicopter from USCGC *Escanaba* flew toward the southeast through the night. Two senior Coast Guard officers were aboard: *Escanaba*'s captain and the commandant of the First Coast Guard District. Three federal law enforcement officers were with them — two from ATF and the third from the FBI. None of the five passengers was in a good mood. The aircraft had refueled on the cutter's flight deck a half-hour earlier, then flown to the roof of the Coast Guard headquarters on Atlantic Avenue in Boston. There, her distinguished passengers had embarked in stony silence. The flight seaward had taken only ten minutes, during which time none of the passengers had said a word to any of the others. As they approached *Escanaba*, the cutter's captain spoke to the pilot. "Fly alongside this so-called yacht for a minute. I want a look at her."

Smoothly transitioning to a near hover, the helo took station on *Seafire*'s starboard beam. The yacht was showing the required running lights, and her white hull was clearly visible in the light of the nearly full moon. The passengers looked at her without speaking for a minute or so.

"I'll be damned," said the commandant, Rear Admiral James Baumgardner. "She really is an old Fletcher. Making good speed for an old lady, too."

Agent Norton of the FBI said nothing in reply. If he had his way, they'd be putting torpedoes into the old bird's gizzard. Norton reached under his coat and touched the holstered pistol under his armpit. Warm from the heat of his body, it felt comforting to his touch, like a small pet. "Can't we just land on her and arrest these assholes?" he asked.

"No way," the pilot replied. "She's got her own helicopter parked on her deck. If we tried to land, our rotor blades would hit hers, and we'd crash."

"Let's go aboard *Escanaba*," said the admiral, and the helicopter began a wide turn to starboard. It touched down on the cutter's landing deck, and four of the passengers disembarked. Then, the helo flew off again, carrying one of the ATF agents. It headed east.

"Captain on the bridge!" shouted the quartermaster of the watch as Commander Peter Goldman stepped into *Escanaba*'s pilothouse. For a moment or two he looked around, pleased at what he saw. Young Lieutenant Monaco had the deck and the conn, and the bridge was fully staffed with competent men and women. His ship had gotten underway in a hell of a hurry with only the duty section aboard, and the watch appeared pretty damn professional. The admiral was looking around the bridge as well, and Goldman could see he'd reached the same conclusion. The captain felt an intense surge of pride in his ship and his troops. Every so often in life, you have to answer a bell in a hurry. *Escanaba* had answered this one very well.

"Lieutenant Monaco," Goldman said, "I'd like you to meet Admiral Baumgardner, Commandant, First District."

Giulia Monaco saluted, and the admiral returned the salute. "We've met, sir," said the lieutenant. "Welcome aboard."

"Thank you, Lieutenant Monaco," the admiral said, "Why don't you give us your report?"

"Aye, aye, sir. Shortly after 1600 hours we received telephoned orders from the admiral's headquarters to sortie in pursuit of the private yacht, *Seafire*. Just prior to that time we'd observed *Seafire* depart her pier in East Boston in a hurried manner. In fact, I had personally remarked at her unorthodox procedures in getting underway. We started engines, cut shore power and communications lines, singled up lines, and were underway within twenty minutes of our receipt of the sortie order."

"Well done, Lieutenant," said the admiral. "Especially as you were short handed."

"Thank you, admiral, but the credit should go to the enlisted men, not me. I just told the chiefs, 'Get us outta here,' and they did.

"*Seafire* had a head start on us that translated to about four miles, once we got going. Then they took a shortcut that gained them another mile or two. They gained a bit more on us through sheer speed, but they've slowed down some recently."

"What was the shortcut?" asked Goldman.

"They went to sea through Hypocrite Channel. At dusk. At twenty knots. I thought about following them, but I chickened out. We went out the North Channel, and around the Graves. It cost us nearly two miles."

"And avoided placing the ship and her crew at an unacceptable risk," said the admiral. "A very wise decision, young woman. Chickens are extremely stupid birds, you know. Avoiding unnecessary danger is not chickening out."

"Yes, admiral," said Giulia Monaco. "Thank you, sir."

Admiral Baumgardner looked at the radar repeater for a moment. "The old lady has led us on a merry chase. We'll put an end to that tomorrow."

Aboard *Seafire*, Bill Jackson watched the radar screen. *Escanaba*'s helicopter was still flying east, more than thirty miles out. Soon, it would be out of radar range, over the horizon. Where the hell are they going? he asked himself. He worried that he'd get an answer soon. An answer he wouldn't like.

Jim Malloy read the dispatch that had just been handed to him. Then he read it again. Handing the paper to Christmann, he said, "Well, Bill, it looks like your friends are going to get bagged, after all. The Coast Guard has upped the ante. Tomorrow morning *Hamilton* is going to get into the act. She carries Harpoon antiship missiles, and it looks like she's going to use them."

For a moment or two, Christmann said nothing. "I don't believe it," he said, finally. "Those things are lethal! They'll sink *Seafire* and kill everybody aboard. How in hell can they justify using deadly force just to stop a ship that has a couple of machine guns aboard, and won't pull over when the cops tell them to? Haven't we learned anything from Waco and Ruby Ridge?"

"They're going to wait until dawn. They'll shoot an exercise missile across *Seafire*'s bow. If that doesn't work, they'll shoot a real warshot, with the explosives removed from the warhead. It'll hit the ship, and do some damage, but it won't sink her."

"And after that?" Christmann asked.

"I don't think they've decided that yet. Theory is that *Seafire* will heave to when the missiles start flying. I tend to agree with that."

Christmann was not so sure. He was thinking of a rookie naval aviator who'd killed four MIGs in four minutes. No, thought Christmann, if they want to stop that ship, they'll have to sink her. He kept his thoughts to himself. "When does this start?" he asked.

"Tomorrow, 0800 hours," said Malloy.

"It would be nice to have a Nightbird up, so we can watch the fun," Christmann said.

"Already laid on," Malloy replied. "I wouldn't miss this for the world."

United States Coast Guard Cutter *Hamilton* was one of a dozen ships of the class that bore her name. In Coast Guard jargon, ship and boat classes are designated by length. The "378s" or "378-footers" were High Endurance cutters — bigger, faster, and able to remain at sea longer than any other ships in the service. The first in the class, *Hamilton* was the oldest, having been launched in 1965 and commissioned in 1967. No youngster, she was nevertheless fully fit, having been overhauled and refitted in a Fleet Rehabilitation and Modernization (FRAM) program in 1987. Part of her rehab had been the removal of some obsolete antisubmarine gear, and the installation of a Harpoon anti-ship missile battery. On this cold morning, some of her missiles were going to fly.

Like *Seafire*, *Hamilton* carried an unorthodox power plant and had no steam boilers. The 378s basic propulsion system was a pair of huge Fairbanks-Morse diesels with 3500 horsepower each. With the diesels driving the twin, variable pitch propellers,

Hamilton could reach a top speed of just under nineteen knots. When she was in a hurry, however, the big cutter had another option — jet power. She carried two Pratt & Whitney FT-4A6 gas turbine engines with combined power of 36,000 horses, enough to move *Hamilton* at nearly thirty knots. Each turbine could be connected to one of the prop shafts. Fuel economy was terrible on the turbines, they were the least fuel-efficient marine engines ever built. On a Boeing 707, for which they'd been designed, they could be throttled back when the plane got to cruising altitude. At sea, the turbines were never throttled down. As *Hamilton* sped to bring her missiles within range of an unseen target beyond the horizon, the turbines were at full power. They were burning three thousand gallons of fuel an hour, a consumption rate twenty-five times that of the diesels. Fortunately, the chase wasn't going to be a long one. At this speed, *Hamilton* would be out of fuel in a day and a half.

The High Endurance cutter had been at sea for over a week when the orders had come to head southwest. Normally stationed in the Pacific, she had returned to Atlantic waters on an urgent mission — to save the cod and haddock on George's Bank. Nearing commercial extinction, these species had been declared off-limits to fishing by both the United States and Canada. A moratorium on harvesting the fish had been imposed to allow the stocks to rebound. Yet, poachers were stripping the surviving fish from the bank, threatening to destroy the resource forever. *Hamilton* was part of the response. Parked in the middle of the Bank for weeks at a time, sweeping the sea with her radars and with her helicopter on the prowl, she was the best defense against the poachers. By coincidence, she was perfectly placed to cut off *Seafire*'s escape.

At 0645, Lt. James Storey, *Hamilton*'s weapons officer, was busy on the cutter's deck. The ship was preparing to fire an exercise missile from her Harpoon battery. The missiles were housed in eight canisters, in two groups of four, mounted on the 0-1 deck below the bridge. Safety procedure when firing an exercise round was strict. The canister to be fired had to be opened and visually inspected to be certain that the missile inside really was a training round and not a warshot. Then, each of the other seven canisters had to be manually disabled to eliminate any possibility of a warbird flying by mistake. This was Storey's job for the moment. Although junior personnel would do the physical work, the actual verification was something he could not delegate. He looked at his watch, there was time enough. The firing was scheduled for 0800, over an hour away. The sun had risen at 0615 or so, and the men who would do the work were beginning to straggle up from breakfast, squinting and blinking in the bright morning light.

Meanwhile, in *Hamilton*'s combat information center, Lt. Bill Martin, the operations officer, was watching as his men tracked their target. Over sixty miles away, she was over the horizon and far out of radar range, yet there she was on the scopes. It was a trick, of course, the target was a simulation. *Escanaba*, herself over the horizon, was tracking the target with her fire control radar. That data, together with Escanaba's GPS position information, was being relayed to *Hamilton* constantly via data link. The 378-foot cutter would never see the target, she didn't have to. Her little sister would be all the eyes she would need.

Bill Jackson was tired. He'd gotten only two or three hours of sleep and he wasn't used to it. He'd insisted that the owners get as much sleep as possible, and, mostly, they had complied. Jackson was certain that the Coasties were up to something, and he wanted his people rested.

The helicopter had caused Jackson's wariness. He'd watched on the air search radar as it flew east at 140 knots until it disappeared. Later, he'd watched it return. The round trip had taken just over an hour and a half. Assuming a quick turnaround, the helo must have flown about a hundred miles each way. Perhaps less, but certainly not more. Why? There was no land out there. There could be only one answer. There was a ship to seaward of *Seafire*, a ship to which *Escanaba*'s helicopter had flown and returned.

At 0600, Jackson had awakened George Holbrook, and told him what he suspected. Holbrook had gone to speak with Roth and Knight in CIC. It was close to seven when Holbrook returned to the bridge. He'd called Suvia Ferris shortly before leaving combat, and she arrived on the bridge with him.

"What's up?' she asked.

"Bill had a theory that there was a ship east of here. Navy or Coast Guard. Unfortunately, he was right. It's the *Hamilton*, a big Coast Guard cutter, and it looks like she's going to start shooting missiles at us."

"What?" said Suvia. "How do you know?"

"Knight and Roth have been working on that computer of theirs all night. They asked it to analyze all of the radio signals from *Escanaba*." Holbrook gestured astern. "They've been talking on the radio. The signal is scrambled, of course, but the computer broke the code."

"What about the missiles?"

"*Hamilton* is about sixty miles away. She's going to fire a Harpoon missile at eight o'clock. It will be a dummy, a training shot. Supposedly, it will scare us into surrendering."

"That would scare a lot of people," interjected Jackson. "Those things fly at about six hundred miles an hour. An exercise model would fly right at us, then veer off at the last minute and parachute into the water. I suppose they'd call us on the radio and say, 'The next one is the real thing,' or something like that."

"Are they still calling us on the radio?" Suvia asked.

"Oh sure," George replied. "Every ten minutes. We don't answer, of course. We're pretending we don't hear them. They know damn well we do hear them, and we know they know we do, but we still pretend we don't. I'm sure that it pisses them off."

"Enough to shoot a missile at us?" Suvia asked indignantly.

"Yeah, but just a dummy missile."

"If they're sixty miles away, how can they shoot any missile at us?" Jackson asked. "We're out of radar range. They wouldn't just fire it blind, they might hit *Escanaba* or some poor lobsterman."

"*Escanaba* maybe, she's close enough to our size. Lobster boat, no. In addition to its own onboard radar, the missile has an optical sensor that recognizes ship types. It will be looking for a destroyer type. To answer your question, Bill, *Escanaba* has us on her fire control radar. Her computer's passing the targeting information directly to *Hamilton*. So far as *Hamilton*'s fire control computers are concerned, we're on her radar as well."

"What are we going to do, George?" Suvia asked.

George Holbrook began to explain about Satan's Cloak.

* * * * *

At 0712, *Escanaba*'s fire control radar went dead. It was still transmitting, but the receiver wasn't picking up any echoes and the screen went blank. At the same time, a number of unusual events occurred on the ship. All of the radios hummed loudly, in a deep and resonant tone, for two or three seconds. The other radars, the air and sea-search units, showed transmission spikes through broad arcs. The passive ECM gear went crazy, showing emissions all over the spectrum, and then it, too, went dead. And, throughout the ship, anyone in a darkened space who was wearing a watch with a luminous dial saw it glow like a beacon. In CIC, the senior petty officer asked the question for everyone, "What the fuck was that?"

Sixty miles away, *Hamilton*'s ECM gear picked up the power surge, and there, too, it caused much consternation. Not nearly as much consternation, though, as when the crew in CIC realized several seconds later that their data link with *Escanaba* had just been severed.

In less than a minute, *Escanaba*'s leading electronic technician had the console open and read the bad news. The fire control radar was a total loss. Massive arcing had fused most of the receiver side into glass. Some parts were simply gone, vaporized. It would be days, weeks perhaps, before the radar could be repaired. They might as well just get a new one. On the bridge, Captain Goldman explained to Agent Norton what it meant.

"Our radar was sending information to *Hamilton*. She used it to develop a fire control solution. Without it, the solution will degrade. Look, *Seafire* is changing course. By eight o'clock the solution will be useless. Who knows where the missile would go?"

"So, why don't we shoot now, while the solution isn't degraded?" Norton asked. He was getting angry again. He'd watched that damned ship get away once. He wasn't going to let that happen again.

Admiral Baumgardner replied, "*Hamilton* probably isn't ready yet. There are a lot of things to do before you can shoot an exercise missile. Safety checks and so forth. The sun's only been up for an hour, I doubt if they could have done them all."

Norton replied in a tone of disgust, "Isn't the Coast Guard's motto *Semper Paratus*? Always Ready? I hate to say this, Admiral, but I haven't seen a whole lot of that this morning!"

Stung by the criticism, the admiral picked up the radiotelephone microphone. "*Hamilton*, this is First Coast Guard District One. Let me speak with *Hamilton* One, over."

In a moment came the reply, as the cutter's commanding officer replied personally, as ordered, "This is *Hamilton* One. Good morning, Admiral. Over."

"I want you to fire that bird now, Tom," said the admiral. "I repeat, fire it now."

There was a moment's pause, and when *Hamilton*'s skipper replied, it was with a tone of real concern. "We haven't completed the safety protocol, Admiral. We can be ready to fire in a half hour, no sooner."

Admiral Baumgardner watched Norton as the FBI man shook

his head in disgust, then made a decision. "Fire it now," he said. "Disregard the protocol. On my authority. Fire it now."

For a moment there was silence on *Hamilton*'s bridge. Her captain looked down at the deck below; several men were working around the Harpoon canisters. "Mr. Storey," the captain said, shouting down from the port wing of the bridge. "Get those men out of there. We're firing in three minutes." Into another microphone he continued to speak. "Combat, bridge. This is the captain. Stand by to fire the exercise missile in three minutes!"

The crew in CIC were caught completely off guard. Their fire control solution was still fresh, but few of the final initialization steps had been taken. Target location was already loaded into the missile, but target profile wasn't. The ops boss realized that he didn't know what the target looked like, and therefore couldn't tell the missile what to look for. "Request target description!" he shouted into the intercom.

On the bridge, the captain, too, realized that he had no idea of the physical characteristics of the ship they were chasing. To the ATF agent who was standing beside him, he said, "Have you seen this ship."

"Sure, yesterday."

"What does she look like."

"Big yacht. Maybe three hundred feet long. Painted white."

The captain relayed the information to CIC. "As soon as the profile data is loaded, I want you to fire. Tell me when you're ready, and I'll free the battery."

Thirty seconds passed, and once again the intercom crackled. It was Lieutenant Storey. "Captain, I must protest. The battery is not safe!"

"Protest noted, Mr. Storey. Report to the bridge and I'll explain what's going on."

Another thirty seconds passed, and Storey stepped onto *Hamilton*'s bridge. Just at that moment CIC reported ready and the captain gave the order to fire. With a roar, a sheet of smoke and flame flashed up and around the bridge. Jim Storey watched with fascination as, for 2.9 seconds, the missile's solid booster hurled her to nearly the speed of sound. Then, as he watched the missile transition to cruise, he realized with horror and disbelief that it was white. It was not the orange practice shot he had just sighted in canister number one. This bird was a live round. "God help us, Captain," he said. "Warshot away."

Steve Roth called *Seafire*'s bridge on the intercom. His voice conveyed agitation verging on panic. "*Hamilton* is calling on the radio. Not scrambled. Says they just fired a Harpoon missile at us by mistake. A real one. It will be here in six minutes."

"Wonderful," said George Holbrook. "Did they say anything else?"

"They said they're very sorry. Shall I reply."

"Yes. Tell them 'message acknowledged.' No, better yet, patch the radio up to the bridge so I can talk to them."

A moment later, Holbrook spoke over the radio. "*Hamilton*, this is *Seafire*. Tell me about this missile. Quickly!"

"It's fully armed," was the reply. *Hamilton* One was doing the talking, although Holbrook neither knew nor cared. "Five hundred pound warhead. I suggest you stop and abandon ship immediately."

"Thank you for the suggestion," George said, the sarcasm clear in his voice. "I might have one or two for you, as well. What is its flight profile?"

"Standard Harpoon. Straight and low with its radar off. About ten miles out it pops up and turns on its radar to acquire the target. The attack phase is a dive."

"Kilo uniform band radar?"

"Affirmative."

"If the radar is jammed, or doesn't work for some reason, what happens?"

"It'll get you anyway. It will circle the last known target position, and search optically. It's programmed to kill a three hundred-foot white-hulled ship. Radar or no radar, it's going to hit you. For God's sake, abandon ship!"

George Holbrook put down the handset and looked at his watch. Four minutes to impact. Something was nagging at his subconscious, and in an instant, he realized what it was. "Jackson!" he shouted. "Reverse course! Tell Finnerty to put on as much speed as he can!" He called CIC on the intercom. "Get the damn Cloak ready," he shouted. "The lasers, too. I'm coming down.

"Let's go down to combat, Suvia!" George said. He bolted from the bridge, and down the ladder to the lower deck in huge bounds, Suvia behind him.

The mood aboard *Escanaba* was one of shock and dismay. Both Admiral Baumgardner and Captain Goldman knew the Harpoon's characteristics. It was a fire and forget missile. *Hamilton* could not destroy it, call it back, or divert it. All control was severed when the bird left its canister. Now, all anyone could do was pray that it would malfunction, though there was little chance of that. Harpoons have a nearly perfect success rate. Captain Goldman ordered *Escanaba*'s helo readied for immediate takeoff to pick up survivors. It was all he could do.

Lieutenant Monaco was on the bridge, watching *Seafire*. At the Coast Guard Academy, she had seen a damage control video, showing HMS *Sheffield* on fire after being hit by an Exocet missile. The fire was so hot that the aluminum in her superstructure was burning. *Sheffield* had been lost, along with many lives aboard her.

The terrible images of the burning ship flashed in Monaco's memory. A live missile, not very different from an Exocet, was going to hit the ship ahead of them in the next four minutes. The horror was overwhelming. As Monaco watched, she saw that *Seafire* had begun a turn to starboard. And, while it was hard to tell at this distance, the yacht seemed to be picking up speed.

"She's turned toward us," said Admiral Baumgardner. "Why?" The radio messages between *Seafire* and *Hamilton* had been in the clear, and everyone on *Escanaba*'s bridge had heard them.

"She probably thinks we have an anti-missile capability," the captain replied. "We don't, of course, but she probably thinks we do. They think if they get close enough, we can help them."

"Maybe so," said the admiral. "Or, maybe they want to be close to us when they get hit, so we can take off survivors. Jesus Christ, what a mess."

"I don't believe this," said Jim Malloy. "I do not fucking believe it." Word that the missile firing had been advanced had come to him only minutes before, and he had rushed to the war room just as the Harpoon had been fired. The recon aircraft had been on station early, thankfully, and live pictures were on screen. All the Nightbird pilot had to do was orbit the op area; controllers on the ground aimed and focused the cameras. *Hamilton* was out of range of the video link, but her radio transmissions were loud and clear. Malloy watched in living color as *Seafire* began her turn toward *Escanaba*, just as Christmann and Tolman ran into the room.

"What's going on?" Christmann demanded.

"A fucking disaster, that's what," Malloy replied. "At least this one isn't our fault."

As he listened to the audio, Christmann quickly agreed with

Malloy's first observation. As to the second, to his personal dismay, he wasn't so sure.

Suvia Ferris was right behind George Holbrook as he hurried into the computer-filled room that they called the combat information center, or CIC. The room was crowded, Bob Knight, the Roths, and Carsons were all there already, George and Suvia made seven.

"Three minutes," said a familiar voice, and Suvia was startled by it. It was the computer's voice synthesizer, and it had been programmed to sound like Walter Cronkite.

"Why did we turn?" asked Grace Roth.

"Two reasons," George answered. "First, we don't want to be where the missile thinks we're going to be. It's programmed to fly to a point, and then look for us. By turning around, we're going to be as far as possible from the aim point. Second, the description those idiots on *Hamilton* programmed into the missile is a lot closer to *Escanaba* than it is to us. If the missile goes after her, I want us to be close enough to try to shoot it down. Normally, she would have a slim chance against a Harpoon. Thanks to us, she now has no fire control radar, which reduces her chances to zip."

"Check," said Steve Roth. "We're doing almost thirty knots. With them at twenty, the range is closing at nearly a mile a minute. Range in three minutes will be about six miles."

"Can you handle that?"

It was Bob Knight who answered. "Don't know," he said. "Hitting a crossing target will be a lot harder than nailing something heading right at us. At six miles, it will be iffy."

"Two minutes," said the voice.

"OK," said George. "Here's the plan. Use Satan's Cloak to blind the missile's radar. Don't shoot the laser unless we're sure the missile is going to hit either us or *Escanaba*."

"Got it," said Steve Roth. "Ready, Bob?"

"Ready," Bob Knight replied. "*Watson*, Cloak to standby."

The computer's voice filled the room. "Cloak on standby. Ready to fire on your order."

"Cloak target will appear to starboard," Knight said. "Cloak target is a kilo uniform band radar. Cloak to fire upon target immediately as target is detected. Cloak is free to fire. *Watson*, confirm."

"Confirming. Cloak free to fire on kilo uniform radar upon detection. Standing by to fire."

"*Watson*, ruby laser to standby. Air action starboard. Ruby laser target will be a missile. Missile will appear at a range of approximately ten miles. Acquire but do not fire ruby laser until my order. *Watson*, confirm."

"Confirming. Ruby laser is on standby. Target is a missile. Ruby laser is not free to fire."

"One minute," said *Watson*. "Missile identified. Tracking missile. Target acquired."

"There it is!" said George, looking at a radar picture on one of the consoles. The missile had popped up from its surface hugging approach, and was finally visible to the air search radar. It was ten miles away, and clearly heading to a point astern of *Seafire*, where she would have been if she hadn't turned.

"Kilo uniform band radar detected. Source is target missile," said *Watson* in his calm anchorman's voice. "Cloak firing. Kilo uniform radar transmissions have ceased. Cloak has ceased firing."

"Small unit," said Steve Roth. "Receiver must have taken out the transmitter when it blew. Too bad it didn't blow up the whole damn missile."

"Thirty seconds," said *Watson*. "Tracking missile. Missile not on intercept course. Ruby laser on standby. Ruby laser not free to fire."

Five miles away from *Seafire*, the Harpoon missile began to search for its prey. The target wasn't where it was supposed to be, and the missile's electronic brain was receiving no information from the radar. Off to starboard, its TV eye could see a possible target. The Harpoon turned to investigate.

"Missile turning," said *Watson*. "Missile inbound."

"Hold fire 'til we're sure," said George. "We don't want to show off our laser unless we have to."

From three miles away, the Harpoon missile compared the optical picture of the ship ahead to the data stored in its onboard computer. Too big, it decided, in the on-or-off, yes-or-no logic of computers. This is not the target. It turned again, heading back toward the initial aim point. From there, it would spiral out until it found its target, or ran out of fuel, whichever came first.

Aboard *Seafire*, on her bridge and in her CIC, there was a simultaneous sigh of relief as the Harpoon missile turned back to port and astern of the ship. "Don't celebrate yet," said George. "That damn thing is going to sniff around for something to hit." Even as he spoke, the radar screen showed the missile making a broad turn to starboard, a turn that would take her close to *Escanaba*.

"*Watson*," said Knight. "Analysis of missile track."

"Missile circling right. Track will intersect a surface target four decimal nine two miles ahead."

There was silence in *Seafire*'s CIC. George and Suvia's eyes met. The surface target was a ship with over a hundred people on it.

▬ ▬ ▬ ▬ ▬

"Sixty seconds to impact," said the voice on the intercom from *Escanaba*'s CIC. Lieutenant Monaco looked to the west, searching for the missile. She saw nothing. The Harpoon was too small and too far away. A strange fear came over her, as once again the film of *Sheffield* in flames played in her mind. Her fear was strange in that it was not for herself. She was afraid for her shipmates, but far more for *Escanaba*. In the movie in her mind, it wasn't men dying. The creature in its last agony was a ship.

"Conventional tactic is to turn away to take the hit astern, Admiral," Captain Goldman said. "But, I'm going to maintain course. We have a lot JP-5 back aft for the helo, plus the helo itself. A beam hit is less likely to croak us than taking the missile astern."

Admiral Baumgardner nodded as Goldman picked up the ship's intercom microphone. "All hands stand by for missile strike. Move as far as possible from the starboard side of the ship. Brace yourselves for impact. Stand, do not sit. Keep your knees flexed, not locked. I will count down to impact. Thirty seconds." Goldman thought wistfully of the Phalanx anti-missile system on *Hamilton*'s stern. That high-speed, computer-aimed cannon would come in handy about now, he thought.

▬ ▬ ▬ ▬ ▬

"*Watson*," said Knight. "Count down time to missile impact on surface target."

"Fifty-four seconds to impact," said the voice of the computer, and George Holbrook looked at the radar. The two ships were still converging at a combined speed of nearly fifty knots. In less than a minute, *Seafire* would be within the effective range of *Escanaba's* three-inch gun.

"*Watson.* Air action port," Roth said. "Target missile. Range ten miles. Identify and acquire."

Almost instantly, the computer replied. "Target identified and acquired previously. Continuing to track target. Ruby laser on standby. Ruby laser not free to fire."

"*Watson.* Ruby laser battery to bear."

"Acknowledged. Bringing battery to bear. Battery bearing on target. Battery locked on target. Range to target eight decimal two miles. Time to impact thirty seconds."

"Wait 'til we're sure it's attacking," George said.

"Can we hit it?" Suvia asked.

"I think so," answered Steve Roth. "At four or five miles, the laser did pretty well in tests against target drones. That Harpoon is nothing more than a drone with a bomb aboard."

"Fifteen seconds to impact," said *Watson.* "Missile diving toward surface target. Ten seconds to impact."

"*Watson,*" said Bob Knight. "Ruby laser free to fire. Shoot."

From the odd-looking housing on the flying bridge, a pencil of bright red light cut through the morning sky. There was no noise, no crash and roar of gunfire, just the red light, unbearably brilliant and completely silent. *Seafire*, ex-*Watson*, ex-*Yellow Rose* fired her first shot in anger without making a sound.

On the video monitor screens in the situation room at Langley, the Harpoon missile was clearly visible, streaking down in its attack dive. None of the people in the room said a word. They merely stared in horrible fascination from their bird's eye perspective as death sped toward *Escanaba* at six hundred miles an hour.

Behind her, Lieutenant Monaco could hear the captain counting down for the crew. Five seconds. There! Off the starboard beam she could see the missile, tiny and deadly in its flight. Five seconds. Once again, the fear overwhelmed her, and she spoke instinctively, saying the words the nuns had taught her long ago. "Hail, Mary," she said, and the world turned to fire.

— — — — —

"Mother of God," said James Malloy, as he watched the screen, trying to decipher what he had just seen. The Harpoon missile had exploded in midair, less than a quarter of a mile from *Escanaba*. And in the instant before the explosion, there had been a line on the screen, a red line, like a stream of tracer bullets. The line had intersected the missile just before it had exploded. Malloy had no idea what the red line was, but he was sure of two things. It had destroyed the missile, and it had come from *Seafire*.

— — — — —

For several seconds after the explosion, there was silence throughout *Seafire*. The missile had exploded so close to the cutter that, at first, the people aboard her weren't sure *Escanaba* hadn't been hit. When he realized that the laser had succeeded, George Holbrook felt no elation whatever, only a profound sense of relief. He checked the radar. *Escanaba* was less than four miles away. Holbrook keyed the microphone to speak to the bridge. "Let's reverse course, Bill," he said. "Just in case these guys show their gratitude by shooting at us."

— — — — —

Malloy watched the real-time color pictures on the screen. *Seafire*, slicing through a high-speed turn, carved a white crescent in the cobalt blue of the North Atlantic. "Gentlemen," he said, "I believe we just watched a private yacht shoot down a Harpoon missile at a range of four miles." Beside him, Bill Christmann was beginning to laugh.

"Now I know why they turned around," Christmann said. "They came back to save the Coasties from their own missile. What did I say about Holbrook? A fucking Boy Scout!"

"I concur. That's *why* they did it. I want to know *how* they did it. There's not a ship in the U.S. Navy, or any other navy for that matter, that can destroy an anti-ship missile four miles away. How did they do it?"

"With a laser," said Christmann, still laughing. "A really big one. Holbrook showed it to me."

"*Seafire*'s turning again," said *Escanaba*'s captain. "God, she's a beautiful ship." The damage control reports were coming in — no damage or casualties. Admiral Baumgardner agreed with Goldman's opinion of *Seafire*'s looks. He, too, was feeling a sense of personal relief. *Hamilton* had fired in haste on his authority. Had there been blood, it would have been on his hands.

"Do you know what I'm thinking?" Goldman asked.

"That what she needs is some racing stripes on that pretty white hull of hers?"

"Exactly. You think so too, Admiral?"

"Of course. Look at her move! What do you make her speed to be, lieutenant?"

Lieutenant Monaco consulted the surface search radar for a moment or two. "Twenty-eight knots at least. Maybe thirty, Admiral."

Goldman chuckled. "I wonder where that speed was last night."

"Perhaps they didn't want to show it to us," said the admiral, as he, too, began to laugh.

"Hey!" said ATF Agent Stern. "She's getting away! That ship must be in range now. Shoot, for Christ's sake!"

"That ship just saved *this* ship from a missile hit," said the admiral in an icy tone. "She may have saved your life and mine. Are you seriously asking me to shoot at her?"

"I'm not *asking*! I'm *ordering* you to shoot. I don't give a rat's ass whose life that ship saved, I want it stopped!"

Without realizing it, Stern had just called off the chase. The admiral, concealing his rage, said, "You, sir, are an official of the Justice Department. I, on the other hand, am a member of a semi-military organization under the general superintendence of the Transportation Department. Therefore, you are not in a position to *order* me to do anything. At the *request* of your agency and the FBI, we set off yesterday in a great hurry after a private yacht believed to be smuggling machine guns. At the *request* of your agency, *Hamilton* hastily fired a missile that could have killed many innocent people. The ship we're chasing may look like the *Love Boat*, but she carries weapons like the Starship *Enterprise*. I don't think you people have the foggiest idea who or what we're chasing. I know I don't. Accordingly, I am ordering this ship and *Hamilton* to return to port. If you want somebody to shoot at those people, call the Navy!"

Agent Stern opened his mouth to speak.

"One more word out of you, and I'll have you thrown in the brig," said the admiral.

Red-faced, Stern turned and left the bridge.

"Your men are tired, Captain," the admiral said. "Running shorthanded was hard work, and they did a good job. Let's take them home." The admiral took a few steps toward the companionway, then turned. "Send a message to *Seafire*, please. From me, personally. Wish her fair winds and following seas. Tell her if she ever wants to join the Coast Guard, I'll paint the racing stripes on her myself!"

As Suvia Ferris stepped onto the bridge, George Holbrook could tell she was bringing good news. For the first time in hours she looked relaxed and happy. George felt a familiar twinge of affection for her and, for once, did not try to make it go away. He smiled in response to her smile and was rewarded to see her brighten even more.

"Interesting stuff on the radio after you left, George. Very interesting stuff. The Coast Guard cutters are returning to Boston."

"Excellent!" said George. Bill Jackson shouted, "Yes!" and thrust a clenched fist skyward. He narrowly missed smashing his knuckles on the overhead.

"We heard the admiral order *Hamilton* back to port. He's figured out that the missile had been loaded with a target profile that matched the ship he was on, and he's not amused."

"I'll bet," Bill Jackson said.

"The admiral had a message for us, too."

"What was it?"

"It was kind of lengthy, but basically, it amounted to 'Thanks.' At the end, another voice came on and added something else. Like an afterthought. I think it was the admiral himself. I didn't understand it, so wrote it down. 'Finex, bravo zulu,' he said. It sounded like a joke. What does it mean?"

Bill Jackson laughed. George Holbrook felt a sudden rush of pride in his shipmates and his ship. "You're right, Suvia," he said. "It was a joke, an inside joke. It means that the training exercise has concluded, and we got a high score."

Suvia considered this for a moment. "It must be a guy thing," she said. "I don't see the humor in it at all."

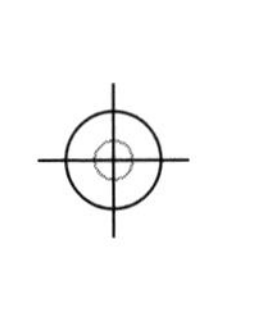

CHAPTER 12

DIRECTOR OF CENTRAL INTELLIGENCE is the title of the senior officer of the CIA. Most people in government use the acronym DCI. At the interface between the worlds of politics and espionage, politicians hold the position more often than spies. The most famous DCI, George Herbert Walker Bush, had gone on to higher political office. Others had gone on to ruin and disgrace. Christmann knew that the current director had no illusions about the former possibility, but he was deeply committed to avoiding the latter. The DCI had made it clear that the *Seafire* situation could evolve into a disaster and bring enormous discredit to the agency, which was already under attack. With the Soviet menace evaporated, a lot of people on Capitol Hill questioned the need to have a

CIA at all. The DCI wanted nothing further to go wrong concerning *Seafire*. Failing that, he wanted somebody outside the agency to be blamed for it.

The meeting was a large one; senior staff from all four directorates of the agency were present. In the three weeks that *Seafire* had been at sea, she had been monitored constantly, in an effort to learn her intentions and ultimate destination. Little had been learned. The ship had headed south, refueling twice. After her dash out of Boston, she had slowed to an economical cruising speed of twelve and a half knots, three hundred nautical miles a day. Now, she was at the island of St. Helena, refueling again. At each refueling point, she had met with a tanker of the Argeriardis fleet. She had taken on fuel in remote bays rather than entering restricted harbors, and thereby avoided placing herself in a position to be boarded and seized by local authorities.

Bill Christmann took a mental attendance. There were nearly twenty men and women in the room, most of whom he did not know by name. The deputy director for operations, DDO, Jim Malloy's direct supervisor was there. Malloy was there, too, sitting beside Christmann. That was a good omen. If Jim had distanced himself from Bill, it would have meant bad news.

Christmann recognized three of the tekkies from the Office of Research and Development. Their boss, the deputy director for science and technology, was talking to the DCI. The second in command of the agency was present as well. Her title was deputy director of central intelligence, DDCI. The deputy director for intelligence was absent, but three of his people from the Office of Scientific and Weapons Research were in attendance. They were speaking with a group of men and women who could be recognized as wonky scientists at a range of fifty yards.

Christmann was bewildered. This wasn't the way the company did business. Twenty people in a room, including four of the top six officers? A meeting of four or five people was considered a crowd. That was why the big building at Langley had so few large conference rooms. Letting twenty people into a sensitive discussion was as good as broadcasting it on C-Span. If they start talking about my warning to Holbrook, Christmann thought, I'm finished.

There was a brief murmur as the DCI began to speak. "Thank you all for coming," he said. Right, thought Christmann. As if we had a choice.

"I know it's unusual for me to chair a meeting such as this," the director continued. "We're in the midst of an unusual situation. As you all know, a private yacht by the name of *Seafire* left the port of Boston three weeks ago. Prior to her departure, the FBI and BATF were preparing to board and search the ship. It appears that the ship's owners somehow learned of that fact and left Beantown in a hurry."

The DCI paused to let his subordinates laugh politely at his small joke, and his eyes met those of the DDO. He, in turn, glanced significantly at Malloy, who then turned his gaze toward Christmann. "Tag, I'm it!" thought Christmann. At least, no one was naming names. Yet.

The director continued, describing the events of October 31 — the dash out of Boston, Satan's Cloak, the Harpoon, and the laser. Then he played the tape of Nightbird pictures, *Seafire*'s turn toward *Escanaba*, and the laser shot bagging the Harpoon. When the tape had run, the DCI swept his eyes over his audience. He had their complete attention. Christmann could read the satisfaction in his face.

"We surmise the following with a fair degree of comfort. One, the people on *Seafire* knew that the cutter was at risk and turned around so they would be in a position to protect her. Two, they must have known that their laser weapon would attract a hell of a lot of unwanted attention, from us and God knows who else. Three, they fired the weapon after deciding that letting their secret out was better than letting people on the cutter die. These points are of little strategic importance, but they may be weighed when making moral judgments later on.

"We have determined the nature of the weapon used. It was a ruby laser. You see them in supermarket checkout lines every day. This one is different in one way, and one way only. It's bigger."

The director of central intelligence paused again. There was a nervous titter in the audience, as people were unsure if they were supposed to laugh at this or not.

"We have done some investigating into this device," the DCI continued. "Not without difficulty. Several of the persons interviewed had spoken previously with agents of the FBI. The bureau people had specifically directed them not to cooperate with us. Imagine that!"

This time the laughter was both general and genuine. The relationship between the FBI and the CIA had been strained for decades. A couple of years earlier, a CIA agent had been arrested for spying for the USSR and, later, for Russia. It turned out that the FBI had been watching him for years, without a word of warning to the company. While the fibbies had watched and waited, CIA informants had died. A lot of people in the agency believed that the bureau had deliberately waited to allow the traitor to do maximum damage to their rival organization. Whatever the truth might be, the people at Langley believed that the FBI was not a friend.

"Despite this, we managed to piece together just what kind of gear the so-called yacht has aboard. Dr. Peter Schroder, of the Office of Scientific and Weapons Research, can tell you more about that. Doctor?"

Schroder stood up. He was a cheerful, roly-poly sort of man, known throughout the Agency for his brilliant mind and bizarre sense of humor. His childhood idol and personal role model had been the Froggy the Gremlin character on the "Buster Brown" TV show. Everyone in his directorate had heard him say, "Hiya-hiya-hiya, kids, hiya-hiya-hiya!" more times than they could count. He was also known for a good Dr. Strangelove imitation, as well as the "It's alive, it's alive!" line from the movie *Frankenstein*. On this occasion, he was serious. At least to start.

Schroder looked around the room, and asked, "How many of you know what Big Dumb Booster was, or would have been?" Two or three hands went up, and he shook his head in a gesture of disappointment. "At the beginning of the space shuttle program, some engineers thought the project was too complex, too high-tech. They proposed a much simpler space vehicle. They would use proven rocket technology and just make it bigger. None of this liquid fuel, external tank, supplemental solid booster nonsense. Just a huge, simple, solid fuel rocket that could get the job done." There was a murmur as several in the group remembered the concept.

"The idea was dead on arrival, of course. It wasn't new. It wasn't cutting-edge. It wasn't sexy. The shuttle was American ingenuity with wings on! Big, old-fashioned rockets were what the Soviets were using. Puh-lease!" Schroder paused, and a small laugh fluttered about the room. "Then *Challenger* blew up and Big Dumb Booster didn't look so dumb after all.

"Something similar happened with the SDI program, the one the press likes to call Star Wars. The scientists were all hot to develop entirely new technology. Pulse weapons, rail guns, particle beams! Zowie! It's Flash Gordon time! One system was supposed to use a small nuclear explosion, which would generate a magnetic pulse, which would generate electricity, which would power a laser, which would destroy the enemy warhead. Talk about Rube Goldberg contraptions. And, we spent billions on this stuff!

"Meanwhile, up in Cambridge, Massachusetts, a guy named Steve Roth came up with an idea he called Big Dumb Laser. Lasers were becoming common. Ruby lasers were used in inventory control, to read bar coded numbers, mostly. Keeping track of freight cars, checking out groceries in supermarkets, and so forth.

Argon gas lasers were used for surgery, repairing retinas and removing tattoos. Roth believed these machines could be increased in size many orders of magnitude, and could focus enough power on an incoming warhead to vaporize it. He got short shrift. Beefing up supermarket technology didn't have the sex appeal that plasma physics had.

"Roth didn't give up. He had the bucks, so he built a couple of prototypes. In tests, they pumped out the power like champs. Cut up anything you put out in front of them. Up close or miles away, made no difference. Very impressive weapons. Unfortunately, Roth had two problems. One, he needed a huge energy source to run the lasers. Plugged into a power grid, they were great. On a ship, a plane, or a space platform, they would be useless. They need more electric power than you can get in any of those places.

"The second problem was aiming. A warhead is small, and it moves fast. Shooting it down from dozens of miles away means aiming the laser beam to millionths of a degree of accuracy. Air bends the laser beam, so does gravity and the earth's magnetic field. It is, after all, just a beam of light. Aiming the lasers required more computer power than any known computers could provide. Roth gave up, and his lasers went into storage. Until last summer, when he put them on his yacht. From the events of October 31, it would seem that the computer and power supply problems have been solved."

Schroder paused again, making sure his audience still was with him. "That brings us to Bob Knight, a buddy of Roth's, and another of *Seafire*'s owners. He's a computer genius. He's worked with Roth for years, including the Big Dumb Laser project. His real passion is AI, artificial intelligence. He wants to be the guy who builds the first computer with a soul, with true awareness of its own existence. My sources say he's getting close. He's been working on a monster of a computer, a thirty-two unit parallel processor that can out-compute anything ever built. Designing programs for it is an enormous task, so he's programmed it to program itself. When the ship went to sea, the computer was aboard."

Schroder paused once more. "Now for the third part of the equation, the power. That's the easy part. That weird yacht had it all along. We obtained the plans. It wasn't easy, but we got them before the FBI did." There was a weak cheer in the room. "They speak for themselves. Take a look." The lights dimmed, and a series of blueprints flashed up on the screen. "From the outside," Schroder continued, "*Seafire* looks like an ordinary World War II destroyer. Fletcher class, I believe they're called. Inside, though, she's unique. Look at the plans of her engine rooms.

"In a normal destroyer, we'd be looking at a steam plant. Fire rooms with boilers and engine rooms with steam turbines to drive the prop shafts. *Seafire* has no steam boilers. She has diesel engines that make electricity and electric motors to make the ship go. The scheme is very simple, and hardly unique. Lots of ships have this system. The *Queen Elizabeth II*, for example. What is unique is the number of engines. So far as we know, the closest thing to *Seafire* is an old icebreaker that the Coast Guard retired a couple of years ago. And she only had ten engines." Schroder paused for the people in the room to marvel at the plans.

"So. Now we know the secret of *Seafire*. She's a technological time machine. Her power plant was designed and built half a century ago. Her weapons are based on years-old technology you can buy anywhere in the world. And she is carrying a computer that can turn the other stuff into the most effective anti-missile weapon on the planet. Which brings us to the hard questions. How do we get *Seafire* back into the good old USA? And, if we can't get her back, should we destroy her so nobody else can get her? I believe that's the moral question the DCI was talking about."

Dr. Peter Schroder smiled benignly and looked around the room. "Any questions?"

George Holbrook and Suvia Ferris were relaxing on the starboard wing of *Seafire*'s bridge, halfway through their afternoon watch. They had the bridge to themselves. *Watson* was steering the ship, as usual, as well as standing a radar watch, navigating, and keeping the log. George and Suvia were OOD and JOOD, but, in reality, they had nothing to do. That was fine with them. For the next two hours, like the previous two, they would simply enjoy the weather and each other's company.

Below them, on the foredeck, Bob Knight and Patty Phelps were watching dolphins play in the bow wave.

"They're standing awfully close to each other," Suvia observed. "What do you think?"

"I don't know. I thought he and Jacqueline were becoming an item."

"No one becomes an item with Jacqueline," Suvia replied. "Brief relationships, strictly physical, are her modus operandi. She was through with Bob a week ago. Then she made a move on you, which you turned down."

George was surprised that Suvia knew about that, and his expression showed it. Suvia grinned. "This week's flame is Paul Harrington," she said.

"How do you know she made a pass at me?"

"She told me. She tells the other women about all of her exploits. Rates the men like a theater critic. Bob, for example, was unskilled but adventurous and energetic."

"Yikes. I'm glad I didn't take her up on her offer of companionship. I would hate to have my prowess panned like that."

"George, that was a rave review. Adventurous and energetic are what Jacqueline's looking for. So far as she's concerned, all men are unskilled. She likes being a teacher."

"I'm still glad I turned her down."

"Why did you?"

The question annoyed George. He looked at Suvia and read in her face that the question was a serious one. He knew why, or thought he did, but he wasn't ready for a serious answer. "I didn't think she'd respect me, afterward," he said with a grin and noted with regret Suvia's expression of disappointment.

"I wonder if Jacqueline's review was what got Patty interested in Bob," George said.

"No. Patty became interested in Bob when she heard that Linda had filed for divorce. Patty doesn't fool with married men. Up 'til now, the only man she's had her eye on was you."

"Me? No way. If it's true, which I doubt, she never gave me any sign of it."

"She gave you signs all right. Seventy million of them on one night alone. You're just too obtuse to notice these things." Suvia laughed. As always, George thought the sound of her laughter was the sound of music.

George watched as a big roller threw spray over the bow, drenching Bob and Patty. They ran, shrieking with laughter, for the door into the deckhouse. They were holding hands. Suvia turned to George and arched an eyebrow. George wondered if it was a sign. He resolved to be less obtuse about such things.

In three and a half weeks at sea, George and Suvia spent long periods with nothing to do but talk and watch the ocean. The watch bill had been expanded. *Watson* could man CIC using human supervision from the bridge. Three pairs of watch standers had moved from CIC to the bridge, changing the watch rotation to one in six. Cutting the evening watch into two short dog watches prevented people from standing the same watch each day. Today, George and Suvia had the afternoon watch. They'd had the first dog the day before, and tomorrow the forenoon watch would be theirs. They'd learned a lot about each other, but little that mattered.

George spoke little of himself. When he did, it was of superficial things. He didn't tell Suvia about his air battle with the MIGs. She had no idea that he'd ever flown in combat, or worked for the CIA. Suvia, too, was reluctant to reveal much of herself. George asked her about her unusual name, which he thought was beautiful, but hadn't said. She'd replied only that it was an old family name from New England.

Phase six, the LNG bomb ship, was a major source of tension between them. Whenever George mentioned it, Suvia became angry and withdrawn, and he would soon become angry as well. So, for much of the time, they spoke of inconsequential things, enjoying each other's company nevertheless.

It was a lovely day, late spring in the southern hemisphere. The ship had left St. Helena on the morning of the previous day, motoring southeast at ten knots. The sky was a brilliant blue, and the sun's warmth felt wonderful. The sea was rough, though, as rollers from the great southern ocean storms marched northward to meet *Seafire*'s bow. The ship's pitching was uncomfortable and speed had been reduced to relieve some of the motion.

The ability to slow down to avoid seasickness was a luxury. The original plan, before the hasty exit from Boston, had been to proceed through the Mediterranean and transit the Suez Canal. Fleeing from the FBI had rendered that route impossible. They'd surely have been boarded in the canal. To reach the rendezvous, they would have to go the long way round the African cape. The trip, nearly nine thousand miles long, would take almost thirty days at a cruising speed of twelve and a half knots. Allowing time for refueling and storms, there was little margin. Now, nearly two thirds of the distance had been covered, and less than half of the time had been consumed. The time margin was more comfortable and allowed the occasional reduction in speed.

George and Suvia were looking for whales when Bill Jackson came onto the bridge. They'd seen several already and were competing to see who'd be first to spot the next one. Whoever did would shout, "Whale ho!" They'd been at sea long enough to find this amusing. When they saw the look on Jackson's face, thoughts of the game faded.

"Trouble," Jackson said and handed a sheet of paper to George. It was a fax, unsigned. George held it so that he and Suvia could read it at the same time.

> EXTREMELY URGENT to George Holbrook:
>
> SEAFIRE must return to U.S. at once. Export of computer technology aboard deemed grave threat to U.S. national security. SEAFIRE will not, repeat WILL NOT, be allowed to enter port in any foreign country. U.S. NAVY WILL SINK SEAFIRE IF NECESSARY TO PREVENT EXPORT OF TECHNOLOGY.
>
> Call me.

"Christmann?" Suvia asked.

"Must be," George replied. "Bill, how did we get this? We haven't accepted any incoming satellite communications since we left Boston." George had shut the satellite telephone receiver down so nobody could send ultimatums to the ship.

"Steve Roth got a call from Nick Argeriardis on the single-sideband radio," Jackson replied. "Using the Argeriardis Shipping Company code, as usual. Told us to turn on the satellite receiver at exactly 1400 Zulu for a very important fax. He did, and here it is."

Zulu time is the military term for Greenwich mean time. On this leg of *Seafire*'s journey, it happened to be local time, as well. The ship had been using the single-sideband radio to communicate with Nick Argeriardis, and others through him. The code was contained in a series of one-time message pads, similar to the old Diana system. Cumbersome and old-fashioned, it was completely unbreakable, so long as nobody ever used the same pad twice. They'd used the code to arrange the refueling rendezvous at each stop on their journey, and for little else.

George wondered how he was supposed to call Christmann. Call information and ask for the CIA? An hour later, after talking to Suvia, George gave Steve Roth a message for encryption and transmission to Nick Argeriardis. Roth, who'd read the incoming fax, looked at what George had written and shook his head. It began with a brief reply to be relayed to Christmann. The rest of the message, the longest part by far, was a shopping list for Nick. God help us all, Roth thought as he read the list. And, God help anyone who gets in our way.

Eight days later, *Seafire* was far into the South Atlantic, only two days short of Capetown. Even though it was late spring in the Southern Hemisphere, the sea was a rough and angry gray. The ship was making hard going of it in heavy seas, her southeasterly heading provided a pounding ride. Shortly after dawn Bill Jackson, George Holbrook, Ralph Dade, and Steve Roth stood together on the port wing of the bridge. They took turns looking through binoculars at a ship three or four miles off of their beam, on a parallel course.

"She intersected our course before midnight," said Jackson, "and maneuvered into that position. She's kept station on us ever since."

"Do you recognize her?" asked George.

"USS *Willis A. Lee*, DLG-4," Jackson replied. "Small world. I sailed on her as a midshipman. That was before they put missile launchers on her. She was just DL-4 then."

"Is she nuclear powered?" asked Roth.

"No, conventional. Four boilers, steam turbines."

"I wonder what she's up to," George said. "Has she tried to signal us?"

"Not yet".

"What do you suppose they're waiting for?"

"I know her CO. He was a classmate of mine at the Academy," said Jackson. "A ring knocker, as we used to say. Always squared his corners. I'll bet he's waiting 'till 0600. He'd never start an operation at an odd time like 0547. He'll get the crew fed, hold quarters, and then do whatever it is he's here to do. Which probably is to board us."

"If you're right, that gives us a less than an hour to figure out what we're going to do. Steve, how accurate are those lasers of yours against small targets?"

"I don't really know. In theory, pinpoint. In practice, who knows? The ruby laser bagged the Harpoon, which wasn't exactly huge. Smaller than that, I don't know."

"Well," replied George, "we may get a chance to find out. Go wake up Bob so the two of you can get your fancy gear fired up."

As Roth left the bridge, Jackson asked George if he really intended to take on the frigate.

"Yes, if I have to," said George. "No, if I can help it."

"Where have I heard that before?" asked Suvia Ferris, who had just joined the men on the bridge. George didn't respond.

In Washington, it was neither spring nor morning. It was early December, officially fall but really winter, a few minutes after midnight. The briefing room in the East Wing of the White House was slowly filling with men and women from several branches of government. Bill Christmann looked around and was amazed. Several members of the president's cabinet were present, and others were expected. The attorney general had arrived with three of her senior staff. The secretary of defense was there with the secretary of the Navy in tow. DCI was making small talk with the director of the FBI. It was a show, of course. The two directors loathed each other, yet in public they chatted and smiled like colleagues. Christmann grimaced. The things we have to do for our country.

Like cliques in high school, various groups and agencies spoke quietly among themselves to the exclusion of outsiders. The CIA contingent had gravitated to the back of the room, resisting any attempt draw them into conversation with people outside the company. The group consisted of Christmann and Malloy, Dr. Schroder and a couple of his wonks. The DDCI was also in attendance, but she was at the front of the room, schmoozing with people of cabinet rank, and pretending not to be a pariah. The agency grunts at the back of the room knew better. They knew they were pariahs. They liked being pariahs.

There were color video screens all around the room, like the big TVs in a sports bar. They flickered into life and conversations faltered as people looked at the images of two ships: one white, the other gray. Murmurs rippled through he crowd, and some nervous laughter. What CNN would give for this feed, Christmann thought.

"My money's on the little white pointer," said Schroder, and Christmann snorted in laughter.

"What do you mean?" asked Malloy.

Christmann answered for Schroder, "In the America's Cup race that Dennis Connor lost, the Aussies called their boat the little white pointer. Their boat was a bit smaller than the American boat, and it was painted white. Pointer is Aussie slang for shark."

Malloy was about to reply, but he was interrupted. The President of the United States was entering the room.

Bill Jackson's prediction was correct. Shortly after six o'clock, a code flag broke out on Lee's yardarm. Jackson studied it briefly through his binoculars and said, "It means 'I am attempting to communicate with you by radio.' So what else is new."

George picked up a microphone. It was hooked into the ship's primary tactical radio circuit, PRITAC, which had been set on VHF Channel 16, an international hailing and distress frequency. The PRITAC and SECTAC radio speaker and microphone arrangements were a Navy setup. Whether they had survived from the *Watson* days, or were a Bill Jackson nostalgia touch, George didn't know. He suspected the latter.

"*Willis A. Lee*, this is the yacht *Seafire*, WAM 4635, over," George said, in a matter-of-fact tone.

The PRITAC speaker crackled. "*Seafire*, this is the *Lee*. Please heave to and prepare to receive a boarding party, over."

George took a deep breath, and spoke slowly and deliberately into the microphone. "Please be advised that these radio transmissions are being tape recorded and will be used at a formal inquest, should you attempt to board us. We are an unarmed yacht, owned by citizens of the United States and other nations, and we intend to go about our business. I suggest that you do the same."

For a moment there was no reply. Then, a different voice came from the speaker. It said, "Please put Mr. William Jackson on the radio."

George glanced for a moment at Jackson, and than handed him the microphone. "This is Jackson. Is that Jim Crawford?"

"Yes, it is," came the reply. "Interesting that you still keep track of the list. Listen, Jackson, I've been ordered to board your ship. I fully intend to do so. Please don't make me use force. My orders are quite specific that I am to use whatever means are necessary."

Jackson turned and said to George. "What do we tell him?"

"Tell him we'll testify at his court martial."

Jackson did just that, speaking into the microphone with the same deliberation that George had used a moment before, and ending with an emphatic, "... *Seafire*, OUT!"

George asked, "Can we outrun him?"

"In a flat calm, maybe. In these seas, no way. He's five hundred feet long and twice our tonnage. He can pound through these swells. We can't."

"What do you think he'll do next?"

"Put a shot across our bow, I suppose," Bill replied.

"Jesus. Can these radio transmissions be heard very far?"

"The FM radio frequency that we're using is strictly line of sight. There's no way anyone more than fifty miles from here can overhear what we're saying. I doubt that there's another ship within two hundred miles, and there are no air routes anywhere near here."

George turned to Ralph Dade, who had been listening all along, but not saying anything. "Go below and get on the satellite phone," said George. "Contact our friends in Washington, if we still have any, and try to get this guy called off." Ralph departed, without saying a word, and George turned to one of the bridge intercoms. He pushed the button which connected him with CIC and said, "Steve, are you tracking the Navy over there?"

"Yes," came the reply.

"In a few minutes he's probably going to fire a shot across our bow. Is this computer of yours fast enough to track the shell in flight?"

"More than fast enough. The program was designed to shoot down incoming warheads fifty miles up. Those shells may be smaller, but they'll be much closer and a whole lot slower."

"OK, then, track it and keep the laser on standby. Don't shoot at the shell unless it's actually going to hit us."

Bill Jackson had gone out onto the wing of the bridge. Through the open wing door, he shouted, "He's lit off mount one!" Everyone on the bridge looked at the *Lee*. The frigate's forward gun mount was moving. The five-inch gun was pointing toward *Seafire*, tracking steadily as the two ships pitched and rolled on the deep South Atlantic swells.

"Standby, Steve," George yelled into the intercom, and turned to watch the frigate.

Lee fired. There was a muzzle flash, and a puff of smoke from her forward mount. The wind quickly tore the smoke astern. On Seafire's mast, remote cameras and high-resolution radars swiveled to follow the flight of the shell, which exploded several hundred yards ahead of Seafire's bow.

"Did we track it?" George shouted into the intercom.

"I'm checking the program analysis now," Roth replied. After a pause, he continued, "It looks like a ninety-six percent probability of a hit if we'd fired."

George Holbrook steadied himself for a moment, assessing the situation and liking the odds. Aloud but to himself he said, "Alright, you son of a bitch." Then into the radio microphone, "This is the yacht *Seafire*. I am speaking to the officers and men of USS *Willis A. Lee*. Your captain is obviously insane. He has ordered you to commit crimes that will place you all in the brig at Portsmouth. I urge you to relieve the madman of his command before it is too late."

Jackson turned to George. "You've done it now. He's not going to take that. No way."

Lee fired again. This time the shot fell much closer to Seafire's bow and the explosion threw water onto her fo'c'sle.

Crawford called again on the radio. "*Seafire*, this is *Lee*. You are suspected of carrying contraband. The International Anti-Smuggling Act gives us authority to interdict such suspects. If you don't heave to, my next shot will hit your ship."

George called Roth and asked how the tracking was on the second shot.

"Close to one hundred percent. Watson's in his self-programming mode. He analyzed his mistakes on the first shot, and adjusted. Next time he'll be better yet."

"Great," said George. "Next time, shoot."

Lee fired for the third time. Almost simultaneously, the beam of ruby-colored light flashed out from the laser on Seafire's flying bridge. Halfway between the two ships, the hurtling five-inch shell exploded in mid air. Everyone aboard *Seafire* cheered and shouted.

Aboard *Lee*, and in Washington, the reaction was different.

A chorus of gasps and exclamations rippled through the White House briefing room. The aircraft orbiting the two ships was picking up the radio transmissions between them, and everyone in the room had expected Lee's next shot to hit *Seafire*. They'd all been briefed on the laser, several had seen tapes of the destruction of the Harpoon. No one, not even Dr. Schroder, had anticipated that the laser could destroy a naval rifle's projectile in flight. "My God," Schroder said. "If they can hit a shell from a ship's gun, they could hit a warhead. It really is Star Wars."

A brief commotion arose at the front of the room as an aide spoke to the DCI. "There's a man on the phone who says it's extremely urgent that he talk to you. It must be important, because Langley put him through. He says his name is Ralph Dade."

"What the hell was that?" Crawford shouted.

"It looked like a laser, Captain," said the XO, a lieutenant commander named Ryder. "It came from that thing that looks like a fire control director up on his flying bridge. Blew our shell up in flight. Jesus."

"Combat, bridge. Fire another round."

Crawford and his executive officer watched *Seafire* with their binoculars. *Lee* fired again, the laser fired again, and the second shell exploded in mid air.

Aboard *Seafire*, Steve Roth called George on the intercom. "ECM gear detects long range radio transmissions from the *Lee*."

George replied, "Crawford's probably calling the Pentagon

for further instructions. Can you put your targeting display on one of the screens up here?"

A picture of the *Lee* appeared on a monitor on the bridge. "Give me a close-up of her mast," said George, and the image shifted and grew. "See those antennas? Shoot them off. Everything but the VHF. We'll let this turkey make a few decisions for himself."

The ruby laser fired again. Sparks and flame flickered on Lee's yardarms like St. Elmo's fire. When the laser stopped firing, George could see that all of the frigate's radio antennas, except for one small VHF whip, had been destroyed.

Lee's bridge was in a state of confusion and disarray. The radio room had just reported that all long-range radio contact, voice and data, had been lost. Crawford was in a rage. He stepped out onto the starboard bridge wing and looked up at the mast. The sight of the smoldering stubs of his antennas drove him into a frenzy. He stormed back into the pilothouse and called CIC.

"Target that God damn laser on top of their bridge!" he shouted. "When you're locked on, I want mount one to commence rapid fire!" Crawford turned to his XO. "Sooner or later that fucking laser is going to miss one of our shells, and one is all it will take." He had barely finished speaking when the five inch gun began to fire, pounding out a shell every two and a quarter seconds.

Seafire was keeping the pace. Every two and a quarter seconds, the ruby laser fired and there was an airburst between the ships. George realized what the frigate was up to, and recognized it as a threat. They were playing a deadly game of catch, and one miss would be fatal. "Steve," he said, speaking to Roth on the intercom, "just how quick are *Watson's* reflexes, anyway?" The reply on the speaker was the sound of Roth's laughter. Several seconds later, the laser beam began to move in tiny increments. As each shell was fired, the laser hit it slightly sooner than the last, and the airbursts were walking closer and closer to the *Lee*. Finally, when shrapnel was clattering off *Lee's* bridge enclosure, and several of her windows had been blown out, Crawford screamed, "Cease firing."

George spoke again to Roth on the intercom. "I want you and Bob to fire up Satan's Cloak. That bozo is trying to kill us. Take out his fire control radar, and his surface and air search radars, too. While you're at it, blast his GPS receivers. I don't want him to be able to give our position to anybody, the way *Escanaba* did. For all we know, there are submarines around here, armed to the teeth with Harpoons and Tomahawks, and God knows what else." A minute later, Roth reported that Satan's Cloak's work had been done. George stepped out onto the bridge wing and looked at the cloak housing, mounted far aft and heavily shielded so its emissions couldn't affect *Seafire*'s own equipment. It really is too bad, he thought, that these gizmos don't make noise. All this firepower and no bang, no smell of burning cordite. Ah, well, you can't have everything. He went back into the pilothouse to called the Navy on the radio.

Captain Crawford was beside himself with outrage. A powerful energy pulse had just swept over his ship, and he was sure it had come from *Seafire*. Every radar set on the frigate had been destroyed. The air search radar cabinet had exploded and started a small fire. The GPS satellite navigation gear was ruined, and the passive ECM arrays were a smoking mess. He was about to speak when the ruby laser fired again, for three or four seconds. "What the fuck are they doing now?" he shouted. A moment later, the Operations Officer called with the answer. "That last burst took out the optical range finder on our fire control director," he said. "We've got nothing, absolutely nothing, to generate a fire control solution!"

The PRITAC speaker crackled on the frigate's bridge, "*Lee*, *Lee*, this is *Seafire*. Can you read me?"

▪ ▪ ▪ ▪ ▪

Crawford replied, "Affirmative." Even over the radio, the tightness of anger could be heard in his voice. Holbrook and Jackson looked at each other, sharing a grim satisfaction.

"I want you to listen carefully," said George. "My fire control system is keyed to your muzzle flash. Our laser will detonate your shell just as it clears the barrel. If you shoot that five-inch again, your bridge is coming right off. If you turn your missile control radar on, I'll fry it like the others. If you put a missile on the launch rail, I'll blow it up and half your stern goes with it. You have nothing to shoot at us that we can't blow up before it gets here. Go home. I repeat, go home, before any of your men get hurt. Over."

George waited, but Crawford did not reply. *Lee* continued steaming parallel to *Seafire*, keeping station as before. Greasy black smoke appeared and billowed out of *Lee's* stack, but her course and speed remained the same.

"Oh, shit." said Jackson. "He's getting ready to ram us."

"What!" said Holbrook.

"That black smoke. He's lighting off more burners to get ready for flank speed. Now what do we do?"

George paced about the bridge while thinking out loud. "There's not a lot we can do. If we turn the ruby laser on their bridge, we're bound to kill a few sailors, and blind a few others. We could use the big laser to punch holes along their waterline, but that might kill somebody, too. Unless we're willing to kill those guys, there is nothing we can do to stop them. Damn." He looked at Suvia, who said nothing. There were tears in her eyes.

Ralph Dade suddenly bolted through the companionway and onto the bridge. "I did it!" he shouted. "The Navy's calling *Lee* off right now!" He looked around, puzzled that his news wasn't being greeted with more enthusiasm.

"That's great," said Suvia, in a tone that didn't match the sentiment. "How did you do it?"

"I got hold of the director of the CIA, himself. He was with the president, and I got the impression that the two of them were watching us on some sort of satellite camera. I told them that we've made copies of the plans and specifications of every piece of gear on this ship. I said that those copies, together with tapes of our computer's operating software, would be delivered to the government of North Korea tomorrow morning at sunup if the U.S. government didn't leave us alone. I told them if they want to see our technology fall into the wrong hands all they have to do is keep shooting at us."

"Christ," said George. "Too bad we didn't think of that approach a couple of hours ago. While you were down below, we've been taking potshots at *Lee*, over there. She's hurting for radio reception capability. Unless they have some really fast carrier pigeons in Washington, there's no way they can call *Lee* off."

"Can't we tell them ourselves?" asked Suvia. "They can hear us."

"Do you think they'd believe us?" replied George.

"We could try," Ralph said. "No harm in that."

"Good point," George said. "Bill, call Crawford, one Academy man to another. Tell him the fun's over and he's wanted at home. Now, Ralph, what's this satellite camera business?"

"Just an impression I got," Ralph replied. "What time is it in Washington, anyway, two A.M.? How come the CIA director and president are up talking and they take my call? I didn't have to explain who I was or why I was calling. It was as if they knew what was going on."

"Steve," George said to Roth on the intercom. "Ralph thinks we may have company of the U-2 variety. Anything on the air search radar?"

"Negative," said Roth. "That doesn't mean anything, though. When they retired the SR-71 Blackbirds, they came out with a new model, the Nightbird. Cosmic top secret. U-2 range and endurance, SR-71 speed, and Stealth technology. There could be twenty of them up there and we'd never see them."

"If there was one overhead, could it monitor our VHF radio transmissions?"

"I'm sure it could and would," Roth said.

Jackson interrupted George, who was about to ask Roth another question. "Crawford doesn't believe me," Bill said. "So much for that idea."

George spoke again to Roth, "Could the Nightbird, if there is one, transmit to *Lee*?"

"Sure."

"Ralph," George said, "go down to the exchange room and call Washington. Tell them to route their traffic to Lee through the Nightbird."

"Why waste time?" said Suvia. "If there's a spy plane monitoring the radio and transmitting the signal to Washington, why bother arguing with the switchboard at Langley. Why not just call up on our radio and say, "Hey, Mr. President, listen up!"

George stared at Suvia for a moment, then grabbed her by the shoulders and kissed her. "You're a genius!" he said.

The White House briefing room was in turmoil. The operation was going wrong fast. While a few of the men and women present were still trying to salvage the situation, the majority were positioning themselves to avoid blame. The chief of naval operations was explaining to his commander in chief that all attempts to contact *Lee* had failed. The president didn't like the news and was blaming the military for its inability to carry out his wishes.

In the back of the room, the CIA group was in high spirits. They'd advised against this operation and its unraveling was sweet. Bill Christmann didn't believe for a minute that his fucking Boy Scout would hand over critical technology to the wackos in

Pyongyang, but he admired the bluff for its audacity and effectiveness. Throughout the room, the words treason and disaster were being muttered, as people speculated that a weapon that could hit thirty-seven five inch projectiles, without missing any, might be able to handle MIRV warheads, as well.

Malloy and Schroder had come around to Christmann's point of view. Throughout her high-tech shenanigans, *Seafire* had avoided causing casualties. She'd gone to the aid of a not-so-innocent bystander and blown significant cover in the process. Giving the North Koreans Star Wars technology could result in megadeaths, and the *Seafire* people must know it. The threat was as empty as a politician's promise, Christmann believed. Malloy and Schroder agreed. DCI and DDCI were scared witless, and didn't know what to believe.

Christmann was about to say something witty to Schroder, whom he was beginning to like immensely, when the speakers crackled into life. Christmann recognized the voice, it was Holbrook's.

"This is the yacht *Seafire*," said the voice. "I'm speaking to the President of the United States."

Silence filled the room as everyone there tried to grasp what was happening. Schroder got it first. "He's figured out the data link," he said. "He knows we're listening. Holy jumping Jesus Christ!"

"We're aware that you are attempting to recall USS *Willis A. Lee* from her attack. Thank you. We are not the enemy, please believe that. Unfortunately, we rendered *Lee* incapable of receiving your messages. We're sorry about that now, of course. It seemed like a good idea at the time."

Holbrook paused for a beat, and Christmann glanced at Schroder. "Insolent bastard," Christmann said. "I love it."

"We believe that you have a reconnaissance aircraft over our position. If you can hear us, then we are correct. If you can't hear us, please disregard this message. Have the aircraft relay your recall message to *Lee* on VHF. Please do it quickly. Things are getting ugly out here. *Seafire*, out."

Suvia had been listening to George as he transmitted in the blind, hoping to reach the president. "What do you think?" she asked. Her tone told George that she had her own opinion, and it wasn't good. "I don't know," he replied. "My guess is that we're going to have to keep fending for ourselves."

Bill Jackson spoke up. "I've got it! The sonar! The Mark 26 sonar! Get the big laser going!"

George glanced at Suvia and then called Steve Roth on the intercom. "Combat, bridge," he said, "main battery to standby." Then, he asked Jackson what he meant about the sonar.

"She has the Mark 26 sonar," said Jackson. "The first one ever built. The transducer dome is a huge rubber bulb on the chin of the bow." He pointed to the TV monitor, still showing *Lee* in close-up. "See that anchor way out there on the cutting edge of the bow. It's put out there so it will miss the sonar dome when it's dropped. When I was on the *Lee*, we always had to be going astern when we dropped anchor. If we were going forward, even slightly, it would take the dome right off and flood half the forward compartments."

George was elated. "So all we have to do is burn through the anchor chain! And if she's going really fast, the pressure of the water will probably flood more compartments. In these seas, she'll have to slow down to a crawl." Then George's elation evaporated. "Which puts us back where we started. Flooded compartments mean drowned sailors. We've got to do this without killing anybody."

"But if he's preparing to ram us," Jackson said, "then he'll get the men out of the forward compartments and close the watertight doors behind them. Even Crawford would think of that."

George nodded. "But we can't shoot until we're positive he's going to ram. Otherwise we can't be sure there won't be any men up forward. Is there any way to tell when *Lee* will make her move?"

"Watch for the squat," Bill replied. When Ralph asked what he meant, he explained, "I keep forgetting you guys were aviators. A squat is the trademark of a real warship, a display of raw power. Destroyers can do it, some cruisers, too. When they accelerate the propellers throw tons of water out from under the stern, and create a partial vacuum. The screws actually dig a sort of hole in the water and the stern sinks down into it."

Suvia said, "Sounds like the seagoing equivalent of laying down rubber on a drag strip. Muy macho."

"Exactly," said Jackson. "On both counts."

Bob Knight called from CIC to say that the argon laser was ready, and George picked up the radio handset for one last try.

"*Lee*, this is *Seafire*, we have learned by radio that you are being ordered to disengage and return to base. If you send men topside to rig an antenna so you can verify this, we won't interfere."

On the *Lee*, the XO looked at Captain Crawford. "He might be telling the truth, Captain. He's not trying to get away. It wouldn't hurt to wait and see if we really are being recalled."

"I don't believe it," said Crawford. "He claims to be an unarmed yacht and then he hits us with weapons out of *Star Wars*. I'm not going to give him time to pull any more cute tricks. What's the status report?"

Lieutenant Commander Ryder sounded miserable. "All men have moved aft of frame fifty. Condition Zebra is set throughout the ship. Damage control parties are standing by. Main control reports ready to answer all bells."

"Very well," said Crawford. Then, louder, "This is the captain. I have the deck and the conn. All engines ahead flank."

• • • • •

"There he goes!" Bill Jackson shouted, and everyone on Seafire's bridge watched Lee's stern dig down. In a moment, she began to accelerate and she turned toward *Seafire*. Steve Roth called the bridge. "*Lee's* on a collision course," he said. "Less than three minutes to impact."

"Start the main laser firing sequence," George replied. "Your target is the anchor chain for the bow anchor. Fire as she bears."

• • • • •

On *Lee*'s bridge the XO was watching *Seafire*, also through binoculars. "*Seafire* hasn't changed course," the captain said. "You don't suppose they really believe that crap about talking to the president?"

"I'm sure they believe it," the XO replied. "What I don't know is if I believe it." Something caught his eye. "Something moving over there, Captain. Up where mount one would be. Christ it *is* a mount of some kind, and it's training on us!"

"What?" shouted Crawford.

"The thing they shot before was a little gizmo up on top of the bridge. It must have been their secondary battery. Now they're going to hit us with the big stuff. Captain, we should break off."

"Shut up, you fool. I'll ask for your opinion when I want it."

"Combat reports one minute to collision," said a sailor.

"Very well," Crawford replied.

"I don't believe it," he said to Ryder. "He's not taking any evasive action at all. He must know we're going to ram him by now."

Ryder looked ill. "Maybe he doesn't regard us as a serious threat." Then, in an alarmed voice, he continued, "Now what the hell?"

As the officers and men on the *Lee* watched, the mount on

Seafire's foredeck began to spout water. Tons of it were streaming out of the housing, over the deck, and out the scuppers. Crawford crowed with derision, "Looks like a damn water cannon. That fool thinks he's going to stop us with a fucking water cannon!"

Ryder moaned, "No, sir! That's a cooling system, Captain. Whatever they're going to shoot at us needs all that water to keep it cool." He turned to the men on the bridge. "Shield your eyes," he screamed, as *Seafire*'s main battery fired.

Several things happened in quick succession. A beam of electric blue light struck *Lee*'s bow. Stanchions and lifelines burst into flame. The blue beam flickered and danced around the capstan, tearing huge chunks of metal out of anchor handling gear and the surrounding deck. Holes were burned in the steel deck, their edges glowing cherry red. Huge sparks rolled around the forecastle.

On *Seafire*, water no longer poured from the laser mount. Instead, great clouds of steam billowed out, and trailing behind the ship like a fog bank. On the bridge, the status report monitor showed a flashing warning:

DANGER — MAIN LASER OVERHEATING.

The blue beam struck the anchor chain as *Lee*'s bow was on the downswing. The chain parted, and the anchor fell into the water. On the frigate's bridge there was a powerful jolt, as the anchor hit the sonar dome, and several men lost their balance.

Seafire's laser abruptly shut itself off. Bill Jackson grabbed the engine control levers, and rammed them to full ahead. Then he turned to watch the *Lee*, which was by then only three hundred yards away and still on a collision course.

On Lee's bridge, the sailor with the headset shouted, "Damage control reports flooding in several forward compartments, Captain. The chief engineer says if we don't slow down the bulkheads may not hold."

"I'll slow down, all right," Crawford said to his XO, "but not until I've rammed that son of a bitch." Then he looked at *Seafire*, which was slipping across the bow from starboard to port. "Damn, he's increased speed. Left standard rudder."

The XO looked at the pitometer log. "We're slowing down, Captain. Must be the weight of water we're taking up forward. If we don't decrease power, we're going to dive like a fucking submarine!"

With the *Lee* losing way and *Seafire* accelerating, the ships were still closing, but *Lee*'s bows were closing on *Seafire*'s stern. *Lee* missed ramming *Seafire* by inches, sweeping just astern of her, to the relief of everyone on both ships, except Crawford. "All engines ahead dead slow," he said, bitterly, and turned to watch *Seafire* leaving him behind. Looking through his binoculars, he verified that the small laser on the flying bridge was still tracking the five-inch gun. This close, he thought, we could hit her with the iron sights in the gun mount. Damn. He sank into his chair with a sigh and asked for damage control reports.

George Holbrook asked Roth what had happened to the argon laser.

"It just didn't lase properly," Roth explained. "The light should have been blue-green, not pure blue. Too little energy went into to laser light, which means too much turned into heat. The circuit breakers tripped out. We'd better not fire it again. We nearly burned out our generators."

George said nothing, and shook his head. He looked aft at *Lee*, now a couple of miles astern and wallowing in the heavy swells. He picked up the radio handset. "*Lee*, this is *Seafire*. Are you in danger of sinking?"

"No, damn you," came the reply.

George turned to Bill Jackson. "You know, Bill, I don't think I like this classmate of yours very much."

"I never would have guessed it."

On the bridge the radio crackled with the sound of a new voice. "*Willis Lee*, this is Nightbird Thirty-one Alfa. Stand by for urgent encrypted message, over." Jackson and Holbrook looked at each other and began to laugh.

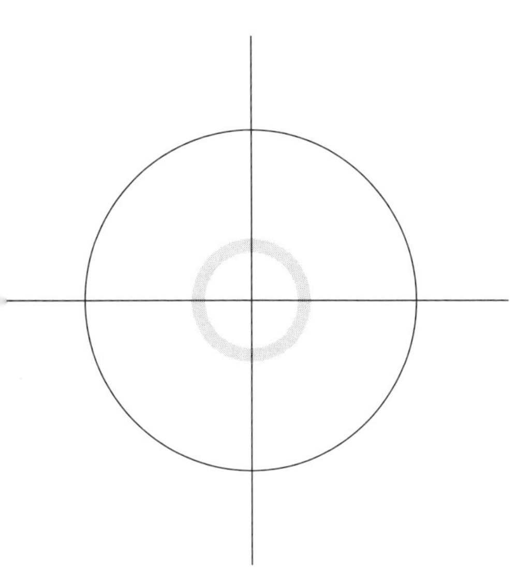

CHAPTER 13

BILL CHRISTMANN was enjoying the view from the top of Table Mountain. To the south, the cape peninsula pointed its bony finger into the southern ocean. Westward, mighty Atlantic swells pounded relentlessly against sheer stone cliffs. North and east lay Capetown, with all of Africa behind her. False Bay was to the southeast. The views were all breathtaking, but Christmann's main interest lay in False Bay, particularly in the western corner known as Simon's Bay. On this day it provided shelter to two ships from the United States.

Christmann reached into an oversized camera bag and removed a pair of Zeiss binoculars, 8x50s. He used them to look into the anchorage at Simon's Town, home base to the South African Navy.

There, resting in the outer anchorage area, were the two American ships. The air was clear, though the ships were fifteen miles away, he could make them out easily. Despite their difference in size and color, they were remarkably similar in appearance. Each had the lean lines of a fast warship. Christmann was amused by the fact that the small white one was the more powerful.

Through his binoculars, Christmann could see *Seafire*'s helicopter being prepared for launch. He was familiar with the machine, having studied its specifications before leaving the United States. It was a Holbrook ExecuStar, a big twin-rotor aircraft that had been modified to fit into the yacht's hangar. Of the two helicopters known to be aboard *Seafire*, this one interested Christmann least.

As Christmann watched, the rotors began to turn, and the aircraft lifted off. It swung wide over Simon's Bay, past the wounded *Willis A. Lee*, and then toward Table Mountain. Christmann looked at his watch. Holbrook was right on schedule. Christmann turned his attention to the *Lee*. She had arrived in Simon's Bay three days ago, he knew, limping around the point of the Cape of Good Hope and dropping her remaining anchor less than a mile from *Seafire*. Prior to entering the anchorage, the destroyer had radioed the yacht, giving assurances that she had orders to leave *Seafire* alone. Still, the CIA agent thought, it must have been a tense moment aboard both ships. In several days, *Lee* would be entering a floating dry-dock, courtesy of the South African Navy. Until then, she would have to wait at anchor, lucky to be afloat.

The helicopter took a little less than eight minutes to cover the fifteen miles, and Christmann watched as it touched down on the pad outside the observation area. Ralph Dade was at the controls. The machine touched down briefly. Holbrook and a woman Christmann knew to be Suvia Ferris stepped out. As soon as they cleared the rotors, the helicopter lifted up and away, sweeping back toward the south.

Holbrook greeted Christmann with genuine affection, and introduced him to Suvia, "Suvia, this is Bill Christmann. The man who sent the fax heard 'round the world."

"An act which I hope I don't come to regret," Christmann said to Suvia. "I'm pleased to meet you." This, too, was a genuine comment. Christmann found Suvia attractive.

"Thank you for coming to meet us," Suvia said. "It's a long way. And thanks for the fax, too."

Christmann hadn't expected to be speaking with anyone other than Holbrook, and Suvia Ferris' place in the equation hadn't been explained. The fact that Holbrook had identified him, Christmann, as the source of the warning fax indicated that she was Holbrook's confidante, at least. Christmann wondered if she were more. Caution made him want to speak with Holbrook alone. What the hell? he thought. I'm dealing with amateurs, the whole boatload probably knows everything, anyway.

"Before we get to the main topic, George," Christmann began, "I want to tell you about that other matter you asked us about. So far, everything you told us has checked out. Much to my surprise, I admit. The case should be wrapped up in a few days."

"That's great," George replied. "Thank you!"

"No thanks necessary. Some of my friends are going to get promotions out of this. If anyone deserves thanks, it's you."

Suvia looked puzzled, and Christmann could see that she didn't know what he was talking about. Before she could ask, he changed the subject.

"The government wants you to return to the United States," Christmann began, getting straight to the point. "Your ship, that is. The technology aboard her could fall into the wrong hands. That risk is unacceptable."

"The wrong hands," George replied. "That's a clever phrase. I'll have to remember it. Just whose hands might the wrong hands be?"

Christmann smiled a cynic's smile. "North Korea. Iran. Iraq. Israel. Syria. Japan. France. Russia. Especially Russia." Christmann made a sweeping gesture at the landscape. "South Africa, of course. Red China. Both Chinas, in fact. Great Britain. Canada. Nantucket. In general, anybody but the United States military."

Suvia said, "All this technology was offered to the United States military years ago and they turned it down."

"Ah, but then, they didn't know it would work. Now they know it works and they want it. Real bad."

"Tell them to make us an offer," George replied. "The technology is for sale, but the prototype isn't. *Seafire* has places to go, and we have people to see. The ship's not for sale, and we're not coming home until our business is concluded."

"They'll stop you if they have to."

"They can try. We're now ASW capable, by the way. Or, did you know that? We've loaded the ordnance pods that convert the Sparrow helicopter into a Sea Sparrow."

Christmann hadn't known; it was one of the things he'd been sent to find out. He was familiar with the Holbrook Sparrow which had several interchangeable ordnance pods available. Strap on the antisubmarine pod, and you had a Sea Sparrow with sonobuoys, two homing torpedoes, and a computer that could nail any submarine in the world. Take off the ASW pod, clamp on the anti-armor pod, and now you have the SparrowHawk, with rockets, either miniguns or a small cannon, and a computer that could bust any tank in the world. Christ, Christmann thought. If they have ASW weapons, what the hell else do they have aboard?

"I know we can't take on the whole U.S. Navy," George continued. "If they want to stop us, they can. But, if they do, the technology will certainly fall into the wrong hands. I guarantee it. We'll give it to North Korea and a few other people on the 'wrong hands' list."

"The problem is," said Christmann, "I just don't believe that. You went out of your way to save the Coasties from their own missile. You figured out a way to stop the *Lee* without hurting anybody. If you gave Star Wars technology to North Korea, thousands, maybe millions of innocent lives would be put at risk. I just don't see you doing that."

"Don't be so sure of that," said Suvia. The bitterness in her voice took both men aback. "If innocent lives have to be put at risk, George Holbrook's the man to do it."

Christmann could see that George was hurt and embarrassed by Suvia's remark, but for some reason chose to ignore it.

"While we're on the subject," said George, "here's something else to tell Washington. From now on, the gloves are off. There's a *Seawolf* class attack sub out there. He's stayed far enough away from us so his torpedoes aren't a threat, and we can handle his anti-ship missiles. We can't stop a torpedo, though, so we can't let him get within range. If he gets too close, we'll sink him. That's a promise."

Christmann raised his eyebrows.

"Look," George continued in a milder tone, "we're not stupid. If the ship gets taken over by the bad guys, they won't get any sensitive technology. The hardware's not exotic. The only thing that's unique are the lasers, and they're just scaled up versions of common commercial tubes. It's the software that's sensitive, and it's protected. It exists only on the fixed disks in the computers. No tape backup. If anyone tries to use the system without voice codes and passwords, it'll scram itself and format all the disk drives. Every bit of data will be erased in seconds. Trust me on this. We're out here to take weapons away from these assholes, not to arm them ourselves."

"Who are these assholes, George?" Christmann asked.

"I don't think we should tell you that," said George.

"Jinnah and the M.L.O.," said Suvia.

George looked at Suvia for two or three seconds. Christmann sensed tension between them. Finally, George said to Christmann, "As the lady said. Jinnah and the M.L.O."

Christmann was only mildly surprised. There were several terrorist groups known to be bidding for the bombs. Jinnah's was among them. "You must be crazy," he said. "Do you know who you're up against?"

"The guy who helped bring down the Marine barracks in Beirut like a house of cards," George answered. "You know the same guy bin Laden hired to blow a hole in the USS *Cole* last month. Yeah, we know who we're up against."

"How the hell did you get into this?" Christmann asked.

George looked at Suvia, who shrugged. He then spent fifteen minutes describing the events since Jinnah first boarded *Seafire*.

When George finished, Christmann was silent. He knew he'd never convince *Seafire*'s owners to bring her home. Doing so would put their families at terrible risk. These people were determined to fight one of the most ruthless terrorists in the world. God help them.

"Do you think Jinnah has gotten wind of your plan to fight?" Christmann asked.

"Not unless his intelligence is better than I think it is," George replied. "Or, ours is a lot worse."

"What do you mean?"

"The only way he could smell a rat would be if he knew we had weapons aboard. Anything larger than small arms, that is. We've carried those for security for years. ATF was behind the raid in Boston, and illegal weapons was the justification for it, but that's not common knowledge. The official story of our dash out of Boston with the Coast Guard in pursuit is that we broke the harbor speed limit while we were testing our engines. We watched the story on CNN. We supposedly apologized and paid a big fine. Jinnah doesn't have the organization to find out what was really gong on, and anyone who has the capability wouldn't bother.

"Only you, the Navy, and the Coast Guard know about the lasers. By now, I suppose, agents of foreign powers know, too. Even if they wanted to help Jinnah, they'd have no way of knowing the information would mean anything to him. Only when the information's bundled, the weapons and Jinnah's involvement together, is there a risk of compromise. That's why I didn't want to tell who our opponent is." George looked at Suvia who showed no sign of remorse.

"OK," Christmann said. "If you're going, then I'm coming with you."

George and Suvia, stunned, said nothing, and Christmann continued. "If I were aboard, Washington would feel more secure about the technology risk. I could recruit some troops, Rangers and Seals, to beef up your security. Your security force is mostly civilian, right? Bodyguards and such, no military types?"

"We have no security forces aboard," said George.

"What?!" Christmann was incredulous.

"No security forces. Just us. If we showed up at the rendezvous with a private army aboard, Jinnah would be gone in a nanosecond. Believe me, we've thought this out. Martial arts experts disguised as engine mechanics. Green Berets making the beds. None of it would work. Jinnah's too smart. He'd see through it."

"Besides that," Suvia said, "I don't think the United States government will want to be involved in this operation. Not even the CIA. Some of what we've done is illegal. Some of what we intend to do is more so. Any involvement, direct or indirect, by any U.S. agency could have disastrous political fallout. Thanks for the offer, but you don't want to be involved in this. You don't even want to know the details."

Christmann considered this for a moment. "I don't see how you can bring this off," he said. "No combat troops, no armed guards, how do you propose to take Jinnah, anyway?"

Holbrook sighed. "You risked your career to send us the fax, the least we can do is tell you what we're up to."

"Needless to say," George continued, "this is in strict confidence. Being able to deny prior knowledge of our plans might be useful to your agency. I expect you'll preserve that option for it."

"Of course."

"Fine. To begin, we divided the operation into six phases. The first three were mostly preparation and the last three are the action phases. Our mission was never to take Jinnah, as you said. We're going to destroy him. That can be done in several ways.

"The first phase was to convince Jinnah that money was being deposited into his Swiss account when it really wasn't. That's happened; it will cause Jinnah major financial embarrassment in the near future. That alone could be fatal to both him and his cause. Phase two was rebuilding the ship. It meets Jinnah's specifications as a research vessel, as well as our own as a Trojan horse. Success in that phase remains to be seen. The third phase was finding all of Jinnah's assassins. Jinnah has hit teams following our families around. We think we've identified all of them, although we can't be sure. People like the Rangers and Seals you spoke about are following them. These three parts of the operation are more or less complete.

"The action phases will take place after Jinnah boards the ship. We'll let him lead us to where the bombs are to be loaded, then we'll try to overpower him. That's phase five. Meanwhile, phase four will be underway. Our paid assassins will kill all of his paid assassins, in the United States and around the world."

"Sweet Jesus," muttered Christmann.

"If we fail to kill Jinnah, and he orders his men to kill our families, there will be nobody to carry out the order."

"You might as well tell him all of it," said Suvia, the bitter edge returning to her voice. "Tell him about phase six."

Christmann felt the tension again.

"Phase six," said George, looking at Suvia. "That's a contingency phase. We hope we don't have to use it. If Jinnah is about to escape and go after our families, we'll blow up the capital city of Makran, and make the world believe Jinnah did it."

"Makran is part of India, by God!" said Christmann. "That would be an act of war!"

"So, you'd better not be around if we have to do it," George replied. "Don't you agree?"

"But why? Revenge?"

"No, of course not. As I said, Jinnah must be destroyed. If we fail to kill him, we can still destroy him as a leader. His trademark is huge, spectacular explosions. If everybody in the world believed he'd blown up his home city in an act of sheer fanaticism, no one would ever carry out his orders again. His own people would hunt him down like a mad dog. As surely as if we'd killed him ourselves, he'd be destroyed."

"But George," Suvia said, pleading with him, "even if it would protect our families, how can we kill innocent civilians by the thousands?"

"What innocent civilians? Those people support Jinnah. He's their hero. Most of the Muslim population of Makran is concentrated in the slums of Makran City. In those areas, Jinnah's like a god. Without those people, Jinnah would be nothing. He's declared war on us, personally. So have all of them. We're the enemy, the Great American Satan. The Marine barracks blow up in Beirut; the Muslims of Makran cheer. The Air Force's Khobar Towers explode; the Muslims of Makran wish they had come down like the barracks in Beirut. Innocent people, my ass! They're like the Germans who cheered the Luftwaffe while London was burning, but cried, 'Unfair!' when the firestorm ate Dresden."

Christmann stared at George. George seemed to check himself, visibly wrestling with his anger. Suvia was starting to cry, and Christmann continued to stare at George in disbelief.

"Damn it all," said George. "If I have to blow up the city, I will." He took a small radio from his pocket, and called Ralph Dade for a ride home.

George strode off toward the helo pad, and Christmann watched him go. Jesus, he thought, either my favorite Boy Scout is capable of mass murder, or he's one hell of a poker player. Christmann was sure he didn't know which. The scary thing was, he doubted that George did, either.

Shortly after eight in the morning on December 7, Kevin Finnerty was standing on *Seafire*'s foredeck. He'd raised the jack precisely at eight. Since her arrival in Capetown the ship had held morning and evening colors with the precision of a military school. Kevin suspected, correctly, that the major purpose of this had been to piss off the Navy guys over on the *Lee*.

Kevin was supervising the raising of *Seafire*'s anchor. He watched as the wildcat wound in the big links of chain. "Up and down," he said into a small radio, when the anchor chain was perpendicular. A moment later, the foredeck shuddered slightly, and the capstan began to turn more easily as the anchor had risen free of the floor of False Bay. "Anchor's aweigh!" he said into his radio, and quickly turned to take down the jack. On the signal bridge, he knew, the steaming ensign would be coming up smartly and the black spherical "anchored" signal would be coming down. Kevin hoped that the sailors on the *Lee* were watching. It would be a shame if all this effort were wasted.

Although technically underway, *Seafire* didn't use her engines until the anchor was aboard and the chain secured with the huge pelican hooks on the fo'c'sle. Finally, when Kevin had completed securing the anchor for sea, the big yacht began to move.

On *Seafire*'s bridge, Bill Jackson watched as Kevin Finnerty left the foredeck. Several of the owners were on the bridge as well, including Holbrook and both of the Dades. Suvia Ferris was not, Jackson noted.

"*Watson*," Jackson said. "All ahead one-third; turns for five knots. Steer course one six five. Acknowledge."

As the computer acknowledged the commands, Jackson stepped out onto the starboard wing of the bridge. On this course, *Seafire* would come up astern of *Lee* and pass along her port side. Jackson was in his best pressed white uniform, with the four gold stripes of a private yacht's captain on his shoulder boards, and gold "scrambled eggs" on the brim of his hat. He was dressed for inspection, and *Seafire* was going to pass in review.

Kevin Finnerty joined Jackson on the bridge wing, as he'd been asked. "OK, Kevin," Jackson said, "we're going to dip colors. When I tell you, pull the ensign about half way down and hold it."

"Why are we lowering our flag?" Kevin asked. "We beat them. They should strike their colors to us!"

"Dipping isn't striking, Kevin. It's a salute, not a surrender," Jackson said, smiling. "It's an old custom. Merchant ships, cruise ships, and yachts if they're big enough, dip to warships as a sign of respect. The warship returns the dip."

"Are we doing this to piss them off?" Kevin asked, hoping he answer was yes.

"Sort of. If we dip, and they're not ready to return it, it will embarrass them. I want to see how squared away their new skipper is. He must know we're leaving. We radioed the port captain for permission to leave harbor over an hour ago. *Lee's* radio room would have heard that and reported it to the captain. If he's squared away, he'll expect us to dip as we go by, and be ready to return it. We'll see.

"Anyway, Kevin, we're supposed to hold our flag at half mast until he dips his. He'll pull his flag down, hold it for a second or two, and then haul it back up. Once his flag is back up, we can haul ours back up. Not before."

"Got it," Kevin said, and hurried aft to the signal bridge.

There was hardly a ripple of breeze as *Seafire* approached the *Lee*, so there was no danger of the frigate swinging at her anchor into the yacht's path. Jackson told *Watson* to steer two degrees to the right, a new course that would bring the two ships within a hundred yards of each other. As he drew closer to the old destroyer leader, he remarked at how little changed she was since he had sailed in her on his midshipman first class cruise. Her weapons were newer, of course, but little else had been altered. He felt a brief pang for what might have been, but forced himself to suppress it. "Ready, Kevin?" he shouted.

"Ready!" came the reply.

Jackson could see activity on the frigate, as *Seafire*'s bow approached a point opposite her stern. It was time. "OK, Kevin," Jackson shouted, "Dip!"

For a moment nothing happened, and Jackson allowed himself a small smile. Caught them off guard, he thought. Suddenly, a sailor in whites ran to *Lee*'s fantail and hauled her ensign down to half-mast. "Remember, Kevin," Jackson shouted, "don't haul our flag back up until he does!"

"Yes, Sir!"

Jackson was puzzled. Several seconds had passed, and *Lee's* ensign was still at half-mast. Suddenly, to Jackson's amazement, sailors began pouring onto the frigate's main deck. Like the man at the fantail, they were all dressed in whites, and in less than a minute, there were more than a hundred of them, lining *Lee*'s port rail, evenly spaced, facing *Seafire*, and standing at attention. Still, the frigate's ensign remained at the dip.

"What's going on?" Kevin asked, but Jackson didn't reply.

Across the still water came the sound of *Lee*'s intercom. "Hand salute," it said, and the sailors saluted as one. More seconds passed, with *Lee*'s men holding their salute and her ensign still at half-mast. The ships were beyond abreast, and were beginning to pull apart.

"Hey, Mr. Jackson," Kevin shouted. "I think they want us to pull our flag up first!"

"Do it!" came the reply.

Kevin hauled away on the halyard, and *Seafire*'s ensign raced back to the top of her gaff. Almost at once, *Lee*'s deck speakers blared the word, "Two!" The frigate's men dropped their salute, and her ensign snapped back to the top of her flagstaff.

Young Finnerty walked forward and stood beside Jackson. For

a moment or two, he watched as the men on *Lee* continued to stand at attention along her rail. "I don't get it, Mr. Jackson. Who was saluting who back there?" Receiving no reply, he turned and looked at Jackson. He saw the silent tears running down the man's handsome black face and falling onto his perfectly pressed white shirt. Showing wisdom and compassion far beyond his years, Kevin walked away and left his captain alone.

Bill Christmann, arriving back in Langley at about the time that *Seafire* was leaving Capetown, was immediately summoned to a meeting with the DCI. A late spring morning in South Africa translated to late fall predawn in Virginia, but in the windowless room at CIA headquarters, it could have been any time of day or year. The meeting was in progress when Christmann entered. Beside the DCI, there was Malloy and his boss, the DDO. Dr. Schroeder and a couple of his tekkies were there, too. Christmann took a chair.

The meeting was like previous ones, but differed in one detail. There were no aerial views of the white ship, since there were no Nightbirds orbiting it. Holbrook had threatened to shoot them down, and nobody was sure he couldn't do it. Christmann, using a secure satellite telephone, had told his superiors about Phase Six the day before. The fucking Boy Scout theory had been blown to pieces, and all of Holbrook's threats were being taken seriously.

Conversation had stopped when Christmann had entered the room. Bill realized they were waiting for him to say something.

"Happy Pearl Harbor Day," he said. Schroder was the only one to laugh.

"Very funny," said the DCI, in a tone that indicated he thought otherwise. Christmann regarded him coolly. It was no secret that the DCI had a fairly low opinion of Christmann, who'd been careful to conceal that the feeling was mutual. DDCI was sitting next to the director. Christmann didn't like her much, either, and wondered if the DCI was boffing her. If he was, Christmann thought, neither of them would be enjoying it. Both would think it was a great way to gain control over the other. Yikes, Christmann thought. I've been in this job too long.

"I suppose we're here to figure out how to keep Holbrook from blowing up the capital city of Makran," Christmann said.

"Actually, no," replied the DCI. "We're here to figure out how he's going to do it. More important, we want to know how he's going to blame it on Jinnah. The consensus around here is that if he's likely to succeed on both counts, we should let him go ahead."

For once, Bill Christmann, notorious CIA wise guy, had no sassy response. He stared at the DCI in stunned disbelief.

George Holbrook was waiting on the flying bridge when Suvia arrived. Around the anchorage the steep hills of Diego Garcia, brown and green in the seasonless tropical sun, rose from the sea. Although it was before nine in the morning, the sun blazed with the power of a furnace.

"Merry Christmas, Suvia," said George, as she reached the top of the ladder.

"What?" she asked, perplexed. When he'd asked her to meet him on the flying bridge, she'd assumed he had some confidential matters to discuss. Jinnah was due to arrive at noon. She had forgotten that it was Christmas Day.

"I wanted to give you your present before our honored guest arrived." He handed her a small package, wrapped in metallic foil, with a matching bow. The foil shimmered rainbows in the light.

"This is terrible," she said, taking the package from his hand. "I didn't get you anything."

"I got this for you in Boston. I hope you like it. Women who are nearly billionaires are damn hard to shop for."

Satisfied that he wasn't mocking her, she began to unwrap the foil, picking carefully at the tape to keep from tearing the wrapping. Inside was a book, a thin volume, clearly not new. It was entitled, *South Shore Town*, by Elizabeth Coatsworth.

"I hope you like it," George said, as she leafed through the pages, puzzled. "Turn to page thirty-nine."

Suvia did and began to read. Her eyes opened wide as she saw the name "Suvia" on the printed page.

"It's the story my mother told me when I was a little girl," she said, her eyes brimming. "Where did you find this?"

"A place called the Brattle Bookstore. They sell old books. There's only that one paragraph, but I thought you'd like it just the same. There's a story about Minot's Light, too."

"Thank you, George," she said, then burst into tears and kissed him, more or less at the same time. Then she fled from the flying bridge. George watched her go, pleased and perplexed, feeling the warmth of her lips on his, tasting the saltiness of her tears.

Shortly before noon, a small fishing boat pulled away from the beach and headed toward *Seafire*. On the wing of the bridge, George used binoculars to study the boat. It carried three men: Jinnah, Syed, and a third man George didn't recognize. The latter controlled the odd-looking outboard motor. George smiled to himself. The third man was probably just a boatman who would take the boat back to shore. As they approached, George went below to meet his guests on the quarterdeck.

George watched as the boat came smoothly alongside the accommodation ladder. Jinnah came aboard first, followed by Syed, who carried two large duffel bags.

"Welcome aboard," George said to Jinnah, in an even tone.

"I'm sure you do not mean that," Jinnah replied, "but I appreciate your civility, nonetheless. Thank you."

"You're welcome. This is an awkward time. Hopefully, we will be able to avoid shouting at each other."

"Hopefully indeed," Jinnah agreed. "Please show us to our accommodation. As Syed is my personal bodyguard, he should have a room next to mine."

"That is how we planned things," George said. "I'll show you to the guest quarters myself."

"Surely a steward could do that," Jinnah said.

"None aboard," George said. "They've all been let go."

Jinnah was suddenly suspicious. "Why is that?" he demanded. Syed began to unzip one of the duffel bags.

"Security," George said. "You and I and the rest of the owners know that your research foundation is a sham. It is best for your interests and ours that no one else ever learns that. Twelve of the owners plus two paid crew brought the ship here from Boston. The two crew are the captain and the chief engineer, who are necessary to teach your men how to operate the ship. All unnecessary personnel were left behind."

Jinnah appeared to relax. "Excellent thinking, Mr. Holbrook," he said. He handed George a slip of paper. "The ship must be at these coordinates at noon three days from now. Until then, Syed and I will take our meals in our rooms. Are you familiar with Muslim dietary restrictions?"

Jinnah and Syed stood on the port wing of *Seafire*'s bridge, defying the heat of the midday tropical sun. Jinnah's moment of triumph had arrived. A little over a mile away, a nondescript trawler was approaching the rendezvous point. The fishing vessel was roughly ninety feet in length and indistinguishable from thousands like it that scoured the Indian Ocean in search of food. It carried Jinnah's men, the handpicked guerrillas who would man and operate the ship he was bringing them. In a few minutes, his dream of a seagoing stronghold would become reality.

Soon thereafter, Jinnah thought with satisfaction, Holbrook would be dead. It was well that most of the yacht's crew had been left behind. Killing the wealthy owners wouldn't trouble Jinnah. Murdering working men and women would. Watching Holbrook die would be sheer pleasure.

As the trawler approached, on a converging course with the big white ship, Jinnah could see the men lining her deck. How impressive the white destroyer must appear to them, he thought. How excited they must be to see my promise fulfilled. As he watched, the men on the trawler began to wave and shout, gesturing wildly in triumph. Several of them brandished automatic rifles, holding their weapons overhead in the universal gesture of joy and defiance. What a day!

A few feet behind the Makranis, in the pilothouse, George Holbrook regarded them with interest. They're well dressed for the occasion, he noted. Jinnah wore crisply pressed fatigues, looking like a young Fidel Castro. Syed was equally correct in his uniform. Although Jinnah was unarmed, Syed carried the Uzi that he never seemed to be without. Such an odd choice of weaponry for a Muslim, thought George. Made in Israel. People say that gold has no politics. George supposed that bullets have no religion. As George watched, Jinnah raised his hand to wave back to the men on the trawler. An imperial gesture. George picked up the intercom handset, spoke briefly, then returned it to its cradle.

One deck below, in CIC, Bob Knight began talking to his computer. "*Watson*," he said. "Surface action port." Knight centered the image of the trawler on one of the video monitors, then increased the magnification until the boat filled the screen. Using a light pencil on the screen's surface, he designated three targets. First antennas, next the base of the trawler's single mast and finally, the pilothouse. When he was done, he continued, "*Watson*, transfer voice command to George Holbrook on the bridge. Do not acknowledge commands on bridge speakers until contrary command is given. *Watson*, acknowledge."

"Acknowledged. No acknowledgments on bridge speakers until further command."

Bob Knight turned away from his monitors. He and Suvia knew what was coming, but the others did not. "George and I worked this over a number of times," said Knight. "If Jinnah realizes that the computer is the key to our operations against him, he's likely to come in here and shoot the place up. George is going to run things from the bridge. We need to go to the exchange room."

Suvia Ferris didn't like this part of the plan; it was incredibly dangerous. Jinnah and Syed would be armed when the laser started firing. She had wanted George to overpower them before taking action against their boat. He wasn't willing to risk any overt action against Jinnah while his organization was still intact, and while the assassination teams were still at large. George decided that even arming himself was too great a risk. If Jinnah found a gun on him, the terrorist might order the killing to begin. The best George could do was keep the number of people at risk to a minimum. George, Jackson, and Ralph Dade, the three ex-Navy men, would stay on the bridge. Everyone else had to take cover and wait.

It wasn't Suvia's style to hide while the action was going on. As George's backup, she knew that her place was anywhere but at his side if there might be shooting. Intensely frustrated, she led the group of owners to the exchange room. Kevin Finnerty, armed with a twelve-gauge riot gun, met them there. They locked themselves in.

George stepped to the starboard side of the pilothouse. Jinnah and Syed, still on the port wing with their backs turned, would be unlikely to hear him when he spoke to the computer. The trawler, now less than a mile away, was flying colorful flags. Her deck was crowded with armed men. "*Watson*," George said. "Battery to bear." Above his head, he could hear the low rumble as the ruby laser mount rotated on its bearing ring, directly above the pilothouse.

Syed and Jinnah also heard the rumble as the laser mount turned to point at the trawler. Standing just beneath it, they could hear the whine of the servomotors as well. They turned and looked up, puzzled, unable to recognize the danger the strange looking object posed.

"Ruby laser free to fire," George said. "Shoot."

The two terrorists were looking directly at the laser as it fired. Even though it was aimed far above their heads, the brilliant red light blinded them temporarily. Instinctively, they turned away. As their vision cleared, they could see the red beam tearing the trawler apart. In the first few milliseconds, the laser cut the radio antennas from the trawler's mast. Next, it went to work on the mast itself; that came down in less than three seconds. Then, the beam shifted to the trawler's pilothouse, cutting like a torch.

Jinnah and Syed watched in horrible fascination for five seconds or more. The trawler broke into chaos. Men who had been jubilant a moment before now dashed about in confusion and panic. The falling mast had injured several of them. It trailed drunkenly over the starboard side, with a man pinned beneath it. The red beam continued to cut big chunks from the burning wooden pilothouse.

Syed and Jinnah recovered from their shock. Jinnah turned toward the open door to the bridge. His fists were balled tightly, his face contorted with hatred and rage. "No!" he screamed at Holbrook. Behind him, Syed raised his Uzi, aimed it at the laser mount, and opened fire. In less than a second, he emptied a thirty-round clip into the open front of the laser housing. Two bullets struck the ruby crystal, shattering it. Sparks and flame erupted from the mount, relays tripped, and power shut down.

Jinnah leaped at Holbrook, seizing him by the front of his shirt. "You fools!" he screamed. "You will all die for this!" Jinnah looked back at the trawler. The flames were growing higher, although several men could be seen trying to extinguish the blaze. "Go alongside that boat! Take the men off!"

"*Watson*, take the conn," said George. "Resume voice acknowledgments."

The familiar voice filled the pilothouse. "This is *Watson*, I have the conn." Jinnah momentarily released his grip on Holbrook's shirt.

"Surface action port," said George. "Previous target. Ram and sink target. Ship is free to ram."

"Confirming. Maneuvering to ram," said the computer, as once again, Jinnah screamed, "No!"

Seafire began to accelerate, and turned to the right, a maneuver that would bring her through 270 degrees and intersect the trawler's course directly on its beam. When nobody said or did anything to stop her, Jinnah pointed at Ralph Dade and shouted, "Syed, shoot this man. Shoot him in the leg!"

Syed, having just reloaded the Uzi, flipped the selector lever to semiautomatic fire, and pumped a single round through Ralph Dade's thigh. Ralph shouted in pain, falling to the deck. Blood flowed, but it wasn't spurting. The shot had missed the femoral artery, George thought.

George Holbrook looked directly at Jinnah, but he spoke to the computer. "*Watson*, this is Holbrook. Code seven. Ramming command cannot be countermanded under any circumstance. *Watson*, acknowledge."

"Code seven acknowledged," said the voice of the computer, full of calm authority.

"All right, you murdering son of a whore," Holbrook shouted at Jinnah, his own rage growing to the very limit of control. "This ship is going to ram and sink that boat of yours, and nobody here can stop it. Your threats are useless. If you kill us all, you'll be alone on a ship full of dead people, with no idea how to get home. And that trawler and everyone on her will still be on the bottom!"

For a moment, Jinnah said nothing. He shook with rage. *Seafire* continued to accelerate, continued to swing through her wide right turn. The burning trawler was dead astern, temporarily out of sight. Suddenly, Jinnah said to Syed, "The computers! Destroy the computers!" Syed bolted from the pilothouse, and Jinnah turned to Holbrook. Once again, the look of triumph shone from the terrorist's face.

George Holbrook knew that Syed and his Uzi would be in CIC in seconds. He spoke without hesitation, "*Watson*. Run program St. Elmo's Fire."

"Confirming," said the familiar voice from the speaker. "Running program: St. Elmo's Fire." After a second or two, the computer continued, "Program complete." Then, just as *Watson* finished his message, the sound of gunfire came from below.

Several seconds passed as nobody spoke. Syed returned to the bridge, ramming a fresh clip of ammunition into his Uzi as he stepped through the companionway. *Seafire* continued to turn in a wide circle, passing through a course that would have intersected the trawler's. Her rudders were no longer under control. "Now," said Jinnah. "There must be a way to steer this ship manually. Unless you find it, I will kill all of you and try to find it myself!"

Holbrook made eye contact with Jackson and nodded. Jackson went to the steering console and pushed the computer override switch. He shifted the ship's rudder, throttled back the engines, and brought *Seafire* on a course to intersect the trawler once more. "Keep your weapon on the black man," said Jinnah to Syed. "If he does anything foolish, kill him." Jinnah returned to the bridge wing, triumphant once again. His triumph was dashed as fire reached the huge store of munitions aboard the trawler. The explosion was enormous: burning cordite formed an orange ball of flame that engulfed the small ship. The fireball rose, twisting and roiling, a thousand feet into the air. When the smoke cleared, there was nothing of the trawler to be seen but bits of smoking debris on the surface of the ocean.

George Holbrook had anticipated the explosion and the moment of opportunity it might give him. He had found a weapon, and as the fireball rose, he had it in his hand. Syed, mesmerized by the explosion, was unaware of the danger until far too late. He barely had time to raise his Uzi before the heavy fire extinguisher smashed into his temple, crushing his skull like an eggshell.

As Syed's body fell to the deck, Suvia came through the pilothouse door with the riot gun. She pointed it at Jinnah and chambered a shell.

"No, Suvia," George said. "We need this one alive."

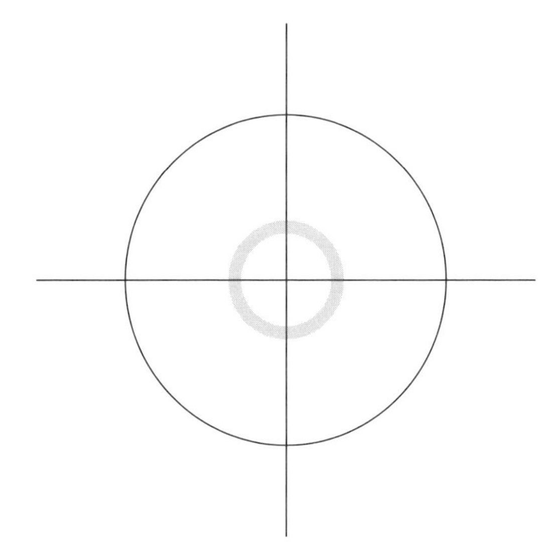

CHAPTER 14

THE RADIO squawked briefly. Raoul, who had been dozing, was instantly awake. The quarry was on the move, said the voice. Raoul nudged his companion, started the engine, and put the car into gear. Here we go again, he thought. Maybe tonight would bring some real action. It had been Raoul who had cut off Chrissy Langone's hand, months ago. He still relived the moment in his dozing half-dreams, grinding his teeth in the satisfaction of savagery. He dreamed, too, of what had been left undone — what he had wanted to do with the girl, things that had been forbidden. Perhaps tonight.

The Fleetwood rolled out of the entrance to Lost Tree, and turned north onto A1A. When it reached Route 1 it turned right, heading north again, toward Jupiter. Raoul followed, mildly perplexed. In the past, the car had taken precautions, sudden turns, doubling back, running yellow lights. Now, it was proceeding like the lead car in a funeral procession, virtually inviting pursuit. Was the driver sure he wasn't being followed? Or didn't he care? Raoul spoke briefly into the radio, calling the man who used the name Jake. There was no reply, and Raoul felt even more uneasy.

"*Que pasa*?" asked Hector, Raoul's companion. "Is something wrong?"

"I don't know. It looks like they want us to follow them. Maybe it's a trap. Jake doesn't answer the radio. That's never happened before. I don't like it."

Hector grunted and turned in the passenger seat to look astern. It was nearly midnight, and traffic on Route 1 was light. If they were being followed, the tail was a very loose one. Raoul tried again to reach Jake on the radio. The result was the same.

Jake would not be answering the radio call, then or ever again. The men who had come for him were professionals. They'd come in silence, like ninjas. Weeks earlier, they'd identified the apartment that Jake was using as a lookout post. The men had money — a modest bribe had produced a key. They'd been in the room, listening, as Jake had ordered Raoul and Hector to follow the Fleetwood. They'd calmly waited while he completed his call and put down the radio. Then they had moved.

Jake's mindset had been that of a hunter. The possibility that he might become prey hadn't occurred to him, and he was poorly prepared to defend himself. His only weapon, a pistol, lay in a drawer of a lamp table. His move to get it was clumsy and obvious. The larger intruder clamped Jake's wrist in a viselike grip before he could reach the drawer. He was still struggling to free his arm when the second man stepped behind him.

Death came easily for Jake. The struggle was over in seconds. The knife stroke was clean and quick and had come before he'd had time to appreciate the mortal danger. The razor sharp blade severed the windpipe and both carotid arteries. He lost consciousness before pain or fear of death could trouble him.

• • • • •

Two or three miles south of the Jupiter inlet, the Cadillac slowed and turned left. It bumped ponderously over the grade crossing of the Florida East Coast Railroad and proceeded west down a dirt road. Raoul's alarm increased, and he considered breaking off the chase. Curiosity, greed, and above all lust made him continue on. Tonight, perhaps, he would have the girl, both her body and her life would be his for the taking. He drove on, west, toward the edges of the Everglades, down the deserted, dead-end road.

Raoul drove with his lights off, following the Cadillac's taillights and the ribbon of sandy road glowing with silvery moonlight. Hector, never much of a talker, was completely silent. Raoul reached under the seat and extracted his weapon, a Glock machine pistol, and placed it next to him on the seat. Hector was already holding his pistol in his lap.

After four or five miles, the Fleetwood stopped, and Raoul stopped his car several hundred yards behind it. Now firmly convinced that he had driven into a trap, he began to turn the car around. The road was narrow, and Raoul didn't want to get stuck in the soft sand of the shoulders, so it took several cycles of backing and filling to complete the turn. Relief swept over him as he accelerated toward the east, back the way he had come, away from the danger behind him. Lights still off, driving as fast as he dared, he followed the silver ribbon of road. When he saw that the ribbon had a black hole in it, it was too late.

■ ■ ■ ■ ■

The huge dark green bulldozer raced at its maximum speed of twenty miles per hour down the narrow dirt road. The driver held the massive scraper blade, as wide as the road itself, bare inches above the surface. He braced himself for impact as the car slammed into the blade. The mid-size Chevy had less than a tenth the mass of the big 'dozer, and its driver felt little more than a solid jolt. The effect on the men in the car would be far greater, he knew. He hoped they hadn't been killed by the impact. He wanted to confront them before they died.

The bulldozer backed a few feet, and the driver peered over the blade. The front end of the car was smashed in. Steam billowed from the radiator. Through the shattered windshield, he could see movement. Good. Using skills his father had taught him, he raised the great blade high, moved forward, and lowered it onto the roof of the car. He increased the pressure, watching the roof buckle and the doors twist as the blade pushed inexorably downward. Over the roar of the big diesel engine, he could hear screaming from inside the car. Good.

Satisfied that the car was flat enough that the men couldn't get out, the bulldozer operator eased the pressure on the blade and climbed down from the cab. He knew the men were armed, so he approached the car cautiously. Standing back from the driver's door, he aimed a flashlight inside. Both men were conscious, struggling to free themselves from the twisted wreckage. Neither had a gun in his hand. He doubted either could produce one quickly.

"Before you die," he shouted to them, "I want you to know why." He shone the light on his own face for a moment, then climbed back onto the bulldozer. Lowering the blade once again, he pushed the smashed car off the road and into a pit he had dug earlier. He could still hear the men screaming as the blade pushed the first mounds of dirt onto the car.

Bobby Langone knew this was insanity. He should have been a hundred miles from this place. His father's instructions had been explicit — use hired talent that wouldn't know who they were working for. In all other cases, even for the lookout in the condo on Singer Island, that's how it was being done. But not in this case. These were the men who had kidnapped his daughter and killed her friend. These were the men who had cut her. This was personal.

The LNG carrier *St. Elmo* was less than three miles from the channel entrance before anyone in the Indian Navy noticed what she was doing. Makran exported liquefied natural gas, and LNG ships were commonplace. Since their cargo was so dangerous, a special offshore terminal had been built. There, the ships could be loaded away from the densely populated areas surrounding the harbor. It was not only illegal for an LNG ship to enter Makranpur Harbor, it was unthinkable.

The harbor was an old one, and small. During the days of sail, a squadron of British men-of-war could barely fit inside. Almost perfectly round, it was protected on three sides by steep hills that rose above it like the seats of a Greek amphitheater. Mak Harbor, as sailors had called it for centuries, was a classic hurricane hole — the favorite shelter during the terrible cyclonic storms that periodically ravaged the region. The same factors of shape and topography made the harbor completely unsuitable for ships carrying explosive cargo.

Lt. Edward Dindial of the Indian Navy was certainly not the first to see *St. Elmo* inbound with a huge bone in her teeth. He was, however, the first to recognize what she was and what she was doing wrong. With outrage, horror, and disbelief, he grabbed the radio handset and began to scream.

Nicholas Argeriardis, Jr. stood on the bridge of the huge ship as she surged ahead at a full twenty knots. He watched the channel buoys swing into alignment as the LNG carrier settled on its final approach course, and checked the radar for the millionth time. The ship was fully loaded and making maximum speed. From the time he gave the order to reverse the engines, it would take the ship a full fifteen minutes to stop. During that fifteen minutes, the ship would travel three and a half miles. The spot he had chosen was precisely in the center of the harbor, so his margin for error was less than half a mile. At twenty knots, *St. Elmo* was traveling a nautical mile every three minutes. If Nick mistimed the order to reverse by more than a minute, the ship would stop either outside the harbor, or downtown in Dockyard Square. Either result would be a disaster.

The radio squawked on the bridge. It was the Indian Navy. Interspersed with a string of presumably Hindu obscenities, came an unmistakable order for the ship to stop. Nick checked the radar once again. It was time. "Full reverse engines!" he shouted. Then, into the radio, "This is the LNG ship *St. Elmo*. We acknowledge your order. Our engines are reversed and at full power." What more could a sailor do? Ah, yes, he thought, there is something. He reached for the lever that sounded the ship's mighty horn.

Mak Harbor, like countless other Third World harbors, was filthy, crowded, and confused. Hundreds of vessels, mostly small, nearly all old, bustled about with casual disregard for any rules of the road. The anchorage was packed, with only a narrow channel from the harbor entrance to the docks. *St. Elmo* came into this channel, howling like a banshee, white water fore and aft. Still going fast enough to throw a huge bow wave, her prop, churning astern, dragged its own maelstrom behind her. All around, terrified boatmen scrambled to get out of her way. Curses and screams of fear and outrage mixed with the trumpeting of the big ship's horn. The harbor descended into chaos.

Nick Argeriardis's eyes flicked back and forth between the pitometer and the radar. Well inside the harbor mouth, he was now concerned that he might have given the order to stop too late. The docks ahead seemed incredibly close, they were disappearing under the bow. The speed drained away slowly — five knots, four, three. Finally, the great ship lost way, and began to creep astern. "Stop engines!" he said. "Drop anchor." Nick stepped out onto the starboard wing of the bridge, pleased with himself. *St. Elmo* was in the center of the harbor.

"OK, Alex," he said to his brother, who had joined him on the bridge. "Here we are. Let's play the tape."

Although none of them had ever seen his face, virtually all of the people of Makran knew Jinnah's voice. Broadcasting for years from clandestine radio stations, the terrorist routinely delivered the equivalent of the Fireside Chat. A mixture of religious zeal and anti-Hindu hate mongering, the rambling speeches were a routine part of life in Makran. When the powerful transmitter aboard *St. Elmo* began broadcasting on the frequency used by the M.L.O., the voice was Jinnah's.

"My brothers and sisters of Makran," it began, starting with Jinnah's familiar greeting, "may God be with you. I have returned to our homeland, aboard the ship that you can see in our beautiful harbor. I have come to bring us freedom at last.

"This ship is a carrier of liquefied gas, and it is fully loaded. I have captured it from the capitalist tycoons of the United States. The crewmen are my prisoners, and they do my bidding. It is I who ordered them to enter the harbor. My men and I have placed explosives around each of the five gas spheres. At my command the ship will explode in a fireball with the power of a thousand suns. All around it will be destroyed, the harbor, the city, the docks. I, too, will be destroyed, as will many of you, my people.

"I will wait for forty-eight hours before doing this. If, during that time, the Indian government irrevocably agrees to grant Makran its rightful status as a sovereign nation, I shall depart and release the ship and the crew. Otherwise, the city and its people will be destroyed.

"Why would I kill myself and my people like this? The answer is a simple one — freedom. For years I have fought for freedom from the Hindu oppressors, to no avail. I am tired of fighting, tired of waiting. We will all have freedom soon, one way or another. We will be free to build a new nation of our own, a nation rooted in the sacred beliefs of Islam. Or, we shall soon rejoice in eternal life in the bosom of God. One way or another, we shall all be free.

"I warn the Hindu, do not try to leave the city. People of Islam, do not let them get away! They will be our slaves in paradise if they die with us in the flames. If there is any sign of evacuation, I will blow up the ship at once! I will blow it up if there is any attempt to board the ship, if any boat or aircraft approaches it. Hear me! Do not doubt that I will do this!

"Be strong, my people, be brave. God is merciful. God is great. As we believe in God, He shall believe in us. I shall not speak to you again until Makran is free. Until then, may God be with you, and goodbye."

The tape ended, the radio was shut down, and panic swept the city.

In Langley, Virginia, Bill Christmann, Jim Malloy, the DCI, and others were watching the news on CNN. A mood of doom and dismay pervaded the briefing room. The story of the crisis in Makran was playing, and everyone watching knew that Jinnah wasn't behind the outrage. It was the international terrorist, George Holbrook, an American with known ties to the Central Intelligence Agency. In the next few days, the North Koreans could get Star Wars and thousands of Makranis could die, all courtesy of the CIA. The consensus that Holbrook should be allowed to proceed with phase six had evaporated. No one would admit having heard of such a consensus. Not even the DCI.

The news archivists at CNN had dredged up some old film of the 1944 LNG disaster in Cleveland. The grainy, black-and-white images were flickering on the screen while the anchorman read his grim copy. "Little is known about the effects of a major LNG explosion," he said. "There are a number of theories, all with support in computer models. Scientists agree on two points. The gas will not explode, like dynamite. It will burn like a torch. That's because it must mix with oxygen in the air before any form of combustion can occur. We have with us tonight a special science correspondent, Dr. Bruce Barnett, a noted physicist. He will explain more about the potential disaster."

"Thanks, Wayne," Dr. Barnett began. He was a distinguished looking sort, with pale skin and snow white hair. "Yes, while scientists agree that the gas will burn, not explode, we disagree on how fast it will burn. The burn rate is critical to all of our computer models. Since there is wide disagreement on the burn rate, the results of computer predictions of the potential fire vary widely."

"Perhaps, doctor, it would help our listeners if you explained what you mean by 'burn rate'."

"Of course, Wayne. The gas in a LNG tanker is a lot like the propane in the tank in a backyard barbecue. Before the gas can burn, it has to mix with air. Before it can do that, it has to turn from a liquid into a vapor.

"Unlike propane, LNG must be kept very cold to keep it in the liquid state. Turning it into vapor, the 'gas' that we're familiar with, requires heat. You literally have to boil the stuff, and it takes a lot of thermal energy. How fast this cold liquid will boil into gas is hotly disputed. Sorry, no pun intended.

"Remember, the liquid gas is cold, extremely cold. Much colder than the water in Makranpur Harbor. Much colder than the freezing point of water. If the gas spills, it will float on the surface of the water, like gasoline, because it's lighter than water. Some physicists believe that the gas is so cold it will freeze the surface of the water. The liquid gas would then be insulated from the warm water below, and the boil off rate would be quite slow. This would result in a less intense fire, lasting longer in time, as much as half an hour.

"Most scientists disagree with that hypothesis. They believe that a slurry of ice would form, rather than a solid sheet of ice. The slush would not effectively impede the flow of heat from the water to the gas."

"You mean like a Slush Puppy?" asked Wayne, trying to enliven the story, which was sounding like Physics 101.

"Slushier, actually. If that happened, the entire cargo of gas could burn in less than five minutes. While I've been talking, you've been playing film clips from the Cleveland incident of October 21, 1944. That involved the rupture of an LNG tank. The heat sources were limited, and the liquid gas got into the storm sewer system. It would travel for blocks, until a heat source boiled off some gas and caused an explosion. It was as if dozens of mad bombers had gone underground, and were blowing up parts of the city at random. One hundred and thirty-five people died."

Wayne kept quiet. He knew his business. Nobody would click to another channel when they could see 135 people burning up in Cleveland.

"Could we have that other clip?" asked Dr. Barnett. "Thank you," he said, as other images filled the screen. "This is the resort known as Los Alfalques. It was a beach and campground in Spain. On July 11, 1978, a butane tank truck went out of control on the coastal highway. It overturned onto the beach, spilling its cargo down to the water's edge, burning the bathers alive. People jumped into the sea to escape the flames, but to no avail. The burning gas floated on the water, and killed the people when they had to come up for air. The death toll in that accident was one hundred and fifty."

Wayne decided that the grisly details had gone on long enough. "There must be a lot more gas in the ship than there was in the tanker truck," he said.

"Oh, yes, far more," Dr. Barnett replied. "The tank truck could not have been carrying more than fifty cubic meters of liquefied gas. The LNG ship has one hundred and twenty-five *thousand* cubic meters of gas aboard. More than two thousand times as much as the tank truck that crashed in Spain."

"Dear God," said Wayne, reacting for an instant as a human being rather than a newsman. "The potential for disaster must be enormous!"

"Wayne," said the physicist, sensing that the anchorman wasn't grasping the magnitude of his story. "That ship has five cargo tanks. The fuel in each one contains energy equal to the bomb that destroyed Hiroshima. If the ship burns, she'll release the energy of five atomic bombs."

"Dear God," said Wayne, repeating himself. The network had put the special report together quickly, and Wayne hadn't been briefed on these details.

"Remember, though," said Dr. Barnett, "it can't explode in a flash, like an atomic bomb. If a tank ruptures and the cargo ignites, a pool of burning gas would spread over the water of the harbor. According to the computer models, heat would rupture the other tanks quickly. Within five minutes, the pool would grow in diameter to nearly half a mile. The flame would be over a mile high and would tilt downwind. The radiant energy from the column of fire would be as deadly as the flash from the Hiroshima bomb. Less intense, but longer lasting. A person a mile away, outside without protective clothing, would receive fatal burns in ten seconds. Lightly constructed buildings two miles away would burst into flames within thirty seconds. Although the gas would be consumed in five minutes, the firestorm it would ignite could burn for hours."

"What do you predict would happen in Makranpur, Doctor, if the ship were to blow up?" asked Wayne, the newsman taking control once again.

"It would be terrible. The harbor's circular, not much more than a mile across. There are slums all around it, crowded with people living in cardboard shacks. The ship's at the center of the harbor. A million people could die."

People around the world were watching CNN at that moment, but in only two places was there anyone who knew what really was going on. One such place was in Langley, Virginia, where a grim little group had just heard the million deaths prediction for the first time. The other place was the salon aboard *Seafire.*

The man who called himself Jinnah found himself once again in the salon, a place he had first visited in triumph some nine months before. He no longer exuded the air of power and menace that had been the source of his strength. Instead, he seemed smaller than his actual size.

"I do not understand," he said. "Why do they think that it is I? I have nothing to do with this! Blow up Makranpur? How could anyone believe that I would do such a thing?"

"Because you told the world that you would do it. On your own rebel radio station," George replied.

"That is nonsense!" Jinnah shouted, getting to his feet. "It is a lie!"

"Sit down, Jinnah," said George. "Of course, it's a lie. Explain it to him, Steve."

"Gladly," Roth said. "Mr. Knight and I have been working on an advanced voice synthesis program for our computers. Not only can a computer speak in a human voice, it can speak in *any* human voice. Yours, mine, anyone's. We chose Walter Cronkite's voice for the ship's computer. We could have chosen Margaret Thatcher's as easily. Or yours.

"A computer aboard *St. Elmo* is loaded with that program as well as tapes of your voice, mostly your propaganda broadcasts. Remember Malta, when you told George that death would be freedom for your followers? We taped that, too. The computer announced, in your voice, that you were about to incinerate yourself and your countrymen. It was quite a speech."

"No one will believe it!" Jinnah shouted, still on his feet.

"Of course, they will," said George. "Everyone knows you're a mad bomber. The Marine Corps barracks in Beirut, the Khobar Towers in Saudi Arabia. You've bragged about those. You've claimed that if your plans had been carried out correctly, the Air Force Towers would have blown up like the Marine barracks. Of course, people will believe it. They already do."

Jinnah sat down again, and once more he seemed to shrink in size. "Why?" he asked. "In God's name, why?"

Half a world away, in Langley, Virginia, the same question had just been asked. It was after midnight there, although the real-time images from CNN showed a small harbor in bright daylight. In the middle of the harbor a ship loomed hugely in the telescopic lens of the news network's camera. On her side, like an obscenity left by a deranged graffiti artist, the ten-foot high letters LNG were painted in white. Bill Christmann ventured an answer to the question. He wasn't even close.

George Holbrook considered Jinnah's question for several seconds. "Because we don't trust you. Because we're afraid of you.

And, because we hate you, for making us afraid.

"Since you first visited us nine months ago, you've been the focus of our lives. All our combined resources have been dedicated to dealing with your threats. We've studied you, analyzed you, tried to predict your reaction to every contingency. Everything we have done since we've known you has been committed to one goal — the utter destruction of you and the Makran Liberation Organization.

"As we studied you, we learned things that commanded our respect. Unlike many terrorists, you're not a coward. You're firm in your faith, and death holds no terror for you. You have a good mind, a military mind with an instinctive grasp of how to seize a tactical advantage.

"It took a while, but we found your weakness. We found the one thing that we could threaten you with that would really matter to you. Your name.

"In a few minutes, we're going to ask you for the coordinates of the rendezvous point, where you were to take delivery of the nuclear weapons."

Jinnah's eyes widened in surprise. "Yes," George continued, "we knew about those. We also want you to tell us whatever codes or signals will allow us to land without opposition, so we can take those weapons away from whoever has them."

"I will die before I will tell you anything," Jinnah said.

"You haven't been paying attention," said George, with a slight edge to his voice. "We know you'd die gladly as a martyr. If you don't tell us, we won't just kill you. We'll kill a lot of your people, and make the world believe you did it. Your name will be reviled for a thousand generations. Your followers will deny they ever heard of you. You'll be the Hitler of the Islamic world."

"You would kill a million innocent people simply to destroy my name and reputation! Are you mad?"

"We doubt the million figure. One hundred thousand dead is

more likely. About the number that just one of those mini-nukes you're after could kill. Are we mad? No more than you, my friend.

"Also like you," George continued, in a somewhat angrier tone, "we're not stupid. Do you think we believe you'd let us go after we gave you the ship? We know what you're planning to do with her — operate her as a floating base for terrorism. Would you let two dozen people live who know that? Hardly. We would have been fish food if we'd done this your way."

"You agreed to my demands," Jinnah said, instantly regretting his words.

"Promises made under duress are void," said George. He, too, regretted his words at once, since he was about to use extreme duress to extract promises from Jinnah.

"Our agreement was a lie. We decided months ago that we wouldn't give you *Seafire* or a billion dollars. You would have used the money to buy nuclear weapons, and used the ship to deliver them. Whatever the cost to ourselves and our families, we couldn't put those weapons in your hands.

"Having decided that, we had to find a way to protect ourselves. Killing you wouldn't be enough. Your followers would want revenge. To be safe, we'd have to eliminate all of them. We're in the process of eradicating the men who have been following our families. We think we've identified all of them, and by now they should all be dead. However, you have dozens of men under arms throughout the world, and hundreds, if not thousands, of unarmed followers. To destroy them all would be impossible. The only effective alternative is to destroy you in their eyes."

Jinnah interrupted, "The weapons have been delivered. The funds must be transferred tomorrow. There can be no deviation. The funds are available; I verified it with the bank. The funds must be transferred."

"There are no funds to be transferred, Jinnah," George said softly. "The money isn't there."

"No," Jinnah replied, "the money is there. One billion dollars. I verified the balance myself."

"There is no money in the bank," George said. "Henri Girard arranged for reports to you of the steadily growing balance. They were all false. A billion dollars did, in fact, go into the bank. All but a few million came right back out.

"Where did a billion dollars go? Some of it was spent to purchase the LNG ship, which we renamed *St. Elmo*. An apt name, don't you think? Most of the money was spent on rebuilding *Seafire*. She is not just an oceanographic research ship. She is also a warship, and unless you agree to *our* terms, we will use her to destroy your base and all of the people there. Having done that, we'll go ashore and take custody of the nuclear weapons, which we know are there awaiting confirmation of transfer of the funds."

George paused, and Jinnah sat, stunned. He turned his attention to the TV screen. CNN was replaying the old film of the disaster in Cleveland. Nearly a minute passed before either man spoke. Finally, Jinnah said, "It would seem that you must destroy Makranpur no matter what I do. Even if I give you the information that you seek, you would still have to destroy the city, wouldn't you? Otherwise, my organization and I would still be a threat to you."

"No," George replied. "We have a plan for that, too. The city would be spared. You would not. We would deal with the remnants of your organization in other ways."

"So, in either case, you intend to kill me." Jinnah's words were a statement, not a question.

"You began this. You declared war on us, and all is fair in war. You wanted our money, because money can buy weapons, because money *is* a weapon. Instead of giving it to you, we used it to defend ourselves. We have no desire to burn your city; but if we're forced to, to protect our families, we'll do it. Believe me, we will. We have no desire to kill you, or anyone else. Yet we shall. Right now, people in our employ are killing people in yours. If there were a way to spare your life, we would. I don't believe there's any way."

Jinnah was quiet for a moment. Holbrook is right, he thought. My faith is strong; death does not frighten me. Yet, Holbrook is wrong at the same time. If millions of people believe me to be a villain, it will mean nothing. God will know the truth; that is all that matters. I will do what I can to save the city of Makranpur; to do so I will give my promises. After all, promises made under duress are void. "Welcome to the world of terrorism, Mr. Holbrook," he said with a bitter smile. "I regard your threats as genuine and I agree to your demands. What, exactly, do you want to know?"

The ExecuStar helicopter lifted smoothly from *Seafire's* flight deck, swung wide around her stern, and flew north, the direction in which the ship was heading. George Holbrook was in the pilot's seat, Suvia was beside him.

"George," Suvia said, "you're not making any sense. From the beginning, you were planning to use both helicopters for your assault. We can still do that, even without Ralph. I can fly. Not as well as you or he, but well enough. Let me take his place."

George knew Suvia was right. He'd planned to use the ExecuStar to carry the assault team, with the Sparrow as a supporting gunship. Bill Jackson had done a masterful job of tending to Ralph Dade's wounded leg. Even so, he was going to be bedridden for days. With Ralph unable to fly, George had changed the plan. The ExecuStar would have to go in without cover.

George pondered the situation for a few minutes. Suvia, realizing what he was doing, kept silent to let him think. His plan kept changing, and each change involved fewer aircraft. If this kept up, he and the others would end up wading ashore. This flight had been planned from the beginning, too — a reconnaissance sweep over the island thirty-six hours before the assault. It had never been his plan, however, to fly the mission in a helicopter or take Suvia along. Both of those changes were recent and both had been forced upon George. He liked neither of them.

Originally, he had intended to overfly the island in the Caproni jet sailplane. Flying high in the late afternoon, he would have used the high-resolution camera mounted in her belly to take pictures. Most likely, Jinnah's people on the island would never have known the aircraft was above them. But, in the hasty departure from Boston, the Caproni had been left behind, and George's subsequent attempts to ship it forward had failed.

When it became apparent that he would have to use the ExecuStar to scout out the island, Suvia had insisted on coming along. As his second in command, she had argued, she needed to know the lay of the land in case he was killed or captured. George had tried to dissuade her, saying that without her body weight aboard he would be able to carry twenty gallons more fuel. In the end, though, she had prevailed in the argument. He would fly the aircraft, and she would snap pictures with her Nikon, using the longest lens that the late afternoon light would allow.

The flight was going to be a long one, nearly four hours. Extra fuel tanks had been installed to extend the ExecuStar's range. Even so, the trip couldn't be made unless the return was shorter than the trip out. While George and Suvia were airborne, *Seafire* would be racing toward them at twenty-five knots. The flight back would be almost an hour shorter than the flight to the island, but the fuel margins were still dangerously thin.

"You know, George, you could be creating your own miniature Bay of Pigs invasion here."

"Bay of Pigs. What do you mean?"

"The secret invasion of Cuba. You must have read about it."

"Of course, I did," said George. "I don't see the connection."

"Air power. Insufficient air power. That's why the invasion failed. You could have the same problem."

"Different situation entirely. The invaders had no air cover, but Castro did. Jinnah's people won't have any more air cover than we will. We'll fly in there in one civilian helicopter, early in the morning. Most of them will be asleep. Those that are awake will expect to see Jinnah get out of the 'copter. We'll jump out, deal with them, and that's that. If we go in there with an air armada, they'll be suspicious, and we'll lose the element of surprise."

"Two helicopters are an air armada?"

"So I exaggerated a little."

"Before Ralph was shot, you were planning to use just such an armada. Or does the element of surprise get lost only if half the armada is being flown by a woman?"

"Of course not. That has nothing to do with it. When Ralph got hurt, I was forced to analyze how the plan would work with only one helicopter. I thought of the element of surprise angle for the first time, and realized that one helicopter was better than two."

"Bullshit," said Suvia, in a bright, have-a-nice-day tone.

"Bullshit?" George replied, trying to sound shocked and offended. Suvia laughed aloud. It had been weeks since he had heard the music of her laughter.

"This invasion of yours is a boys' club, plain and simple. No girls allowed."

"That's just the way the assignments worked out."

"Sure. GI Joe Langone, who's sixty years old and has a bad heart, hits the beach at dawn. Little me, twenty years younger and a hell of a lot more fit, stays behind."

"He's a good shot."

"Give me a break! I'm a Texan, remember?"

"Suvia, some of the people who cut off his granddaughter's hand may be on that island. Do you think he'd let me leave him behind?"

"No, I guess not."

"We won't be taking any prisoners on that island. We're going in shooting and we'll keep shooting until all the bad guys are dead. If anybody tries to surrender, we're going to pretend they didn't and shoot them anyway. Are you prepared to do that?"

Suvia didn't reply.

"It wouldn't be fair to let you fly the SparrowHawk. You're a good pilot, and someday you'll be one of the best. But combat flying is different. You'd be taking an intolerable risk."

"My choice."

"Takes two to fly the SparrowHawk in combat. Are you willing to have somebody else risk his life to your inexperience?"

"I'll fly it alone." Suvia's affect was flat, without trace of laughter or anger.

"Can't. Pilot flies it and shoots the rockets. They're unguided. They go where the aircraft is pointed. Not very effective. The main weapons are the machine guns. Gunner aims and fires them. Pilot can't. Suppose the turbine takes a round and disintegrates. Could you disengage it and go to autorotation before you crashed? Have you ever put a helicopter into autorotation? No. How many hours do you have in a Sparrow? Thirty? Fifty?"

Suvia didn't reply. She was turned away from George, staring at some imaginary object on the horizon.

"Suvia, I'm sorry. I don't want to hurt your feelings. We need you on the ship. You're the second in command, you have to be ready to take over if I get shot down. Having you shot down with me isn't going to advance the cause very much."

"All right," she said, facing forward once again. "I'll be a good girl and do what I'm told. How much longer until we get to this fucking island?"

George looked at her, startled by the obscenity.

"Your assumption that men are more capable than women of cold blooded killing is interesting," Suvia continued, her tone relaxed once again. "I'll have to tell you about Lucretia Borgia some day."

The helicopter approached the island a few minutes before sunset. George had followed a course that had taken them to a point about five miles west of the island. He then turned to the east, so that their final approach would bring them in out of the setting sun. Suvia began taking pictures when they were about three miles out.

They had known little about the island before the flight. All of the charts of the area were small scale, lacking in meaningful detail. The island bore a Creole name that probably meant something like, 'This would be a nice place to live if it had any food or water on it.' The vegetation was sparse and desert-like, since the low hills along the island's spine weren't high enough to coax moisture out of the tropical winds.

The island was shaped as the chart had shown it, like a fat banana, with a broad bay on the convex side, to the north. There was nothing resembling a harbor, and the bay would offer no shelter in a blow. George looked for signs of shipping and saw none. Nor could he see any aircraft on the ground. Good, he thought. Anyone on the island would be stuck here until somebody else came to take them off. Crossing the water's edge at the west end of the island, George spotted the encampment. It consisted of six or seven tents in two distinct groups. Two or three people came out of one of the tents at the sound of the helicopter. Suvia clicked away with her motorized Nikon. Two or three more people came out of another tent. One of them had a rifle. George decided it was time to leave.

The ExecuStar approached *Seafire* in complete darkness. George had programmed the ship's course into the helicopter's GPS navigation computer, and had flown down it on a reciprocal heading. In the clear air, he had spotted the ship's running lights ten miles away. With no wind, the ship didn't have to turn to allow the helicopter to land. George had about fifteen minutes' worth of fuel left, however, and decided to hover for a few minutes to allow the ship to slow down.

"What's that?" asked Suvia, gesturing toward the water astern of *Seafire*. George pivoted the aircraft to see where she was pointing.

Seafire was decelerating, but she was still making better than twenty knots, and leaving a huge wake. It frothed from under her counter and streamed, arrow straight, toward the southern horizon. The wake was plainly visible for miles in the tropic darkness, shining with a radiance of its own, glowing with the cool light of a trillion fireflies.

"Bioluminescence," said George, after he had watched the light show for a few moments. "Sea life, disturbed by the ship's passage, giving off light like a firefly does."

"It's beautiful," said Suvia. "Why haven't I seen it before?"

"It only occurs when the water has a lot of life in it. You probably never happened to be outside when it was around and the night was dark enough to see it."

"It's magical. What did you say it was called?"

"Bioluminescence. Some people call it phosphorescence, but that's not technically correct. A lot of people call it seafire."

"Seafire. Is that where the ship's name came from?"

"Yes."

"I never knew what the name meant. Never thought about it, I guess. *Seafire*. What a beautiful name."

"Like Suvia," said George. The words were out of his mouth before he knew they were coming, and they took him and Suvia equally by surprise. They sat in silence, waiting for the ship to slow down. They watched the river of cool fire flowing below them, neither able to think of anything to say.

George Holbrook had been dreaming when the knock came at his stateroom door. Half asleep, half awake, he'd been thinking of

Suvia Ferris. After the helicopter had been secured on the flight deck, he and Suvia had stood together on the fantail for over an hour, watching the glowing wake and talking about the future. In less than two days their plan would have met with success or failure. Either way, the long adventure would be over, and, barring catastrophe, they would each return to their normal lives. George, who should have been getting some sleep, or thinking about invasion tactics, was unable to do either. All he could think of was Suvia, and how he would miss her when she returned to her own world.

The knock came again, soft and tentative, and George rose to open the door. Suvia wore a silk gown, the one Helen Dade had given her. A creamy off-white, and very expensive, it flowed lightly over her, touching gently here and there to reveal provocative hints of the woman under it. George stood, mesmerized at the sight of her.

"Aren't you going to ask me in?" she said, with the familiar hint of laughter in her voice. "I'd really be embarrassed if somebody came down the passageway and caught me dressed like this." She gestured with her hand at her nightgown, and the movement swept the translucent silk across her breasts.

"Please come in," George said, stepping back from the doorway to let her pass. He closed the door behind her, and locked it. Suvia turned and smiled at him at the sound of the bolt snapping home.

"Do you always sleep in your clothes?" she asked, sitting on the edge of the bunk and folding her hands in her lap. George was wearing a tee shirt and khaki trousers.

He sat on the bunk next to her. "Never know when I might get called up to the bridge." He ran his eyes up and down her in a deliberately salacious way. "You'd cause quite a stir if general quarters were called and you ran up there in that outfit."

"Let's hope that doesn't happen for a while, then."

"Why, Suvia? Do you have something in mind?"

"Don't make this any harder for me than it already is. I was taught to wait for the man to make the first advance. Trouble is, a girl could die of old age waiting for you to make a move."

George touched her cheek with his hand, running his fingers down her jaw line to her chin. Gently, he pulled her mouth to his and kissed her. They held the kiss for a long time. "I'm glad you came," George said. He felt Suvia's breath catch and quicken. He felt his own heart begin to race in his chest. He kissed her again, and the world began to swim dizzily.

"I am too," she replied, pulling him to her.

For the first time in his life, George Holbrook made love to a woman that he actually loved, and who loved him in return. Together, they took each other to places George had never dreamed of, and she had nearly forgotten.

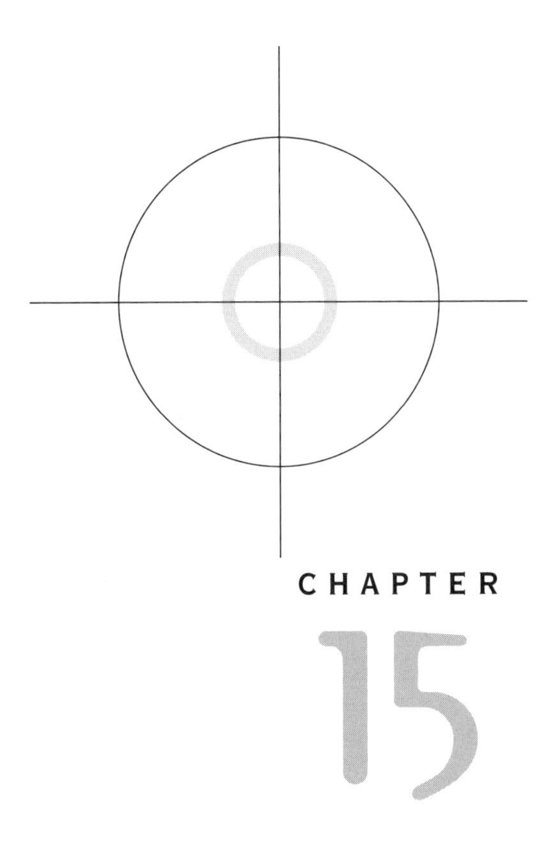

CHAPTER 15

GEORGE stood alone on *Seafire*'s flight deck in the predawn darkness. The ship lay motionless in the shallow bay. The engines were silent. Only the faint rumble of the electric service generators disturbed the peace of the tropical night. In an hour or so, it would be dawn of the last day of the year.

And perhaps the last day of George's life.

He looked at the island, a dark mound, barely visible in the moonless night, less than a mile away. There was no moon, but George knew that the white ship could be seen from the shore, if anybody was looking. This possibility had been discussed the day before. George and the others had agreed that the risk of discovery was slight. The island was a terrorist camp, not a military garrison. Lookouts would most likely not be posted. Even if the ship were noticed, Jinnah's men probably would assume that their leader was in command.

That, and a thousand other issues had been discussed the previous day. *Seafire* had followed an oblique course, not turning directly toward the island until after dark. The final approach had been timed to take place after midnight. Shortly before four A.M. the darkened ship had glided slowly into the bay, using only one engine. She had not anchored, merely stopped. With no wind and little current, the anchor wasn't needed, and the noise it would have made could have been heard ashore. George and Bill Jackson had scanned the beach with night vision scopes, and detected no activity. George had wondered if people ashore were looking back with night observation devices of their own.

George and the others had made the final preparations for the assault as the ship had made the approach to the island. They had developed Suvia's pictures, and made a rough model of the island. They'd studied it, as well as the pictures, for hours. They would attack in near darkness, at the earliest light of dawn, so they'd memorized the island's details as best they could.

Waterless and far from any other land, the island was uninhabited. Several hundred feet high at its highest point, it was mostly barren rock, with patches of stubborn vegetation clinging to life here and there. Most of the vegetation was on the southern side of the island, the side away from the bay. It was there that Jinnah's men had set up camp.

George's plan was simple. He would fly the ExecuStar to a landing zone on the ridge just above the terrorist's camp. Approaching low from the north, the helicopter probably wouldn't be heard by the terrorists until it crested the ridge at the landing zone. He wouldn't land, just touch down lightly while Roth, Carson, Wilson, and Knight got out. They'd move quickly to a patch of high ground just above the encampment. From there, they would have a clear field of fire, down into the camp, from a protected higher position. Meanwhile, George would fly the helicopter to a point south of the camp, and hover. Joe Langone, Paul Harrington, and Bill Jackson would still be aboard, with an M60 machine gun and an M19 grenade launcher. Langone, who had demanded the job, would pump grenades into the tents. Anyone who came out would be caught in a crossfire between Jackson and Harrington's machine gun and four laser-aimed assault rifles on the heights above. It would be a nasty bit of work, but it would be over quickly.

Suvia Ferris had briefly renewed the argument that two helicopters firing into the tents would be better than one. George had been firmly opposed. They would have no way of knowing if their approach had been detected. A single passenger helicopter probably wouldn't attract gunfire at first sight. The SparrowHawk, with weapon pods hanging all over it, probably would. It was the old air armada argument, of course, but Suvia had realized that George was right.

The idea of bringing *Seafire* close to shore in the bay came from similar logic. If the helicopter's approach were detected, it would be better that the terrorists could see that it had come from the yacht, which was parked and presumably waiting for the nuclear weapons transfer. In addition, having the ship close provided the evacuation route if the tide of battle turned foul. The evacuation plan was as simple as the plan for the assault. Suvia and Helen Dade would take *Seasmoke*, the big Magnum powerboat, to the beach, under cover of machine gun fire from two M60s mounted on the wing of the bridge. They would pick up the men, Dunkirk style, and speed back to the ship. Everyone on the ship shared George's degree of comfort with this plan. They all hated it. But, with both lasers out of action, it was the best they could devise.

Much of the day had been devoted to weapons training. With the exception of Ralph, who was still unable to walk, all of the men and women had fired the assault rifles, grenade launchers, and machine guns. They had been learning to shoot the weapons for weeks, of course, but this had been the final session. Everyone had practiced, even those who weren't planning to participate in the assault. Plans might change. As George had predicted, the aiming lasers on the assault rifles were ineffective in bright sunlight. The dots of red light were too dim to see unless the target was quite close. In the predawn darkness, however, that wouldn't be a problem.

All this and more tumbled through George's mind as he waited for his small assault force to assemble on the flight deck. The hourly CNN reports had told them that the standoff with *St. Elmo* was holding. Yet two things were in George's mind more than anything else — Suvia Ferris and the Bay of Pigs.

After their night of lovemaking, George and Suvia had tried to behave as they had before, as friends and no more. They'd failed. They'd been like newlyweds, unable to take their eyes off of each other. Helen Dade had been the first to notice. Soon, others were catching on as well, even some of the men. George and Suvia had neither noticed or cared. And, after the long day of planning and practice, they'd retired early, citing the need for a good night's sleep. Nobody had believed them, of course, and they hadn't cared about that, either.

George wondered if he and Suvia had a future together. Whether or not they had a future at all. Which led George to think about the Bay of Pigs. What if Suvia was right? He wondered about this, questioning his plans, doubting his decisions. What if there are a hundred guys on that island, not the dozen or so we expect? What if Jinnah, locked up in a makeshift brig, had been lying when he said there was no arrival code or password? What if this does turn into a small scale Bay of Pigs?

This was nonsense, George knew. He and his troops were as ready as they ever would be. There was no time to revise the plans. The assault had to take place on this morning. The funds were to be transferred at 9:00 A.M. Zurich time. When the transfer failed to take place, there would be hell to pay, and the weapons would be gone. The Indian authorities weren't going to let *St. Elmo* sit around forever in Mak Harbor, either. Today had to be the day and sunrise would be too late. The time for doubts and questions was over. George needed to concentrate on executing the plan he had, not wishing he had a better one. He knew this, so he forced himself to think of Suvia. It wasn't hard.

He was thinking of her when his assault team appeared on the flight deck. They shuffled around, letting their eyes adjust to the dark. George looked them over. God, he thought, what a motley crew. Middle-aged businessmen dressed up as soldiers. A bunch of geriatric commandos, George thought, recalling Ralph's joke. Their Kevlar body armor made them look fat. George knew, though, that they were all in pretty good shape. If you didn't count Joe's bad heart.

Even the ExecuStar looked strange, sitting on the flight deck with the doors off. It reminded George of a time, long ago, when he'd taken his father's car on a date. He'd driven the black sedan a mile or so, then stopped to take off the hubcaps. He'd thought it made the car look cool. In fact it had just looked silly. So, too, the ExecuStar, a staid commuter trying to look like a Huey. Stop it, George said to himself. He looked at his watch, and the glowing dial told him that it was almost time. He was putting on his own Kevlar flak jacket when Suvia came out of the hangar. He stepped away from the others, so he could say goodbye to her alone.

"George," she said, "don't say anything like, 'Don't worry, Suvia. Everything will be fine.' It's bad luck. That's what Richard said the morning he went off to fight that oil fire." There wasn't enough light for George to see the tears in her eyes, but he could hear them in her voice. Strangely, he felt no jealousy at her mention of her late husband's name. Two days earlier it would have made him crazy. The realization of that fact amused him, even as he was touched by her words.

"I love you, Suvia," he said, and pulled her head under his chin, hugging her tight against him. "I hope it's OK to say I love you."

Time to leave, George knew, so he released her from his embrace.

"Yes, it's more than OK. I love you, too, George," she said, and turned back into the hangar. Then, she turned again, a brittle smile on her face. She said, "That's a cute little butt you've got there, Mister. Try not to get it shot off, y'all hear?"

"Yes, Ma'am," George replied, smiling as well, and she turned to leave. He watched her go, then turned to prepare the ExecuS-tar for combat.

In Langley, Virginia, the telephone rang in the situation room. Malloy picked it up. He listened briefly, then put the handset back into its cradle. "Hah!" he shouted, beaming. "Got 'em!"

"Where are they?" asked Christmann.

"Damn island in the Indian Ocean that nobody ever heard of. The peeping toms at NSA picked the ship up on one of their satellites a couple of hours ago."

The DCI jumped to his feet, face reddening. "A couple of hours! Why weren't we told immediately?"

"Because we're the CIA, and everybody hates us," said Christmann. Jesus, he thought. This turkey runs the company and he hasn't figured that out yet.

"Don't be flippant with me, Christmann," the DCI said, his face even more florid.

"He's right, boss," said Malloy, in a matter of fact tone. "I'm sure that's exactly why. They were ordered to cooperate with us. That pissed them off, so they'll obey the letter, but never the spirit, of the order. I'm sure somebody over there deliberately let the information age for a while, like fine wine, just to show us what they think of us."

Christmann looked again at the DCI, whose face was as red as an expensive cut of beef. That man, he thought, belongs on a low-salt diet. "Can we get a Nightbird up?" he asked.

The DCI's color was fading. "We already have one over Makranpur Harbor," he said.

"Don't we have more, in Diego Garcia, maybe?"

Malloy responded to Christmann's question. "Sure. We keep a few of them there all the time. Helps us keep tabs on the latest genocidal outrage in Africa."

"God, you're a cynic, Malloy," said the DCI. It was the friendliest thing he had said in thirty-six hours. "There is another Nightbird there, I believe. I'll have one sent up. And if it takes a couple of hours to get airborne, I'll flap my arms really hard, fly over there, and personally shoot it down with my Walther PPK." He strode out of the room.

There may be hope for the Old Man yet, thought Christmann. If only he'd quit using words like flippant. The last person Bill could remember using the word was Eve Arden in *Our Miss Brooks.*

The heat-seeking missile struck the ExecuStar squarely on its port engine. It had been fired just as the helicopter had reached the beach on the north side of the island. George had been flying fast and low, and the homing missile had approached more from the side than below. The port turbine disintegrated immediately, showering the aircraft with shrapnel, mostly turbine blades, knife sharp bits of hardened metal. Things were happening too fast for George to assimilate. The stab of fire to his left, the sound of an explosion, the shudder of the aircraft and the cries of pain in the cabin all startled and confused him. His pilot's brain reacted instinctively. Even before he'd fully comprehended what had happened, he knew his aircraft was in trouble. He did what any pilot would do. He grabbed all the altitude he could get.

In a little more than two seconds, George had regained control. As in most twin rotary wing aircraft, the rotors were slaved to each other. Swinging through intersecting arcs, they had to maintain equal speed at all times. Although the blades were usually driven by both engines, they could be powered by either alone. Declutching the port engine, George powered up the starboard one, pulling up hard on the collective to give himself the cushion of safety that altitude provides to any aircraft. By then, he'd become aware that he'd taken a missile hit. Achieving stable flight, he felt a brief sense of relief, only to have it shattered as the starboard engine began to fail. Shrapnel from the port engine had sliced through the starboard engine's oil line; it would seize in seconds. The ExecuStar was going down.

"Hang on," George shouted to the others. "We're going to have to land. The engine's about to buy it. I'll try to get us back to the ship."

In the seconds since the missile strike, the ExecuStar had flown over the ridge and almost completely across the island. Anxious to avoid flying past the missile shooter again, George gambled on the length of time that the helicopter could stay in the air. He flew south, over open water, then swung to the west. Still over water, he cleared the western tip of the island, and set a course for the ship. Hang on baby, he thought. Give me sixty seconds, and we'll be aboard.

"*Seafire*, this is George," he said into the radio microphone, "We've taken a missile hit, and we're heading back to the ship. Please turn on the lights on the flight deck." He could see the ship fairly well in the faint predawn light, but he wanted the best visibility he could get. The missile that had hit him was probably one of the mini-Stingers stolen from the armory in Germany. George was sure that its range was less than the distance between *Seafire* and the beach, so there would be no harm in lighting up the ship. A squawk burst from the radio in response to his message, but he ignored it.

"Anybody hurt back there?" George asked, recalling the shouts of pain he'd heard just after the missile strike.

Steve Roth replied, "Yeah, Joe. Pretty bad. Me, too, but I'll be

OK. Just get us back to the ship, George. We'll worry about the injuries then."

George looked at the engine instruments and read bad news. If anyone in the world knew that a Holbrook ExecuStar couldn't stay in the air for sixty seconds with one engine gone and zero oil pressure in the other, it was George Holbrook. "Shit!" he said aloud, as a terrible thought struck him. "Life jackets!" Nobody aboard was wearing one. Instead, they were wearing heavy bulletproof vests. If the ExecuStar went down into the sea, people were going to drown. Once again, George turned his crippled bird around, and headed toward the island.

"*Seafire*, this is George again," he said, keying the radio. "We're going down pretty soon now, and I'm not certain we can make it back to the ship. I don't want to risk crashing into the water. We're heading for the beach at the west end of the island."

There was more noise in his headset, and George tried to ignore it. Vaguely, he recognized Suvia's voice, shrill and questioning, but there was no time for him to respond. In seconds, the ExecuStar was going to stop flying. Every bit of his skill and attention had to be directed to getting it onto dry land. Very soon now, he knew, the starboard turbine was going to turn from friend to foe. When it stopped turning, it would act as a brake on the rotors, and the helicopter would drop like a stone. Before that happened, he would have to put the helicopter into autorotation, the rotary wing equivalent of a glide. If he did it too early, they wouldn't make it to the beach. If he waited until too late, they would crash. George was no longer reading the engine instruments; according to them, the turbine was already dead. Concentrating instead on the sound and feel of the aircraft, he waited for the last possible moment to disengage the engine.

The helicopter was a hundred yards from the beach when George decided that the engine was finished, and transitioned to autorotation less than a second before it stopped with a bang. Skimming over the water, he slowed the helicopter, canting its nose up, using the energy of its airspeed to keep the rotors turning. Finally, he pulled back on the cyclic control and up on the collective, to flare into a soft landing. Nothing happened. The hydraulic pressure was gone, the controls were dead, and the ExecuStar crashed into the sea.

Nick Argeriardis was a nervous wreck. The sun had just risen, and he'd slept no more than a few minutes during the night. He, too, had been watching CNN. According to "unnamed sources," the Indian equivalent of Delta Force was preparing to storm the ship. The logical time for them to strike would be at night. Dawn should have brought relief to Nick. Instead, it merely brought exhaustion.

The main source of Nick's anxiety was his knowledge of the two timetables for ending the standoff in Mak Harbor. On the radio, the bogus Jinnah had announced that the ship would be destroyed at noon on January first. That deadline was thirty hours away. It would never be reached. The Indian Army had announced it to lessen the chance of a commando raid. Logically, they would wait to see if negotiation could end the crisis before launching a raid that could end in disaster. If they had known the real deadline, Nick thought, they would have come last night.

The decision to detonate the explosives, or not to, would be made within a few hours. Probably before noon. For what must have been the hundredth time, he asked himself the question. Will I actually blow this ship up if they tell me to? The answer was the same. We'll see when the time comes.

"Four or five hours!" The DCI was livid, his face crimson once again. "That's not acceptable! What's the excuse now?"

"No bird available," Malloy replied. "Simple as that. There are four Nightbirds assigned to that sector. We've had one in the air over Mak Harbor on a continuous basis for the last day and a half. That takes at least two airplanes, usually three."

"How does that translate into a four or five-hour delay?"

"One of the four airplanes is in the middle of an engine replacement. It won't be back in operation for two more days. Another had a hydraulic failure on its last rotation over Makran. It won't be fixed for four or five hours. When it is, we'll send it to check out the yacht. That will leave us without backup for the two planes alternating over Makran, but we can probably handle that. Unless you want me to drop the coverage over Mak Harbor, though, that's the earliest we're going to get a bird over *Seafire*."

The DCI pondered for a minute. "No, we have to know what's going on with the LNG tanker. Keep the coverage there. I doubt we'll miss much by waiting a few hours to check out that damn yacht."

It took Holbrook several seconds to realize the ExecuStar wasn't sinking. The water where it had crashed was only three or four feet deep. The wrecked helicopter was sitting upright on the bottom, with the floor of its cabin awash. A good landing is any landing you walk away from, George thought, a euphoric wave of relief sweeping over him. He remembered the line from his earliest days of flight school at Pensacola. A landing you can wade away from is pretty good too, he decided.

"OK guys," he said. "We're sitting ducks out here. Let's get ashore and set up some sort of defensive perimeter before the opposition gets here. How are we doing for casualties?"

"Joe's really bad. Semiconscious," Steve Roth said. "I've got a splinter or something in my arm, but it won't bother me."

"Everybody else OK?" George asked, and got affirmative replies from Knight, Wilson, Jackson, Harrington, and Carson.

"Good. Bill, take the grenade launcher and as many grenades as you can carry. Peter, you take the M-60. Alex, the M-60 ammo boxes. Paul, Bob and Steve, two rifles each and as much ammo as you can handle. I'll take Joe."

"George, this is *Seafire*," Suvia said into the radio handset. There was no reply. In the five minutes since she had watched the ExecuStar splash into the water, her spirits had fallen and risen at a dizzying pace. The horror of the crash had been replaced with joy at the sight of the men wading ashore. Then had come the new horror of seeing one of the men carrying another in a fireman's hold. Even with powerful binoculars it was too dark, and the beach too distant, for her to tell who was who. The uncertainty and anxiety were intolerable. She called on the radio again. Again, there was no answer.

George Holbrook surveyed the situation. As a defensive position, it wasn't altogether bad. They were behind a small berm at the west end of the island. In front of them was a relatively flat piece of ground. It was roughly triangular, about two hundred yards wide and long. The makeshift beachhead was at the apex of the triangle; the end of the ridge that ran east and west along the island was at the base. Jinnah's troops could reach the base of the ridge without hindrance from the *Seafire* contingent. After that, though, the bad guys would have to cross two hundred yards of open ground. Unless Jinnah could mount an Iranian-style human wave assault, George decided, he and his friends could hold them off. For a while, anyway.

George took a quick inventory. After getting everybody ashore, he and Jackson had waded back to the helicopter twice, retrieving ammunition and other supplies. They had the M-60, with two boxes of belted ammunition for it, and a fair supply of projectiles for the grenade launcher. They'd retrieved all the M-16 rifles, and verified that their laser sights were working. There were dozens of clips of ammunition for the rifles. For firepower, they were in good shape.

Other supplies were a problem. George hadn't planned for a sustained campaign. They had carried no food, and very little water, aboard the helicopter. The medical kit was a good one, though. Thank God, George thought. Jackson was using it to dress Joe Langone's wounds as Steve Roth bandaged his own arm. George watched Jackson jab a morphine syrette into Langone's thigh. Now, he said to himself, how the hell do we get out of here?

As George asked himself the question, the snarl of powerful engines drifted across the still water of the bay. "Christ!" he said, "they're firing up *Seasmoke*." He grabbed for one of the handheld radios.

"*Seafire*, this is George," he said.

"George, thank God!" came Suvia's voice in reply. Even over the radio, he could hear the relief in her voice. "I've been calling on the radio. What's going on there? We're coming to get you right away."

"Suvia, I think we should wait before you try to do that. We're in a pretty good defensive position for the time being. If you try to come ashore in *Seasmoke*, the guy with the missile launcher might bag her, too. Hang on while I try to think of a way around that, OK?"

"All right, George," Suvia replied, with obvious disappointment. "Tell us what's happening. Is anybody hurt?"

"Joe Langone's in rough shape. He got hit with some shrapnel, turbine blades probably, in the neck and shoulder. We've patched him up as best we can. I'm afraid he may be having a heart attack. Bill Jackson's doing what he can." George paused for a moment, with the mike still open, transmitting the sound of his own breathing. "Christ, what a mess," he said, without realizing it. "Steve Roth got a piece of metal in his arm. He pulled it out himself, and he's going to be fine. No other injuries, thank God. It was a damn good thing we were wearing flak jackets."

Bob Knight poked George in the arm and pointed. They could see movement at the base of the ridge. George nodded, and motioned for his friends to stay down. The sky was brightening rapidly at the approach of sunrise. In the growing light, he could see several men tentatively venturing out onto the open ground. "Call you back in a couple of minutes, Suvia," he said into the radio. Then he turned it off, put it down, and picked up one of the rifles.

"OK, guys, let's hold our fire," he said. "Don't even turn on the sighting lasers until they get closer. I don't think they could have seen the helicopter crash, and they may not have seen us come ashore. If we let them get well out into the open, we may be able to bag a few of them before they can get back into cover. Selectors on automatic. Short bursts, just like we practiced. Bill, you use the M-60. Forget the grenade launcher."

George watched the small group of men approach. Five in all, they carried assault rifles much like the one in George's hands.

"Steady, guys," he said. "They don't know we're here. Bill, keep the M-60 down and out of sight until we start shooting. Paul can feed the ammo belt. I know it will take a couple of seconds to get it up and into action. Better that than they see it too soon."

"Right," Bill replied.

Peering over the top of the berm, George could see the men approaching, now almost halfway across the clearing. "I don't think they have any idea we're here," he whispered. "They're about a hundred yards away, coming slowly. Five of them. Turn on the sighting lasers, but point them into the dirt. Let them warm up. When I say, go, we're all going to stick our heads up and start shooting. I'm going to go after the one on the left. Bob, your target is the one on the right. The other three are grouped in the middle. Alex, Steve, and Peter can take them as a unit. Got it?"

"Got it," said the others, more or less in unison. For an instant, the absurdity of the situation struck George. This would be funny if nobody had gotten hurt, he thought. Saturday Night Live goes to war. "Go!" he said, and raised his rifle. Over the years, he'd become a fairly competent marksman. He hoped he still was.

The approaching terrorists stopped about sixty yards from George's ambush site when they saw the heads pop up. The sky was bright enough for George to see the face of the man on the left, his expressions of fear and surprise. At first, the man seemed unsure of what to do, turn and run, or bring his weapon to bear. He was still trying to decide when the disk of ruby light came to rest on his chest and George fired. The M-16 kicked in George's hands, the muzzle pulling up and to the left. He compensated, pulling the red dot back onto target, firing another burst. Beside him, he could hear the sound of his friends, firing in controlled bursts, just as he and Jackson had taught them. Adrenaline flowed through his veins, the smell of gun smoke filled his nostrils, and his ears rang with the sound of gunfire. "Die, you bastards!" he screamed, ramming a fresh clip home and shifting targets. His first target, the man on the left, was down.

Suvia Ferris paced the deck anxiously, desperate to know what was happening on the beach. Once more, nobody was answering her calls on the radio. The sound of automatic weapons fire echoed across the water. What the hell is going on? "I'll tell you something," she said to Helen Dade, beside her on the wing of the bridge. "If the MLO doesn't kill George Holbrook, I just might kill him myself."

The skirmish was over five seconds old before George and the others began to take any return fire. Three of the five terrorists were down, and the other two were running the other way. Their comrades, still in cover east of the open area, provided erratic and ineffective covering fire for their retreat. Bill Jackson got the M-60 into action when the two fleeing figures were still a hundred yards from safety. They had no chance. They ran straight ahead, directly away from the machine gun as the tracer rounds bored into their unprotected backs. Both were down within seconds.

Guns on both sides fell silent, and George surveyed the battlefield in the light of the newly risen sun. Five enemy dead. No new casualties for the *Seafires.* Not bad, he thought, as a slight movement caught his eye. One of the terrorists was still alive, and trying to crawl into cover. "Oh, no, you don't," said George, and switched his M-16 to semiautomatic. He fired once. The man jerked, and was still. Feeling neither satisfaction nor remorse, George put down his rifle and picked up the radio.

"God damn you, George," came Suvia's unexpected reply to his call. "We're going crazy out here. We can hear all of this shooting and you don't answer on the radio. Two of the men with you have wives here, and they want to know if their husbands are all right!"

"We just set up a little ambush for the opposition. I turned off the radio so they wouldn't hear it as they approached. Sorry if we worried you, but we were all too busy to call. We won this round, Suvia. We got five of them, and none of us was hurt. I think they'll leave us alone for a while."

"That's good. Have you had a chance to think about getting back to the ship?"

"Yeah, but I haven't come up with any great ideas, I'm afraid. If you come for us in either the Sparrow or one of the boats, you'll get killed before you're a quarter of a mile from the beach."

"What if I move the ship in closer?"

"With the reefs, the closest you can get is about a mile. Even then, the run for *Seasmoke* is a full minute. You'd be exposed to gunfire on the way in, and the engine exhausts would make a great missile target on the way out. Same with the Sparrow, except with her, you'd have to make three trips to get all seven of us. Let me think for a while, Suvia. I'm sure I'll come up with something." From the sound of his voice, Suvia could tell George really didn't believe that. Neither did she.

The man who called himself Jinnah sat in *Seafire's* main salon. With him were Suvia Ferris and a young man she called Kevin. The latter was armed with a riot shotgun. He and another man, much older, had come to Jinnah's cell, with the odd invitation to the salon. Mrs. Ferris wants to talk, they had said. This will be interesting, Jinnah had thought. He hadn't been wrong.

Jinnah regarded the woman across the table with almost clinical interest. She was the embodiment of all that he and his organization opposed and despised. A capitalist, very rich and very white. Her blonde hair, green eyes, and fair skin were the mark of the racial elite, like the snob Brit kids who had taunted and humiliated him at Oxford. Shameless in her dress, face and hair uncovered, she had summoned him, a man, a leader of his people, to negotiate with her. As if she were his equal! No wonder the West was in a moral decline.

"It's very simple," she said. "I propose an exchange of hostages. We take you ashore, and you join your colleagues there. They let our people come back to the ship. We leave. You leave. End of story."

"Why would I agree to this? My people will soon destroy Holbrook and the others. Tonight, surely, if not sooner."

"And we will destroy you. Here and now. Kevin will blow your brains out. Is that a good enough reason?"

Jinnah was shocked by the vehemence of Suvia's response. "No," he said.

"Look," Suvia said, in a calmer tone. "Your organization and ours have been a disaster for each other ever since we met. It's cost us hundreds of million dollars to fight you. We've had a girl's hand cut off, men shot, one of whom is probably dying right now. You've had a boatload of your people blown up and five more of them shot this morning. Syed's dead. We could end up with a firestorm in Makranpur with tens, maybe hundreds of thousands of casualties. Do you want that? Do we want that? Of course not.

"I propose a truce. We let you go. You let us go. We pretend we never met each other."

"What about the ship in the harbor at Makranpur?"

"The captain calls the police. Jinnah has disappeared! All of his men are gone, over the side with SCUBA gear in the night. By now they are lost in the slums of Makranpur. The threat to destroy the city? A bluff, a magnificent gesture of defiance."

For the first time in days, Jinnah smiled. "That has a ring of truth to it. Was that the plan, if you had succeeded in killing all of my men on the island?"

"Something like that," Suvia said. "We never intended to destroy the city except as a desperate last resort."

"I doubt you would do it even then."

"If we're forced to, we will. For God's sake, haven't we done enough damage to each other. Let's break off. You get on with your holy war and we'll get on with our lives."

"It is not that easy. Some men on the island expect payment of one billion dollars. When there is no transfer of funds, there will be unpleasantness."

"Tell them the truth. You had a nice extortion scheme worked out, but the victims started shooting. You negotiated a truce that let the sellers get off the island with their merchandise and their lives. They'll be disappointed, but they'll hardly blame you."

Jinnah considered the woman's words for several minutes. His options were limited, but much less so than an hour ago. He smiled at Suvia. It was a salesman's smile, showing all of the brilliant white teeth, the teak colored skin crinkling at the corners of the handsome dark eyes. "Just how would you propose to carry out this 'hostage exchange'?"

At noon Helen Dade slipped *Seasmoke*'s mooring line from the boat boom on *Seafire*'s port side. Suvia sat at the controls, and Jinnah was in the seat nearest the stern. As he had done constantly for the past four hours, Kevin Finnerty kept the shotgun pointed at Jinnah's chest. This arrangement, and a hundred more, had been carefully negotiated. Neither side trusted the other, of course, both had good reason not to. Each step of the operation, from who got into and out of the boat, and in what order, had been fought over with the rancor born of mistrust. Finally, with the last detail agreed upon, the transfer was to begin. Suvia turned the powerboat's bow toward the beach and proceeded at the agreed speed of twelve knots. It would take her precisely five minutes to cover the nautical mile between the ship and the island.

"Finally!" said the DCI, as the monitors flickered into life. He studied the screens for a moment. "Now what the hell are they up to?"

Malloy and Christmann watched the images. The island reminded Christmann of a skinny pinecone, like the ones that had grown on a neighbor's tree when he was a kid. Brown in the blue and green water, it looked dried out and dead. "Hey!" he said, "check out the tip of the island. Can we get magnification there?"

"Christ," said Malloy, as the image shifted and grew. "It's a helicopter. Looks like it crashed."

"It's Holbrook's ExecuStar," Christmann said. "I recognize the rotors. Or what's left of them. Check the beach. Is that a defensive perimeter there?"

The image shifted again, and all three men recognized the formation. On ultrahigh magnification, they could make out seven men in a shallow depression, backs to the water, with weapons pointed inland.

"Jesus," said Christmann, "for a guy who's so critical of CIA screwups, he sure doesn't learn from them. This looks just like the damned Bay of Pigs."

Suvia Ferris grounded the big Magnum gently on the sand and coral beach. She had the Arneson surface piercing drives raised almost out of the water, to keep them from being damaged as she landed. The landing spot had been negotiated to the inch. It was between the positions of the two opposing groups, equidistant from each. Like a spy swap at the Brandenburg Gate, the balance of the standoff had to be maintained throughout the exchange. Each side knew the other would exploit any advantage. Both sides knew about promises made under duress.

The first move was from the Holbrook camp. Paul Harrington, Steve Roth and Peter Carson approached the boat, unarmed, carrying Joe Langone. While Kevin Finnerty continued to guard Jinnah, Peter climbed a boarding ladder that Helen had placed over *Seasmoke*'s side. Then, Peter and Helen pulled Joe's unconscious body into the boat. Finally, Steve and Paul got aboard.

With this part of the transfer complete, it was Jinnah's turn to move. Moving slowly, with Kevin aiming the riot gun at his chest, he climbed down the ladder and waded ashore. Kevin followed him, using one hand on the ladder, and cradling the shotgun with the other. Jinnah walked ten paces up the beach, then turned and sat down, as agreed. Kevin squatted at the water's edge, riot gun still at the ready.

Suvia Ferris made eye contact with Jinnah, and cocked her head in a questioning gesture. Jinnah responded with a curt nod, and Suvia waved toward George's little fort. Bill Jackson, Alex Wilson, and Bob Knight all stood up and began to walk toward the boat. Each was carrying an assault rifle. Fifty feet from the boat they stopped. As Jinnah watched, they removed the clips from their rifles, and put them into their pockets. Then they jacked the rounds out of the chambers of their weapons. Satisfied that the rifles were empty, and would take several seconds to be brought into action, Jinnah nodded again, and the three men waded toward the boat. Bill Jackson gave Jinnah a mock salute as he passed. Jinnah ignored it. He stood up, nodded at Kevin, turned around, and began to walk inland.

"Hey!" shouted Kevin. This wasn't the way it was supposed to happen. He was pretty sure, at least. Mr. Holbrook was supposed to come over to the boat, and then Jinnah would go inland as the boat pulled back. That was how it was supposed to be. Jinnah was leaving too soon. "Hey!" he shouted again, and fired the shotgun over Jinnah's head. Jinnah broke into dead run, zigging and zagging like a halfback, and Kevin fired again. Jinnah kept running, and the island erupted in gunfire.

"Kevin, get into the boat!" Suvia screamed, as bullets splashed all around the Magnum. "George," she shouted, as loud as she could, "Get over here!"

"Go Suvia!" George shouted, "Go! Go! Go! I'll cover you. GO!"

Suvia was about to argue, to shout back across the hundred yards of beach, but George had started firing the M-60, and there was no way she could be heard. Kevin came boiling over the gunwale, just as three or four rounds struck the boat, punching fuzzy holes through the fiberglass hull. Bill Jackson got a clip into his rifle, and lit up the laser sight. It was useless. The ruby light was completely washed out in the light of tropical noon. Aiming along the iron sights, he squeezed off a short burst of fire, knowing it would be ineffective. Then George found the range with the M-60, and the fire toward the Magnum became lighter and more erratic. Jackson stopped shooting and sat down, watching as the M-60 fire chopped through the area from which the opposition had been shooting. Suddenly, the M-60 stopped, and George shouted again. "For God's sake, Suvia, GO!"

A bullet smashed through the windshield, and struck the seat inches from Helen Dade. "Oh, God," Suvia said, and put the engines into reverse. Backing out fifty yards, she dropped the Arneson drives, pulled the wheel over hard, and threw the engines into gear. The big boat leaped forward, swinging in a tight arc toward the open water. "Hang on!" she cried, as she swung the wheel back and forth, making the boat zigzag as Jinnah had done as he'd run away. Bitter tears streaming down her face, she drove the Magnum toward *Seafire*.

The Nightbird was ten miles up, and while her gyro-stabilized cameras were rock steady, the pictures weren't. The tropical sun had heated the island's bare rock, and currents of warm air swirled upward. The small group in Langley could see the action, but it was if they were looking through moving fun house mirrors. As they watched the powerboat pull away from the island, the room was quiet.

"Analysis," said the DCI, his tone curt, clipped, imperious. Christmann and Malloy exchanged glances.

"Hey, boss," Christmann replied, "you've been on this job, what? Two years now? I know you're a politician, not a spy. But I don't think you're as dumb as you pretend to be, if you get my drift. So, why don't you give us *your* analysis, and we'll tell you if we agree."

The DCI looked at Christmann hard for several seconds. Was this a challenge, he wondered, or a friendly overture? He guessed the latter, his politician's instincts serving him well.

"Prisoner exchange. Guy in the boat gets traded for the guys on the beach."

"And ... " said Malloy, making eye contact with Christmann.

"And it went wrong," said the DCI. "Guy in the boat took off before the trade was done."

"Notice anything else?" Christmann asked.

"People on the ship are using conventional weapons. Small arms. They could have cleaned house with either of those damn lasers of theirs. They didn't use them. I assume they're not operational."

"Very good, sir," said Christmann. "Who do you think the guy in the boat was?"

"Jinnah. Had to be. Eight for one trade. Had to be the big guy."

"Who got left behind on the beach?" Malloy asked.

"Holbrook. No question."

"Why?" asked Christmann.

"Rear guard action. Stay behind to cover your buddies while they get off safely. For the last couple of months, one of my best agents has been telling me that George Holbrook is a fucking Boy Scout. Based on that, I've got to assume that it's him in that foxhole. I mean, who else? Without heavy weapons, there's no way they're going to get him off of there before nightfall. After dark, the bad guys are going to sneak up on him, and he's dead. He must know that. He must have known that when he covered the boat leaving the beach."

Bill Christmann looked into the eyes of the director of central intelligence, seeing the man, as a man, for the first time. "There's no way we can get him out of there, is there?" he asked.

"I'm sorry Bill," the DCI replied. "We both know there isn't."

"Shall I recall the Nightbird?" Malloy asked.

The DCI glanced at the president, who shook his head. "No, Jim, even if we can't do anything, I want to watch this play itself out."

George Holbrook's analysis of the situation was equally grim. It was 1:30 in the afternoon. Sunset would be around six. It would be completely dark by seven. His chances of surviving the night were slim. He'd used the last M-60 ammunition covering the Magnum's retreat, and the grenade launcher's limited range made it virtually useless. Swimming to the ship was out. If the sharks didn't get him, the sea snakes would. George had never been much of a swimmer, anyway.

George smiled bitterly to himself. I may not survive this night, he thought, but I'll make damn sure Jinnah doesn't, either. He pulled the Night Mariner binoculars from a pocket in his camouflage shirt. He could never kill all of Jinnah's men, single-handed. George knew he was good, but not that good. He knew with grim certainty, though, that before he died he could get through or around them, and take Jinnah down.

"*Seafire*, this is George," he said into the radio. As usual, it was Suvia who replied. He felt a pang of regret at the sound of her voice. "Let's go to the scrambled mode," he said. "Jinnah's boys have radios and I don't want them to hear this." He switched the radio to the secure setting.

"Can you hear me, George?" asked Suvia, her voice distorted but understandable.

"Fine, how about me."

"You sound like Donald Duck, but I can hear you well enough. Oh, God, George, how are we going to get you out of there?"

"That's what I'm calling about, Suvia. You're not. There's no way to do it. It would be foolish to try. Leave me here and get the hell out."

"That's nonsense!" Even with the scrambled transmission, George could hear the indignation in her voice. "Leave you behind to be killed? Never!"

"Suvia, with the reefs, you can't get *Seafire* much less than a mile from the beach. The weapons you have aren't effective at that range. The boat and the helicopter are easy targets, they'd never get in, much less in and out. The longer you wait, the better the chance that somebody's navy is going to show up. We've killed at least five men today, and we're not in international waters. Go now. I'll fend for myself."

Several seconds passed, and Suvia didn't respond. "How's Joe doing?" George asked.

"The same. He's resting comfortably. We're optimistic." Suvia was lying. Joe Langone had been dead for over an hour.

"We'll wait until nightfall, George," she continued. "I'm sure you'll figure out a way to get aboard by then. In the meantime, what shall we do about *St. Elmo*?"

"That's why I wanted to use the scrambler. We can't put this off any longer. Send the signal: 'EXECUTE PLAN B.'"

NICK ARGERIARDIS read the message and said a brief but fervent prayer. For two days, he had been waiting for orders such as these. Now, preparing to carry them out, he wondered if he and his shipmates could possibly escape the coming fire. "Holy Mother," he said, concluding his prayer, "please help us get the hell out of here."

Quickly, Nick called the ship's company to meet with him. With two exceptions, every man in the hand-picked crew was a relative of his, none more distant than a second cousin. The exceptions were two Texans. Both were explosive experts who worked for the fire fighting division of Ferroil. He grimaced as he thought of what they would be doing in the next few hours. If we survive this, he thought, it will be a genuine miracle.

The mood was grim in the makeshift command center outside Makranpur. The most elite commandos of the Indian Army had been assembled and briefed. They were eager to storm the ship. Confident of their skills, they longed for the chance to save the city and capture or kill Jinnah. They all hated him, and he had eluded them for a long time. Success would bring them honor and glory beyond any soldier's dream. Their commanding officer, a full colonel, was arguing with the provincial governor. The argument was heated, and not particularly polite.

"Colonel," said the governor, a civilian explaining tactics to a career soldier, "we've been through this before. I don't doubt the skill or courage of your men. Your plans are well conceived and will probably succeed. The risk of failure is small, but the consequences of failure would be catastrophic. Jinnah might have time to detonate the explosive charges. If somebody starts shooting, that could start a fire. A million people could die. The smallest risk of failure is unacceptable!"

"We risk disaster by doing nothing, governor," the colonel replied, a soldier explaining politics to a politician. "I know we might not succeed. No military operation is risk free. I think the risk is small compared to the chance that Jinnah will blow the ship up if his demands aren't met. We risk more by inaction than by acting. If we try and fail, our effort will be applauded and our failure forgiven. If we fail by doing nothing, there will be neither applause nor forgiveness."

The governor considered this point. He knew that the colonel had covered nearly every contingency. An assault on the LNG ship would have to come from the water, not from the air. Jinnah was known to have anti-aircraft rockets. Helicopters would be sitting ducks, and if one crashed onto the ship, an explosion would be inevitable. Also, Jinnah had promised to detonate the explosive charges at the first sign of any assault. Helicopters are noisy, and would be heard minutes before the assault force could get aboard the tanker.

Any form of assault that could result in a firefight was also ruled out. One stray round could ignite a conflagration.

The colonel's plan was, the governor conceded, the only one possible. The commandos would swim to the ship, dressed in black like ninjas during the darkest part of the night. Three of the leaders, all Sikhs, would climb the anchor chain, a logical place for a sneak attack. There probably would be guards there, however at three or so in the morning, the guards would be likely to be drowsy, if not asleep. The Indian soldiers would be unarmed, except for their hands and edged weapons. There would be no firefight. The three pathfinders would kill any guards they found on the foredeck. This would be done in utter silence, a particular skill of the colonel's unit. Then they would lower knotted ropes over the sides of the ship. Thirty more men would come aboard and fan out through the ship, silently killing everyone they could find. Then they would locate and disarm the explosives.

The governor considered the things that might go wrong. The list was endless. Failure was a real possibility. Yet, he knew, inaction could yield the same result. There were political considerations. Nasty ones. If the assault failed and the ship exploded, the governor would survive. If he did nothing, and the ship exploded, he would be a dead man, and not just politically. The governor felt shame that this factor had entered into his considerations. Nevertheless, it had.

The governor was aware of a more shameful consideration. The colonel was a Hindu like himself. Most of the Indian Army garrison in Makran, and all of its officers, were Hindus or Sikhs. The local Muslim population regarded it as an army of occupation. The governor suspected that, to some in the Army at least, the ship blowing up wouldn't be viewed as a disaster. There would be terrible loss of life, but virtually all the victims would be Muslims. If a Muslim terrorist wants to kill a million Muslims, why should we risk Hindu lives to stop him? The governor, proud of his Hindu heritage, was appalled that some of his fellow Hindus could think such a thing. The terrible things we do to each other in the name of religion, he thought.

"There's nothing like a crisis to promote introspection," said the governor.

"What?" asked the colonel.

"Never mind. Implement your plan. Do it tonight."

The governor looked at his watch. It was a little before three. In twelve hours, he thought, the crisis would be resolved, one way or another. Behind him rose a great commotion. The room filled with shouts of alarm and dismay. He turned to look at the harbor, and his heart sank into the black depths of despair. *St. Elmo* was on fire.

George Holbrook watched *Seafire* move. She had drifted a few hundred yards during the past several hours. Now she was motoring slowly back to a position abeam of the beach where the hostage swap had taken place. Pulling up to the edge of the shallow water, the ship stopped, a little less than a mile from shore. Some of Jinnah's men decided they could hardly miss such a target, and fired several bursts from their automatic rifles. George had no doubt that they were hitting the ship, but at such a range, the nearly spent bullets would do little more than chip the paint.

George gathered up his weapons and ammunition. After dark, his position at the end of the island would be untenable. He'd have to move inland before then, if he was to have any chance of surviving long enough to kill Jinnah. But to cross the two hundred yards of open ground, he'd need a diversion.

George had asked Suvia for one, and *Seafire* was moving into position to provide it.

Suddenly, the air filled with the roar of powerful engines, and *Seasmoke* appeared. The big Magnum rounded the ship's stern at sixty knots, and headed for the beach. Oh, God, no, thought George, as he grabbed the radio.

"No!" he screamed, in the clear, non-scrambled mode. "Go back! It's suicide!"

Suvia Ferris, at the Magnum's helm, looked like the Michelin tire man. She and Helen Dade had dismantled a half dozen flak jackets, and Suvia was swaddled in Kevlar. She was armored, head to foot, as bulletproof as she could be. She was also incredibly hot, and cranky as a result. "Shut up, George," she said, "we know what we're doing. Hide and watch."

Gunfire erupted from the island, as Jinnah's men all began firing at once. All around *Seasmoke*, the rounds struck the still surface of the water, pock marking it with flecks of white. The boat zigzagged briefly, then turned to starboard, back away from the beach. A new roar arose over the shallow bay, far louder than the sound of the Magnum's engines. An ear-splitting buzz, like a fire alarm, tremendously loud. A stream of tracer fire poured out from the wing of the ship's bridge.

"Christ!" George said to himself. "It's one of the Miniguns."

The situation room in the basement of the White House was getting crowded. The president had arrived several minutes earlier, along with his security advisor, and several people from State. Virtually all of them were watching the pictures of Makran Harbor, of *St. Elmo* belching smoke and fire. As usual, they were waiting for information from other agencies. Once again, it was the NSA whose input was most urgently needed. The Nightbird had picked up the scrambled messages between Holbrook and Ferris.

The NSA was in the process of breaking the scrambler codes and processing the tapes into intelligible audio. The task should have taken minutes. Two hours had gone by, and still no tapes. Christmann wondered if the NSA people knew, or cared, that the president himself was fuming. Malloy and Christmann were certain that the message had something to do with the LNG tanker, but what was the message? When smoke appeared aboard the tanker, Christmann thought he knew.

Despite the action in Makran, Christmann, Malloy, and the DCI were watching another monitor. They had seen the powerboat racing toward the beach. Like Holbrook, they'd decided it was a suicidal move. Then, the boat had turned away, and *Seafire* had started shooting. Really shooting.

"What the hell is that?" asked the DCI.

"Looks like a Minigun, a 7.62 light aircraft machine gun, said Christmann. "M134, I believe. Six barrel Gatling gun, electric drive. Fires a hundred rounds a second."

"Standard equipment on the proper yacht," said Malloy. "Very useful for marlin fishing."

"The Holbrook SparrowHawk carries a Minigun in one of its configurations," Christmann explained. "You can have rockets plus twin M60 machine guns, or no rockets and a single Minigun. Load according to mission. Trained crew can switch pods in five minutes. They must have had a SparrowHawk pod in the hold someplace and pulled the Minigun out of it."

"Look at that!" the DCI shouted. On the island, men had stopped shooting at the Magnum. They were in full rout, running away from the hail of bullets, up and over the ridge, onto the island's south side. Several had dropped their weapons as they ran. Three had fallen and lay still on the rocks.

As quickly as it had begun, the skirmish was over. All of Jinnah's men were sheltered behind the ridge, and *Seafire* stopped shooting. Once again, the Magnum turned toward the beach. When it was about halfway between the ship and the shore, Jinnah's men began to fire at it again, this time from sheltered positions along the top of the ridge. The Minigun fired again, but the range was too great for it to provide effective suppressing fire against men shooting from such positions. With bullets striking the water all around it, the boat turned for the final time, around the stern and into the shelter of *Seafire*.

The president and his party had diverted their attention from the burning tanker to the brief firefight. "Am I wrong, or did that little boat just go out there to draw fire from the island, so people on the big boat could see where the opposition was and pound the hell out of 'em?" the president asked.

"For a guy who never served in the military, he figures this stuff out pretty fast," Christmann said to Malloy. "Not as fast as the boss, though." The DCI heard this. Christmann had meant him to.

George Holbrook ejected the empty magazine from his rifle, and rammed another one home. He slammed the operating lever back and forth with undue force, out of disgust with himself and his weapon. As they had fled from the fire of the Minigun, several of Jinnah's men had offered themselves as excellent targets to George. He'd hit none of them. It wasn't buck fever, George was sure of that. It was the damn laser sight. The daylight was still far too bright for George to see the aiming dot, and the iron sights on top of the laser tube were junk.

Otherwise, George was pleased with the result of the latest skirmish. In the confusion, he'd sprinted away from his foxhole at the end of the island without notice. Hidden among scrubby vegetation a few yards inland from the northern shore, he was out of sight of Jinnah's troops, in a place they couldn't investigate without exposure to fire from the Minigun.

"Hey, Suvia. Nice move," George said into the radio, still using the scrambler.

It took Suvia several seconds to reply. She was stripping off the Kevlar padding that was roasting her alive. "Next time, we'll get you out of there."

"Suvia," George replied, "the purpose of that diversion was to get me some maneuvering room. So when it gets dark, I can track Jinnah down and kill him. Quit trying to figure out ways to come and get me. As long as Jinnah's alive, I'm not leaving."

"Rudder amidships," said Nick Argeriardis. "Engines back dead slow." He felt the deck shudder under his feet as the huge ship began to gather sternway. Glancing over the side, to be sure that *St. Elmo* was moving backward, he said, "Let the anchor chain run!" and his brother, Ted, spoke into a radio. On the foredeck, a small party of men released the gear securing the anchor chain, and it ran free as the ship backed away from her anchor. In less than a minute, the bitter end had gone over the side, and *St. Elmo* was underway.

"Stop engines. Engines ahead full," said Nick. He looked ahead, where visibility was poor. Thick smoke billowed up from the area of the cargo tanks, and it carried toward the bridge as the ship gained headway. "Take the wheel, Ted. Steer for the harbor entrance if you can see it. Steer 135 true when you can't. I'm going to talk to the people ashore." He stepped out onto the starboard wing of the bridge, and looked forward over the cargo deck. Smoke and flame seemed to be everywhere. Small groups of men were darting about, exchanging bursts of automatic weapons fire. Christ, thought Nick, if we bring this off, we'll deserve an Academy Award.

The smoke and flame generators had been installed weeks earlier, all carefully placed to minimize risk of igniting the cargo. Even though Nick knew this, the sight of open flames on a ship carrying flammable gas unnerved him. So did the sight of his cousins and nephews shooting at each other with Uzis, even if they were firing blanks. My turn to act, he thought, and stepped back into the wheelhouse.

"This is the LNG ship *St. Elmo*," he said into the radio, having switched to an emergency channel. "We must speak to the authorities ashore. We have a terrible emergency!"

The reply came almost instantly. "This is the governor of Makran. We see smoke and flame. We hear gunfire aboard. What is happening?"

Nick looked at the pitometer readout. *St. Elmo* was making less than five knots. Fully loaded, her top speed wasn't bad, but her acceleration was pitiful. Keep 'em talking, Nick, he said to himself. We won't be able to outrun anybody for a half-hour or so.

"The situation is critical," Nick replied, allowing his genuine excitement to color his voice. "The ship's company has broken out and we've retaken the bridge and the engine room. We've disabled some of the explosive charges, but we don't think we've gotten all of them. There have been casualties on both sides, and Jinnah has started several fires. We can't fight the fires with Jinnah's men shooting at us. We're taking the ship out of the harbor, in case the cargo tanks rupture. Please don't try to stop us or to put any men aboard. That might force Jinnah to blow up the cargo tanks."

"Please stand by," the governor replied. "I must talk with my military advisors."

"Take all the time you want, Governor," Nick replied, but not into the radio. "The longer the better." Again, he looked at the pitometer. Six knots and climbing. Through the smoke he could see the entrance channel, and the open ocean beyond it. In ten minutes *St. Elmo* would be outside the harbor. In an hour she would be in international waters, making twenty knots, and plunging into heavy seas. It would not only be illegal to board her, it would be virtually impossible. She'd have escaped.

Suvia Ferris had never been into *Seafire's* engineering spaces before. Looking at the huge circuit breakers in the electrical switching array, she couldn't help thinking of the birthing room in Frankenstein's castle. "How much longer?" she asked.

"Less than an hour," Steve Roth replied. "We'll be done by five." Suvia watched as Roth, Alex Wilson, Bob Knight, and both Finnertys wrestled with lengths of copper cables as big around as a man's arm. One by one, the circuit breakers, which protected the ship's main power plant from overload, were being bypassed. It was a gamble, of course. Designed to lase in the blue-green spectrum, the laser had overheated when it produced a pure blue light. Roth and Knight believed that if more power had been applied, it would have produced blue-green light and far less heat. More power, more efficiency, they thought. If they were wrong, the ship's engines could all be destroyed in less than a second. Dozens of fires could break out at once, destroying the ship like the *Achille Lauro*. The laser was indeed a Star Wars weapon, it was a light saber. *Seafire* could live or die by that sword of light.

"Put the tape on the speakers in here," the DCI said. NSA had just decoded George and Suvia's scrambled transmissions. After a moment, her voice filled the room.

"I don't understand, George. I thought you wanted *St. Elmo* to be blown up. That was the plan, wasn't it? Blow up the ship if all else fails. All else has failed, hasn't it? Am I missing something?"

"If I'd said to execute Plan A, would you have done it?"

"Yes. I think so."

"Suvia, my love, I've been wrong all along about this. You've been right. I've been trying to convince you and everyone else how ruthless I was. The one person I couldn't convince was me. I can't kill thousands of innocent people. Not to save my life. Not to save Ralph's kids. Not even to save you."

"What happened to your theory that they support terrorism, and aren't innocent at all?"

"Most of the Muslims in Makran are as guilty as Jinnah is. I still believe that. They encourage terrorism and they deserve to taste some themselves. But somewhere in the city, just as the ship blows up, there'll be a newborn child drawing his first breath. He'll suck up a piece of the firestorm and turn his lungs to ashes. The kid's never supported Jinnah, he's never had a chance to. If we kill him, and a thousand like him, we'll become the terrorists. Jinnah will have won. He'll have turned us into monsters like himself."

Many seconds passed. When Suvia spoke again, it was clear that she was crying. "Keep your head down, George. We're holding a council of war in ten minutes. I'll call again from the meeting. Keep thinking, damn it. There has to be a way to get you out of this."

The tape ended and the situation room was silent, except for the soft sound of somebody weeping near the back. Probably one of the women from the State Department, Christmann thought. On the monitor, they could see the LNG tanker, engulfed in smoke and flame.

"I don't understand," the president said. "Holbrook told the Ferris woman not to blow up the tanker. But they're setting fire to the ship anyway. Was there a mutiny? Did they get their signals crossed? What's going on?"

From the back of the room, not far from the weeping woman, came the sound of a man's laugh. A classic belly laugh, deep and resonant, it belonged to Dr. Peter Schroder. "What ever you do, Mr. President," he said, "you must pay no attention to the man behind the curtain." Schroder laughed again, and the president wondered if he'd gone crazy.

"Are you telling me that all this is a sham, blue smoke and mirrors?" the DCI asked. As he spoke, the monitors showed a huge explosion, and a fireball fifty feet in diameter rose from *St. Elmo's* stern. The pictures from CNN were better than those from the Nightbird, and everybody studied the cable TV monitor. In the crisp image, they could see the ship continuing on, apparently undamaged, gathering ever more way as she headed out of the harbor.

"God in Heaven, you're right!" shouted Christmann, jumping to his feet. "It's brilliant! It's beautiful! Look at the pictures on CNN. Listen to Rolf, for God's sake. Jinnah, the madman, is trying to kill his own people, while the valiant sailors risk their lives to save the city. It's all bullshit! One hundred percent grade-A bullshit, and everybody in the world is going to buy it. Holbrook's winning, by God. He's destroying Jinnah, right in front of our eyes. He's destroying the MLO And nobody, absolutely nobody, gets hurt."

"Except Holbrook," said the president. "I was never a soldier, but if he's on that island after dark, I think he's dead."

Silence in the room confirmed the president's opinion. He continued, "I don't suppose there's any way we can get him off of there?" Again there was silence. That answered his question.

The call came a half-hour after *St. Elmo* had cleared the harbor entrance. Nick had expected it, of course. In fact, he'd expected it much sooner. "*St. Elmo*, this is the governor of Makran again. You are ordered to heave to and await a boarding party. We will be coming aboard to capture and arrest Jinnah and his accomplices, over."

"Negative, negative!" shouted Nick. "We can't stop, we can't even slow down. The worst fires are aft, the wind of our passage is keeping the flames away from the cargo. If we catch Jinnah, we'll hold him in the brig, and make arrangements to turn him over later. If we blow up, he'll blow up with us and save you the expense of a trial. For God's sake, please stay clear and let us try to save our own lives!"

The radio was silent for a minute or two, during which time the ship got another half mile closer to international waters. Then the governor called again.

"I understand your need to keep moving. However, it is imperative that you do not leave the territorial waters of the Province of Makran. I suggest that you begin to circle. A fast frigate of the Indian Navy is underway. She has fire-fighting equipment aboard. Allow her to come alongside, her men can help you with both of your problems."

Nick looked at the GPS readout. Twelve minutes to the border, and wherever the fast frigate was, it wasn't anywhere in sight. Nick stepped out onto the wing of the bridge, and took an Uzi from one of his cousins. Triggering the weapon and the radio microphone at the same time, he treated the governor to the sound of close-up gunfire. Then he said, "Governor, I have to go! Jinnah's men are trying to retake the bridge!"

Nick Argeriardis handed the machine pistol back to his cousin, and turned off the radio. "They have twelve minutes," he said, "maybe eleven, to figure out what to do, and then to do it. I don't think they can." He looked astern, marveling at the trail of smoke. For the first time in several days, he felt himself relax.

"George, are you there?" Once again, Suvia was using the scrambled mode on the radio.

"Still here," he replied. As if I could be anywhere else, he thought. Then he realized she'd been asking whether he was still alive.

"It's getting late," she said. "Do you have any ideas?"

"Yeah, I'm working on one. I still want you guys to leave. On the way, swing around the south side of the island and shoot it up with the Minigun like you did last time. Jinnah and his men still don't know I've moved. Try to drive them up and over the crest toward where you beached *Seasmoke*. I'll be the grouse hunter and you can be the drovers."

"We've been thinking along those lines too," Suvia said. "We can do better than the Minigun. We've gotten the big laser back on line." George wondered how they were going to keep the argon laser in action. The damn circuit breakers tripped every time they fired it. Of course, they could bypass the circuit breakers, like putting a penny in the fuse box. Fine if it works. Sets the ship on fire if it doesn't. George knew there was no point in trying to talk Suvia out of doing it. He pondered his plan for a moment more and decided to add a refinement.

"Tell Ralph to have the ship do something predictable when she circles the island," George said. "He'll know what I mean."

George scrambled uphill on his belly to a point where he could see Jinnah's men. He switched his radio to the clear mode. "Good work, Suvia," he said, "if we get those maggots out into the open, that big laser will turn 'em into puffs of pink steam."

Clearly Jinnah had overheard the transmission, as George had hoped. The terrorists moved away from the ridge, toward better shelter on the south side of the island. He illuminated the laser sight on one of the rifles. The dot was dim but visible in the late afternoon sun. Resisting the temptation to take a shot or two, he settled in to await developments. This actually might work, he thought. On a scale of one to ten, with ten being euphoria and one being utter despair, George's spirits rose to a qualified five.

Suvia Ferris put down the radio microphone. George's plan was a good one, as far as it went. She would add some refinements of her own. She hadn't told George about them, because he would have tried to talk her out of them. Far too late in the day for arguments. Time to tie her hair up and get things done.

Most of Seafire's company had gathered in the recreation room, surrounded by the video arcade game machines. In four rows of eight, the thirty-two machines sat, waiting for players, in the cool, semi-darkness where the ship's library had once been. Steve Roth flipped the master switch, turning all of the games on at once. The machines came to life, screens flickering as they emitted a chorus of game sounds. Roth seated himself in front of Pac-Man, one of the prized antiques of the collection, and fiddled for a moment with the controls. The dots and monsters disappeared, and the words ENTER CODE filled the screen.

"What was USS *Watson*'s old hull number, again?" he asked, to no one in particular.

"Four eighty-two," said Bob Knight, standing behind him.

"Thanks," Roth said, and he began to punch at the one or two player buttons on the machine. As he did, 111100010, the binary number equal to 482, appeared on the screen. Five seconds passed. A message appeared:

> IF YOU ARE FINISHED, PRESS 1;
> OTHERWISE, PRESS 0.

Roth pushed the one player button. The screens on all of the video games went blank. After a second or two, they all lit up again. This time, they were all showing the same image. A string of ones and zeros appeared on the screens, scrolling down faster than the eye could follow. Finally, the scrolling binary numbers froze, and the screens went blank again.

"This is Watson," said the familiar voice of the computer over speakers mounted in the machines. "Memory reload partially complete. Security interlock program running. If security code is not given by an authorized voice in ten seconds, all programs will be erased from memory."

Steve Roth smiled. "Watson, come here! I need you!" he said, wishing Ralph could hear him. Ralph loved puns.

"Security code accepted," said the computer. "All processors on line. Parallel processing synchronization program running." A pause, then, "Synchronization complete."

"Watson, computer status report," Roth said.

"Central processing units operating nominally. Peripheral units in command information center are missing."

"I don't understand," Suvia said. "I thought Syed destroyed the computer. All we had in here was backup."

"Other way around," Bob Knight replied. "Main computer has been here all along. It's a parallel processor, thirty-two units that operate together as one. George, the devious bastard, had us hide them in these video games. The boxes in CIC were front-end machines, what we call a firewall. When Syed shot them up, Watson's security program kicked in and he shut himself down."

"Watson," said Roth, "take control of the engineering plant. Start engines." All engines had been shut down while the switching gear was being rewired.

"Please specify engines to be started," Watson said.

"All of them, my dear Watson," said Roth, smiling again.

"Acknowledged," the computer replied. "Engine starting sequence has commenced."

Across one of the screens a series of binary digits began to scroll again. Another screen said:

ENGINE #1 BEGIN STARTING SEQUENCE.

The vital signs of the engine — pressures and temperatures — appeared as data on the screen. In the engine room, the starter motor whined, and the huge thirty-two-cylinder diesel came to life.

On the island, George Holbrook watched as a faint haze of diesel smoke appeared from *Seafire*'s stack. He felt a thrill of excitement and allowed himself a larger measure of hope.

On *Seafire*'s bridge, Jackson stared out over the bow as he felt the vibration of the engines.

In the pilothouse, Ralph Dade sat in the captain's chair, with his wounded leg stretched out in front of him like an English lord with gout. He watched Bill Jackson, wondering what the man was staring at.

In main control, Finnerty could see that another engine was starting. "Hey, Kevin, there goes number six," he said to his grandson. "Why don't we go up to the bridge where we can see what's going on? Nothing for us to do down here. Damn scab computer's stolen our work."

Suvia Ferris watched one of the CRTs in the game room. The readout of engine status had just changed. It read:

ENGINES ON LINE 6

MAX AVAILABLE SPEED ....22 KNOTS

HORSEPOWER AVAILABLE................15,000

POWER AVAILABLE TO
WEAPONS SYSTEMS............10 MEGAWATTS

As he climbed out of the hatch above Main Control, Finnerty paused for a moment, struck by a thought. *Seafire/Watson* was over fifty years old, and this would be the first time that she would have all of her engines running at one time. I hope the old lady doesn't shake herself apart, he said to himself.

Steve Roth watched as Suvia left the game room. When she was gone, he looked at a screen. It said:

ENGINE #10 BEGIN STARTING SEQUENCE.

Suvia Ferris asked Bill Jackson to give her a hand on the signal bridge. "Sure," he said. Puzzled, he followed her. She was carrying a blue sail bag from Ted Hood's loft in Marblehead. He watched as she opened the bag and pulled out a huge flag. It was thirty feet long, a holiday ensign made of spinnaker cloth.

"Do yachts usually carry battle ensigns?" he asked.

"Don't make fun of me, Bill," she said. "*Seafire* was built as a warship. She's going to do what she was built for, and she should have a decent flag when she does it."

"Didn't she lose her virginity when she took on the *Lee*?"

"Heavy petting, Bill, that's all. She wasn't shooting to kill. And the fishing boat wasn't a real challenge. Today, she'll do what she was destined to do. Flying a proper flag."

Suvia left the signal bridge and Bill looked up at the giant flag, rippling slightly in the barely perceptible breeze. He smiled, but his eyes welled with tears.

When Finnerty and his grandson arrived in the game room, the engine status CRT had changed again. It said:

ENGINES ON LINE 12

MAX AVAILABLE SPEED ....32 KNOTS

HORSEPOWER AVAILABLE................30,000

POWER AVAILABLE TO
WEAPONS SYSTEMS............20 MEGAWATTS

In the engine room engine number fifteen was starting.

- - - - -

On the island, Jinnah watched with interest and concern. He assured his men that they were safe, since they had a solid ridge of rock between them and the ship, and, unlike artillery, lasers can't shoot people on the far sides of hills. He joked about the flag, and reminded his men to stay on the south side of the island.

The ship vibrated noticeably. In the salon, old framed photographs of USS *Watson's* sisters at war shook quietly against the bulkheads, seeming to come alive. Grey ships fighting Kamikazes off of Okinawa, or on convoy duty in the cold North Atlantic. It was as if ships long dead were stirring in their deep and silent graves.

Bill Jackson stepped into the game room, and looked at the engine status screen. It read:

ENGINES ON LINE 20

MAX AVAILABLE SPEED ....37 KNOTS

HORSEPOWER AVAILABLE................50,000

POWER AVAILABLE TO
WEAPONS SYSTEMS ....31.6 MEGAWATTS

On the island, like Jinnah, George watched the ship. He could tell by the sound and by the volume of diesel smoke that she was lighting off her entire power plant. He hoped the old hull would stand the strain.

Cheering broke out in the game room. Bob Knight and the Roths hugged and congratulated Finnerty, and Suvia pounded him on the back. "You've done a wonderful job. Every engine started without hesitation. Every one. I don't believe it." The status screen told the final score:

ENGINES ON LINE 24

MAX AVAILABLE SPEED ....41 KNOTS

HORSEPOWER AVAILABLE................60,000

POWER AVAILABLE TO
WEAPONS SYSTEMS............40 MEGAWATTS

Seafire was ready for war.

Finnerty and Roth came up from the game room to join Ralph Dade and the others on the bridge. Ralph still sat in the captain's seat, his leg resting on the brace that Finnerty had welded to the base of the chair. "Ready, everybody?" he asked.

"As ready as we'll ever be," Bob Knight responded.

"OK *Watson*," said Dade, "let's show these people what the old lady can do. All ahead, flank."

"Acknowledged," said the computer. "All engines ahead, flank."

In the engine room, the rows of huge switches looked like something out of Dr. Zarkov's lab in the old Flash Gordon movies. State of the art, circa 1942. The first switch closed with a blue flash, and, beneath the ship, the twin screws began to turn. Another switch closed, then another, and another. The screws turned faster, and cavitation bubbles began to appear at the tips. The switches closed more quickly then, with blue sparks flashing down the line like a row of dominoes. The ship began to move forward, slowly at first, the huge screws throwing tons of water out from under her.

George Holbrook watched *Seafire* from the beach. It looked as if Neptune's giant hand was pulling her down by the stern. George called on the radio. "Pretty impressive squat for a yacht. I thought only 'real warships' could do that."

"You thought right," came Ralph's reply. George wondered briefly why it was Ralph who was conning the ship, instead of Bill Jackson.

Jackson stood on the wing of the bridge and overheard the conversation through the pilothouse door. He watched the stern hunker down into a torrent of froth as the ship gathered way, leaving *Seasmoke* behind at anchor. "Time to go," he said, and hurried aft.

The ship shook herself like a wet dog as she accelerated. A wet greyhound. In the salon, glasses rattled in their racks behind the bar. Two or three bottles of champagne exploded. The pale liquid soaked quietly into the expensive carpeting, fifty years overdue.

In the game room, and on the bridge as well, video monitors displayed the ship's speed. The figure changed constantly, with numbers to the right of the decimal moving too rapidly to read, and the whole numbers passing through thirty-four, thirty-five, thirty-six.. Another screen showed a chart of the waters around the island, with a tiny ship superimposed. Dotted and dashed lines indicated course and track. The little ship on the screen executed a gentle right turn as, on the bridge, the wheel swung right with no one touching it. George Holbrook had been wrong. Ralph Dade wasn't conning the ship. *Watson* was.

- - - - -

Jinnah watched the ship disappear around the headland. Through his binoculars, George watched Jinnah arguing with two or three of his men. George could tell from their gestures that they recognized the threat of *Seafire* circling the island to catch them exposed. One or two men started toward the crest. George chambered a round in his rifle.

Seafire had circled halfway around the island and was now completely hidden from Jinnah's men by the headland. At slightly more than forty knots, her wheel swung hard to port, and she leaned into a sweeping, spectacular, high-speed turn. Still at forty knots, she completed a U-turn and headed back the way she had come.

A great deal of visible consternation broke out among Jinnah's troops. For a moment George thought they would go for the fake and scramble over the crest, into the lines of fire of the argon laser and George's rifle. At the last moment, though, Jinnah called them back. Perhaps he suspects the misdirection play, George thought. His heart sank as he watched Jinnah send a scout to the headland. George could see *Seafire* again. So would Jinnah's man, in a few moments. On the crest of the ridge, Jinnah's lookout had scrambled to a protected spot. Pointing toward the north, he gestured wildly, and George knew his final plan would fail. He called Ralph on the radio.

"Nice try, but they didn't go for it," he said. "Take the ship home and leave me here to deal with Jinnah."

"Don't give up the ship," Ralph replied. "Phase seven begins in thirty seconds."

"Phase seven? There never was a phase seven!"

"There is now."

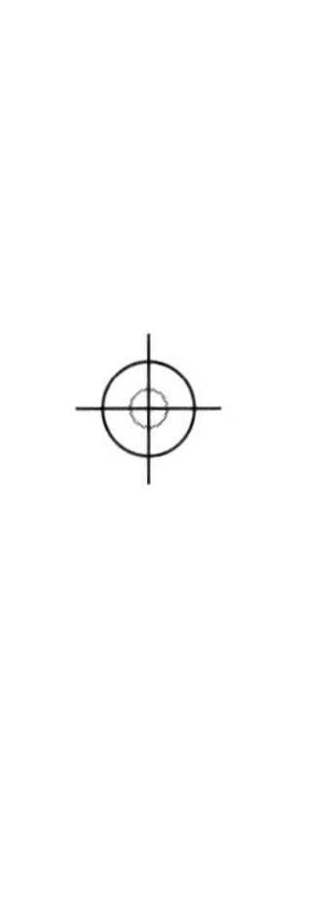

THE SPARROWHAWK flew as low and as fast as Suvia dared fly it. In full ground effect, its rotor tilted forward to drag the machine through the air. Suvia sat at the controls in the pilot's seat with Bill Jackson, the gunner, in the right hand seat. Nervous about the lack of altitude, he made the mistake of looking back and down at the same time.

"Shouldn't we be up a little higher?" he asked. "We're leaving a wake."

"Don't worry, I know what I'm doing. It's strange. I can actually feel the control surfaces, as if I were part of the machinery. Maybe it's adrenaline. All of a sudden, I really know I can fly this thing."

Jackson groaned, half in jest. He looked at her hands on the controls. She had them in a death grip, her knuckles gleaming white. He groaned again, not at all in jest.

"Are you sure you can fire the machine guns, Bill?"

"I can shoot them, but hitting anything is another story."

"No problem," Suvia said with a maniacal laugh. "You can start a stampede without actually shooting the cows. You just have to spook 'em."

He looked down at her feet, as they rested on the pedals. She was wearing cowboy boots. "Yippee kiyo," he said, and Suvia laughed again.

George heard the thumping sound of the rotor blades, even though the helicopter was still out of sight. He realized that Suvia must be flying and called again on the radio.

"What the hell do you think you're doing?"

Ralph Dade replied from *Seafire*. "Classic pincer movement. Clausewitz would be proud."

Furious, George screamed into the radio, "Suvia, get the hell out of there before you get yourself killed!" His voice was drowned out by the sound of the helicopter's arrival.

The SparrowHawk reached the beach only seconds after it came into view. It streaked across the surf with rotors and skids scant inches above the tops of the breakers, machine guns spraying tracer rounds all over the island. Even George, five hundred yards from Jinnah's men, was forced to hit the deck as stray bullets whined about. The terrorists panicked and began to scatter. Several began to run toward the crest. George looked to the north. *Seafire* was decelerating, gliding into the bay on momentum alone. Tons of water cascaded over her foredeck. Now what the hell? When *Seafire* had sprinted out of the bay, she'd left *Seasmoke* behind, unmanned, at anchor. Or so he thought. Now he could see people aboard her.

Jinnah bellowed at his men, and they turned to look at him. He was standing up, rather than diving for cover as machine gun bullets whined past him. "Dogs and cowards, sons of whores. Run away, all of you. I will fight alone, like a man!" The helicopter passed over his head, and he still didn't flinch. Jinnah's men, taking courage from his display of bravery, ashamed of their own cowardice, rallied around him.

"OK , kids, let's go," said Patty Phelps, as she hauled herself up from *Seasmoke's* floorboards. The bulk and weight of her flak jacket made the movement awkward, and she nearly knocked Alex Wilson over, as he struggled with a heavy bag of gear. He grunted something at her, angry and unintelligible. She guessed that he was still fuming that she, rather then he, had been put in charge of the small amphibious force.

"Cut the anchor line," she said to Paul Harrington as she started the Magnum's engines. *Seafire* was gliding into her planned position, just outside the reefs. Patty's assault group was supposed to hit the beach just as she got into position, so she could give them fire support with her laser, if it worked. If it didn't, Patty's group would join George to lay in wait on the north side of the island, to ambush Jinnah's men when Suvia drove them over the ridge. If that worked.

"Hang on," she said to her five passengers. "It's going to be a rough ride at the end."

George Holbrook watched the Magnum gain speed and head toward the beach. This was another part of Suvia's plan she hadn't told him about. If we get out of this alive, he decided, I'm going to talk to her about insubordination. He turned his attention back to Jinnah's group. Damn, there were a lot of them. He'd guessed that there could only be a dozen or so left. Twice that many were grouped around Jinnah. God knew how many more were out of sight.

Patty throttled back as *Seasmoke* approached the shore, and quickly realized that she had done it too late. She had planned to run the Magnum right up onto the beach, so she and her troops wouldn't have to wade ashore. She hadn't planned on doing it at nearly forty knots. The initial jolt, as the hull hit the sand, threw the passengers violently forward. The boat slid across thirty yards of sand, and was still going nearly twenty knots when it ran into a huge rock.

"Nice landing, Patty," Alex Wilson said, as she took inventory of her body parts. She'd taken most of the impact with her chest against the steering wheel, which was now bent like a pretzel. It hurt to breathe, and she guessed that a rib or two might be cracked. She was fit to fight, she decided, and if Alex was up to sarcasm, he couldn't be hurt too badly either.

"We've got to get away from this boat," Patty said. Peter and Emily Carson had managed to stay in their seats, and were unhurt. Jacqueline Girard tended to Paul Harrington, who was unconscious and bleeding from a gash where his head had hit the dashboard. "Shit!" said Patty. She forced herself to concentrate on the mission, on what to do next. She could blame herself for her bad driving later. If there was a later. "Let's move out."

Four minutes later, Patty moved out again, heading southeast with Alex Wilson. The Carsons headed southwest. Each team of two gunners would set up a firing position on opposite sides of the most likely path of the terrorists. They had left Paul about fifty yards from the wrecked Magnum, in the best hiding place they could find, with Jacqueline as his nurse and bodyguard.

George watched the helicopter complete its pass and circle east to make a second run. He was about to call again on the radio when a man came over the crest, less than fifty yards from his position. Hiding behind a stunted bush with tiny leaves and huge thorns, he hunkered down to watch the man. George's heart pounded in his chest. He couldn't shoot while the man was still visible to Jinnah and his troops. Shooting would give his position away and ruin his chances of killing Jinnah. The scrawny bush provided miserable cover; George couldn't believe the man hadn't seen him.

The terrorist watched the SparrowHawk fly east as he took several steps downhill, away from the crest. George rose to a crouch and shouldered his rifle. Suddenly the man noticed *Seafire* gliding into the bay, and *Seasmoke* speeding toward the beach. He turned abruptly toward the crest, and began to run. "Shit," said George. He switched the selector to single fire, centered the ruby laser dot an inch above the man's right ear, and squeezed off a round. The man fell silently; the head shot had killed him before he could utter a cry. Even as the man fell, a huge blow struck George in the back. The impact threw him forward in a heap; shock kept him immobile. It took George several seconds to realize what had happened. He'd been shot in the back.

Suvia completed her circle around the headland, and headed toward the beach for a second pass. "We came in too fast," she said, angry with herself. "We were supposed to drive them north, but we were past them before they could run. Damn! Now we've lost the element of surprise. They'll be shooting back this time, and we'll be going more slowly. Hang on."

"Let's go," Bill replied, as he watched muzzle flashes wink at him from the island.

George lay still, in a loose fetal position on his right side, head slightly downhill, feet pointing toward the crest. He'd managed to hold onto his rifle as he'd tumbled, and he still had it clutched against his chest. He could see the man who'd shot him, approaching cautiously, rifle at the ready.

George took inventory. The flak jacket had stopped the bullet, but none of its kinetic energy. His kidneys and lower spine had absorbed the shock. He was beginning to feel pain. That was a good sign. He wasn't going to die just yet.

In *Seafire*'s CIC, Polly Harrington watched the monitors with growing alarm. With the sun lower in the sky, heating the air less, the cameras produced sharper images. She'd watched the Magnum crash ashore and recognized her grandson as the one who had to be carried out of the wreckage. Now, the party of two heading eastward, which looked like Alex and Patty, was about to walk into an ambush. Grace Roth had tried to warn them on the radio, but they didn't respond.

"Steve, we need that laser now," Polly said. "We can't wait for Jinnah to come over the ridge. There are four men waiting to bag Patty and Alex. We have to cover them with the laser."

"Agreed," Roth replied. "*Watson*, commence main battery firing sequence." Bob Knight turned to a monitor with an infra red display. Using a light pencil, he marked the thermal signatures of the four waiting terrorists as targets. "*Watson*," he said. "Main battery. Fire for effect."

Nothing happened.

"*Watson*," Roth shouted. "Main battery status!"

"No power. Main battery switches must be manually reset."

"Shit!" said Roth. In the fight with the *Lee*, it hadn't just been the circuit breakers that tripped. The thermal overload protectors on the main switches must have gone as well. Why hadn't we checked that? "Bob, come with me. You too, Finnertys." The four men bolted from CIC leaving only Grace and Polly behind.

Patty reacted quickly as four terrorists opened fire from a range of a hundred yards. She dropped flat into the prone shooter's position and fired three quick bursts, ignoring the pain in her ribs. The men reacted by diving into defensive positions, and Patty took the opportunity to ram a fresh clip into her M-16. The range was too great for the laser dot to do any good, so she scanned for targets with the open sights. She suddenly realized that Alex hadn't fired, and turned to see if he had been hit. He hadn't. He was running away. As she watched, he dropped his M-16 and continued in a mad dash back toward the beach. "Fucking coward," she said to herself. "I should have known."

George Holbrook watched the man who'd shot him. He was about seventy yards away, to the west and slightly down slope. George cursed himself for concentrating on the man to the east without watching his own back. Moving as little as possible, he verified that the ruby laser was still turned on. He hoped that it hadn't been knocked out of alignment when he'd been knocked over. Still minimizing movement, he switched his rifle to full automatic. He knew he had eighteen rounds in his clip and one in the chamber. He'd use all of them at once. At best, he'd get one chance for survival. There wasn't any point in saving bullets for a second burst.

George watched the man approach. God, he was wary! Neither his eyes nor his weapon wavered, the man fixed both on George with fierce concentration. To kill him, George would have to raise his rifle, bring it to bear, and fire. That would take at least a second. More than enough time for the man to shoot George again. Worse, the closer he came, the less likely the Kevlar vest would stop a bullet. George forced himself to be calm and still, waiting for the opening that might never come.

The man's concentration gave George his opportunity. With his eyes riveted to George, he didn't see the loose rock in his path. He stepped on it and it rolled under his foot. He stumbled slightly, instinctively fighting to steady himself. He released his two-handed grip on the rifle, spreading his arms for balance. For that moment, the rifle wasn't pointing at George. The man's finger wasn't on the trigger.

George Holbrook struck like a cobra. Moving only his arms, he slashed up and out with his rifle, swinging it through a wide arc toward the startled terrorist. Even before the weapon was bearing on the man, George was firing, using all his strength to pull the muzzle toward the target. George watched the flickering laser dot sweep across the man's chest, and fought to pull it back. Before he could, the rifle stopped firing and the slide locked back. It was empty.

Seconds passed and George waited, ears throbbing from the sound of gunfire, legs still immobile from the blow to his spine. The terrorist was facing George, both hands on his weapon again, but it seemed too heavy for him to raise. Slowly, it slipped from his grasp as he sank to his knees and collapsed. Of the nineteen rounds George had fired, eighteen had missed him completely. The nineteenth had passed cleanly through his heart.

Intense relief swept over George, but it was short lived. He could hear gunfire from over the ridge. Suvia was making another pass at the beach. He stood up, forcing himself to ignore the pain. His right leg collapsed under him and he fell. Using the rifle as a crutch, he hobbled up to the crest, flopping heavily onto his belly at the top. He quickly checked that the rifle's muzzle was clear of dirt, ejected the empty clip and rammed in a fresh one. Finally, he used his binoculars to see what was going on. "Shit," he said, once again, and grabbed the radio.

Suvia was trying to drive the terrorists up and over the ridge. Instead of flying toward the beach, she was flying parallel to it, sideways, with the helicopter's nose pointing toward Jinnah and his men. Jackson was firing short bursts from the twin M60s. Jinnah's men were shooting at the helicopter. And Jinnah, George could see, was loading a heat-seeking missile into its launcher.

"Suvia!" he shouted, "get the hell over to the other side of the island. Jinnah's loading his missile launcher!" George briefly considered taking a shot at Jinnah. It would be useless, he knew. Even with the laser sight, five hundred yards was just too far.

Suvia stopped crabbing the helicopter and headed toward the beach again, standing the aircraft on its nose for acceleration. Oh, God, no, George thought. She's going to fly right over Jinnah, and show him her tailpipe when she's past him.

Bill Jackson fired the M60s as the helicopter swooped over the terrorists once again. Their return fire was heavier than before. As she crossed the surf, Suvia felt a jolt, and the helicopter began to vibrate. Jinnah finished loading and swung the launcher toward the aircraft. He fired hastily, and too late, as the SparrowHawk was pulling out of range to circle the headland again. The missile homed in on the jet exhaust, but fell short and struck a rock outcrop on the headland as Suvia turned behind it.

"Jesus H. Christ!" said Suvia. "That was too damn close."

"Tough to start a stampede when the cows can shoot back."

"We've got to keep trying, Bill."

"I wasn't suggesting otherwise."

"I know."

"Am I imagining things, or is this machine vibrating?"

"Somebody probably shot a hole in one of the rotor blades," Suvia replied. "If we keep the speed down, it might not come apart."

"Suvia!" George's voice blared over the radio. "For God's sake get out of here. The best pilot in the world can't dodge a heat-seeking missile. Go back to the ship before you're both killed!"

"Damn it George! An hour ago you said you weren't going to leave as long as Jinnah was alive. Well, neither are we. Quit telling me to leave and tell me how to fight him!"

George was silent for a moment. "The missiles are lethal. The only way to neutralize them is to stay between Jinnah and the sun. Up-sun, the infrared heads will never see the 'copter, the sun will blind them. If you get down sun of Jinnah, you're dead. Circle way out to the south, out of range, and come at them from the west. The sun is pretty low in the sky. If you come in with it directly behind you, the heat sensor on the missile won't be able to lock onto your exhaust."

Suvia looked at Bill Jackson. He nodded approval. "Great idea," he said. "Why don't you fire a couple of rockets at them, this time? Maybe that will stampede the damn herd."

"Right," Suvia said, arming rockets one and four.

Slowly recovering feeling in his legs, George watched the SparrowHawk circle to the south of the island, out of range of Jinnah's rockets. Suvia would try to force the terrorists into the ambush she had set. Not a bad plan, he allowed. He judged the weakest link to be Suvia's ability to herd Jinnah's men with her helicopter. I'll do more good as a drover than a hunter, he said to himself, and began to move south, half limping, half crawling.

Patty Phelps knew she was about to die. Her greatest fear was that it wouldn't happen quickly. She had killed two of the four men she and Alex had encountered, but the other two had overpowered her when her M-16 had jammed. One man held her from behind, his strong arms wrapped around her chest. The pressure on her injured ribs was agony. The other, a small man with rotten teeth, stood in front of her, grinning in triumph. He said something, vehemently, in a language she didn't recognize. He spat in her face. He drew his knife. He leered at her, brought the knife to his lips, ran his tongue across the blade. Patty reeled in fear and horror at the obscenity and menace in his filthy display. The message was clear. He was going to rape her.

With his knife.

The man holding her shifted his grasp to her arms, so the bearded one could open her flak jacket, then her blouse.

She watched his animal look of hungry gloating as he stared at her naked breasts.

Then his head exploded.

The sight, a geyser of blood, brain and bone, was horrifying, but not as horrifying as the sound — like a watermelon hit with a baseball bat. Then, a second later, came the distant report of a heavy rifle. A sniper's rifle.

Five hundred yards away, Alex Wilson grunted in satisfaction as his man went down. He worked the bolt, chambering a fresh round. He watched through the telescopic sight as Patty struggled with the man holding her. The terrorist tried to use Patty as a shield, fighting to keep her between him and Alex. She twisted and turned, finally pulling free and throwing herself prone on the ground. For a second or two, the man froze, unsure of whether to run for cover or try to pick Patty up. A second or two was too long. Alex's heavy bullet struck him in the chest and blew pieces of his spine out of his back.

Alex savored the strange satisfaction of having killed two men. He pondered his utter lack of remorse. Holbrook was right, he said to himself. I'm bloody good at this. From his sniper's nest on the peak of the hill, he scanned the island, looking for targets.

As the helicopter approached, Jinnah had to face directly into the sun. He could barely see the aircraft, much less fix the infrared sensor on it. When Suvia fired the rockets, he was taken completely by surprise, expecting only more of the same ineffective gunfire. The rockets struck the ground and exploded less than thirty yards away, startling Jinnah so badly that he inadvertently fired his missile. It streaked off to the west, homing in on the sun.

Suvia turned to her gunner. "You're getting pretty good with those guns," she said. "What do you say we try the same move again. Maybe this time I'll do better with the rockets."

"Your first try wasn't that bad," Bill replied. "You were pretty close to target. Same maneuver? Let's do it!"

Once again, the SparrowHawk circled the island to approach from the west. Diving again out of the sun, Suvia fired rockets two and five. They struck about fifty feet from the terrorists' position. Her accuracy was improving. This time however, Jinnah held his fire until the helicopter had passed overhead. Suvia and Bill realized their mistake, and knew what was coming. "Tell me when he shoots," Suvia screamed. Bill, looking aft, saw Jinnah jump up from cover, wait for the launcher to lock on target, and fire the heat-seeking missile. Bill yelled, "Now!"

Suvia's hands flew over the controls. She cut the throttle, shifted to autorotation, armed and fired the two remaining rockets. She pulled hard up on the collective, using the rotor's inertia to gain a few feet of altitude. At the rear of the helicopter the glow of the jet exhaust died just as the two rockets ignited and flew away. The heat-seeking missile followed them, seduced by the heat of their exhaust, passing right under the aircraft. On the verge of a stall, Suvia got power back to the rotor just in time to stay out of the water.

"Whoa!" shouted Bill.

Suvia brought the SparrowHawk into a hover on the north side of the island. They were out of sight of Jinnah's men, and in full view of *Seafire*, which had come to rest in the bay. For a moment or two, neither said anything. Death had come very close, and they fought to regain their composure.

"Suvia, where on earth did that maneuver come from?"

"I don't know," she said, still shaken. "It seemed like a good idea at the time."

"It was brilliant, Suvia. It was incredible."

"George kept lecturing me how important autorotation is, so I had Ralph talk me through it. Thank God he did. It wasn't all that brilliant, though. I should have fired only one rocket, not two. Now we're out of them."

She and Bill looked at *Seafire* again. Mount One was still spewing water.

Polly and Grace watched the monitors as the terrorists closed in on Alex's position on the hill. He'd shot two or three of them, but more kept coming. They had him within range of their automatic weapons. He'd lost the sniper's advantage of being able to shoot without taking return fire. Pinned down by several guns, his only defense was to pop up for quick, ineffective shots. In a minute or two, the attackers would overrun his position.

"Steve, how soon before the laser's on line?" Polly shouted into the intercom. "We need it now!"

"Start the firing sequence," he said. "We'll be clear when it fires."

Alex raised his head for another shot as bullets struck the rocks all around him. His target was a man in a white shirt, carrying an

AK-47. He was recklessly charging Alex's position and screaming, "Allah Akbar." Alex had to risk a careful shot, or the man would be on him in seconds. The terrorist's chest filled Alex's scope as he fired, and he watched the deadly red rose bloom over the man's heart. The other terrorists hesitated for a moment, and Alex chambered another round.

"*Watson*, shoot," said Polly Harrington, as soon as Grace had designated the targets with the light pen. In Main Control, the huge knife switches began crashing down in sequence. Steve Roth screamed at Bob Knight, still wrestling with switch number twenty-four. In seconds, he'd be electrocuted.

The men were close now. Alex no longer used the scope. He chambered and fired round after round, at the maximum possible rate of fire with his heavy bolt action rifle. The first man to reach him got there just as Alex emptied the magazine. The terrorist raised his rifle, then disappeared in a flash of blinding blue-green light.

Steve Roth rushed to where Bob Knight had landed. The massive jolt of electricity had hurled him clear across main control. Roth was overwhelmed with relief to find him both alive and conscious. Together, the men checked Bob for injuries, as a foul odor of ozone and something else wafted about. Finally, they identified the smell — burning hair. Other than bruises from crashing into the bulkhead, Bob's only injury was loss of body hair. The fireball had burned it completely off both his arms, from knuckles to elbows.

▬ ▬ ▬ ▬ ▬

The men storming the sniper nest reversed field in full retreat. Alex felt a bit sorry for them as they scattered and ran in terrified panic to escape the laser beam. For the world's most powerful computer, firing a weapon with the speed of light, they might as well have been standing still. The blue-green light flashed again and again, and each time it flashed a man became a smoldering heap of flesh. The sickening scene reminded Alex of moths flying into a bug zapper. These aren't moths, Alex told himself. They're maggots, and they deserve to die.

Below him, about three hundred yards away, one man had managed to evade the laser by hiding behind a huge boulder. Alex looked at him through the rifle scope. He was using a hand-held radio. Calling Jinnah to warn him about the laser, Alex guessed, and reloaded his rifle's magazine. "Left one for me, did you, Steve?" he said as he squeezed off a shot with the cool deliberation of the sniper he'd become. "Thanks."

▬ ▬ ▬ ▬ ▬

Suvia realized the helicopter's vibration had gotten worse. She called George. "We have a pretty heavy vibration. We think a bullet hit one of the blades. How serious is that?"

"Damn serious!" he replied. "Those blades are carbon fiber. If the hole is on the trailing edge, the blade might hold together or it might not. If the hole's on the leading edge, the blade is bound to tear itself apart."

George was about to tell Suvia, for the hundredth time it seemed, to go home. Instead, he said, "I just said the best pilot in the world can't dodge a heat-seeking missile. I was wrong. She can. Make another pass. This time I'll contribute more than criticism to the war effort."

Suvia looked at Bill. "Time is running out if this scheme is going to work," he said.

"I agree. Let's have at 'em one more time."

"Yes, Ma'am," Bill said.

"I remember a pitcher for the Boston Red Sox," said Suvia. "They called him the Spaceman. He used to say that when his breaking stuff wasn't working, there was nothing to do but challenge 'em with his fast ball. The problem with this diving and zooming, Bill, is that you don't have a stable platform to shoot from. How about coming in nice and stately and holding our fire until we're close enough to do some effective shooting?"

"You realize that a stable platform to shoot *from* is a stable platform to shoot *at*, don't you?"

"Yes."

"OK, let's do it."

Once again Suvia circled the island to the east. Bill looked closely at her. Her grip on the controls had become relaxed, her knuckles no longer were white. Her lips were slightly parted, her nostrils flared. Her expression was of calm determination.

The helicopter approached from the south, just as it had on the first pass. It proceeded slowly, 'stately' as Suvia said, but still very low. The terrorists began firing, and several rounds struck the aircraft. The canopy was hit, and spider web patterns appeared in the plastic, but the SparrowHawk flew on. Finally, as they crossed the surf, Bill commenced firing.

Jinnah stood up, accepting the challenge. Tracer rounds swarmed around him as he aimed the missile launcher. He, too, was holding his fire, the missile in the launcher was the last one. His men rose to stand beside him. As one, they fired at the advancing helicopter, ignoring the incoming fire. The lights in the sight indicated a soft lock-on, a near certain kill. Jinnah's finger tightened on the trigger. He hesitated, waiting for the hard lock, waiting for the shot that could not miss. As he waited, a dime size circle of ruby colored light appeared between his shoulder blades.

George Holbrook had moved. He'd crossed the ridge and hopped and hobbled nearly five hundred yards. He was only a few yards behind the terrorists, who were busily firing at the helicopter, unaware of his presence. He stood in the classic offhand firing position, left elbow pointing at his left foot, right forearm parallel to the deck, as he steadied the ruby laser sighting beam of his M-16. On his face was the same look of calm determination Bill Jackson had just seen on Suvia's. He squeezed the trigger, leaning into the weapon, pulling down against the upward kick of full automatic fire. The rifle's muzzle flashed, and spent cartridges swarmed out of the ejector port like angry bees.

The bullets struck Jinnah's upper back in close succession, physically driving him forward with their impact. As he toppled forward, George continued to fire, pushing Jinnah downward. The launcher fired as Jinnah fell, the missile striking the ground a yard in front of his feet. Spewing flame, it screeched and spun like a child's top, exploding just as Jinnah fell on it.

Two of Jinnah's men had turned toward George and were bringing their rifles to bear even as the missile exploded. The blast knocked them down, and hurled Jinnah's broken body several feet into the air. It twisted and spun for a moment, a grotesque pinwheel, then landed, a lifeless heap of bloody rags.

The stampede began. The terrorists screamed in panic, dropped their weapons, broke ranks and ran. One man knelt in front of George, arms outstretched in a gesture of supplication. George rammed a fresh clip into his rifle, switched to single fire, and shot him in the forehead.

Suvia swung the SparrowHawk into a hover several yards to George's right. Together, George and Bill fired into the backs of the fleeing men. Less than a dozen made it up and over the ridge.

▪ ▪ ▪ ▪ ▪

Ralph Dade sat in his chair on *Seafire*'s bridge, watching the island through the big Zeiss binoculars. "Here they come, right on schedule," he said.

Bob Knight and Steve Roth were back in the game room. "*Watson*," Steve Roth said, "maintain sighting cameras in infra red mode." The tiny figures moved across the screens, like video game characters, as they scrambled for safety. Cross hairs locked in on one and followed it across the screen. Grace Roth groaned and said, "Oh, my God, we can't do this. They're retreating, trying to run away and save their lives. We're homing in on their body heat."

"How about the girl's hand in the freezer, Grace?" Steve replied. "How much body heat does that have?"

"God forgive me," she said. "*Watson*, shoot."

In the engine room the huge switches flashed and crackled, and a full forty megawatts of power flowed to the argon laser. It fired a perfect, tight beam of blue-green light. Cool water flowed over the deck, without a trace of steam. The only steam the beam produced was on the island. It was pink.

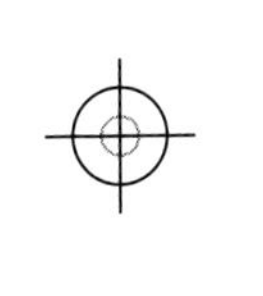

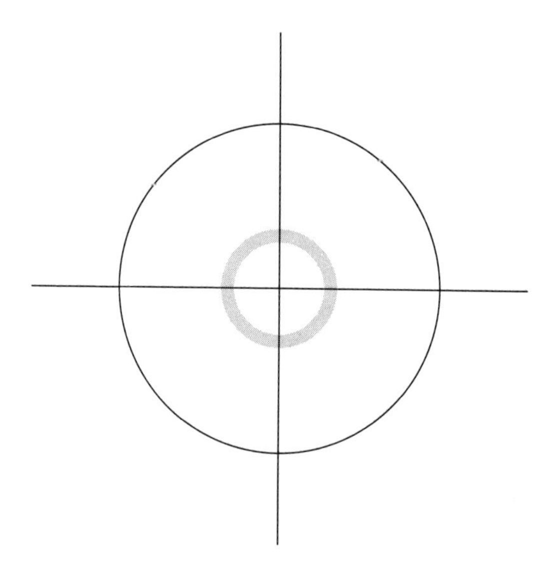

EPILOGUE

THE F-14 pilot had completed his rotation on combat air patrol, and flew inbound from point Alpha, the imaginary turning point astern of his carrier. Below him lay the North Atlantic, cobalt blue in the March sun. Ahead, the carrier USS *Theodore Roosevelt* steamed into the wind, ringed, as always, by her protective screen of destroyers. Today, the pilot noted with interest, one of them was white.

Ralph Dade watched the huge Sea King helicopter hover over *Seafire*'s flight deck, hoisting an object aboard with its winch. Around the ship's helicopter platform, a squad of Marines stood guard with rifles at port arms. Signs posted around the deck carried the yellow and black radiation warning emblem and the legend,

"No Unauthorized Personnel." Ralph watched two men in moon suits carry a box out of the hangar while a third man, also in protective clothing, monitored the other two with a Geiger counter. One of the Marines told Ralph to leave. He opened his mouth to protest, then shrugged and went back into the ship, limping slightly.

Ralph found most of the *Seafire*'s owners talking happily in the salon. It was George Holbrook's birthday, the first day of spring, and the mood was festive. George and Suvia had chosen this date to transfer the bombs. The Jinnah affair was to end exactly one year after it had begun.

Not everyone was still aboard. Paul Harrington had flown back to the States to see a plastic surgeon about the ugly scar on his forehead. Bob Knight had flown home from Rio in response to an invitation from Linda to try to reconcile. Polly Harrington had left at Trinidad, to wage a campaign to get Paul into medical school. Patty Phelps sat next to Alex Wilson, who was telling Bill Christmann how brilliant George's plans had been, and how everyone had supported George from the beginning. "God, Alex, you're so full of shit," she said and punched him on the upper arm.

"Cor blimey," Alex replied in a dreadful Cockney accent. "She's a littul spitfire, she is. When Oi saw her wif me littul telescope, arf nekkid and wrestlin' with that Ay-rab bloke, Oi knew she wuz the girl for me."

The men laughed, the women booed, and Patty gave Alex another shot in the arm. Ralph grunted and took a seat next to Steve Roth.

"How's the leg?" Steve asked.

"Getting better. The orthopods in Sydney said it will take some time for the stiffness to go away completely."

"Got to keep exercising it, I suppose."

"That's right. I was out walking around the deck a few minutes ago. Went aft to watch the Navy loading the nukes, and the damn Marines ran me off! On a private yacht, *my* private yacht, this guy with a rifle tells me to take a hike. Can you believe it?"

"Sure. It's 'cause you're unauthorized," said Roth.

"I helped recover those things, how come I'm not authorized," Ralph replied, still miffed.

"You're a civilian. Those are weapons. Only military types are authorized to mess with weapons," said Roth, with happy sarcasm.

"Damn military lost 'em in the first place," replied Dade, gruffly.

Bill Christmann had just entered the salon. "Ancient history," he said. "Besides, it was the Army that lost them. As far as the Navy is concerned, the Army isn't particularly authorized, either."

"Jesus," said Ralph, "we brought those things half way around the world. If I were going to steal one, I'd have it by now."

"You were in the Navy, Dade, you know better than to apply logic to a military situation."

Christmann looked at George and Suvia, who were holding hands and talking quietly to each other in a corner. Ralph caught his glance and said, "They're courting."

"Courting? Do people still do that?"

"Yeah, I guess that's what you would call it. They have two law firms and twenty CPAs figuring out what the tax consequences would be if they got married. Isn't love wonderful?"

Suvia made a face at Ralph, and George said to Christmann, "Thanks for keeping your side of the bargain. Now, I wish you hadn't."

"What are you talking about?" asked Ralph.

"I made a deal with Christmann last summer," George explained. "If we got the bombs back, we would let the CIA take credit for recovering them. Their side of the deal was to do some checking into the old court martial charges against Bill Jackson. They did just that, and they had some interesting results."

"Jackson has been cleared," said Christmann. "A couple of senior Navy officers and a Marine general have been sacked and will probably stand trial. Unfortunately, most of the people who framed Jackson are dead, but those who are alive are going to the brig."

"The bad news, for us, anyway," said George, "is that the Navy wants Jackson back. They'll give him back pay, four stripes with retroactive seniority, and command of a guided missile frigate. He's up on the bridge, talking to an admiral, who presumably is making him an offer he can't refuse."

"George," said Christmann. "Do you remember that talk we had last summer? When you told me what I could do with an exploding cigar?"

"Yeah, I do. I meant to apologize about that."

"Remember when you told me about those three nukes, and how surprised I was that you knew?"

"Yes," George answered, wondering where this was going.

"Did I blink an eye at the number three?"

"No. Why? Should you have?"

"Damn right, I should. Sheer professionalism made me keep a straight face. There were six nukes stolen in Germany, not three. And I didn't let you know, did I?"

"So why are you telling us now?" Suvia asked. "Surely, this bunch of civilians doesn't 'need to know'."

"Oh, no!" George said. "Not us. This exercise was personal. Jinnah was our enemy. No way we're going to hire out to the CIA to retrieve more missing nukes!"

Christmann said nothing. He just smiled and waited.

"Tell me," Suvia said. "Are these remaining missing items anywhere near the water?"

Christmann smiled at Suvia. It was a warm, friendly smile that pissed Holbrook off enormously. "Suvia," he said, "I thought you'd never ask."

On *Seafire*'s bridge, the admiral was just finishing his pitch.

"That's about it, Mr. Jackson. Even if you don't take the deal, the Navy will try to make things right. You'll get an honorable discharge, and pay and allowances to the day you left the service. There has already been a press release declaring your innocence; 'the Navy deeply regrets,' and all that.

"But the Navy really does want you back. We need senior people of color for young black officers and men to look up to. You are going to be a sort of hero now, going up against the Khaki Mafia like you did. Your getting four stripes would be good for morale and help with recruiting. Aside from that, officers with command potential are extremely valuable. The senior brass have seen the reports of your, er, activities of late. So have I. You're qualified for command in my book. If you were an aviator I'd put in for you as skipper of my flagship.

"So, that's the deal and I hope you take it. It's a good one. The Navy's downsizing again, and commands are hard to come by."

Bill Jackson was silent for a moment. He stared out over the bow as he had the night he talked with George Holbrook.

"Admiral, it's a wonderful offer. If you gave me a dollar for every night I've stood right here and dreamed and prayed for an offer like that, you'd lose a year's pay. A command! That was too much to hope for. Just a two-bit job as a lieutenant (j.g.) on a tin can. That's all I wanted. Anything, just to serve in the Navy again. On a warship.

"A year ago I would have taken the job, Admiral. But not now. You see, I already have a command. And Mr. Langone, the guy who was killed, left me his share of this ship. I'm a part owner."

Bill smiled at the admiral, and continued in a lighter, almost jocular tone, "A part owner, Admiral! That's more than you can say about that carrier of yours. And, as far as guided missile frigates are concerned, I came across one of those recently and I wasn't overly impressed. Damn thing couldn't even handle an unarmed yacht! I'll bet we could even take on your carrier, Admiral. You'd launch your Tomcats and we'd pick 'em off with our lasers like shooting skeet."

Jackson became serious again. "No, Admiral. Tell the Navy

thanks, anyway. I already have command of a warship. She'll probably never fight again, but she has a fine crew and she's mine for as long as I want to have her. If you were me, Admiral, would you trade?"

The admiral had seen the films — the skirmish with *Lee*, the Harpoon missile attack. He'd been on the command bridge of the carrier earlier, when *Seafire* had detected a Russian submarine nearly a hundred miles away, far beyond the range of any of the task force's sonars. The jokes about a yacht in the screen had stopped, and dozens of officers had hurried to ASW plot to listen to the eerie sound of *Seafire*'s active sonar. Jackson wasn't joking, the admiral knew. The yacht was a warship, one of the most powerful afloat. He didn't respond to Jackson's question. He smiled instead, and said, "You know, Mr. Jackson, I'd love to know more about this sonar of yours..."

"Bill," Suvia said to Christmann, "what exactly happened at Jinnah's funeral? The authorities in Makran imposed that news embargo. I'm dying to know what happened. Do you know?"

"Yes, I do. But *I'm* dying to know how come there was a funeral at all. How did you accomplish that?"

"George, you tell him. It's gross."

"After the shooting stopped, we went ashore," said George. "We located the nuclear weapons fairly quickly. We figured that it might help our cover story if *St. Elmo* had some dead terrorists aboard when she pulled into port. So we packed up Jinnah and a half dozen of his men, the ones that had been shot with bullets, not the laser, and stuck 'em in one of our freezers."

"Jesus," said Christmann.

"Yuck," said Suvia.

"Anyway, we set course for Australia, so we could get Ralph's leg fixed, and arranged to pass within a hundred miles of *St. Elmo*.

Her helicopter came and got the very stiff stiffs, and flew them aboard her. Into her freezers they went."

"Double yuck," said Suvia.

"The crew on *St. Elmo* arranged to repatriate the remains of Jinnah and his men. The crew said Jinnah had been shot while trying to blow up the ship, and the bomb he'd been holding had exploded right under him. His wounds matched the story perfectly."

"Amazing," Christmann said. "Obviously, they believed it in Makran. A funeral was planned for Jinnah. Believe it or not, some people wanted to give him a hero's farewell. There was a funeral procession through the streets, and it was met by an angry mob."

"Hindus?" George asked.

"Hindus and Muslims together. It was an ecumenical mob. They beat the bloody hell out of the mourners, ripped Jinnah's casket open, and hacked his body to pieces. Apparently, most of him was eaten by stray dogs."

"A fitting tribute," said George. Suvia made a face at him.

"Needless to say," Christmann continued, "Jinnah's not a popular guy in his old neighborhood. And there's nobody, absolutely nobody, who has anything good to say about the MLO, or will admit to ever having supported it. Mission accomplished. The Makran Liberation Organization no longer exists."

"Thanks, Bill," Suvia said. She squeezed George's hand. He squeezed back.

"Other business," said Christmann, briskly. "Kevin Finnerty's probation violations have been taken care of. The probation officer was a real jerk, by the way. Said he didn't think a presidential pardon was valid for car theft."

"A presidential pardon," Ralph Dade said. "I don't believe it."

"Neither did Kevin's P.O. Told me the president could only pardon federal crimes. So I made a call, and in five minutes, this guy has a new letter on his desk. It's from the governor. Not only does he issue a pardon of his own, he tells the P.O. that if he tries to give Kevin a hard time he'll be out of a job."

"That's wonderful, Suvia," Ferris said. "Kevin's a free man."

"I wouldn't say that. Unless a year of military prep school and four years at the Naval Academy is your idea of freedom."

"Jesus H. Christ," Holbrook said in feigned exasperation. "Quit stealing our crew. First Jackson, now young Finnerty. You're a one-man press gang."

Christmann laughed. "Don't blame me. It was the president's idea. The appointment to Annapolis is from him, personally. He loves you guys. You should have seen him when Jinnah's troops broke and ran into the laser beam. He was jumping up and down and yelling like a wild man. You'd have thought that the Razorbacks had just won the Super Bowl."

"College teams don't play in the Super Bowl," Suvia said, with a straight face. "That's for pro teams."

"I believe you Texans have an expression," Christmann said to Suvia. "About teaching your grandmother..."

"I was just trying to be helpful."

"Right. Anyway, I saved the best for last," Christmann said. "The Intelligence Oversight Committee in Congress has authorized repayment of *Seafire*'s expenses in recovering the bombs. Let us know what it cost you, and we'll cut a check out of one of the 'black' accounts."

"Gross or net?" George asked.

"What do you mean?"

"Well, you see, this is kind of embarrassing, with me working for a bunch of capitalist running dogs and all that, but we sold off *St. Elmo* at a profit."

"And..."

"And we found a good spot market for the cargo of liquefied gas. It was a cold winter in Japan."

Christmann was dumbfounded. "Don't tell me you broke even on this."

"Actually, we did a little better than that."

Christmann was beginning to laugh when Bill Jackson entered

the room. “What did you say to the admiral?” George demanded. Everyone in the room waited for the answer.

“I told him that he and the Navy could shove their offer up their stern tubes.”

Amid cheers, Jackson added, “In a nice way, of course.”

Suvia Ferris turned to George and asked, “Should we tell them?”

“Sure, why not,” he answered, squeezing her hand again.

“Tell us what?” asked Helen Dade, expecting a wedding announcement.

“George and I are expecting a baby,” Suvia replied. “I flew ashore to see a doctor when we were off the coast of Brazil. It’s a little girl. Her name is Suvia.”

AFTERWORD

AS I MENTIONED in the preface, this is a work of fiction. However, it is not science fiction.

All of the ships now exist or existed in the past. The Coast Guard cutters are actual ships; some are still based in Boston. *Hamilton* really has jet engines. *Willis A. Lee* (DL 4) was the flagship of DesRon 24 out of Newport, RI, when I served on her in the late 1960s. Her sonar dome and anchoring requirements are accurately described. Unfortunately, she never became a guided missile frigate. She was decommissioned in 1969.

The Navy really built USS *Watson*, as I have described her. Her engine rooms contained twenty-four General Electric diesel-electric locomotive power plants. Their combined output was, indeed, forty megawatts of electricity. Construction was halted on January 7, 1946. For those who find this hard to believe, check the *Dictionary of American Naval Fighting Ships*, Volume 1, 1959, Navy Department, Office of CNO, Naval History Division, Washington, DC. *Watson*'s listing is on page 304.

LNG ships identical to *St. Elmo* were built at the General Dynamics shipyard in Quincy, MA, during the late 1970s. The thermal energy contained in each of their five cargo spheres is roughly equivalent to the Hiroshima bomb. The physics of a "worst-case" LNG fire are as I have described them. The disasters in Cleveland and Los Alfalques are historically accurate.

The C-130 Hercules missions began and ended as I described them. The famous *Jane's* organization has videotape of the retrorocket Herc crashing and burning at Area 51.

I believe that something very like the Nightbirds actually exists. At the time the SR-71 Blackbirds were retired, the Skunk Works was at it again, working on a project called Aurora. It was to be a stealthy Mach 6 aircraft with a 200,000-foot ceiling. As of this writing, you can see sketches and specifications on the Federation of American Scientists' website, www.fas.org/irp/mystery/aurora. According to information on that website, Aurora may be flying today.

The *Star Wars* weapons are based on projects that were actually considered during the old SDI program and are now declassified. You can verify this by perusing back issues of *Scientific American*. The Navy actually considered a blue-green argon gas laser as a potential antisubmarine weapon. According to an article entitled "Ray Guns Warm Up in N.M." in *The Albuquerque Journal* on December 10, 1999, the Defense Department has begun testing something very like Big Dumb Laser at the White Sands missile range. This article also can be found on the FAS website.

It is estimated that a significant number of helicopter crashes could be avoided if pilots were better trained to autorotate and regularly practiced doing it. The recent tragic loss of life aboard a

Massachusetts State Police helicopter is thought to have resulted from this.

It is possible to create a supercomputer by running thirty-two high-end PCs in parallel. Actually, sixteen will do the trick. See Article on page 1, column 1 of the *Wall Street Journal* dated December 14, 1998.

The account of Fort St. Elmo and the Turks' heads at the Siege of Malta is accurate.

Muhammad Ali Jinnah was the person most responsible for the creation of Pakistan and was its first president. The quotes attributed to him and Mahatma Gandhi are accurate.

The story about the little girl in the lifeboat is true. The book that George gave Suvia, *South Shore Town*, really exists. There are still women named Suvia living south of Boston.

The island of Makran does not exist. The name comes from a strip of coastline straddling the border between India and Pakistan. There is a lot of oil and gas in the Andaman Basin.

I have described Boston Harbor and Cape Cod Bay accurately. Hypocrite Channel and the Graves are exactly where I have placed them. A shortcut through the Channel, assuming one managed to avoid Halftide Rock, would save a mile or two. Check NOAA Chart Number 13267.

The story about Minot's Ledge is true. Minot's Light still flashes, "I L-O-V-E Y-O-U."

ABOUT THE AUTHOR

STUART M. VAN TINE is a lawyer and partner in a mid-size Boston firm. He served as a commissioned officer in the U.S. Navy from 1965 through 1969 aboard destroyers in the Atlantic and Mediterranean, as well as a tour ashore with the Brown Water Navy in Vietnam's Mekong Delta.

This is his first work of fiction.